THE
CURE

DOUGLAS E. RICHARDS

A TOM DOHERTY ASSOCIATES BOOK
NEW YORK

THE CURE

A Tor Book
Published by Tom Doherty Associates, LLC
175 Fifth Avenue
New York, NY 10010

www.tor-forge.com

Tor® is a registered trademark of Tom Doherty Associates, LLC.

ISBN 978-0-7653-7410-3

Tor books may be purchased for educational, business, or promotional use. For information on bulk purchases, please contact Macmillan Corporate and Premium Sales Department at 1-800-221-7945, extension 5442, or write specialmarkets@macmillan.com.

First Edition: September 2013
First Mass Market Edition: September 2014

Printed in the United States of America

0 9 8 7 6 5 4 3 2 1

To my parents, Ron and Sandy,
and my sister, Pam,
for their undying love, support, and encouragement

Special thanks to Mike Koenigs, Ph.D., Assistant Professor of Psychiatry at the University of Wisconsin, for sharing with me what it's like to enter a prison and enclose oneself in a confined space with a ruthless killer, all in the name of science.

You're a braver man than I.

THE
CURE

PROLOGUE

———

ERIN PALMER SHOVED the tip of a huge slice of pizza into her mouth and ripped off a piece hungrily. "Mmmm," she said. She was starving.

She was already on her second bite while her parents and little sister, Anna, were still reaching toward the gargantuan pie in the center of the table to pick up their first slices.

"That was *amazing,* Erin," said her father, in an exaggerated tone. "You've got hands like a magician." He turned to Erin's mom. "Did you see that, Cheryl? She was so fast, it almost seemed like there was a piece already missing when the waiter put it on the table."

Her father was teasing her, but Erin knew he wasn't really troubled by her bad manners. He had already apologized for getting such a late start on dinner. It was a little after seven thirty and they usually ate at six. Anna had eaten a big snack after school, but Erin had been at soccer practice at the time with other sixth graders from around the area, and hadn't eaten in what seemed like forever.

"We do have talented children," noted her mother in amusement.

"Are you sure you don't want to try tennis, Erin?" asked her dad. "I mean, you're amazing on a soccer field.

But anyone with hands that quick should find a sport where you can actually, you know . . . *use your hands*."

Erin groaned. Her parents wouldn't miss one of her games for the world, but she knew her dad wasn't a fan of soccer, even though he claimed otherwise. "I thought soccer was your favorite sport," she challenged playfully.

"It is," replied her dad with an impish grin. "I mean, if I had the choice between winning a million-dollar lottery or watching a soccer game—well, that would be a very tough call."

"You should take the lottery, Daddy," suggested Anna sagely.

Kids, thought Erin. There were just certain things they didn't get. While Erin was almost twelve, her little sister was only eight and a half. "He was just kidding, Anna," she said. "It really wouldn't be a hard choice." Erin turned to her father. "Be honest, Dad, if I wasn't playing, would you *ever* watch soccer?"

"Well . . . maybe a few games every four years during the Olympics," he said with a twinkle in his eye.

"Ah-*ha*," said Erin triumphantly. "I knew it wasn't really your favorite sport."

"Erin, *any* sport that you or Anna play is my favorite sport," her dad replied earnestly, and her mom nodded in agreement. Looking into their adoring eyes, Erin knew they both absolutely meant it, which made her feel warm inside. They had a way of doing that. Her parents were funny and smart and kind, and they loved her and Anna with a passion that showed every instant of every day.

The Palmer family continued chipping away at the massive pizza, although at an ever-diminishing rate as their hunger began to ebb. When they had finished, and were waiting for the bill, Ted Palmer announced that he needed to stop by his office for just a few minutes on their way home.

"How come?" said Anna.

"I have to check up on Mrs. Sinclair's puppy. A black Lab. I spayed her late this afternoon and Mrs. Sinclair asked me to keep her 'til morning."

"What's her name?" asked Anna.

"I told you," replied her father with a straight face. "Mrs. Sinclair."

"*Daaad*," squealed Anna. "Come *on*. You know I meant the dog."

"Catherine."

Anna took a second to digest this. "The dog's name is *Catherine*?"

Her father nodded. "Really. I swear it. I might have gone with something else. But then again, she's not my dog."

"Is she cute?" asked Anna.

Ted Palmer rolled his eyes. "Are you *kidding*? Have you ever seen a black Lab puppy that wasn't absolutely *adorable*? They don't make them any other way." He paused. "The truth is that dogs actually *evolved* to be cute. To be irresistibly adorable and appealing to humans; the species at the top of the food chain."

As a veterinarian, he had explained the theory of evolution many times to his daughters. Erin totally got it, but she wasn't sure Anna did. At least not completely.

"Interesting," said Erin's mom. "Never thought about it, but I guess the first species that evolved to become man's best friend got a pretty good deal."

"A *great* deal," said Ted Palmer. "There are almost eighty million dogs in this country. And most of them are treated like royalty. Meanwhile, wolves, which are superior to dogs in every survival characteristic there is—with the exception of their appeal to humanity—are an endangered species."

"What about cats?" asked Anna.

"Good point. Cats have a different friendship with humans than dogs, but they haven't done too badly either."

"I think I might want to be a vet someday," said Erin out of the blue.

A slow smile came over her father's affable face.

"Yeah, me too," chimed in her little sister.

"Sure," said her mom wryly. "No kid ever dreams of being a patent attorney."

"Not true, Mom," said Erin quickly. "Um . . . that was my second choice."

"Sure it was," said Cheryl Palmer with a grin.

"Girls, you're both very young," said their dad. "If you decide to become vets, that would be great. But a lot can happen between now and then—so you should keep your minds open to other things."

"Like becoming a patent attorney?" said Erin.

"Now let's not get *crazy*," said her father, fighting to keep a straight face.

Her mother threw a balled-up napkin at him while both girls giggled.

Minutes later they had left the restaurant and were heading toward Ted Palmer's office, sure they would never need to eat again. Night had fallen and the sky over the serene town of Medford, Oregon, was spectacular, as usual. There was no industry for many miles around, and although the Oregon rains came all too often, when the sky was clear the star field and moon were dazzling.

The Palmer Pet Clinic was located in a secluded

wooded area about a quarter of a mile from any other sign of civilization along a narrow, semi-paved road. Douglas fir trees and ponderosa pines surrounded the clinic and towered above it. It was a serene, tranquil setting that Ted Palmer thought pets and their owners alike would appreciate. He had decorated the inside with posters of puppies and kittens in humorous poses and had painted each room either a light blue or mint green.

They pulled around back, and as soon as her dad unlocked the door, Erin and her sister raced ahead to where they knew the black Lab would be—past two exam rooms, through an inner door, and inside a large room that was a combination pharmacy and recovery area.

The cage of interest was on top of a long table in the middle of the room. Anna reached the crate the dog was in first.

She let out a bloodcurdling scream. A scream unlike anything Erin had ever heard come from her sister. A primal scream as loud and shrill as only a girl of eight could produce.

The puppy had been butchered. Mutilated.

Erin saw the dog only seconds after her sister and thought her heart would explode. She fought to take a breath and comprehend what she was seeing. She couldn't bear looking at the poor animal, but she couldn't look away. *Physically couldn't.* As though she were paralyzed. The animal had been crippled and both of its floppy black ears had been sliced off. Its downy-soft black fur was matted with dried blood over the entire surface area of its small, broken body.

Erin seemed unable to turn her head, but threw her eyes out of focus so they wouldn't continue to take further inventory of the damage to the poor dog. She bent over and vomited onto the floor just as her parents came charging through the door in utter panic, able to tell the difference between a scream of absolute horror and a more run-of-the-mill variety their youngest daughter might issue.

Erin's father took one glance at the black Lab's remains and gently but hurriedly pulled both of his daughters away from the crate, ushering them into their mother's arms, one on each side. Erin turned and emptied the remaining contents of her stomach onto the floor and then pressed into her mother's side once more.

Ted Palmer spun around the room, searching for something—anything—he could use as a weapon in case whoever did this was still on the premises.

It was too late. Alerted to their presence by Anna's screams, a man was standing calmly near the opposite door to the room, waving a gun with its barrel extended to an unnatural length. Even though Erin was still a few months away from her twelfth birthday, she had seen enough action shows on television to recognize the long attachment as a silencer immediately.

The man approached and the entire family retreated as he did so, their backs against a table along one wall. Above their heads a strip of wallpaper, three feet wide, ran along the border between wall and ceiling, depicting the repeated image of a Dalmatian puppy playing with a ball.

The intruder tilted his head as if annoyed. "My luck has really been bad this week," he said as though looking for sympathy. It was as if the bad luck he was speaking about involved something mundane, like a paper jam while he was printing, rather than being interrupted after mutilating a helpless animal.

"Take anything you want," said Ted Palmer. "Just leave us alone."

The man smiled serenely, but did not reply.

"If you tell us what you're doing here," said Cheryl Palmer, "maybe we can help you."

"The cops have been after me," the intruder explained, as though trying to be cooperative. "I don't think they really *understand* me," he added, as if he couldn't figure out how this could be. "But that isn't uncommon, I guess. Anyway, I'm trying to keep a low profile. The cops almost had me a few miles from here, but I gave them a head fake and came this direction on foot. I assume this is your pet clinic," he said, looking at Ted Palmer. "When I stumbled across it, I knew it was perfect. You're kind of out of the way, and you've been closed for several hours. I thought this would be a great place to stay out of sight for the night." He shook his head as though reprimanding a child. "And now you've ruined that."

Erin found it almost impossible to breathe, as if her throat had constricted entirely closed. She pressed even more tightly into the crook of her mother's arm and watched her father's face. She could tell his mind was racing furiously. "Sorry about that," he said calmly. "I've got some bigger crates in another room. You can padlock us inside until you're ready to leave. We won't cause any trouble. You can stay the night like you planned."

"No," he said sadly. "I appreciate the offer. But I'm afraid that won't do at all."

In that tiny instant something inside Erin felt a dread beyond dread. It was an instant frozen in time that presaged a horror beyond comprehension. The intruder was clean-cut and looked normal in every way, but his eyes were totally . . . dead. Lifeless. As if they weren't connected anywhere. There was no feeling. No emotion. No *mercy*.

He moved his arm just slightly and fired at Erin's mom in one smooth motion, and her entire face seemed to explode. Ted Palmer screamed and lunged at the man, but a slug exploded through the center of his body, just above his stomach, and blood spouted from him like water from an opened fire hydrant. His momentum carried him three more steps before he crashed into a glass bank of pharmaceutical cabinets, filled with a variety of bottles and other medical equipment. Several pieces of glass drove into his face, neck, and arms, releasing additional streams of bright red blood to add to the gore and exposed intestines.

Noooo! screamed Erin internally; a wail of anguish that wasn't vocalized but which permeated every inch of her body and mind, threatening to tear away her sanity. Anna screamed beside her, her vocal cords not paralyzed, but the scream barely registered with her older sister. Erin felt weak and dizzy and her heart thundered in her chest. Both of her parents had been taken from her between one blink and the next. It wasn't possible. It *couldn't* be.

The intruder glared at Anna with such withering, dead-eyed intensity that her screaming stopped as though he had thrown a switch. He tilted his head and sniffed. "Did someone puke in here?" he said, glancing down at the floor for the first time and seeing two separate piles of semi-digested pizza and breadsticks.

"Let's go in the other room and get away from this mess," he said calmly, his expression not changing in the slightest.

Both girls were sobbing and whimpering uncontrollably now. The intruder pulled little Anna away from her fallen mother and locked an arm around her waist with an iron grip. Anna tried to bite his arm, but it was a halfhearted effort through hysterical sobbing and he backhanded her across the face so hard Erin thought her sister's head might fly off. Anna screamed through her tears, her face a rictus of pain and terror.

"Don't do that again," said the man.

He turned his cruel, cold eyes on Erin. "Come on," he said. "Let's go. Don't dawdle." When she hesitated he kicked her leg with the front of his hard shoe. The pain was so great Erin thought her leg might be broken, and she nearly lost consciousness, something part of her realized she would have welcomed.

"Let's move," he said again.

The man carried Anna with him into the adjoining room and Erin limped behind him. He found a dog collar and slipped it over Erin's neck, leashing her to a desk.

"Stay here," he ordered, moving a few yards away and clamping his large palm over Anna's tiny mouth. "Since you both interrupted what was supposed to be a private evening, you deserve what you get," he pointed out.

He turned to face Erin. "So here's what I'm going to do," he said calmly. "I'm going to see how much pain your sister can take. And then I'm going to kill her. While you watch. How does that sound?"

Erin had slumped to the floor without being aware of it and was making mindless mewling sounds. She was still conscious but paralyzed in mind and body. The horror of what she had seen, and what was happening to her and her sister, had overwhelmed her mind's capacity to absorb shock, and her centers of reason were retreating deep within her consciousness, creating an out-of-body persona to take over and buffer the horror her mind could not have survived otherwise.

"No objections?" said the man. "Good. Remember, this is your fault. You had no business coming here after hours." He smiled serenely. "Do you know what sex is?"

Erin continued whimpering, making no reply.

The intruder produced a scalpel from some unknown location, one with dried blood covering it from the helpless puppy he had butchered, and stabbed it into Anna's arm. She screamed over and over again into the man's palm and writhed against him, trying to get free, but he held her body and mouth with a force she couldn't begin to break. He removed the scalpel from her arm and glared at Erin with his ice-cold eyes. "Answer my question or your sister gets punished."

He paused. "So let me ask again, do you know what sex is?"

Erin fought to reply, but couldn't. She had learned about sex in health class that year and had had a short discussion about it with her parents. It was disgusting, and it had been hard for her to believe this is how babies were really produced, but the answer to his question was *yes.* She struggled with all of her might to form this simple word, but her mouth wouldn't cooperate.

Erin's eyes turned to her sister, a wonderful, innocent girl she couldn't have loved more. She was suffering horribly. And Erin couldn't utter even a single word to save her further pain. She felt so ashamed. But she could barely breathe through her sobs, and she couldn't find a way to speak.

The inhuman monster raised the scalpel to strike again when Erin, out of desperation, managed to move her chin up and down a single time, hoping a nod of yes in response to his question would satisfy him.

"Good," he replied. "Now we're communicating. Now, do you know what *anal* sex is?" he asked with a warm smile.

Anal sex? Erin had a vague idea the word *anal* might have something to do with the butt, but she had no idea what the butt could possibly have to do with sex. Once again she was unable to speak, but she was able to— barely—shake her head no.

"No?" said the man, obviously delighted by this response. "Well, I have good news for you. You're about to find out. Your sister here may scream, but trust me, she's going to enjoy this. I promise. And then when I'm done, I think I'll skin her alive. Do you know what that means?"

Erin wasn't sure but she managed to nod. Anything to get him and his dead eyes to stop talking to her, asking her questions. The man was pure, distilled evil. How could anyone be this cruel? And he was so calm. He might have been talking about the weather as he spoke of torture and murder. He had killed her parents, two wonderful people who would never hurt anyone. And he was about to do the same to Anna and her. He would destroy their bodies and end their lives with as little thought or regret as someone else might have when turning off a light.

He reached for his waist and seconds later his pants fell down around his ankles. Erin was still sobbing but had no awareness that this was the case. All the pain and horror in the world had turned into an ice pick, stabbing at her psyche, robbing her of her mind and her will to move. Her will to live.

Deep inside her consciousness a tiny voice was ashamed of her behavior. She could easily remove the collar from around her neck. She should run. Scream. Get help. Somehow attack this monster. Find a weapon and come at him.

But she couldn't break free from the paralysis that gripped her. And even if she could, nothing she could do would change her fate. Not against pure evil of this magnitude. The man was a snake who had hypnotized its victim, his dead, soulless eyes having completely shattered her psyche, as surely as his bullets had shattered her parents' bodies.

As the man reached for his underwear to pull them down, one hand still clamped tightly over Anna's mouth, the door from the pharmacy burst inward and Erin's father stumbled into the room, making an awkward path toward the intruder and his youngest daughter. His intestines were still fully exposed, and he had lost most of his blood, yet there was a look of superhuman determination in his eyes, and Erin somehow realized that only his love for his daughters could have possibly kept him alive for this long.

The intruder reached for his gun with an untroubled expression, but as he was swinging it around, Ted Palmer stumbled and landed at the man's feet.

The intruder lowered the gun and shook his head in mild amusement. "Don't tell me you want to watch too?" he said.

Erin's father lurched forward and stabbed at the man's lower leg. He had concealed a small syringe filled with unknown fluid and he drove it deep into the intruder's flesh, using the very last of his strength. Her father fell away from the man and an instant later allowed death to finally take him.

"Great," the intruder complained to Erin. "Now I have to find out what he just injected me with." He paused in thought. "I guess I'll have to move up my timetable."

With that he put both hands around Anna's small head and yanked. Erin heard a horrible crack, like a thick tree branch snapping in two, and Anna's head went limp and lolled to the side.

The man turned to Erin. "I guess it's just the two of us now. I'll find out what was in that syringe, and then you'll get to experience the fun of anal sex for yourself. You're in for a real treat."

The man smiled, took one step, and then fell to the floor, his eyes glazing over. He convulsed a few times and then his heart stopped.

Whatever Ted Palmer had injected had finally taken its full effect.

A small part of Erin Palmer felt a shallow relief, but the intensity of her suffering remained crippling. She was vaguely aware of time passing, but everything was a blur. She continued sobbing softly until she finally fell into a welcome unconsciousness.

The next morning, Emily, her father's nurse, came in to work to find a scene straight from a charnel house. An hour later, the building swarming with police and two psychologists, Erin still hadn't moved, now curled up into a fetal position.

It was as though she had died inside, even though her body was still living. Her father had given every last ounce of his strength to save his daughters' lives. And Erin had done nothing. Now she was totally alone in the world. Alone with her cowardice and shame. And alone after suffering a loss so great it nearly stripped her of her sanity.

A female psychologist cleaned Erin up gently and gathered the young girl in her arms, carrying her away from the grisly surroundings. Feeling a compassionate human touch helped Erin's psyche reemerge from its hiding place for just a moment.

Why had this happened? a voice inside her head demanded of an uncaring universe. How could that man have taken *everything* from her? How could God allow such evil to exist?

Erin tilted her head and caught the eye of the counselor. *"Why?"* she whispered hoarsely, her voice pleading.

This would be the last word Erin Palmer would speak for the next twenty-seven days.

PART ONE

SCIENTISTS DECODE PSYCHOPATHS' BRAINS
Science Illustrated, May/June 2012

Psychopaths suffer from an antisocial personality disorder, expressed in a marked lack of empathy, conscience, and sympathy . . . Psychopaths either do not feel fear or simply disregard it . . . Psychopaths are thought to be predisposed to commit violent crime. It has been estimated that while only 1 percent of the population are psychopaths, they make up 11 to 25 percent of all prison inmates.

. . . In healthy individuals, viewing morally offensive pictures activated an area in the amygdala, whereas this area was not activated at all in psychopaths. The amygdala is involved in emotional processing.

[Researchers] examined the "connecting roads" in the brains of psychopaths who had been imprisoned for murder, multiple rape convictions, strangulation . . . The study demonstrated that the white matter connecting the orbitofrontal cortex, the amygdala, and the vision-related centers of the brain was markedly weakened in the group of psychopaths as compared to a control group of healthy individuals.

STUDY FINDS PSYCHOPATHS HAVE DISTINCT BRAIN STRUCTURE
Chicago Tribune, May 7, 2012

The study showed that psychopaths, who are characterized by a lack of empathy, had less gray matter in the areas of the brain important for understanding other peoples' emotions.

Blackwood's team used magnetic resonance imaging (MRI) to scan the brains of forty-four violent adult male offenders in Britain . . . The crimes they had committed included murder, rape, attempted murder, and grievous bodily harm . . . The results showed that the psychopaths' brains had significantly less gray matter in the anterior rostral prefrontal cortex and temporal poles than the brains of the nonpsychopathic offenders and nonoffenders.

These areas of the brain are important for understanding other people's emotions and intentions, and are activated when people think about moral behavior, the researchers said. Damage to these areas is linked with a lack of empathy, a poor response to fear and distress, and a lack of self-conscious emotions such as guilt or embarrassment.

1

⚬⟋⟋⟋⟋⟍⚬

ERIN PALMER PARKED her fifteen-year-old Dodge Intrepid, which continued to be more reliable than it had any right to be, especially given the time it spent in the relentless desert sun, and checked herself in the rearview mirror. Her hair was pulled back into an ugly, severe bun so tightly that it looked as if she had an oversized forehead. She removed a pair of glasses from a case—glasses containing large, strangely shaped lenses set in thick, brown plastic that seemed to clash in every way possible with the contours of her face—slipped them on, and checked her makeup, which added fifteen years to her face and left the impression of wrinkles rather than a silky-smooth, flawless complexion.

She exited the car and adjusted her drab but professional outfit, which had virtually no waist and was cut in a way that made it unclear to anyone seeing her from the neck down if she was a man or a woman, covering every inch of her body more surely than a burka.

She left the car and walked past a sign that was surrounded by cacti and sagebrush, a tiny oasis of landscaping in an otherwise barren and uncared-for desert landscape. The sign read, Arizona State Prison Complex—Tucson.

Another day at her home away from home.

As she approached the entrance, the main yard came into view within the fenced-in perimeter, the coils of razor wire on top of the tall fences looking as lethal and intimidating as ever. Inmates exercised or conversed in small clusters throughout the dry, dusty yard, every last one of them wearing orange: some wearing cotton slacks and an orange T-shirt, some having chosen orange sweats in the chilly morning desert air, but all of the clothing stamped with giant black letters, ADC, which stood for Arizona Department of Corrections.

She submitted to scanning and security procedures with a mechanical detachment and finally walked through two heavy metal doors that slid open before her, triggered by a guard manning a control station. The doors were programmed so that the second door wouldn't release until the first door was closed behind her, so that for just a moment she was trapped between two impenetrable doors, in what she'd learned was called a *sally port*. As she cleared the second door, which slid shut behind her with a solid *thunk,* she waved her thanks to the guard behind her.

To Erin's right a familiar sign read, Welcome to ASPC, Tucson—Medium Security Prison. *Medium* was a misnomer if ever there was one. No one was getting out of this facility unless they were *let* out.

"Alejandro," said Erin cheerfully to her favorite prison guard, who met her just inside the grounds. "Good morning."

"Good to see you, Erin," he said, having long since become completely comfortable using her first name, which she had insisted upon, rather than the Miss Palmer he had used in the early days. He began to escort her to the side yard where she would spend the entire day.

"How was your daughter's birthday party this weekend?" asked Erin.

"She loved it," he said with a big smile. "The balloon guy was a big hit. And a lot less expensive than a magician," he added.

Erin nodded. "Good choice. Those magicians can be hit or miss. And you got the added benefit of the kids getting to keep the balloons when your guy was finished."

They entered a side yard, whose most distinguishing feature was a massive trailer that was parked dead center—a long rectangular container that had been unhitched from the cab of an eighteen-wheeler. Makeshift wooden stairs led up to its entrance.

Inside the trailer there was carpeting, an office, an all-important air-conditioning unit, and a smooth, white, doughnut-shaped MRI apparatus, with a perpendicular platform emerging from the bottom of the doughnut hole. The platform would slide the heads and upper torsos of patients inside the white torus, which generated a potent magnetic field, so they could be bombarded with radio frequency pulses and have their brains mapped. The trailer may have been mobile, but it now seemed as permanent a fixture in the prison as the fences, and it was an office Erin had occupied for three or four days a week for many years.

When they arrived at the trailer, Erin handed Alejandro a printed list of names. "I've got a pretty packed schedule today," she said.

"When *don't* you have a packed schedule?" he replied in amusement.

They chatted warmly for another five minutes and then he left, returning a few minutes later with a man named John, dressed in orange, although not restrained in any way.

"Welcome back, Miss Palmer," said John affably. "How was your weekend?"

"Good," she said flatly; noncommittally. She made sure she always acted professionally, but was never friendly. But this wasn't always easy to do. The man in front of her now was even more charming than most of the men she worked with—and that was saying a lot. He was relaxed and confident. He was of average height but managed to look trim and appealing, even in prison orange. He had striking blue eyes that stood out against jet-black hair, a masculine and very symmetrical face, and no tattoos or piercings to mar his classically handsome features.

"Are you ready for today's session?" asked Erin, keeping her voice monotone.

"Absolutely," replied John enthusiastically. "Wouldn't miss it for the world."

Yes, he was the total package. He was handsome and charming and smooth as silk. He had also, three years earlier, beaten a young couple into a bloody paste with a tire iron. They had been out on a date and had paused during a stroll for an extended kiss, leaning against his car as they did so and inadvertently scratching it.

When it was over, John calmly carried the tire iron he had used to kill them to a nearby field, buried it, and returned to his apartment, where he had showered off to remove the significant amount of blood that had splattered on him, ordered a pepperoni pizza—since he had worked up quite an appetite—and settled in to watch a movie on cable.

Since this had happened at night and there were no witnesses, it was more luck than skill that had enabled the police to finally catch him five months later. When asked if he felt remorse for what he had done, a look of disbelief had come over his face and he had said, "Why should I feel remorse? They got what was coming to them. I had just gotten that car repainted the week before. They didn't care about me. Why should I care about them?"

Erin forced herself to remember the exact reason John was here every time she met with him. He smiled at her pleasantly. "Let's do this thing," he said, straightening his orange shirt.

Erin nodded, keeping her face impassive. *Yeah,* she thought grimly, *this John is a real charmer all right.* She took a deep breath, motioned him into the trailer, and then followed.

Alejandro watched them both enter, waited for the door to shut, and then walked purposefully over to his post near the entrance to the trailer.

2

ERIN HAD BEEN in graduate school now for over five years, and her thesis should have been completed already, but it was at least a year or so away. The truth was that she didn't much care. She had bigger goals than this, and was in no hurry. And even though her thesis advisor, Professor Jason Apgar, mouthed platitudes about her needing to speed it up, she did great work, marred only by a few unfortunate incidents that had been found to be totally unrelated to her work. Graduate students were slave labor, and she required almost no supervision, had a mind as sharp as a razor, and was more dedicated than anyone in the school. She knew Apgar wouldn't rush her to get her Ph.D.

As John filled out a standard questionnaire, her mind wandered to the first time she had met Jason Apgar. She had been accepted into six graduate programs, and she had set up a meeting with him before committing to a school. Her first visit to the University of Arizona. Her first visit to Arizona, period.

The school was an oasis, about a square mile in area, in the middle of Tucson's Sonoran Desert, at the foot of a barren mountain range, one of five minor mountain ranges surrounding the city. A significant portion of the main campus had been designated an arboretum, and plants from around the world were labeled along a self-guided walking tour, which naturally included plenty of cacti. While it wasn't Princeton or the University of Chicago, both of which she had been accepted to, it was highly regarded academically, especially in her field of interest, and it formed a thriving social community of forty thousand students. Yes, it was as hot as the surface of the sun in the summer, but during most of the academic year it was sunny and pleasant, and she had been assured that the school took its air-conditioning very seriously.

After touring the campus and grabbing a quick lunch, she made her way over to Dr. Apgar's office for her scheduled meeting. He shook her hand and motioned for her to take a chair sitting in front of a desk so cluttered with stacks of scholarly papers and miscellaneous items that he had to rearrange several tall stacks so they could have an unobstructed view of one another.

"Thanks so much for taking the time to meet with me, Dr. Apgar. I really appreciate it."

"Not at all," he replied. "And please, call me Jason."

She acknowledged this request and he continued. "I understand we've accepted you into the department, but you haven't committed yet."

"That's right. I wanted to meet with you in person before making any decisions."

"So I take it you have interest in my work, then?"

"Very much so," replied Erin. "I've read all of your papers with great interest. Your work with prison inmates is fascinating. More than that," she amended. "It's *groundbreaking*."

Apgar couldn't help but smile. "Thank you," he said. "I would wholeheartedly agree with you on that, but my modesty prevents me."

Erin laughed.

Apgar raised his eyebrows. "The school is very keen to get you here, Erin. They sent me your records, and I can see why. Top GRE scores, top grades, a course load that was very broad, lots of neuroscience to go along with psychology, even molecular biology. You took on a course load that would break the backs of most students, and performed extremely well. Very impressive."

She nodded in acknowledgement.

"So what questions can I answer for you?" he said. "I can tell you about the graduate program's course requirements, research requirements, teaching requirements—whatever you want. I can talk about the culture here. The climate. Anything I can do to help you make your decision."

"Thank you, um . . . Jason," she said awkwardly. "But what I'd really like to do is learn more about your research with prison inmates. Your methodology and conclusions were fairly straightforward—and very profound. But I had some questions about the nuts and bolts of what you did."

"Okay."

"So I know you conducted MRIs on prisoners. And I know what you found. But *how* did you do it? In practice? Did you actually go into a prison? Or were the prisoners brought to a medical facility?"

"The entire study was done on prison grounds," he replied.

She nodded slowly. "Yeah, that makes sense for security reasons. But I never would have guessed they're set up to do MRIs in a maximum security prison."

Apgar smiled. "They aren't. But it turns out there are a number of companies that have mobile MRIs for rent or lease. The rental units are quite nice. It's like they've put a doctor's office inside the trailer of an eighteen-wheeler. You just order one up. A driver brings it to the prison, is screened, drives through the gates, sets up the trailer in the prison yard, and then drives off in the cab. The trailer is parked there for months or years at a time."

"That has to be pretty expensive."

"Not as much as you might think," he said. "And my lab has been awarded a significant amount of grant money—more than enough to cover it." He paused. "And I did the study in a medium security prison, by the way. Not maximum."

Erin's eyes narrowed. "I don't understand. According to your paper, you studied serial rapists, murderers, and torturers. How are these people not in maximum security prisons?"

"How much do you know about psychopathy?" he asked her.

She paused as if searching her mind. She suspected she knew almost as much about the condition as he did. "A little," she lied.

"If you know anything, I'm sure you know that psychopaths are not psychotic. It's unfortunate these two words are so similar, because this has caused tremendous confusion in the general public. People use the abbreviation *psycho* to stand for both conditions, but most of the time they use the word *psycho* as a stand-in for *crazy.* With respect to *psychotics,* this is true. They *are* crazy. They kill because little green men inside their heads tell them to. *Psychopaths,* on the other hand, are chillingly sane. They know exactly what they're doing at all times. And why. They just don't care. They have zero conscience."

Erin nodded.

"They are also the most manipulative human beings in existence. And the smoothest liars. And they don't feel fear, or guilt, or remorse, or doubt. If you catch them in the most bald-faced of lies, this doesn't embarrass them in the slightest—or trip them up. They just switch gears or introduce even bigger lies to cover it up." He paused. "And they never take responsibility or blame for anything they do. John Wayne Gacy tortured and murdered thirty-three young men and boys and buried them in the basement of his house, but was quoted as saying that he saw himself more as a victim than a perpetrator."

Erin fought to maintain a look of interest even though all of this information she knew as well as her own name. "Fascinating," she said.

Apgar nodded. "But getting back to your question," he said. "The decision as to what type of facility a prisoner is put into isn't entirely dependent on the crimes they've committed, but also their behavior while incarcerated. The ones I was dealing with all *started* in a maximum security facility, of that you can be sure."

Erin nodded. If he had but said this simple sentence to answer her question she would have grasped the situation immediately, but she knew she would have to wait patiently while he connected the dots for her.

"Psychopaths aren't crazy and they can be the most charming and cooperative beings on the planet to get what they want. So they are brilliant at manipulating the system. They tend to be model prisoners. The kind who are eventually transferred to medium security facilities. They enroll in counseling, take classes, pretend to become born-again Christians, anything to play the system. Not all violent criminals are psychopaths. The ones left behind in the maximum security facilities are violent for a host of other reasons, but don't have the psychopath's gift for manipulation."

"I see," said Erin with a smile. "When you explain it that way, medium security makes sense."

"But don't get me wrong, if you've never been to a prison, medium security will seem like maximum security to you. Medium isn't the same as none. You still have the high fences, nasty coils of razor wire, guards, and multiple doors you have to get through to enter the prison."

"Was it hard to get the psychopaths to participate in your studies?"

He shook his head. "Not at all. We pay them a dollar

an hour, but even if we didn't, they'd be happy to do it. What else are they doing?"

Erin raised her eyebrows. "A dollar an hour?"

Apgar smiled. "We actually debated if this was too much. We pay students twenty-five an hour to participate in studies. But that would be a king's ransom to prisoners, who are paid more on the order of one to three dollars a *day* for their work in prison. Which they can spend in the prison canteen or in other ways I'm not sure I want to contemplate. It would be unethical to pay them more, because this would be seen as coercive when we're asking them to sign the informed consent forms." He paused. "But boredom isn't the only reason they're eager to help. It gives them another chance to be manipulative and try to exploit the system. That's why they're so happy to undergo group therapy and any other rehabilitation programs offered by prisons. Believe me, they don't want to get better. They're quite happy with themselves, and never question their own behavior, seeing it as totally rational and rewarding. Group counseling just makes them *worse,* because they're able to use it as a learning experience. They don't learn the error of their ways. They learn how to make better use of psychology to manipulate and deceive others. As if they weren't good enough at this already. Studies have shown that psychopaths who participate in this kind of counseling are *more* likely to commit violent crimes when released than those who don't."

Erin knew that she should act surprised by this result, since it wouldn't be intuitive that prison programs that had such positive effects on normals would totally backfire on psychopaths, but she was too eager to get back to the subject. "Okay," she said. "So you enter the prison, pass through the heavy doors and checkpoints, and then what? You go to the semi and a guard brings you each subject according to a schedule?"

Apgar nodded. "Right."

"I'm trying to picture it. So are their hands cuffed behind their backs? In the front? Are their ankles cuffed also?"

Apgar shook his head and looked amused. "No. They aren't restrained in any way."

Erin digested this for a few seconds, looking as though she wasn't quite sure if she believed him. "So how many guards go with you into the trailer?"

"None," said Apgar.

"None?" repeated Erin incredulously.

He sighed. "I know you're picturing Hannibal Lecter in his prison cell wearing one of those scary masks over his face. The kind of psychopath who would kill you if he could get near you for a second. But it doesn't work that way in real life." He paused. "At least it hasn't so far," he added. "Knock on wood."

"But these men have committed savage, brutal acts."

"I have to admit, it took a while getting used to. The first time I was alone in a contained space with someone who was in prison for torture and murder, I was . . . a little nervous."

"A little?"

"Okay, I was stressed out of my mind. But it worked out. And other researchers had been alone with these people before, and there had never been an incident. The prisoners have far more to lose than to gain by trying to harm a researcher. They make some good money—at least relative to the prison economy—and they get a diversion. If they pulled anything it would be a one-way ticket to a maximum security facility forever. And a long, long stint in solitary confinement."

"Still. I'd think you'd want at least *one* guard."

"I *did*. Believe me. Especially in the beginning. But you can't. The work is conducted under researcher/subject confidentiality. So no guards, no video monitors, no audio. Just me and a violent psychopath. And this works out for the best. You'd be surprised how many of them, knowing I can't repeat anything they tell me, will boast about other crimes they've committed. Rapes, murders, robberies—the works. I can't repeat it, but made anonymous, this information helps enhance my research results. They wouldn't say a word if a guard were present."

"I have to admit, this is something I would have never considered."

"They love the fact that I'm sworn to silence. This is carefully explained to them at the outset. Unless they tell me of someone in current jeopardy, or talk about a prison break or a violent act they're *planning* to commit—in the future—I'm sworn to secrecy."

Erin tried to imagine what it must be like to sit in a trailer in the middle of a prison alone with these inmates, and felt her skin crawl.

"And they truly are incredible at manipulation," continued Apgar. "You think you're prepared, but you're not. Even researchers who have studied psychopathy their entire lives get taken in." He shifted in his chair. "Early on, there was an inmate I interviewed before I saw his file. He had me absolutely convinced he was falsely accused—had just been the victim of circumstance. He spent an hour telling me what had happened in incredible detail. He fell in love with this girl who told him she was twenty. But she was really seventeen. The father found out and was totally unreasonable, making sure he was prosecuted to the fullest extent of the law for statutory rape. The father had connections, so he made sure this poor guy had the book thrown at him."

Apgar paused, remembering. "It's difficult to explain how convincing he was. Unless you were there. How articulate and persuasive. At the end of the session, I was ready to march into the warden's office and fight for this guy's freedom. Become his personal advocate. But then I checked his file." He shook his head, and a troubled look came over his face. "The guy had raped and beaten three girls under the age of fourteen. There were photos in the file." He shuddered. "He had cut them with a razor and their faces looked as though they had been at the wrong end of a wood chipper. It's a wonder they survived."

Lava-red hatred flashed across Erin's eyes, but only for an instant. Not long enough for Apgar to detect, even if he had been paying close attention.

The professor leafed through a stack of papers on his desk and pulled out a single sheet. "I felt like the biggest idiot in the world to have been taken in, but I've swapped stories now with many others in the field, and it's happened to all of us. That's why when you're dealing with a psychopath, you can't let your guard down for an instant." He handed her the page he had been holding. "This says it about as well as anything I've read. I use it in the graduate course I teach, Psych 850."

Erin looked down at the sheet and began reading.

Good people are rarely suspicious: they cannot imagine others doing the things they themselves are incapable of doing. Then, too, the normal are inclined to visualize the [psychopath] as one who's as monstrous in appearance as he is in mind, which is about as far from the truth as one could get... These monsters of real life usually looked and behaved in a more normal manner than their actually normal brothers and sisters; they presented a more convincing picture of virtue than virtue presented of itself—just as the wax rosebud or the plastic peach seemed more perfect to the eye, more what the mind thought a rosebud or a peach should be, than the imperfect original from which it had been modeled.

Erin finished and turned her gaze back to Apgar.

"Any idea who wrote that?" he asked. "Where it's from?"

Erin had recognized it instantly. It was from *The Bad Seed,* by William March. She faced Apgar and shook her head. "No idea."

"It was written by William March, author of *The Bad Seed*. The novel was turned into a film and a Broadway play. You should see it sometime."

No thanks, thought Erin. "Yeah, maybe I will," she said.

"Anyway, I know most people are fascinated by the idea of working with psychopathic killers. Believe me, when I was doing this research and it was fairly well known, I was a big hit at cocktail parties. Like you, everyone is interested in what happened after I entered the prison. But after I made my discoveries on the differences in their brain structure compared to normals, I've turned to other research projects. I haven't studied psychopaths for six months now."

For the next thirty-five minutes, Apgar went on to describe several other research projects going on in his lab, and his plans going forward.

Erin asked a polite question or two along the way, but mostly waited patiently for him to finish. She had known from the start she wanted to join his lab. The purpose of the entire exercise had been to get a feel for his personality, and she liked what she saw. Not that she even *needed* to like him. It was only necessary that she not *hate* him. And she had decided he would be a pleasure to work with only a few minutes into their discussion.

When he had finished describing the last of his research projects she leaned forward and stared at him intently. "Professor Apgar . . . Jason," she corrected. "How would you feel about taking on another graduate student? I'd love for you to be my thesis advisor. If you're okay with that, I'm willing to commit to Arizona immediately."

"I'm flattered," he said. "And I'd welcome the chance to take on someone with your impressive background. I have six grad students in my lab now, but I have ideas for enough projects to occupy fifty of them. In which research area would you see yourself working?"

Erin took a mental breath. "I'd like to revisit your work with psychopaths. Further define the differences in their brain structure. Test how their brains react to various other stimuli. I'd want to devote myself a hundred percent to this area."

Apgar's eyes narrowed and his face scrunched up in disapproval. "I thought you were asking questions about this for the same reason everyone does. I had no idea you were thinking of actually doing this sort of work *yourself.*"

Apgar leaned back and rubbed the back of his head absently. "You do realize you'd have to go into a prison like I did—a lot. Frankly, that's why I didn't pursue this project any further, even though there's clearly additional fertile soil to till. It's just not exactly the work environment I wanted to spend any more time in." He grinned. "Not exactly the tweed jacket and pipe existence I envisioned for myself as a professor."

Erin laughed. His personality couldn't have been further from this stereotype.

"Are you really prepared to be left alone, one on one, with a psychopathic murderer?" said Apgar, serious once more.

"Yes," said Erin, but it came out far more timid and uncertain than she had wanted. "*Yes,*" she repeated, stronger this time. "I can hardly wait," she added wryly, raising her eyebrows.

He studied her for several long seconds. "So why so interested in psychopathy?" he asked. "I mean, when you ask young women what they want to do when they grow up, working with psychopathic killers doesn't usually make the top of the list."

Erin lowered her eyes, trying to conceal the intense emotional pain that had flared up in response to this question. So what would she tell him? That her family was brutally murdered by a psychopath while she watched? That she had been emotionally crippled by the experience for a long time? That she had only managed to regain a semblance of equilibrium by vowing to devote her life to studying the evil that had rained down on her and her family?

Would she tell him she had spent year after year training her mind and body so that she would never feel helpless again, becoming an expert in multiple martial arts and with multiple weapons?

No. Of course she couldn't. She knew Apgar's history well. He had pioneered brain-imaging techniques and had mapped the brain and studied emotional reactions extensively before he had conducted his studies with psychopaths, an obvious extension of his work. He hadn't begun with an interest in psychopathy. His impetus to study this condition was purely intellectual. While hers was a tad more . . . visceral.

So acknowledging the role her past had played in her current interests was out of the question. Apgar might question if she wanted to settle a vendetta rather than push back the frontiers of human knowledge. Instead of being worried about what an inmate might do to her, he would worry about what she might do to *them*.

Numerous scientists had found their calling in response to personal tragedy. Researchers who had devoted themselves to finding a cure for Parkinson's or Alzheimer's after having watched a parent or grandparent suffer from these horrible afflictions. How many oncologists had chosen this field because they had been helpless to prevent cancer from slowly and horribly choking the life out of a loved one? Erin's devotion was no different. And maybe Apgar would see it this way.

But maybe not. Many would view her passion to study psychopathy quite differently than they would view the passion of an oncologist who had lost a loved one to cancer. Apgar could be one of them. So she wasn't about to give him an honest answer and take this risk. Fortunately, the records of what had happened, and her subsequent counseling, had been sealed. This was a secret she was prepared to take with her to her grave.

So instead of the truth, she responded to his questions with platitudes about coming across his work and recognizing the breakthrough nature of it. Of always having been fascinated by psychopathy after seeing *The Silence of the Lambs* and other such movies.

When she was done, he studied her for a few seconds longer and then said, "You do realize that movies and the media sensationalize the condition. Just so you know, while up to one percent of the population can be classified as psychopathic, a very, very small percentage of these are the Hannibal Lecter type. Vanishingly small. Even among the prison population."

"Yes, but even the ones who can fool the system—the doctors and lawyers and politicians—are almost always engaged in cons, or white-collar crime, or unethical behavior. And they leave endless shattered lives in their wakes." Seeing Apgar's eyes widen, Erin hastened to add, "I mean, you'd have to guess that, wouldn't you? At least I would. Or am I wrong about that?"

"No," said Apgar with an amused look. "Good guess. I couldn't have said it better myself." He sighed. "Will you at least let me try to convince you out of this?" he asked.

Erin shook her head. "I'm afraid not," she replied, and then with an incandescent smile added, "like you said, this is the kind of stuff that's endlessly fascinating to people. So I may be in what you might call a . . . hostile . . . work environment, but at least I'll be a hit at cocktail parties."

Apgar couldn't help but laugh. But he still wasn't entirely convinced. "Look, let me preface this by saying I'm happily married and not hitting on you or anything." He smiled sheepishly. "But you must know you're a beautif . . . that you're, ah . . . quite attractive. There haven't been any incidents with this type of research, for the reasons I explained. But psychopaths have poor impulse control. And the ones you'd be interacting with will all be men, after all. Men incarcerated in an all-male prison year after year after year. Sending you alone into an enclosed room with them would be tempting fate. You have to be aware of your effect on men. I'm not sure I'd feel comfortable sending you alone into a room with normal men, who have *great* impulse control."

Erin frowned deeply. She had a flawless complexion, a figure a bikini model would envy, and a grace and agility that had arisen from years of training in martial arts and other forms of self-defense. Her hair was a deep chestnut-brown, and glowed with health and vigor, and her features were strong but delicate.

"I really thought the prisoners would be bound," she admitted unhappily. "And that you'd have a guard in there with you." She shook her head in determination. "But no matter. I'm sure I can find a way to overcome this little . . . problem. I'm willing to bet I can make myself look pretty hideous. I can wear clothing so that inmates will barely be able to tell I'm a woman, let alone a woman who might have any physical appeal."

Apgar sighed. "At the risk of being accused of sexual harassment, that would take quite some doing."

Erin smiled back sweetly. "Thanks for the compliment," she said. She paused for several seconds and then, in a level just above a whisper but with undeniable intensity, added, "But I think you'll find that when I set my mind to something, I don't let anything get in the way."

* * *

ERIN'S MIND RETURNED to the present. Had it really only been five years since she had met Jason Apgar? Sometimes it seemed like five days. But for some reason, today it seemed like an eternity ago. An eternity in which she had given herself a literal prison sentence, just as surely as if she had been convicted by a judge.

She had intended for this to be a normal session with the human monster named John, who could casually beat two people to death over some scratched paint. She would strap goggles containing a visual LED display over his eyes, pack his head with pillows, and slide it and his upper torso inside the doughnut-shaped MRI device. Then she would take a baseline. Finally, she would begin collecting new data.

Simple and routine.

But it wasn't to be. John insisted on talking. In a different way, and about a different subject than he had ever spoken of before. After thirty minutes he showed no sign of slowing down. He seemed filled with remorse. And Erin believed him.

And, strangely, she was as horrified by this turn of events as she was elated.

3

"YOU MUST BE the hardest working woman on this campus," said Lisa Renner. "And that's really saying something."

Erin Palmer smiled. "Okay, so I'm a bit driven. I confess. But I don't think I'm *that* bad."

They arrived at their destination, a cozy Greek restaurant on the outskirts of campus, and waited to be seated.

"Are you kidding me?" said Lisa. "Sharing an apartment with you is like having an apartment to *myself.*" She grinned. "Except that some mysterious stranger is nice enough to pay half the rent. It's a good deal if you can get it."

Erin laughed. Actually, she felt as though she had gotten the better end of the deal. She couldn't be more thrilled to have found Lisa Renner. Erin's roommate of several years had done the unthinkable two months earlier—she had finished her Ph.D. and had taken a postdoc on the other side of the country. Erin had been wrapped up in her research as usual, and had been slow to realize that the few people she was close enough with to want as a roommate were happy with their current living arrangements, and she was forced to advertise for someone to room with. Urgently. Either that or learn how to beg for money on street corners.

Graduate students were notoriously overworked and underpaid. In her case, she received some funding from grants and for teaching undergraduate courses, but she would have to get a substantial raise just to be considered *poor.* Lisa, a third-year history graduate student who also found herself running low on funds, had come along at exactly the right time seven weeks earlier, and they had hit it off immediately.

Lisa was possibly the sweetest girl Erin had ever met. She was hardworking but spontaneous. She was relentlessly upbeat and full of life, both qualities that Erin knew she needed to work on. At twenty-four, she was three years younger than Erin, exactly the same age that

Erin's sister, Anna, would have been, and Erin was surprised by how quickly she'd come to love this quirky, endearing history student.

"Okay. I work late a lot," confessed Erin. "But I have been getting better since you moved in. I mean, I'm here, aren't I? On a Monday. Having an actual lunch with a friend at an actual sit-down restaurant."

As if on cue the hostess appeared and led them to a small, isolated table against the window.

When they were seated, Lisa shook her head slightly and pursed her lips in a classic *what-am-I-going-to-do-with-you* gesture. "I do appreciate you coming to lunch with me," she said. "But I had to practically put a gun to your head to get you to do it."

"Well I'm glad you did," said Erin. "Keep forcing me to remember I'm a human being."

Lisa brightened. "Well, you teach once a week, right? So why don't we do this every week on your teaching day?"

Erin realized that while this might have seemed impossible only three weeks before, now it was actually worth considering. Because the unimaginable had happened. She had achieved the results she had been working toward.

Perhaps.

Preliminary results were breathtaking, true, but they were still preliminary. She would need to confirm and refine these results for several months by doing careful, rigorous, statistically significant science. Only then would she be able to shout *eureka,* if only to herself—and to Hugh Raborn. But if her initial success *could* be duplicated, repeatedly, she really would be able to throttle back, enjoy life a little. But she couldn't agree just yet, and certainly not without a little banter. "Lunch every week?" she said in amusement. "Now that's just crazy talk."

"It'd be good for you," said Lisa. "You just admitted that yourself. Just cut your office hours in half and use this time to bond with your roommate. Come on, does anyone ever visit you during your office hours anyway?"

"Well, there was this one guy once. In 1943 . . ."

Lisa laughed as the waitress came over to take their order. Lisa ordered a massive plateful of food, while Erin ordered a gyro sandwich and water, declining to add an appetizer or at least a side dish or two as Lisa urged her to do.

"If I had your figure," said Lisa as the waitress left, "I'd be ordering everything on the menu." She frowned. "Which probably explains why I *don't* have your figure."

Erin suppressed a smile. "Come on, Lisa. You're not in the least overweight. I bet we weigh exactly the same."

"Yeah, but you're a few inches taller, and your weight is, ah . . . *distributed* better." She sighed. "Let's face it, if I were going into a prison, I wouldn't have to wrap gauze around my chest every day like you do. My breasts would hide out just fine in that ugly, baggy outfit of yours."

"From what you've told me, Derrick doesn't seem to have any problem with your figure."

Erin's roommate raised her eyebrows. "He does seem to be a bit insatiable, doesn't he?"

Derrick was finishing up an MBA, and he and Lisa had started dating just four weeks earlier—but they were seeing more and more of each other and the trajectory looked promising.

"So did he call you today?" asked Erin.

Lisa beamed. "He did. I think I really like this guy. I

mean *really* like him." She shook her head and frowned. "But you've really freaked me out, Erin. Before I met you, I didn't even know how to pronounce the word *psychopathy*. I would have said psycho-pathy instead of psy-*cop*-athy."

Lisa gazed up at the sky as if pondering a long-ago memory. "Those were the good old days," she said. "Seven weeks ago. When I was blissfully ignorant of not only the pronunciation of this word, but the fact that fricking one percent of the fricking population is fricking psychopathic. Now I'm totally paranoid. I'm seeing psychopaths everywhere. I mean, take career politicians. Are there any who *aren't* psychopathic?" She shook her head. "Thanks, Erin."

"That isn't fair. You asked *me* what percentage of the population were psychopathic. *I* didn't bring it up. What was I supposed to do, lie?"

"*Yes*," said Lisa emphatically, but with an amused twinkle in her eye. "I really like this guy," she added. "But he does fit the characteristics of psychopaths you told me about. He's bright, handsome, smooth, totally at ease in social situations, articulate . . ."

"Sounds like a real monster," said Erin wryly.

"I'm serious," complained Lisa. "Didn't you say these people are great at manipulating you to like them?"

"Look, just because psychopaths fit a certain profile doesn't mean that normal people can't fit that profile also. In fact, far more normal people have these qualities than psychopaths. They just have a soul as well." She raised her eyebrows. "Which is always a nice feature." The corners of her mouth turned up into an amused smile. "But sometimes a pickle is just a pickle."

"As opposed to a psychopath?" said Lisa.

"Right."

Lisa considered. "Okay. But he still *could* be one, couldn't he?" She looked intently at Erin. "You're always so busy on the weekend with your ninety-hour-a-week work schedule, but this coming weekend you've got to meet him. I don't care if I have to take him to your lab and pull you away from the computer. I mean, if anyone would know if he was a decent guy or a monster in hiding, you would."

The waitress appeared with their food, set it down in front of them, and left.

"Hey, even the experts can be fooled," said Erin. "Fairly easily. I mean, I'd have a far better chance than you would of figuring it out, but I wouldn't be infallible. Did you Google this guy?"

"*Of course,*" snapped Lisa, as if her roommate had just called her an idiot. "No bodies chopped up and found in his refrigerator—at least as far as I can tell." She leaned forward. "I can't even imagine working with these monsters year after year. If I've become paranoid, I can only imagine what this has done to you. I mean, how can you trust *anyone*? Is that why you don't have a guy?"

Erin had just torn a large bite from her gyro and motioned for her friend to give her a few seconds to finish chewing and swallowing. She did, set her gyro back down on the plate, and said, "Okay, I'll admit trust isn't my strong suit. But I've been in relationships before. Really."

"When was the last time you were in one?" challenged Lisa, taking a sip from the Coke she had ordered.

"Two years ago."

"So . . . what? You've been doing one-night stands since then?"

Erin rolled her eyes. "Oh yeah, one-night stands are

ideal if you aren't the trusting type. Nothing like going home with a total stranger." She shook her head. "I'm not a one-night stand kind of girl."

Lisa's eyes widened as she hurriedly swallowed the bite she had just taken. "*So you haven't been laid in two years? Are you kidding me?* No wonder you seem a little stressed out most of the time. I'm amazed you don't *explode*. Just spontaneously erupt into a ball of repressed sexuality. We have to find you a guy."

"Two years isn't *that* long," said Erin.

Lisa just ignored her. "We have to find you a guy," she repeated.

"Uh . . . thanks," said Erin. "I know you mean well. But I can take care of that myself when the time is right. Let's get back to Derrick."

"Wow, that was the least subtle attempt to change the subject I've ever seen. I'm not giving up on this. You're a workaholic, we've established that. And I like you far too much not to want to help you. I can't even imagine how depressing it must be to work with murderers and rapists in prison all the time. I'm taking it upon myself to counteract the gloom of that place. Just think of me as the self-appointed ray of sunshine in your life."

"And you're doing a great job," said Erin. "In fact, I just might start calling you *Ray*." She paused. "So *now* can we change the subject?"

"Okay," said Lisa. "But I'm making this my mission. I'm warning you."

"Warning received. Now let's get back to Derrick."

"Okay. Why not? He is my favorite subject, after all." She stared at her roommate. "So give me some advice. There has to be some way to spot a psycho."

"Psychopath," corrected Erin.

"Yeah, I get it. People use *psycho* to refer to *crazy*. You told me. But whenever I say it, just know I'm referring to the people you study, okay? The evil but sane people. Anyway, how do you spot them?"

"I could tell you a possible way, but you aren't an expert. You'd probably misdiagnose most of the time."

"You're probably right, but tell me anyway. Now you've piqued my curiosity."

"Okay. You know how people use their hands when they talk? Humans are wired that way. Even when we're on the phone and the other person can't see us, we do it—although we don't ever think about it or realize we are. This gesturing increases when we're trying to get across a difficult concept. Next time someone you're talking with is searching for the right word and it's on the tip of their tongue, watch their hands. They'll be more active than ever—as if these movements will help them find the memory or convey the meaning. Am I making sense?"

"Perfect sense."

"Good. And if you're using a second language that you aren't as comfortable with as your first, your hand movements increase in amount. Probably for the same reason. Well, emotions are a second language to a psychopath. They don't really have them. They know the words but they can't hear the music. Hook an EEG up to a normal and their brains respond differently to a word like *chair,* and an emotionally charged word like *torture.* Not a psychopath. Their brains react to these words *in the exact same way.* They're like color-blind people who teach themselves to fake seeing color. So when they're trying to voice something emotional they move their hands more than normals would." She paused and raised her eyebrows. "Like I said, emotions are a second language to them."

"Fascinating," said Lisa. "And scary as hell. But you're right. This doesn't help. I have no idea how much an average person uses their hands. I mean, I'll start paying attention now, but I'd hate to kick Derrick in the balls because he spoke with his hands."

Erin laughed. "I'm sure Derrick would hate that also."

"I know what we can do," continued Lisa. "If Derrick and I start getting really serious, you can put him in your MRI machine and scan his brain. Then we'd know for sure."

"Haven't you already told him what I study?"

Lisa frowned. "Yeah. You did come up. The mystery roommate. So you're saying he'd probably figure out that's what we were doing. That he might not appreciate it that his girlfriend thinks he might be a psycho."

Erin opened her mouth to respond when her phone vibrated in her pocket. She pulled it out and read the caller ID. "Sorry, it's my boss. I need to take this."

The phone conversation lasted less than a minute, but all the sunshine that this discussion with Lisa had let into Erin's life quickly vanished.

"Erin?" said Lisa worriedly, not having to be an expert in body language to know that something was very wrong.

"Sorry, but I have to go," said Erin, shoving the last of her sandwich into her mouth and chasing it down with a long drink of water.

"What is it?"

"Seems the dean of my department wants to see me

and my advisor in his office," she replied. "Immediately. If not sooner."

"What about?"

"I have no idea," replied Erin. She frowned deeply and then added, "But, apparently, he isn't a happy camper."

4

ERIN AND HER thesis advisor sat before the desk of Dean Richard Borland in two brown leather chairs that looked stately, well padded, and exceedingly comfortable, which only went to show that you couldn't judge a chair by its appearance. Whoever had designed the chairs must have been the world's leading expert on the human body to be able to design one this unsuited to the human posture.

Erin watched the dean's glowering face and wondered if he had bought these chairs on purpose to unsettle his visitors. Not that he wasn't fully capable of making visitors squirm and become miserably uncomfortable all by himself.

The dean handed her a section of the *Wall Street Journal* once she was fully locked into the torture chair, doing so with such contempt that he threw it on her lap more than handed it to her. She glanced down. It was one of the weekend sections of the paper that boasted the highest circulation of any in the country. The lead story, which took up the entire front page of the section, top and bottom, and continued onto the next page was entitled, "The Psychopaths Among Us."

Erin handed the paper to Apgar beside her, having

learned on her way here that he didn't have any better idea than she did as to why the dean had demanded an audience, and why the man seemed so unhappy. Apgar scanned the title as well.

"Have you seen this?" demanded the dean.

Erin and her advisor both shook their heads no.

"Really?" said the dean to Erin pointedly. "I find that hard to believe." He leaned toward her with a scowl. "Since you're *quoted* in it."

Erin blanched. "What are you talking about?"

"Don't tell me you didn't know."

"I didn't know. I don't read this paper. And there has to be some mistake. If I had spoken with a reporter from the *Wall Street Journal*, believe me, I'd remember it."

"Can you give us a few minutes to read this, Richard?" said Apgar.

Dean Borland fumed but nodded, handing Erin the same section from a second copy of the paper he had on his desk. She and Apgar read silently while the dean drummed his fingers on his desk impatiently.

The story spoke of the progress being made in the study of psychopathy, especially focusing on the differences in brain physiology that were continuing to be uncovered almost every year now. And then the story got to Erin, who was quoted on the second page. She was introduced as a graduate student at the University of Arizona, studying differences in the brains of psychopaths and normals, both with respect to their structure and the electrical patterns given off in response to certain stimuli. The article went on to say:

Ms. Palmer says that her ultimate objective is to perfect a diagnostic that can identify a psychopath from the electrical patterns of their brains—and do so remotely. "The technology isn't quite there yet," she explains. "But great progress is being made on two fronts. First, scientists are learning how to pick up electrical impulses from the brain to control artificial limbs, video games, and the like. If we can download movies wirelessly, we should be able to detect brain waves wirelessly—at least from a short distance. The trick is to find identifiable differences in electrical patterns between psychopaths and normals, which is one of the things I'm working on. My ultimate goal would be to develop a device you could have on your key ring that would vibrate, or alert you in some other way, when a psychopath is within fifty feet. An early warning system."

The article continued, this time switching gears to another topic in the study of psychopathy. She and Apgar finished the article at about the same time, and she wasn't mentioned further.

Erin glanced at her advisor and winced before turning to the dean. "This is from *years* ago," she explained. "*Three* years ago to be exact. It's from an interview I did with a tiny local paper." Her features darkened. "Can a reporter *do* that?" she demanded. "I mean, a reporter can't just take a quote I gave to another paper and use it three years later like it's a fresh one," she finished, her voice filled with outrage.

The dean shook his head in disgust. "Well, I'm guessing a reporter *can* do that," he snapped. "Since this one *did*." He eyed Apgar. "Why wasn't I told about this interview three years ago then?"

"It was harmless," replied Apgar. "I didn't even know about it until the paper put it online. It was small-time. Even when it was posted online it hardly got any hits. And I made it very clear to Erin that she had stepped on a land mine and never to think about saying anything like that again. Who could have known it would go national three years later?"

The dean ignored Apgar and turned his focus back on Erin. "You've really stepped in it this time—whether it was this weekend or three years ago. Makes no difference. As if your research wasn't controversial enough. I had reps from the ACLU calling me all morning, and any number of news stations and papers. You do realize we survive on grants here, right? We do solid research. Not flamboyant research. Or controversial research. And we don't show-boat."

"What did the ACLU want?" said Apgar.

"What do you think? You know, or you wouldn't have told Erin she hit a land mine three years ago. They were outraged! And I don't blame them. Talk about infringing on civil liberties. What Erin says she's trying to accomplish—in the name of the University of Arizona, for Christ's sake—is a modern-day Scarlet Letter."

"Look, I know why it was wrong," said Apgar. "But Erin's heart was in the right place, even though her head was in the wrong one. And I bet most of the people who read this article would love to see a project like this succeed. Psychopaths destroy lives, even the ones who aren't violent criminals. In a perfect world, it would be extremely useful to know who fell into this category."

"I'm sure it would be," said Borland. "So you could discriminate against them. Even if they were never arrested or convicted of any crime or wrongdoing. A device that would turn every citizen into their own private thought police, convicting other citizens to a lifetime of being shunned on the basis of their brain-wave patterns alone. And if this isn't bad enough when the test is accurate, what about false positives? If even one in a hundred was a mistake—can you imagine? Wives leaving their husbands. 'Wow, he was a loving husband and father, but my key ring vibrated—so he must be a psychopath. Who knew?' "

The dean shook his head angrily. "I've seen the research proposals for every student in the department. And this was never mentioned. Were you both trying to hide it from me? Is this some kind of stealth project?"

"*No*," said Apgar emphatically. "Because it *isn't* a project. Erin was just speculating. Three years ago, she did hope to initiate a second phase of research, geared toward wireless detection of psychopaths. But she hadn't yet written up the proposal or discussed it with me. When I read about it online, I told her the same thing you've just told her; that a project like this would be fraught with controversy and unintended consequences. She understood what I was saying and agreed with me. Yes, she's still trying to identify differences in electrical patterns between psychopaths and normals. But not for the purpose of creating a remote diagnostic. I promise you."

"That may be so," said the dean, "but that doesn't change the fact that no one will believe it. You think they're going to believe me that this misguided project—a gleam in the eye of a raw young grad student—was aborted before it started three years ago? When the goddamned *Wall Street Journal* has her quoted, *yesterday,* as saying this is a research goal of hers? A research goal, by extension, supported by the *University of Arizona*?"

Erin knew the vast majority of people would be thrilled to have the device she had so carelessly described. Ironically, only a short while ago her roommate had been clamoring for a way to conclusively test for psychopathy. And there was no doubt that even if mistakes were made, lives would be saved on balance. But she had come to agree with the dean. She had developed her thinking on this subject far beyond that of either the dean or her advisor, of that she was sure, and she was paying a terrible price, emotionally, for this evolution.

Apgar had, indeed, gotten her to think deeply on this subject three years earlier, and she had been doing so ever since, which had led her to a deep study of philosophy and ethics and to a seismic shift in her thinking. She had ultimately come to concede the validity of his—and now the dean's—point of view on this subject. And it couldn't be very fun for the dean to get outraged calls from the ACLU and others, especially since he had the responsibility of protecting the university and the department from controversy.

Erin took a deep breath. "We can demand a correction," she said. "I'm pretty sure they can't do what they did here."

"Yeah, good luck with that," said Dean Borland dismissively, as though she had just fallen off the turnip truck. And in this case, maybe she *was* out of her league. The media had considerable power, and the last thing she needed was more controversy—or more of a spotlight on this topic.

"Ever since Jason completed *his* work," continued the dean, "I've had to deal with conservative groups, worried that if we proved the brains of psychopaths were truly structurally aberrant, these monsters might use this information as a defense at trial. Insisting they had no control of their actions. And now I have liberal groups worried about discrimination *against* psychopaths, for Christ's sake. That's my dream, to be a punching bag for both ends of the political spectrum. Just shoot me now."

"Look," said Apgar. "I know you feel like we've kicked a hornet's nest. And we have. But this will blow over before you know it. I'm sure it will."

"Yeah, I'm sure it will also. Because I'm pulling Erin from her project."

Erin's eyes widened. "What!" she said. "You can't do that."

But even as she said this, like half of a schizophrenic personality, a weary voice whispered to her to let it go. That this would be for the best. She was so tired. Tired of deception. Tired of guilt. Tired of wrestling with issues of ethics and morals so thorny the densest rosebush seemed like a downy pillow by comparison. How easy it would be to cave, to use this as an excuse to stop what she was doing and bring the one foot she had hanging over the abyss back to firm ground. But something in her wouldn't let her. Not after she had come this far. Despite the severe price it was extracting, she couldn't leave matters unfinished.

"Look . . . Erin," said the dean. "I'm doing you a favor here. You have more than enough data to get your Ph.D. and move on. Write up what you have and then find a nice university—one not named the University of Arizona—to do a postdoc. Jason should have forced you to begin writing up your thesis six months ago anyway."

"But I'm at the most important part of the research," said Erin, fighting to keep her voice calm.

"This isn't a discussion," said the dean.

Erin's mind raced. Ideally she could use two or three months of further study. To confirm, and polish, and refine, and measure. To get her scientific arms fully around the phenomenon. But she could get to a quick and dirty confirmation fairly quickly. It wouldn't be ideal, but it would have to do.

Erin blew out a long breath. "Okay," she whispered. "You're right." She paused for a few seconds to make sure the dean digested the fact that she was surrendering without a protracted battle. "Just give me two weeks to wrap up what I'm doing," she added casually, as though this was a request that was *beyond* reasonable. "And then I'll pull the plug."

"No. You're off the project. Effective immediately. When this meeting ends, I have to return dozens of calls. And you can bet your ass I'll be telling them you were removed from this project the instant I became fully aware of it. This will be just the beginning of damage control. God knows how I'll explain why I wasn't aware of it earlier."

Dean Borland shook his head. "Consider yourself lucky that I let you go on *this* long," he added. "You were a hair away from being removed from the project a year ago. I don't know if you're bad luck or what. But as good and dedicated a student as you are, trouble follows you. There are a number of groups around the world visiting prisons and studying psychopaths. So how is it that all of them combined have had one test subject die during their studies, and you've had *three*? *In the past two years.* This project was damned from the beginning."

Erin was speechless, but Apgar didn't have this same

problem. This decision impacted him as much as it did his student. As her advisor, Apgar would be a coauthor on the scholarly papers that would come from the research. "Richard, these unfortunate deaths are a separate issue," he insisted. "Having nothing to do with the *Wall Street Journal* piece. So I hope you didn't factor them in to reach your decision. Two prisoners had a stroke and died in their sleep. Yes, it was one in a million, but one-in-a-million events happen. Every day. The pathologist verified their strokes had nothing to do with Erin's research activities."

"Okay, two deaths are one in a million," responded the dean. "But then add in her being attacked in the trailer. I don't believe in curses, but if I did, this project would be cursed. Three inmate deaths. What are the odds of *that*?"

"Would you have preferred I let him kill me?" said Erin angrily. "Would that have helped the odds? Two inmates and a grad student dead?"

"No, of course not. Although you could have told us you were a female Chuck Norris earlier. Before this happened, Jason and I used to wonder if we were insane for agreeing to let you do this project in the first place. If we would have known how easy it was for the hundred-and-twenty-pound damsel to strike a lethal blow against the two-hundred-pound, weight-lifting inmate, we could have saved ourselves the trouble."

"I didn't mean to crush his windpipe," said Erin. "It was self-defense, and I struck harder than I realized. But why rehash any of this? I can only second what Dr. Apgar has said. The prison conducted a thorough investigation of all three deaths, and I was exonerated. If I hadn't been, the prison wouldn't have let me continue.

So that's in the past. It isn't fair to link that case and this one."

"Yes it is," said Borland. "Because I've already been asked about these deaths today by the media. The media and the ACLU don't have to do much digging into your research to learn about these incidents. It's not like they're hidden. They just pop right out. I have no doubt some people will wonder if you're *studying* inmates, or picking them off one by one, *Ten Little Indians* style."

Erin frowned deeply. "The thing about the wireless psychopath detector was a mistake. I admit that. But one I made years ago and didn't repeat. The other incidents happened, but I had nothing to do with them. Please don't do this," pleaded Erin. "Not now. Just give me a single week."

The dean shook his head, his expression even grimmer than before, if this was even possible. "I'm sorry," he said in a tone that suggested he really wasn't. "But you're done. As of this second. And no power on earth is going to change that."

5

"GOOD MORNING, ERIN," said Alejandro cheerfully as she entered the prison grounds and the heavy steel door slid shut loudly behind her.

"Morning," she said, adjusting her hideous and useless glasses and trying hard not to look as nervous as she felt.

She had ended her meeting with Dean Borland by

making sure he knew how much she disagreed with his decision, but also making it clear that she was prepared to respect it. She would halt her current study and begin writing her doctoral thesis. He was right. This was long overdue, and she had enough data for two doctorates.

She had assured both the dean and her advisor that she would inform prison authorities immediately that her study had come to an end, and make arrangements for the mobile lab to be removed from the yard once and for all. She had also told them she would be taking a two-week vacation to sort things out in her head and get a new lease on life, starting immediately. She would get a fellow grad student to fill in for the two missed teaching days this would entail.

After they had left the dean's office, Apgar had apologized profusely for what had happened, and told her she was the most impressive graduate student he had ever had. She thanked him for trying to defend her and reassured him that her thesis would make him proud.

But she had no intention of pulling up stakes. Not when she was this close.

"I know you won't believe this," she said to Alejandro, "but I'm actually taking a vacation soon." He had often told her she spent more time on the prison grounds than the inmates, and encouraged her to do just this.

"No!" said the guard in mock horror. "Say it isn't so."

Erin forced herself to smile. Her actions needed to appear perfectly normal, no matter how nervous she was on the inside. "I'm afraid it's true. I finally decided to take your advice, Alejandro."

She sighed. "But here's the bad news. I have a lot I want to accomplish before I go. So I'll be working far more hours than normal for at least the next few days. And seeing far more prisoners."

"Is that even possible?"

"You wouldn't think so," she admitted. "But I'm planning to be very efficient. The inmates will be in and out. Like an assembly line. Each examination will be much shorter and more focused than usual."

Her research would be quick and dirty. But she would have her confirmation. She hadn't run a marathon to be stopped just a few blocks short of the finish line. Too much was at stake to let an academic bureaucrat stand in the way—even if he was right—which she knew in her heart he probably was. So she would forge ahead at top speed, not even stopping for the weekend, which luckily wasn't a necessity, since a prison was the ultimate 24/7 establishment.

As Alejandro left to bring her the first prisoner on her lengthy list, she pulled out her cell phone and called her advisor, knowing he wouldn't be in for another hour yet. She took a deep breath and tried to steady her nerves. The phone rang and then was kicked over to voice mail. She waited for his message and the beep, her heart beating faster than normal. This kind of deception wasn't like her. But then again, she had been engaged in a vast deception for years—so maybe it *was* like her. She wasn't sure *who* she was anymore.

She heard a loud beep and began. "Jason, this is Erin. I just wanted to let you know that I've notified the prison I won't be coming back. And Mobile Medicine will pick up their MRI trailer later today, although, according to the lease, they'll still bill us 'til the end of the month. If you need me for any reason while I'm away, feel free to call my cell. Anyway, give my best to everyone in the lab, and I'll see you in a few weeks. And thanks again for giving me a chance to do this work—and for defending me."

Erin ended the connection and stared off into space. If Apgar or the dean happened to call the prison this week, things could get very ugly, very quickly. And while they probably wouldn't call, there were no guarantees. So she was working on borrowed time. At some point, something would happen to tip them off that she had lied to them and hadn't yet pulled the plug. So she was in a race to the finish line. If she were caught, she was almost certain she could kiss her Ph.D. good-bye.

Alejandro returned with yet another in an endless series of men dressed in orange. The first of the morning. The first she would see in direct violation of the dean's edict. This one was named Tony, and he had robbed three convenience stores, wearing a Homer Simpson mask, killing the clerk in each store with a single bullet between the eyes.

Erin told Tony the visit would be shorter and more focused than usual.

"Too bad," he responded with a friendly smile. "You know how much I enjoy your company."

She nodded but didn't reply. If only she hadn't seen his record, or known him for what he was, she might have enjoyed his company as well.

Erin braced herself psychologically. It was going to be a long, long day. The first of many.

6

—∿∿—

FIVE STRESS-FILLED DAYS and fifty-seven prisoners later, looking over her shoulder the entire time, expecting to be found out at any moment, Erin had her answer.

Her preliminary results had been confirmed. And then some.

She had purposely not breathed a word of her progress to Hugh Raborn in California. She hadn't wanted to raise false hopes, only to later uncover sharp, exposed nails beneath what at first glance looked like a plush, inviting carpet. During her recent discussion with Raborn, she had been careful not to even hint that there was anything newsworthy to report. She hadn't mentioned that she had been pulled from the project, or that she had been forging ahead against direct orders.

So should she call him now? Tell him the great news about their joint project?

She had finished her work by noon on Sunday and was all set to call him that night when she had an inspiration. This was the pinnacle of their work together. This news warranted more than just a video chat. It called for a celebration.

Everyone she knew was always encouraging her to open up, to be more spontaneous. So what better time to do it? Her entire lab thought she was on vacation, anyway, so why not take advantage of that and *really* get away for a few days?

And she had never even met Hugh Raborn. Sure, they had Skyped many times over the past few years, but for this, the ultimate achievement, she wanted to meet him in person. She had previously proposed coming out to San Diego to meet him, but the few times she had found a seam in her busy schedule, he was traveling. This was bad luck, certainly, but since he seemed to travel more than any ten people she knew, combined, it wasn't entirely surprising—just disappointing. His travels usually led him to centers of biotechnology excellence like Boston, Washington, D.C., and the Bay Area. Unfortunately Tucson wasn't on this list, and his duties as an executive and his travel schedule had so far precluded even a brief visit to the university to meet her.

If the truth were to be known, they had a great working relationship. And while she had made some feeble attempts to arrange a meeting, she suspected neither of them were sure this was a good idea. What if an actual, physical meeting somehow changed the dynamic between them? Why take any risk with such an effective relationship? If it wasn't broken, why try to fix it?

But Erin knew her roommate was right. She did need human companionship. And a healthy dose of affection would do her psyche a world of good as well at this point. Hugh Raborn was older than she and wasn't exactly a movie star, but she found him quite attractive. And he was single. Maybe she'd have her one-night stand. Maybe more than one night. They had become quite friendly, and although they mostly discussed the project, they had certainly connected on an intellectual basis. He would be thrilled by her unexpectedly quick breakthrough, and if she made her visit a surprise, delighted by this gesture.

Besides, one of her good friends, with whom she had

become quite close when they were both winning medals at regional eighteen-and-under martial arts tournaments, lived in San Diego. So instead of holing up in her apartment until her fictitious vacation ended, she could get out. Go to the beach. See a friend. Clear her head. And maybe ignite the beginning of a romance.

Erin called her friend, Courtney, in San Diego. After catching up for fifteen minutes, Erin got to the point. "How do you feel about a visitor?" she said.

"You're coming to San Diego?" said Courtney excitedly.

"I am. I've decided to be spontaneous for once." She paused. "Which means that the visit is on short notice. Sorry about that."

"Better short than never, I always say. And my apartment is your apartment. When are you coming?"

"I'm on the earliest flight in the morning." The flight between Tucson and San Diego was little more than an hour. "I'll be in by nine."

Erin filled Courtney in on her plan to surprise Hugh Raborn, and possibly seduce him, without telling her about what they had been working on, or that she would be leaving the university sooner than she had expected. She would save that for when they were together. Maybe she would apply for a postdoc at the University of California, San Diego. Living in the most perfect climate on earth was tempting, and this way she could be close to both Raborn and Courtney.

"If Hugh Raborn is in," said Erin, "and I'm not even going to check before I come—how's that for spontaneous? Anyway, if he's in, with any luck, I won't need a place to sleep Monday night."

"I've seen your effect on men, Erin. You won't need *luck*. Well, as long as he's not taken."

"He's not."

"And he's not gay?"

"No, he's not gay." Erin paused in thought. Raborn had mentioned he wasn't in a current relationship, but he hadn't spoken much about past ones either. "At least I don't *think* he is," she amended. "I guess there's only one way to find out."

"I have to admit, I'm intrigued by this new side of you."

"Yeah, I'm full of surprises," said Erin. "I should be the poster child for *Girls Gone Wild*," she added wryly.

Erin waited for the laughter to subside on the other end of the phone. "How does this sound?" she continued. "We'll definitely get together on Tuesday, whenever you can. And I'll plan on spending the night at your apartment Tuesday night, if that's all right with you."

"Absolutely," said Courtney. "And I think I can switch some things around at work and take the day off Tuesday, so we can hang out the entire day."

"Fantastic," said Erin happily.

"And if your . . . friend . . . isn't in, or if things don't work out, we can have dinner Monday night and you can stay at my place then as well."

"I really appreciate it, Court. And sorry for putting top priority on this guy for Monday."

"Are you kidding?" said Courtney. "I'm psyched for you. I can hardly wait to hear all about it when you wander in Tuesday morning," she finished in amusement.

7

—❧—

ERIN LEFT THE airport rental car lot in a white Ford subcompact. Soon she was accelerating onto the I-5, which would lead her to her destination in La Jolla, Asclepius Pharmaceuticals, in only fifteen or twenty minutes.

Hugh Raborn had been an executive at Asclepius for a number of years, but claimed not to have been there when the company's unfortunate name had been chosen, one that didn't exactly roll off the tongue. Asclepius, Raborn had explained to her, was the Greek god of medicine and healing. Somehow, he had never become a household name in the real world, even though he was the son of Apollo and the father of two famous daughters, Hygeia, goddess of health, cleanliness, and sanitation, and Panacea, the goddess of universal remedy.

Erin couldn't shake the ever-increasing certainty that she was making a fool of herself. You couldn't just barge in on a busy man's life unannounced and expect him to drop everything and wine and dine you like it was the night of the high school prom. He might not be in at all, or he could be in high-level meetings that he couldn't get out of.

On the other hand, this was news he'd been waiting for much of his adult life. She knew how much it meant to him. This should be one of the rare occasions when even the busiest executive could allow himself the luxury of canceling his schedule for the day and celebrating in style. He owed at least this much to her. He had re-cruited her, after all, and it was she who had taken the lion's share of the risk while he remained insulated from it.

Erin reflected on her seemingly innocent interview with a local paper three years earlier. It was incredible how dra-matically this seemingly minor event had changed the course of her life, *and was still changing it.* There were moments in time at which a seemingly small, unimportant event could be amplified in unforeseeable ways, creating ripples that grew into tidal waves, affecting lives, and even the world, in profound ways.

A chance contamination of a single one of Fleming's *Staphylococci* culture dishes had led to the world's first antibiotic, penicillin, marking a revolution in medicine, and saving countless lives. Or, on the more mundane side, how often had Erin heard stories of people meeting their future spouses because of one-in-a-million chance occurrences—like a blown tire on a highway or a ran-dom restaurant choice.

Erin's interview with this small Tucson paper had cer-tainly become one of a few pivotal tipping points in her own personal history, of that there could be no doubt. Not only had it led to her recent removal from her project and difficulty with the dean, but two years earlier it had been the reason Hugh Raborn had first contacted her, changing the course of her research, and the course of her life, in ways she could not have foreseen.

He had called her and introduced himself, and told her he was considering sponsoring her research. She had sug-gested talking to Apgar, but Raborn had said he wanted to speak with her first.

"What can I do for you?" she had said.

"I'm vice president of Neuroscience Research for Asclepius Pharmaceuticals. We're a small biotech company in San Diego with about three hundred employees. We do research on cardiovascular and central nervous system diseases like epilepsy."

As he was speaking, she Googled the company on her laptop, getting the spelling of Asclepius close enough that Google suggested the correct one, which she accepted. The company's Web page was impressive—very sleek and high end.

She hit the Executive Management link and ten thumbnails came up immediately. Raborn's picture was the third one down. He was thirty-six. Erin knew this was young for someone so accomplished, but from his picture she would have guessed he was even younger. He had a full head of jet-black hair and appeared to be trim and in excellent shape.

"I came across an online article last week in which you were quoted," continued Raborn, while she studied his picture.

Erin winced. The interview she had given the year before to the *Tucson Neighborhood Journal* had been placed online, along with considerable other historical content from the publication. The great thing about the Internet, or the worst thing, depending on your perspective, was that an article never died. Forty years from now, the occasional searcher might still stumble over this piece, long after the *Tucson Neighborhood Journal* wasn't even a memory. Apgar had also seen this interview online ten months earlier and had chewed her out good for speaking publically about such a project, or even considering it. He made it clear that this was *not* something on which she would be working, now or ever.

"Anyway," said her caller, "I was intrigued by your goal of a psychopath early warning device."

"Um . . . thanks," said Erin uncertainly.

"I had an . . . unpleasant . . . run-in with a psychopath about fifteen years ago. I'd prefer not to go into details, but it opened my eyes to the monsters among us. If I would have had one of the gadgets you spoke of, it could have saved . . ." He paused. "It would have been very good."

Silence came over the line, and Erin had a sense that this Hugh Raborn was collecting himself.

"Since then," he continued, "I've made myself an expert in the field. I was already a neuroscientist, so I was well equipped to study the problem of psychopathy from a number of angles."

Erin was intrigued. She had no intention of showing any of her cards, but perhaps Hugh Raborn was a kindred spirit. Each had been the victim of this human plague. Maybe this man would share her dedication and commitment, but with a larger wallet and greater access to key people and resources.

"Go on," she said evenly.

"While I would, personally, strongly support the development of a device like the one you propose, I think you'll find you'll get a huge amount of resistance to the idea."

Erin suppressed a groan. *Now you tell me*, she thought in amusement. Where had he been when she had agreed to speak with that amateur reporter in the first place? He could have saved her from a very irate thesis advisor.

"While a detector would be very useful," he continued, "I suspect it would create so many legal and ethical controversies that it would never be used. And my research suggests there aren't enough differences in the electrical patterns between psychopaths and normals anyway. When they are thinking certain thoughts, perhaps, but you'd miss them ninety-nine percent of the time." He paused. "So a few years ago, I came up with an even better idea. One with a greater chance for success than the one you're working on, even though this may seem counterintuitive."

Erin's mind jumped ahead and tried to guess where he was going with this, but she drew a blank. Raborn remained silent for several seconds, probably to build the suspense. If so, it was certainly working.

"I'm listening," said Erin.

"My idea is to treat the condition as a disease," he said calmly. "And cure it."

Erin shook her head in disbelief. "Cure it?" she repeated. "*Cure* psychopathy? You've got to be kidding me."

"Not at all," said Raborn. "Why not? I've read every last paper on the differences in the brain structure of psychopaths and normals, including the one written by your advisor, Dr. Apgar. And if I do say so myself, I'm as good as it gets at molecular biology and pharmacology."

"Impossible," said Erin. "Who knows how many genes contribute to a psychopath's aberrant brain structure? We're finding more differences every year. You'd have to find all the genes, and then modulate them in just the right way to remodel the brain."

"Very good," said Raborn approvingly. "You're up on your molecular pharmacology. Turns out I *have* found them all. All eight."

"I find that very hard to believe. Genes that contribute to this type of brain physiology don't just advertise themselves. Even finding a single one is a needle-in-a-haystack exercise. I don't care how good you are."

"This is true. But along with my considerable expertise, I spent a lot of my personal fortune to attack the problem. I obtained DNA samples from psychopaths and normals and had the entire genomes sequenced."

Erin considered. When the genome was first sequenced, it was an accomplishment akin to sending a man to the moon, a worldwide effort to decipher the more than three billion base pairs in the human genome, which would fill thousands of volumes the size of encyclopedias if actually printed out. The effort had cost billions of dollars and had taken a decade. And this was just to get to a rough draft, which had been accomplished at the turn of the millennia. Only twelve years later, the entire sequence of a human genome, taken from a psychopath or a saint, could be deciphered for under ten thousand dollars in a matter of weeks. And presently, after additional years of further progress, it was far faster and less expensive even than this. This increase in speed and reduction in cost was even more profound than that seen in the computer industry, and was nothing short of miraculous.

"The goal, of course, was to compare them," continued Raborn. "Find all key differences between the genome of a normal and the genome of a psychopath. I paid a team of mathematicians a small fortune to devise algorithms I could use to sort through the billions of bytes of data and possible permutations. The program eventually identified eight genes that differed, each contributing to the condition."

"*If* that's true," said Erin, making sure her emphasis on the word, *if,* was unmistakable, "you've done an amazing piece of science. It's a great first step. But it's still a first step—up Mount Everest."

"Allow me to continue," said Raborn. "I was able to devise a gene-therapy cocktail that makes use of genetic engineering techniques to replace the abnormal sections of these genes."

"All eight of them?"

"Yes."

"So you're suggesting you've succeeded? That you've found a cure for psychopathy?"

"That's what I'm saying. It took dedication, a new approach, and a stroke of genius. And I won't lie to you—a tremendous amount of luck. But I think I've done it."

Erin considered hanging up, but decided he would just call back. She needed the conversation to reach its logical conclusion. "If true, this would be breakthrough work. So why hasn't this been published in a peer-reviewed journal?" she asked, knowing the answer already. Because the snake oil Raborn was selling would never make it past the level of scrutiny required to make it into a prestigious journal.

"I'm keeping this my own little secret for now. I've been working on this—in secret—every spare second I could get for the past few years, and hiring others to help with certain pieces of the puzzle. Without telling them the true nature of the project. Not yet."

"Look, no one would be more excited than me if you could truly find a way to reverse this condition. But for the sake of argument, even if you could replace these eight genes with normal versions, that doesn't mean you'll have a cure. Who knows what will happen? And you can't even test it in animals, because there aren't any animal models of psychopathy."

"Well, there is one. Nothing that approximates the full syndrome. But I'm sure you know that rodents with

septo-hippocampal lesions share some psychopathic behaviors. I used this model in the early going. But I also
sequenced the mouse genome, and found mouse analogs
for all eight genes. Sure enough, if you knock these genes
out, mice show the same aberrant behaviors as those with
septo-hippocampal lesions. And more."

"So you created psychopathic mice?"

"Right. The same abnormal genes and the same behaviors, at least as far as can be identified in an animal of
this limited intelligence. Then I corrected these genes.
When I did, I corrected the condition as well. The mouse
brains were restored to normality. It took hundreds of experiments, but I was able to reverse their psychopathy."

There was a very long silence. "I don't want to seem
rude," said Erin, "but I should probably come right to the
point. I don't believe you."

Raborn laughed. "I don't blame you. Shows you're
sane. It wasn't easy, even after I corrected the genes.
What I found is that the normal versions of these genes
all work in concert to create the normal condition. And
there is a delicate interplay between all of their gene
products. So it's a two-step process. Just replacing the
genes isn't enough. Because even if you have normal
genes, if you don't make sure they are activated in just
the right way, that they are all being expressed—dosed,
if you will—at the precisely correct levels, you still get
the psychopathic condition. In fact, if normal genes aren't
expressed correctly, you could make the condition worse
than if you hadn't fixed them at all. So the trick is to not
only fix the genes, but determine the levels needed, and
modulate their expression accordingly."

Erin shook her head. If she hadn't believed this was

possible before, Raborn certainly hadn't helped his case by explaining it was even more difficult than she had thought. She wasn't a molecular biologist, but cells had numerous complex mechanisms for controlling genes. There was a lot going on at the molecular level, and trying to understand such a complex interaction, let alone measure it, had to be fantastically difficult. "And you were able to determine the precise levels needed for all eight genes?" she asked skeptically.

"Unfortunately, no. It wasn't for lack of trying, but this proved to be an intractable problem. Even with mice. I ended up having to arrive at the answer through trial and error. As far as I can tell, there is no other way. It took many hundreds of attempts to get it right. Much as you might have to try hundreds or even thousands of combinations to stumble on the one that would open a padlock." He paused. "For the modulation of these genes, theory doesn't help. It has to be determined empirically."

There was a long silence on the line.

"I know my call is out of left field, and what I'm telling you sounds utterly fantastic. But I urge you to look up my credentials and read some of my work, which is quite rigorous. And I'd be happy to send you all of the data I've generated so far. I think you'll find it quite eye-opening."

Erin considered. "Okay, for the sake of argument, let's imagine that you send me your data and it's everything you claim it to be. So if it is, why haven't you initiated clinical trials in man to try to get this cure of yours approved?"

"That's the rub," said Raborn, the enthusiasm in his voice giving way to weariness. "This therapy will *never* be approved. Not using the standard drug-approval pathway. First, the FDA likes to see efficacy in two animal species, if possible, and I only have one. One that hasn't even been designated as an appropriate model yet. And even if they accept my model, the therapeutic window in mice is too small to ever get past them. The effective dose and the lethal dose are too close for comfort. Even though I have theoretical and experimental reasons for believing the therapeutic window will be larger in man."

"For something this important, won't the FDA take that into account?"

Raborn laughed. "I see you haven't had many dealings with the FDA. They'd make a steel pipe look flexible. Trust me, they'd never let me begin a trial."

Erin's eyes narrowed. "I see. Why do I have a sick feeling that I know why you called me?"

"I need your help, Erin. I could sense your passion in the article I read. Your drive to give society a tool to deal with these monsters. It came through, loud and clear. And you're one of only a handful of researchers going into prisons and studying psychopaths, and taking MRIs of their brains on a daily basis."

"You want me to test your therapy on my inmates, don't you?"

There was another long silence on the line.

"You're out of your mind," said Erin.

"It's the only way. It has to be done empirically."

"Sure. And I go to jail."

"No one will ever know. I'll give you the therapeutic cocktail, and separately, the eight genes whose precise modulation is critical, at a wide variety of expression levels. You just have to add them to the mix in every possible combination until you find the one that works. It won't be easy, since we can be all but certain the delicate balance of these genes that does the trick in mice won't be the same balance needed in man. It took me hundreds of experiments, and it might take you the same. But when you've found the right combination, you'll see a complete reversal of the condition. The brains of your psychopathic subjects will read as normals. Their amygdalas will light up when given emotionally charged words. And as I mentioned, these abnormal genes would not only be replaced, but expressed correctly. So their brain structures will revert to normal—they will *be* normal—at the level of their DNA. *Right down to their sperm and ova.* And your MRI data will be there to document the entire thing."

"That's how it's *supposed* to work. But if there is one perfect combination of gene expression levels, I'm guessing there's at least one *imperfect* combination. A combination that is lethal. How many mice did you kill along the way?"

"Surprisingly few," said Raborn. "The vast majority of the wrong combinations do nothing. And as I've said, the therapeutic window with mice is very tight. It should be wider in man. So there is even less chance of hitting a lethal combination."

"But you have no idea really. Less chance doesn't mean no chance."

Erin heard a sigh at the other end of the phone. "No. There are never guarantees when testing experimental medicines. Test subjects have lost their lives in the name of clinical research and will do so again. It's unfortunate that this has happened. But that's the nature of drug development. It's a risk we have to take if we ever want to bring important new drugs to the world."

"This is true, but in FDA-sanctioned trials, these patients give their informed consent. The benefits and risks are carefully explained to them before they sign on. They know there is a chance things could go wrong, but they are volunteers. Going in with their eyes open."

"Look, Erin, you know that even if the FDA *would* allow a trial, psychopaths would never volunteer. They're all convinced there isn't anything wrong with them—it's the rest of us who have the problem." He took a deep breath. "Erin, you're working with violent offenders, most of them repeat offenders. And when they get out they'll do it again. You know they will. They have no conscience, no soul. If a few of them don't survive our trial, this will be a tragedy. But nothing like the tragedies they've already caused in countless lives. And will again."

"I won't do it," said Erin emphatically. "There is nothing you can say that will get me to change my mind about this. Period. I agree with what you say. And I have a history with a psychopath myself. I decided early on to study this condition, but not at the cost of my own soul. I vowed not to ever let this work erode my own moral standards."

Just after she had decided on the course her life would take, Erin had stumbled across a famous quote from Friedrich Nietzsche: a warning. *Battle not with monsters lest you become a monster,* he had written. *And if you gaze into the abyss, the abyss gazes into you.* She had taken this admonition to heart, determined not to let her work with monsters turn her into one herself.

"I'm not asking you to lower your moral standards.

Just to reconsider them. I'm asking you to look at the big picture. Think of how many lives you'd be saving if you could wipe this scourge from the face of the earth. I'm not suggesting you *kill* psychopaths to get rid of them. All I'm asking is to *cure* them. Turn them into humans. Give them back a soul. You'd be doing them the ultimate service."

Raborn paused for just a moment to let his points sink in and then pressed forward. "And think about the thousands and millions of victims around the globe you'd be saving. Not just the victims of violent crimes, but of swindles, and heartbreak, and manipulation. Now and for all future generations. If you knew the death of a few of these remorseless killers you study in prison would save tens of thousands of lives, tens of thousands of rape victims—often children—wouldn't this be worth it? And again, not just for this generation, but for all eternity. The total decrease in human pain and suffering would be monumental. Incalculable. And I'm not even saying any of your subjects will die, because I don't think they will. But if I'm wrong, and a few did end up dying, are you saying they wouldn't have died for a noble cause?"

"I won't do it," said Erin.

But she said it with far less conviction this time. And she made no move to end the conversation.

8

ERIN PARKED THE Ford rental car in the large parking lot shared by Asclepius Pharmaceuticals and several other biotech companies in the industrial park. The sky was a vibrant blue, and exotic, tropical vegetation could be seen everywhere a visitor looked. Streams and small fake waterfalls wound their way along the common grounds of the biotech park, and the modern buildings were all four stories tall and made of blue-tinted glass, only the engraved marble obelisks in front of each differentiating one from another.

Here goes nothing, thought Erin nervously. Would Raborn be in? How would he react to her surprise? And where would she be spending the night?

She tried to convince herself that it was fun not knowing. Her life had become too programmed, she decided.

During her last conversation with Raborn, he had made no mention of travel, so she had high hopes that he would be in. If not, maybe she'd treat herself to the zoo or Sea-World before she met Courtney for dinner. One way or another, she was determined to have a fun, relaxing vacation, and stay well clear of any of the local prisons. In fact, as far as she was concerned, she was done with prisons forever.

She eyed Asclepius's lobby for a moment, but decided against this route. In for a penny, in for a pound. No use coming this far only to spoil the surprise by having a receptionist let Raborn know she was here. Sure, it was awkward to meet in the flesh after two years of a great Skype relationship. But Courtney had insisted that once Raborn saw Erin in spectacular 3-D, he would never be satisfied with Skype again. Especially if she was able to seduce him.

Raborn's office was inside Asclepius's vivarium, located within a nondescript building not officially affiliated with the biotech park, a few blocks away from their main offices, unlabeled so as not to attract attention from animal rights activists. She approached the entrance, a glass double-door, and pulled. She wasn't entirely surprised to find it locked, especially since there was a keycard scanner affixed to the wall nearby.

She peered inside. As expected, she couldn't see any animals, but she did spot a young technician in a white lab coat walking purposefully toward a door leading deeper inside the facility. But he was walking *away* from her.

She quickly rapped on the glass. A few seconds later, the tech changed directions and opened the door halfway, his body blocking the entrance. "Can I help you?" he said.

Erin smiled. "Yes. I'm an old friend of Dr. Raborn. In from out of town. But I was hoping to surprise him."

The tech eyed her up and down, but didn't find anything suspicious about her. She was wearing light cotton pants and a blue blouse, fairly form-fitting. The outfit was tasteful, but left little room for hidden weapons, cans of paint, or other items a militant animal rights activist might bring. And her beauty was disarming. If she was an activist, the tech decided he might consider joining the movement himself. "Old friend, huh? You don't look old enough to be anyone's old friend," he said flirtatiously.

She threw him a thousand-watt smile. "Okay, you caught me," she said. "I'm actually a young . . . ish . . .

friend of Dr. Raborn. He told me his office was at the back of your vivarium. Is he in today?"

The tech threw the door open and stepped to the side. "You're in luck. I just saw him in his office fifteen minutes ago. Do you want me to take you to him?"

"That would be great," said Erin.

The vivarium was an expansive stainless-steel complex. A high-throughput, fully computerized animal-processing plant. It was designed to facilitate animal experimentation and it performed its function flawlessly. Erin had never been in one, but she knew all about them. Animals were routinely sacrificed for the sake of science across the world, in immunology classes in undergraduate and graduate school, and for experimentation of every kind.

Pharmaceutical companies were typically filled with well-meaning animal lovers who had no choice but to develop a clinical callousness toward the many animals that were sacrificed. The FDA required that experimental drugs be tested in animals, and even required companies to administer higher and higher doses of their drugs until exactly half of the animals tested were killed—a dose called the Lethal Dose 50, or LD50—before allowing a drug to be tested in humans.

"Would you like me to tell you about the facility while we walk?" asked the young lab tech.

Erin realized she had been openly gawking. "That obvious I'm a tourist?"

"Pretty much," said the tech. "But that's okay. We've all given plenty of tours to friends and relatives." He began walking and turned back toward Erin. "So we house seven different species here: rats, mice, rabbits, guinea pigs, gerbils, hamsters, and Yucatan mini-pigs."

"Yucatan mini-pigs?"

"Yeah. They're about eighty pounds and they look like fangless wild boars. So don't be thinking of the adorable little pink ones that you see in children's zoos."

"Got ya," said Erin.

"Animals are delivered, put in cages with barcodes, and placed in separate rooms by species. Water is purified and piped into each cage automatically—computer controlled. Humidity, temperature, air quality, and lighting in each room are carefully monitored as well."

"Right. Making sure you eliminate all extraneous variables from your experiments."

"Exactly." He waved his arm toward a doorway. "Those are the surgical suites. I won't take you in, but they're pretty much what a human surgical suite would look like. We go beyond government mandates when it comes to anesthesia and are as humane as we can possibly be."

She nodded grimly. Billions of chickens and other food animals were killed each year, maybe even each week for all Erin knew, but for some reason a vivarium run by a pharmaceutical company just seemed more like a horror chamber. She wasn't sure why.

What was truly remarkable was her mind's ability to partition itself. To create a nearly impenetrable barrier to block out, not just the memory of the night she lost her family, but the emotional content of these memories as well. She was now in a facility that did experimentation on animals, which might be expected to trigger her memory of a mutilated puppy. And it did. But only for an instant, before another part of her mind was able to clamp down on this and push it away. After years of nightmares and debilitating fear and mistrust of others as a child living with her aunt and uncle, of waking in the middle of the night screaming, drenched in sweat, her mind had, mercifully, made an adjustment that had allowed her to live a normal life—free of her demons.

For the most part.

"Carcasses are taken out through the unsterilized side of the building," continued the lab technician, "bagged, and thrown into large freezer units. We have an outside service remove the ones we make radioactive during the experiments."

"Where do they take them?"

The tech tilted his head in thought. "Good question," he said. "I really don't know. Wouldn't you rather ask where the nonradioactive ones go?" he added with a smile.

"You read my mind," said Erin, returning the smile. "Where do the nonradioactive carcasses go?"

"I'm glad you asked. These are donated to the San Diego Zoo and put on the menu for the carnivores there."

Erin raised her eyebrows. "I guess if their polar bears start glowing in the dark, you know you've mixed up the carcasses."

The tech laughed and continued walking. As they approached a long black lab table, made of a substance that was smooth and seemed as hard as concrete, the tech said, "You may find this a bit . . . grisly."

A row of glass cylinders were aligned on one of the black benches, one every two feet. Attached to each apparatus was a single pink, throbbing, disembodied reddish-pink mass, about the size of a small pebble, continuously being bathed in a solution, half of which contained experimental drugs. Each fleshy mass, which could only be a heart, continued beating rhythmically as though unaware it was now without an owner. A thin wire led from each heart to a computer monitor that recorded the frequency and force of each contraction.

"Rat hearts," said the tech.

The hearts beat with inhuman speed. *Thump thump! Thump thump! Thump thump!* Erin's lips curled up in disgust. *Grisly was an understatement,* she thought. "So rat hearts will keep beating, even without the rat," she mused. "Who knew?"

The tech took a quick detour into a doorway where a female lab technician in a long white lab coat held a rat by its tail. She set it down and deftly placed a two-pronged metal probe, which resembled a small tuning fork, quickly into the rat's beady red eyes, while simultaneously pressing a button that delivered a powerful jolt of electricity directly into them. The rat went into a convulsion and she carefully recorded the duration of this in a lab notebook that was open on the table.

"Ah . . . I think I've seen enough," said Erin. She was able to seal off her traumatic memories, but there was no need to push it. "Not that I don't appreciate the tour. This was really interesting, in a *torture-chamber-straight-out-of-a-horror-film* sort of way. But I should be surprising Dr. Raborn while the surprising is good."

The tech nodded. "You got it." He led her another thirty yards, took a left, and stopped in front of an office. The outside had a placard that read Dr. Hugh Raborn, M.D./Ph.D., Vice President, Neuroscience.

Erin's pulse raced. The moment of truth had arrived.

Raborn's door was open and he was busily typing into his computer as they approached. Erin stood at the door, ignoring the butterflies in her stomach and hoping her face wasn't flush from the excitement she was feeling.

"Dr. Raborn, an old friend of yours is here to see you," said the lab tech, gesturing toward Erin standing slightly behind him.

Raborn looked up from his computer and his eyes fell upon Erin. He looked her up and down for several seconds, his face expressionless. Finally, he turned back to the technician. "Troy, if this is some kind of joke, I'm afraid I'm missing the punch line."

Erin's jaw dropped open at the sound of his voice. For just a moment she was unable even to speak.

"She said she was an old friend of yours and wanted to surprise you," said the technician, inching away from Erin and now studying her suspiciously.

Raborn shook his head. "I've never seen this woman before in my life," he insisted.

9

ERIN FELT DIZZY and could barely breathe. This was certainly the face she had seen on her computer monitor for years, there could be no doubt about it. Same name, same credentials, same company.

But it wasn't the same man.

She could hear the difference in his voice immediately. The man she knew so well was more of a tenor, whereas this one had more bass. The other spoke perfect English, but there was a hint of an accent that she had never been able to really define—although since he had been born and raised in the U.S. it must have been a regional accent that he was trying to change or conceal. The man in front of her spoke with no accent whatsoever.

What was going on?

What kind of game was he playing?

It was totally impossible for him *not* to be the man she had worked with for two years. Not only was he Hugh Raborn in appearance, but his title and company were those of the man she knew. People could put on different voices if they wanted. Celebrity impersonators could sound exactly like just about anyone.

But if he *was* just acting, just screwing with her mind for some reason, he would still have betrayed at least a hint of recognition during the first instant he had seen her outside of his office. And he had not. No one could fake their reaction to a complete surprise that well. No one.

On the other hand, this *had* to be him. No other explanation was possible.

So should she challenge him? Make a scene and insist he use his real voice? Her instincts told her not to. She needed to have time to think things through.

All of this analysis flashed across her mind in seconds. "My mistake," she croaked. "I guess the surprise is on me. I feel like an idiot. The friend I wanted to surprise is also named Hugh Raborn, and also lives in San Diego. But it just goes to show, you shouldn't Google people and try to surprise them without checking first."

Both Raborn and the tech named Troy eyed her as though she were a terrorist with a bomb strapped to her chest. Raborn looked as if he was deciding if he should call the police.

"Sorry about this," continued Erin. She immediately turned to the lab tech. "Troy, if you could lead me out of here, I'll get out of your hair right away and find the right person."

Raborn's eyes narrowed. "She didn't take any pictures, did she?" he asked Troy.

The lab technician shook his head. "None."

"Did she have her cell phone out at any time? She could have snapped off a bunch without you realizing."

"No. She never had it out."

Raborn caught Erin's eye and sighed. "Look," he said, "I know you'll never understand this, but we try to be as humane as we can be. Testing in animals leads to drugs that save millions of human lives throughout the world. Most of us are animal lovers. Really. I have two dogs at home that I love like children. But we don't have any choice. We're required to test our drugs in animals before we test them in humans."

Erin winced. "I'm really not here about animal rights," she said. "And I don't mean you any harm. I just made an innocent mistake. You can both escort me out of here if you'd like." She frowned deeply. "I'm just as eager to leave as you are to see me go."

10

ERIN PULLED OFF the road into a mini-mall and parked so she could take stock of what had just happened. Her mind was reeling.

She was faced with two impossible conclusions. Either Raborn had an identical twin, a doppelgänger—who just happened to share his name, title, and company—or he was playing some kind of sick game. She still didn't believe he could have faked his initial reaction to her so completely. So maybe he *had* known she was coming. As unlikely as this was, it seemed to make more sense than the alternatives.

She was engaged in illegal activity for him, after all. Maybe he had decided to pretend not to know her. So if she were caught, he could deny everything. He hadn't seemed the type. But the more she thought about it, the more she couldn't think of any other explanation that could possibly fit the facts.

Her hands balled into fists of their own volition. So if she called him in private, would he suddenly admit that he knew her, and make up some excuse for his charade? Would he apologize profusely?

You'd think he could have given her some indication. A wink. Anything. He could have told Troy he wanted to personally escort her from the premises, and then while alone with her whispered that he wanted to keep their relationship clandestine for reasons he would explain later.

Or had she been working with someone who had multiple personality disorder? That would be ironic, she thought. Maybe one of his personalities was psychopathic, and the other was a crusader against psychopathy.

She removed her phone from her pocket and took a deep breath. She hit the speed dial to Raborn's private cell phone. This ought to be interesting. She was furious, and if he thought she'd be forgiving him in this lifetime, he was seriously deluded.

So much for romance, she thought bitterly.

The phone was answered on the third ring. "Hi, Erin," said an enthusiastic voice. "How are things?"

The voice at the other end was one she knew well, not the one she had just heard at Asclepius. *"Don't give me that shit!"* she spat. "What kind of game are you playing here, Hugh? If you didn't want to admit you knew me, you could have at least winked or something."

"What are you talking about?" said Raborn.

"What I'm talking about is you pretending not to know me when I visited your office, you shithead. What I'm talking about is you putting on another voice all this time we've been Skyping. What, do you use a different voice for each of your accomplices?"

"You visited Asclepius?" said Raborn in alarm.

Erin shook her head in confusion. She wanted to reach through the phone and choke him to death, tell him that of course he knew she had visited Asclepius, but there was something in his tone that compelled her to take his question seriously. "Yes. I wanted to surprise you."

"Uh-oh," said Raborn. "That couldn't have gone well."

"You were there. You know exactly how it went."

"I wasn't there. You must have spoken to the real Dr. Hugh Raborn. Who had no clue who you were." He paused. "I'm sure you're pissed off beyond words right now. And I don't blame you."

"So why don't you explain what the hell is going on."

"Well, obviously I'm not Dr. Raborn. I lied to you. But I had good reason," he hastened to add.

"Let me guess. You're his identical twin—but with a different voice."

"No. No relation. I just needed credibility when I contacted you the first time. And I knew you'd check my background. So I took his identity. When we video chat, I have software that turns my face into his for transmission."

Erin shook her head adamantly. "Impossible," she said. "No technology is that good. Your lips and expression match your words perfectly. If there was software out there that could instantly transform your every last expression and lip movement onto a template face, and do it so seamlessly that it could fool someone over dozens of calls, I'd know about it."

"I'll explain everything," said the voice at the other end of the line. "Really."

"What should I even call you?" she said angrily, her rage intensified even further by the extreme hurt she was feeling. She had been betrayed by someone she had come to think of as a friend and scientific colleague. A man for whom she had made a pact with the devil to assist.

"You could just stick with Raborn, if you want. After two years, using a different name for me might not be ideal."

"Not *ideal*?" spat Erin. "Continuing to use the name of someone you've been impersonating, *someone you're not,* isn't exactly what I'd call ideal either. So what's your name? Your *real* name this time."

"Drake."

"Is that a first or last name?" said Erin.

"Both," he said, and then before they could discuss it further he added, "Look, Erin, I don't blame you for being furious. But I know you'll understand once I explain things. But before we go any further, tell me why you came to visit unannounced."

"Are you suggesting this is my fault? Because I attempted a surprise? Look, I don't have to explain *my* actions. You have to explain yours."

"I'm not blaming you in any way," he replied quickly. "This is entirely my fault. One hundred percent. I deceived you and I'll explain why to your satisfaction. But before we go further, I'd like to know. A surprise visit to San Diego isn't at all like you. So I have a guess as to what it might be."

She considered her response for several seconds and then said, "Your guess is right. I found it. I found the combination that reverses psychopathy."

"Outstanding!" he whispered exultingly. "Unbelievable! I thought it would take another year at least."

"So did I," she admitted. And then, as if testing it on for size added, "Drake."

She had gotten lucky. She had won the lottery. There was no guarantee her efforts would ever succeed, since mice and men were not the same, after all. And even if a cure existed, it could easily have taken her years more to find. And there could have been more fatalities than just three, although given the suspicion that these were beginning to arouse, if one more fatality had occurred she would have had to pull up stakes immediately, with or without a cure.

"I found it about a month ago. I didn't want to tell you until I'd confirmed it in a large number of inmates."

"And it worked on all of them?" said Raborn/Drake excitedly. "Total reversal in each case?"

"Yes. Within a few days of administration. On over fifty subjects. Not just the physiology, but the brain patterns in response to emotionally charged words. Everything. We have the absolute cure for psychopathy."

"Incredible."

Erin nodded. In the grand scheme of things, this made the parting of the Red Sea seem like a cheap parlor trick.

"Congratulations, Erin. I know you took all the risk, and the heat. I'm forever in your debt." He paused. "So what was the winning dose combination?"

"That's one of the things I was coming here to tell you. But now I don't know which end is up. I'd be an idiot to trust you with this after you've just admitted to a grand deception, starting the first second we ever spoke. I was prepared to tell Raborn. Not Drake," she added pointedly.

"Whoever I am, I'm still the one who made this possible. This is the culmination of considerable time and financial resources on my part. You *have* to tell me. *Right now.*" There was suddenly a menacing edge to his voice.

"I don't *have* to do anything. And I won't. Not until I understand what's going on here."

A heavy sigh came over the phone. "You're right," he said. "Sorry. I've got some trust to earn back. Okay, keep the combination secret. That's fine. But once I've explained why I've done what I've done, you'll understand. Then you can give me the secret and we can cure this condition once and for all."

"Are you even in San Diego . . . Drake?" she asked, purposely using this name more often than she normally would to begin to train her mind to a new reality.

There was a pause. "No. I live in Arizona, believe it or not. Near Yuma. Why don't we plan to meet tomorrow afternoon at the University of Arizona Student Union. On your home turf. In front of the bookstore entrance. I'll tell you everything. Say one thirty?"

Erin had the almost irresistible urge to agree, but as desperate as she was to get to the bottom of his deception, she couldn't do that to Courtney. She *wouldn't* do that to Courtney. Especially since her friend had called in favors to take the day off to be with her.

"I have business here in San Diego," said Erin. "We'll have to make it Wednesday at one thirty."

"What business could possibly be more important . . . "

Drake stopped abruptly, and Erin could imagine him almost literally biting his tongue. He had spoken with a fanatic intensity she had never heard in his voice before.

"Okay," croaked Drake, as though making a studied effort to speak calmly, but forgetting his teeth were clenched. "Wednesday at one thirty it is."

"It occurs to me . . . Drake," said Erin, "that I don't even know what you look like."

"I'll send photos to your phone before our meeting," he said. "I look forward to seeing you at the bookstore. Lunch is on me."

"You're damn right it is," said Erin. "And this had better be good."

"It will be," he assured her. "Trust me."

She ended the connection. Trust was the *last* thing she intended to give the man who had been impersonating Hugh Raborn. He had betrayed her for two years, and she had no idea what was really going on. She intended to take paranoia to ridiculous levels.

And he must have known she now had far less trust in him than she would have for a total stranger, which was why he knew to suggest a meeting place that was crowded and out in the open. Even so, even given her expertise at hand-to-hand combat, she intended to be prepared for this meeting, and take nothing for granted.

Something stunk so bad in Yuma that she could smell it in San Diego. She would go into this meeting with Raborn . . . with Drake . . . with her eyes open. And her concealed carry loaded.

11

THE MORE ERIN considered the situation with Drake, the more nervous she became. He seemed confident he could straighten it all out, but what if he was a psychopath himself? His actions seemed to fit the profile. Was he the one psychopath on earth who actually wanted to cure himself? Unlikely. There were doubtlessly many layers to this onion.

But if he was a psychopath caught in a lie, he would do just what he was doing. Roll with it. Come up with a web of even smoother lies to cover his tracks.

Whether he was a psychopath or not, she had to be prepared for him to tell her more lies, weaving a tapestry of deception that was utterly convincing somehow. So no matter what he told her when they met, she'd be a fool to trust him. It wasn't enough to go to the meeting prepared for a physical trap—she needed to be prepared for a psychological one as well.

What she really needed was a way to check up on what he told her. She needed to stalk him after the meeting was over and they had parted ways. His words were sure to be convincing—but his actions? If he told her he lived in Yuma and she followed him and learned otherwise, then she would know for sure he was still lying to her. But if his actions matched his story, then she could start to believe. She needed to be paranoid, but she also didn't want to be boxing at shadows if he did tell her the truth.

Courtney would be at work until dinner, so she had plenty of time on her hands. She Googled "GPS tracking devices" on her phone. Endless links appeared immediately. She scanned down the page. The Spy Gear Superstore caught her eye. Spying was exactly what she wanted to do after her meeting with Raborn—with Drake—was over in two days' time. But was there really an entire store—no, an entire *superstore*—devoted to spying? Was there anything you *couldn't* get through the Internet?

She touched the link on the screen and was taken to the superstore. Hundreds of "most popular products" came up on the screen.

Erin shook her head in disbelief as she slid her index finger down the screen, scrolling. Was this for real? Pens with cameras inside? *Neckties* with embedded cameras? Really?

Hidden cameras appeared to be the site's biggest sellers. Cameras in sunglasses, alarm clocks, hats. You name it, someone had put a camera in it. Apparently, nanny-cam technology had come a long way.

Erin continued scrolling down. Invisible ink? Seemed a bit juvenile for this site. Lock-picking tools. Night-vision equipment. Her eyes narrowed. A flash drive preloaded with software that, when downloaded to another computer, would allow the owner of the "spy drive" to record and monitor all activity on the host computer from their own; everything from keystrokes to Skype sessions. She couldn't imagine how anything like this could possibly be legal.

She next came to listening devices. She had seen cheap versions of these advertised on television, which the announcer claimed were useful for amplifying sound to help people better hear their televisions, or live performances from the backs of crowded theaters. But while these legitimate claims were being made by a voice-over, the commercials showed people using these devices to eavesdrop on private conversations, which had always made Erin's stomach turn. The device shown on the Web site was orders of magnitude more sophisticated than the ones she had seen before. It was a six-panel snap-together parabolic dish for only—only!—nine hundred dollars, which could apparently pick up a conversation at almost four hundred yards.

She found the link to GPS devices and searched through them. There were a wide variety, but one in particular was perfect for her needs. It was about the size and weight of a dime, and could be attached to clothing. It used a tiny battery, and rather than doing any work itself, it synched up with the target's cell phone, causing the cell phone to beam a signal to the person who had deployed the device, providing its location. Parents and employers could already get software that allowed them to track the cell phones of their kids or employees— which Erin thought was a scary trend. This device did the same thing, only with more stealth and less permission.

Erin pasted the name of this device into the search bar and looked for a bricks-and-mortar store that would sell it in the general vicinity, along with directions. A half hour later she arrived at the winning store, a place called Modern Electronic Surveillance, and pulled into the parking lot.

Just as she turned off the engine her cell phone vibrated.

She checked the caller ID, but it only told her it was an unknown caller.

"Hello?" she said tentatively, wondering who might be calling.

"Erin Palmer?" said the caller, a man with a deep voice.

"Yes."

"My name is Steve Fuller. I'm with a company called Advanced Science Applications."

"How did you get my cell phone number?"

"Sorry to intrude on your privacy, Miss Palmer. I tried you at home, but your roommate mentioned you had left for a visit to San Diego. She thought I might be able to catch you on your cell."

Erin turned the key slightly, just enough to get power to the car, and lowered the windows. "What can I do for you?"

"We're a very well-funded private company involved in a lot of cutting-edge, next-generation science. Your research in psychopathy has recently come to our attention. We also understand you're close to finishing your doctorate. We'd love the chance to persuade you to come work with us when you have."

They must have seen the *Wall Street Journal* piece, thought Erin. But if so, they would immediately come to the same conclusion that everyone did after considering a psychopath early warning device. Well, everyone but her, that is. That it was a device society would never sanction.

But a cure—that might be more interesting to industry. Did they suspect her secret activities over the past two years? She shook her head. She was being silly now. The incident with Drake had her jumping at shadows.

"Thanks for the interest," she said. "But industry really isn't my thing. And there's no way you'd have any interest in me if you really understood my work."

"I understand how you might think that. But I believe I can convince you otherwise. You'd have unlimited funding. No need to write grants, no need to worry about campus politics. And your compensation would be higher than I'm guessing you could imagine."

"Why would you possibly be willing to spend so much money on my research?"

"I'll explain that to you as well. If you could just meet with me at our facilities for a few hours, I can answer all of your questions. And I'd be very surprised if I couldn't persuade you to join us."

"When did you have in mind?"

"Actually, since you're in San Diego already, I was thinking we could take advantage of that. That's why I was eager to call you before you returned to Tucson. Do you have any free time tomorrow?"

Erin frowned. She had decided to take a single day to relax at the beach with a friend—the first time in years—and suddenly everyone wanted to schedule critically important meetings for that exact day. "I'm afraid not," she replied.

"What about Wednesday at noon? I'm prepared to be very flexible."

Erin considered. She had no idea what this was, but for some reason her intuition was warning her she needed to find out. Something didn't add up here. It was a strange coincidence that this mystery company was located in San Diego, but if she didn't clear this up it would gnaw at her. She would wonder what they knew, who they were, and why they had interest in her. As if she didn't already have enough gnawing at her as it was.

If she agreed, she'd have to extend her stay and text Drake that they'd have to move their meeting back a day. Two enigmas vying for the same time spot on Wednesday. What else could possibly be thrown at her today? She paused for several seconds and considered what to do.

Screw Drake, she decided finally. He had deceived her royally for over two years, so it would serve him right to have to wait an extra day for the information he so desperately wanted. Provided he could even convince her there had been a purpose to his deception.

"Wednesday at noon will work," she said.

"Fantastic!" said the caller. "If you can tell me where you'll be on Wednesday morning, I'll have a car pick you up and take you to the San Diego heliport. The one we fly out of."

"Heliport?" said Erin. "You aren't located in San Diego?"

"Very close—at least as the crow flies. We're just outside of Palm Springs. An easy helicopter ride, but with all the twists and turns through the mountains, it's a longer drive than it should be. And I don't want to inconvenience you any more than I have to. But I'll have a helicopter fueled up and ready to go, and we'll get you here in no time. I promise to get you back before dinner."

This was a new wrinkle, and once again she wasn't sure she liked it. "Could you hold on a minute?" she asked.

"Sure," said the man named Steve Fuller.

Erin quickly Googled "Advanced Science Applications" on her cell phone. The Web site was very slick, and there was even a recruiting page that made specific mention of the company's fleet of five helicopters intended to shuttle their employees to Stanford, UCLA, Silicon Valley, and the numerous other high-tech centers in California an employee might want to visit.

"Sorry about that," she said into the phone a few minutes later. "I'll tell you what. If you send directions to the heliport to my phone, and the time you want me, I'll get there myself. No need to send a car. And understand that I only packed casual clothes. I wasn't expecting to be interviewed."

"Sounds great. And casual is fine. We already know we want you. This is more of you interviewing *us*. And I appreciate your flexibility to meet with us on such short notice."

Erin waited while Fuller sent directions, confirmed that she had received them, and then ended the call.

She threw her head back against the headrest and rolled her eyes. She was going from one fishy situation to another. Was it surreal, alternate reality day? She didn't trust this situation as far as she could throw it.

If this Steve Fuller did know about her activities, she would be at his mercy. She had broken the law. She was in this up to her neck. Three men had died. To make matters even worse, one of the deaths had occurred immediately after she had administered one of the test treatments in the trailer, and she had deliberately covered it up with a fake story about being attacked, and by roughing up a man who was already dead. Yes, all three men were convicted killers, but she would still be sent to prison for years, maybe decades. And not as a researcher either.

It was unlikely that Fuller knew. But he *was* awfully eager to talk to her. And she was a nobody. There was no way he would be giving her the VIP recruiting treatment on the basis of a pie-in-the-sky remark about working toward a remote psychopathy detector quoted in the *Wall Street Journal*.

She continued to search the Internet for more intel on Advanced Science Applications but came up completely empty. Other than their Web site, she didn't get a single hit. For a company with this high of a profile, this was astonishing. And highly troubling.

She next searched for Steve Fuller, who had to be pretty high up in the company to be able to send cars and schedule helicopters. He had a common name, but searching the name in combination with the company name, science in general, and business, didn't get her anywhere either.

Things just kept on getting stranger. And Erin Palmer couldn't help but feel more unsettled than she had in a long, long time.

12

ERIN FORCED HERSELF to put both Drake and Steve Fuller out of her mind later that night and Tuesday while she was with her friend, although she wasn't entirely successful. The good news was that she wasn't entirely *unsuccessful* either, and managed to get reacquainted with the concept of actually having fun for long stretches at a time. She told Courtney that Hugh Raborn had been out of town, after all, and her friend was very supportive and genuinely disappointed for her.

If only her friend had known the truth. On the other

hand, it wasn't as though *Erin* knew the truth either, she realized.

Erin had traded texts with Drake and he had agreed to change their meeting to one thirty on Thursday, at the same meeting place, although the tone of his texts didn't fully conceal the fury she knew he was feeling at a further delay. She could only imagine how pissed off he really was. She had also changed her flight to a day later as well as her rental car.

Now all that was left to do was learn why this mysterious company had taken such an interest in her, and take a ride in a luxury helicopter.

The heliport used by Advanced Science Applications was in one of the most isolated spots in all of San Diego County. San Diego was a tropical paradise with a perfect climate, at least along the coast. But venture even ten miles inland and it could warm up quickly, with temperatures often climbing from ten to thirty degrees over this distance, and with brown, rather than green becoming the dominant color of the landscape. Home prices and population tended to fall the farther inland one traveled going east, and the closer to the Mexican border one traveled going south. The heliport was located a full fifteen miles east of the coast and only a few miles north of Mexico, so it was very rocky and very sparsely populated.

Erin had used Google Maps to do a virtual recon of the area. She wasn't about to get inside a helicopter with this strange caller when neither he, nor his company, had left much of an Internet footprint, and when he was far more interested in her than he had any right to be. Beyond that she wasn't sure why this situation had rattled her so much, but she wasn't going to enter the helicopter until she had satisfied herself that she wasn't walking into an ambush, although why her instincts were screaming to her this might be the case wasn't entirely clear. But she had learned to trust her instincts.

She laughed out loud as she thought about this further. She had trusted her instincts when it had come to Hugh Raborn, now a mystery man named Drake, and how had *that* worked out for her? The recent track record of her intuition was pretty miserable, she had to admit. Even so, she wasn't quite ready to abandon her gut feelings just yet.

Erin pulled into the lot of a small Episcopal church, which probably attracted a significant fraction of the sparse citizenry of the area on Sundays and other occasions but which was now deserted. It was surrounded by a few palm trees that looked more dead than alive. If not for the sign, the white, eight-foot-tall wooden cross sticking up from the roof, and a concrete parking lot, the structure could easily have been mistaken for a very large, very boring house.

She parked her car so that only the front of it peeked out from behind the building, lowered her window, and pulled out a pair of high-powered binoculars she had bought along with a GPS tracking device—and one additional item. One even pricier than the binoculars. Thank God for credit cards. At her pathetic income, it would take her a year to pay off these spy gadgets.

She got her bearings and searched for the heliport with her binoculars. She found it, as expected, about two hundred and forty yards distant. There was only one helicopter sitting there, and even through binoculars as powerful as a small telescope, it looked like a radio-controlled toy, parked in the center of a light gray concrete slab the size of a basketball court, surrounded by a gate and fence. Inside the fence, along with the copter, was what looked like a maintenance shed and a small, self-serve gas pump, dispensing whatever kind of fuel helicopters used. Several cars were parked inside as well, in an area clearly designated for such use.

Based on its relative size compared to the cars, the helicopter was on the large side, probably able to seat eight or more passengers, and was an absolute beauty, exuding corporate opulence. But it didn't have the company's name painted on it, which Erin considered yet another red flag.

She made out a man sitting in the cockpit, the size of a figurine, who was almost certainly the pilot making preparations for imminent liftoff—they were expecting her at any minute. Two men were standing next to each other near the helicopter, dressed casually, who gave the clear impression, despite their diminutive appearance through the binoculars, that they could easily get jobs protecting the president, and both appeared to be scouring the road leading to the heliport for signs of her.

Erin removed the parabolic listening device from its leather case and assembled it by snapping together six separate panels. Fully assembled it was about the size and shape of an oversized umbrella without the spokes, with a thick black microphone in the center and a short, grooved, gun-grip handle. The parabolic dish was fairly light, about the weight of three equivalently sized umbrellas, but it came with a tripod, which she hurriedly set up. She adjusted the dish/tripod assembly until it was pointed directly at the heliport.

Fortunately, the chopper blades were still. Had they not been, they would have drowned out all conversation in the area. It took Erin three or four minutes to adjust the three-band equalizer on the listening device to bring up the frequencies and tones she wanted, but sure enough, just as advertised, she suddenly could hear the conversation over two hundred yards distant in her headphones as though it were taking place next to her. She felt a twinge of guilt listening in like this, but if this operation was legitimate and their intentions pure, no harm would be done. And if their intentions were *not* pure . . .

The two men made small talk for another few minutes. She watched through the binoculars as the taller man— four inches high instead of three—checked his watch. "She's late," he said.

The other man didn't respond.

"Well, it's not like there's any danger of her being delayed by traffic around here," explained the taller man.

"Maybe she's in the john," said the other. "And we're not in that much of a hurry anyway. Although I am curious to see if she's as hot as advertised."

"This is a helicopter, Adam, not a singles bar," said the taller man, more in amusement than reprimand. "I brought it up because I'm wondering if she got cold feet. Fuller said he was surprised she agreed to fly out on such short notice without doing more checking. Or asking him more questions."

"And he used the Advanced Science Applications routine?" said the shorter of the two.

"Right," said the other man.

"Did he actually use his real name with her?"

"He did. Which surprised the hell out of me. That's getting rare for him."

The other man said nothing. Perhaps he shrugged, but Erin couldn't make it out at this distance.

Just great, she thought miserably. Fuller rarely used his real name. And the corporate identity must be fake, since one of the men had said it was just part of a *routine.*

Why was truth suddenly such a precious commodity? Was she wearing a sign around her neck that said *Lie to Me*? She had begun to feel paranoid and ridiculous pointing a fricking satellite dish at these men, but not anymore.

Erin saw movement out of the corner of her eye and jumped so high she nearly hit her head on the ceiling of the car. Two men, both athletic looking and clean-cut, were standing by the door with grim expressions on their faces.

She had been so intent on listening to the conversation hundreds of yards away, and the headphones had been so effective at blocking out local sound, she hadn't even heard their car pull up and park on the other side of the church. They had left the doors open so as not to risk the slightest sound alerting her to their presence.

She took off her headphones as one of the men reached in through the fully open window, removed the keys from the ignition, and slipped them into his pocket. Sitting in a cramped position inside a car was as poor a defensive position as one could get—or offensive position, for that matter. Before she did anything else her instincts—which had now redeemed themselves after their failure with Raborn—told her she needed to change this. She threw open the door, slid out of the car, and rose to a standing position in one smooth motion.

The two men backed a few steps away as she did. They both ran their eyes up and down her body, no doubt looking for signs of a weapon.

"Well this is unfortunate," said one of the men, gesturing to the tripod and parabolic dish. "And unexpected. You need to come with us."

"Who are you?"

"We're with the people you're going to meet."

"Give me back my keys!" she demanded.

"You do realize that actively intercepting private conversations is illegal," pointed out the man who had done all of the talking, while his partner continued to stand quietly beside him.

Erin didn't reply. She had no idea if this was true or not. It might well be, but she guessed that even if it was a crime, it was almost surely just a misdemeanor.

"Come with us, and we'll, ah . . . *escort* you . . . to your helicopter."

Who were these men, and how had they found her? Erin didn't believe in coincidence—not for something like this. Which meant they had been tracking her somehow. When they realized she had stopped for an extended period, they must have decided to break cover and check things out. If they had been physically following her, she would have seen them on the largely deserted roads she had taken to get here, and they would have arrived sooner. They had probably tracked her cell phone.

Erin shook her head in disgust. "Tracking people via their cell phones," she said, "*without their permission,* is against the law too."

The look of surprise in both men's eyes told her that her hunch had been right, although their expressions returned to impassive almost immediately. "I don't know what you're talking about," said their spokesman pleasantly. "But we should go. We don't want to be too late."

"Thanks," she said with an insincere smile, "but I've changed my mind. I think I'll pass on this meeting, after all. Please send my apologies to, ah . . . Steve Fuller."

"I'm afraid we've gone beyond that now. The problem is that we have no idea just what it is you managed to overhear. So now you don't have a choice. You *are* coming with us."

"No," she said calmly but defiantly. "I'm afraid I'm not. I'll take my keys now," she added.

The years she had spent learning multiple martial arts, the many hundreds of hours she had spent training and competing and winning tournaments when she was a teen, had been in preparation for exactly this moment. She had never been forced to use her training in an actual physical confrontation, but she had been physically and mentally prepared to do so for countless years. She had vowed never to be helpless, or freeze up, or even hesitate. *Never again.*

As a soft, helpless child she had looked into the eyes of pure evil, of utter ruthlessness and utter lack of mercy, and these two men could not intimidate her now. They clearly had no idea just who it was they were dealing with. In the looks-can-be-deceiving department, she would take grand prize.

"I'm afraid I'll have to keep your keys for now," said the man, all traces of friendliness having left his voice. "You need to come with us. I don't want to have to use force," he said pointedly.

"Yeah. Me neither," replied Erin, an intense, hard gleam in her eye.

There was something about the calm, confident, matter-of-fact way she said this that unsettled both men.

They glanced at each other and then both began to reach for their guns at the same time.

They never made it. Erin executed a devastating roundhouse kick that connected with the silent partner's head, and he dropped like an anvil to the cement of the parking lot, unconscious before he hit the ground. Erin landed lightly in a crouched position well before he completed his fall, and in a continuation of her original move, swept the other man's legs out from under him before he could react, and he, too, catapulted to the ground.

To his credit, the man who had been their spokesman recovered immediately, and showed considerable athleticism jumping back to his feet to face her. For fifteen seconds he showed impressive skills of his own, blocking the flurry of blows she threw at him and even attempting a few of his own, without any of them landing. For a moment, Erin had a flashback to her many tournaments, when she had faced opponents who were very good, but not as good as she was. Her current opponent was firmly in this category.

She sensed that he was coming to the same realization. As well trained as he was, she expected him to switch tactics and try to change this from a martial arts contest into a wrestling match, where his superior strength would win the day. He rushed at her to do just this, attempting to tackle her and bring her to the ground, but she had been prepared and sidestepped his rush, landing a sideways kick to his knee as he passed, causing it to buckle and him to crash to the ground. She could have taken out his entire knee, but had purposely modulated the blow so as not to do permanent damage to such a vital part of his anatomy. He whirled and drew his gun, but she kicked it from his hand and scrambled for it, grabbing it while he was still on the pavement.

She didn't recognize the make of the weapon, and its weighting was unusual, but she didn't have time to dwell on this as she extended it toward her adversary. He brought himself to a sitting position, nursing his knee.

"Hands up!" she ordered.

He raised his hands slowly above his head.

"Now," she said icily, "I'll ask again. Who are you?"

"I'd like to ask you the same thing," he replied.

He tilted his head and gazed at her with an expression reflecting both respect and admiration. "What did you do to the frail, geeky graduate student we were told to keep tabs on?"

"What in the hell is going on here?" she demanded. "What is this all about?"

"I'm afraid I can't tell you that," he said. "I'm just hired muscle. Although apparently not as good as I thought I was," he mumbled. "But the man you need to speak with is the man who wants to speak with you."

"What's your name?"

"Alan."

"Okay, Alan. Is keeping me in the dark really worth your life?"

"Look . . . Erin," he said. "I'll happily tell you everything I know. I was told you were a science grad student named Erin, shown your picture, and told to keep tabs on you."

"That's it?"

"That's it. I wasn't even told you had . . . skills." He glanced down at his injured knee. "And that might have been a useful piece of information to have."

"I don't believe you."

"I don't know what else I can say. I do what I'm told. I've very well paid. And I'm kept totally out of the loop. The people I work for take their privacy *very* seriously."

Something in his tone made Erin believe that this Alan, if that was truly his name, was probably telling the truth. If he was, further attempts to elicit information would be a dead end, and she had no idea how much time she had before these men were missed and reinforcements arrived.

So what now? She looked around hastily. She was in the middle of nowhere and couldn't exactly blend into a crowd, either human or vehicular. They could track her cell phone and she was certain they knew the make, model, and license plate of her rental car. They also knew she was scheduled to fly back to Tucson at eight o'clock that night, so it would be a simple matter to watch the San Diego International Airport. All of this meant that if she tried to run, she wouldn't stand a chance.

Which only left one thing. Offense. An audacious plan began to take shape in her mind. But she would need to get the two men by the helicopter away from it. And for that she would need a diversion. She would need Alan to cooperate.

Which begged the question: what was she prepared to do to gain this cooperation? Would she finish the job she had started and blow out his kneecap?

Even as she considered this she knew she wouldn't, no matter what was at stake. Yes, she had skirted the law by testing the anti-psychopathy therapy. She had gone over to the dark side. And yes, she had been a little rough with these two men. But that had been in self-defense. She couldn't just maim a man, no matter what. It wasn't in her, and she found herself relieved to realize this.

"Okay, Alan. I need for you to do exactly what I tell you." She lowered the gun and pointed it at his knee. "The second you cross me, I take out your kneecap, understand?"

She couldn't actually do it, but that wouldn't stop her from bluffing.

Now if only he didn't decide to call her bluff . . .

"I'll cooperate," he said with a sigh. "But you should know you're holding a tranquilizer gun. You aren't taking out anyone's knee with that. Please keep in mind that even when I pulled this weapon, you were never in any danger of being killed. Or maimed," he added pointedly.

Erin glanced at the gun in her hand and swallowed hard. She had thought she was doing pretty well for an amateur. But not as well as she imagined. She made her way quickly over to Alan's partner, keeping the gun—the tranquilizer gun—trained on Alan as she did so. His partner was still unconscious, although breathing, and she quickly found a 9mm Sig Sauer semiautomatic pistol and another tranquilizer gun. She removed the semiautomatic and returned to where she had been.

"Thanks for the tip," she said. This time she raised the 9mm and pointed it at the man's kneecap. "So let me try this again. Do what I tell you, or never walk again."

Alan sighed. "What do you want me to do?"

"Call your friends by the helicopter over there," she said, gesturing due north toward the helipad with her head. "Tell them you found me a mile to the north of them, but I managed to find a dug-in position and I'm armed to the teeth. Give them the location and ask them to assist. Whatever you have to do. If they haven't jumped in a car and headed in the opposite direction from us within three minutes, I'll carry out my threat."

She couldn't believe she was doing any of this. She was a graduate student. A scientist.

Yet somehow she felt able to channel strategy from some of the fictional characters she had read. She tended to gravitate toward thrillers in her reading, as long as they didn't feature overtly psychopathic characters. It was true that many thriller villains were technically part of the psychopathic 1 percent, but this was okay as long as they were after money or power, and not serial killers or rapists out to torture and maim for the fun of it. This hit too close to home.

Good fiction tended to have considerable elements of truth in it, and while she had never experienced any situation remotely similar to the one she faced now, she had been introduced to countless such situations through novels and always found herself trying to think her way out of them along with the books' heroes and heroines. As though she had been subconsciously preparing her mental faculties for this kind of trouble along with her physical ones.

So what was she forgetting? Was she making all of the right moves?

After a few seconds of intense thought, she realized she had forgotten something. If fiction had taught her anything, it was that credit cards could, and would, be traced by a group such as this. So hers would be useless.

She wasn't a petty thief, but they had started this— whatever *this* was.

"Wait," she said. "Before you call your colleagues, throw your wallet over to me."

The man frowned but did as instructed. Other than a driver's license, which identified him as Alan Smith, he had no credit cards or other forms of identification. She wasn't surprised. She found a thick sheaf of twenties in his wallet and removed them. She tossed the wallet back to him. "Sorry about that," she said. "Be sure to have your wealthy boss reimburse you."

She rifled through his partner's wallet as well and removed considerable additional cash, keeping the gun trained on Alan the entire time. Both men had been loaded, probably because they didn't carry credit cards.

"Okay," said Erin, nodding to the north. "Now call your buddies over there at the heliport and get them to leave."

She slid the headphones for the parabolic listening device over her head, but only placed one of the two soft cups over an ear. The other ear she kept free. "I'll be listening to both ends of the conversation," she said. "So don't try to get cute."

The man glanced quickly from the headphones on her head to the large parabolic dish pointing toward the helipad. He nodded, almost approvingly, and the corners of his mouth turned up into the slightest of smiles. "I wouldn't think of it," he said evenly.

13

———

ERIN WAS BELTED in the backseat of the car so Alan wouldn't think it was a good strategy to slam on the brakes, and made sure she was behind the passenger's seat to maximize the distance between them. Alan's partner had returned to consciousness, briefly, until she had shot him with a tranquilizer dart and left him in the church parking lot.

Alan had done a masterful job of getting the two men by the helicopter to leave in a hurry, but they wouldn't be gone for long once they realized they had been misled. Fortunately, even taking winding roads they arrived at the heliport gate almost immediately. Erin crouched down even lower in the seat, the gun still pointed at the driver, as he entered the gate code on the metal keypad and the gate slid open.

Alan parked near the helicopter and motioned for the pilot, now standing outside of the aircraft, to walk over to the car. As he neared the driver's side, Erin shot Alan in the neck with a tranquilizer dart and jumped out of the backseat, training the gun on the pilot as Alan slumped forward against the steering wheel.

The pilot raised his hands without being asked.

"Inside the helicopter," she ordered. *"Let's go."*

The pilot glanced at his colleague slumped over in the seat, and nodded.

They entered the helicopter, which was as opulent as Erin had guessed. The passenger cabin was spacious and contained cushioned captain's chairs, made of soft, ivory-colored leather, well spread out and with enough leg room to satisfy a seven-footer, along with a bar, cabinetry, and large-screen television. The pilot quickly made his way through the luxurious cabin on his way to the cockpit, with Erin maintaining a safe distance behind him.

"Get this thing in the air!" she demanded the instant he reached the cockpit. "Now!" Erin had so much adrenaline coursing through her body she wondered if she could rocket into the sky without the aircraft.

The pilot worked several switches and the blades on top of the helicopter began to turn, quickly picking up speed. Moments later the flying limousine left the confines of gravity behind and lifted gently into the air.

"Where to?" shouted the pilot. Neither one of them had bothered putting on headphones to facilitate conversation.

Good question, thought Erin. She knew she would have to be her sharpest to get out of whatever it was she had gotten herself into. While adrenaline muddled the thoughts of some, for her it had the opposite effect. When she was giving a presentation in front of a large crowd, the adrenaline would hit, and suddenly she was more articulate than she had ever been, constructing dazzling sentences during tough stretches of the talk that had tripped her up in rehearsal.

"Just gain altitude," she shouted back to the pilot. "I'll let you know in a minute."

So where *would* she go? Could the chopper make it all the way from San Diego to Tucson? And if so, how long would this take?

She shook her head. Bad idea.

She considered ditching her cell phone so they

couldn't use it to track her, but her instincts told her to save it for later. After all, they had to be able to track their own helicopter, using a transponder, or whatever you called those things aircraft carried that broadcast their locations.

So knowing they would track her, what did that suggest?

First, she needed a short trip, so they wouldn't have time to guess where she was going and plan a welcoming party, or send another helicopter after her. Second, since they would know exactly where she was, she needed to be able to get lost quickly after she landed. If she landed in the middle of a desert, she could never hide. But if she landed in the middle of a major city . . .

"Fly to downtown LA," she shouted. "At best possible speed. I'll tell you where to land."

The pilot nodded, eyeing her gun warily. The helicopter banked and shot northwest.

"How long?" she shouted.

The pilot shrugged. "About thirty minutes."

She knew he could land on top of a flat building or skyscraper, with or without a helipad. But after thinking it through she decided against it. Landing on an actual helipad might be the better play.

So where would you find a helipad in the middle of a busy city? After a few minutes, she had it.

They rode in silence, other than the steady beating of the blades, and Erin focused on staying alert and keeping the pilot in her sights. When downtown LA came into view off in the distance, she said, "Take us to Cedars-Sinai Medical Center in West Hollywood. Land at their helipad."

"You know I won't have clearance," shouted the pilot. "What if another helo is landing or taking off?"

"Then try not to hit it," she said, rolling her eyes.

Five minutes later they landed at the helipad, a large circular expanse of concrete with a six-foot-wide yellow strip painted all around its circumference. The second the blades began to slow, Erin shot the pilot in the leg with a tranquilizer dart.

She still couldn't believe she was doing any of this, but this was no time to be squeamish. The pilot would be just fine, which she wasn't at all sure was true in her case. She opened a glossy, lacquered storage compartment, shoved the Sig Sauer and tranquilizer gun inside, and then exited the craft.

The helipad had a fantastic view of the Hollywood Hills, interrupted only by a large Macy's next door, but she didn't have time to enjoy the scenery. Fortunately, the helipad was currently deserted and she rushed through a door and into the hospital.

Minutes later she exited the facility and made a beeline for Macy's. She quickly purchased an entirely new outfit, the least expensive clothing she could find, including socks, shoes, panties, and even a baseball cap, and changed, throwing her own clothing away.

She knew she was being ridiculously paranoid, but she had read too many books, and watched too many movies, in which the bad guys had managed to plant tracking devices on the hero's clothing—which is exactly what she had planned for her meeting with Drake, an irony that wasn't entirely lost on her. And the penalty for being too paranoid wasn't nearly as high as the penalty for not being paranoid enough. Besides, even if they *couldn't* track her clothing, if she kept it on it would help them identify her, whereas this new clothing might throw them off.

She was about to leave the store when she thought better of it. Instead, she bought an additional T-shirt and tied it into a ball around her phone as she exited onto the sidewalk. She scanned the busy streets around her, looking for both a taxi and a pickup truck. She spotted the pickup truck first and tossed the cotton shirt-ball, with her cell phone inside, into the open bed of the truck as it passed. As she had hoped, the shirt muffled the sound of this maneuver and of the phone sliding around in the back well enough that she doubted the driver would realize he was hauling extra cargo. With any luck, this pickup truck would draw pursuit away from her and buy her additional time.

Three minutes later she caught a cab. "Take me to the main bus terminal," she said as she slid into the backseat.

The driver, a swarthy, unshaven man with a huge gut said, "You mean the Greyhound terminal?"

"Um . . . yeah. That's the one," she said.

As they drove, Erin thought about her next move. It could be that she had vastly overestimated the trouble she was in, the resources this organization had, and their interest in her. But then again, maybe she hadn't. She felt she had no choice but to assume they would spare no effort to locate her—although she still couldn't begin to hazard a guess as to why.

But if they were as capable as she feared, they would know she had landed in LA and would camp out at LAX. They also might be able to trace her if she tried to rent a car.

Which left a bus. She couldn't imagine they would

expect *this* move. No one took buses anymore. She was proud of herself for coming up with the idea. Even if they did guess she would take a bus, she hoped the last destination they would expect her to choose was the most obvious: Tucson, Arizona.

But this was where she would go, purchasing her ticket with cash.

After all, she had a date with the man who had called himself Hugh Raborn. And it was one she still intended to keep.

14

～～～

THE BUS DIDN'T arrive in Tucson until just after midnight. It was an agonizing trip. Erin only managed to sleep for two or three hours and felt naked without her phone. And these were the least of her worries.

She considered going to the police, but knew she couldn't. Not until she had an idea of what she was dealing with. She had been responsible for the death of *three men*. This fact impacted her more now than it ever had. She had avoided thinking about this for some time, but she was a murderer. Plain and simple.

How had she let her life come to this? It was like a nightmare from which she couldn't awaken. Had she become just as monstrous as the people she studied?

Maybe so.

And while she had been sure no one knew of her involvement with these deaths—other than Drake—she was now forced to question *everything*. Maybe others did know, after all. Which meant going to the police might be a very bad idea. Especially since *she* had been the one who had just assaulted two men, used a tranquilizer gun on these two and one other, and hijacked a helicopter.

This had all been in self-defense, but it would be her word against a wealthy organization, and she had no doubt whom the police would believe. Even so, she doubted Steve Fuller's people would report what had happened to authorities. She imagined the helicopter pilot would invent a story to cover up his landing at Cedars-Sinai. An accident. Wrong coordinates. He felt dizzy and needed to land before he passed out. Something like that.

Upon arrival in Tucson, Erin took a cab to the Saguaro Inn on the outskirts of town and checked in under an assumed name, paying cash in advance for the room. The motel was a one-story structure in the shape of a large L, with a small lobby at one end and a rectangular parking lot offset twenty or thirty yards from the inn. It was fairly cheap, but not seedy. The rooms were good sized, didn't smell of mildew as could happen at the bottom of the lodging food chain, and were otherwise clean.

The saguaro cactus, pronounced with a *w*—sa-*whar*-oh—was native to Tucson, and could grow to over seventy feet tall. True to the motel's name, two impressive specimens of the cactus, which looked like green, prickly telephone poles with arms pointing skyward, abutted each end of the L, rising three stories into the sky.

Erin loved the giant saguaro, but on this night she was in no mind to notice them, or to care. The bed in her room was comfortable, but she still tossed and turned until three in the morning before finally managing to fall into a fitful sleep.

When she awoke she took a long, hot shower and tried to clear her head. Too much was going on and no matter how hard she tried to use her considerable powers of reason to solve the puzzle, the big picture continued to elude her. The small picture did, too, for that matter. She just didn't know enough. But she decided not to mention anything about Steve Fuller to Drake until she knew more; her gut instincts, hit-or-miss as they had proven to be, guiding her once again.

She still had the GPS tracking device she had purchased in San Diego, but nothing else. She couldn't risk returning to her apartment for her gun, and she couldn't possibly complete the purchase of one before her meeting with Drake. She thought for a few minutes and then used the motel phone to call a few pawn shops. The second one she called had a Taser in stock. It wasn't much, but she'd feel far less naked with this in her pocket— along with a phone.

She took a cab to the pawn shop and then to Walmart, where she bought a prepaid, disposable cell phone, before grabbing a bite to eat and returning to the motel. She told the desk clerk she would be staying for a second night, paid, and then set off in a cab for the university grounds to meet Drake.

The cab dropped her off on a circular road that abutted the University of Arizona Student Union, the absolute center of campus both physically, socially, and sustenance-wise, since the school had a large undergraduate population and no cafeterias. The union had a large food court, spread out over several stories, and teemed with students at all hours of the day and night, especially since most were on meal plans, paid for in advance by their parents, and every eating establishment in the union accepted a preloaded plastic CatCard, which could be debited for meals with a single swipe.

Erin stood outside the door to the bookstore, which was open to air but shaded from direct sunlight. It was nearing one thirty, the tail end of lunch hour, and the place was less a madhouse than it had been. Still, it was teeming with throngs of students carrying backpacks and wearing clothing of all types emblazoned with Wildcat logos and the familiar red and blue of the university.

She had only been waiting a minute or two when a man, about five eleven in height, broke from the crowd and approached her purposefully. She tensed and realized she had never had the chance to look at the photos of Drake he had sent over, and probably wasn't in possession of her phone when he had. She couldn't imagine whoever was after her could have tracked her here. Even so, she wasn't prepared to let down her guard no matter what. It wasn't as though she could trust Drake any more than she could trust Fuller.

The man approaching appeared to be about thirty years old and was handsome, not in a rugged way, but in a friendly, approachable sort of way. He had sandy hair and deep set, expressive blue eyes.

"Erin Palmer?" he said when he was within a few feet of her.

She was about to say something like, "You must be Drake," when she realized with a start that this wasn't him. The voice was all wrong—again. She tensed even more and examined him for weapons, although it was unlikely he would do anything that would attract attention with this many people around.

"Who are you?" she demanded in low tones.

"I'm Kyle Hansen," he said matter-of-factly, just stopping short of adding, *of course,* as if his name was supposed to mean something to her. He looked confused by her blank stare.

"Drake couldn't make it, so he sent me instead," he added, as though reminding her of this rather than explaining it for the first time. At her continued blank stare he winced. "I'm sorry," he said. "Drake told me he texted you about this several hours ago, and even sent my picture."

Erin nodded. That would explain a lot. "Yeah, well . . . I had a little trouble with my phone," she said, as her mind leaped ahead to try to assimilate this unexpected development.

What new game was this? Who was this Kyle Hansen and what could sending him to meet with her possibly accomplish?

The man she had known as Hugh Raborn had insisted he would explain his multiyear ruse to her. Since she and he were the only ones in existence who knew about the psychopathy cure and her work testing inmates—at least she continued to cling to this supposition—a surrogate would be useless.

"Sorry again," replied Kyle Hansen earnestly. "We didn't mean to surprise you."

"Look, I'm sure you're a very nice guy. And I'm sorry that you had to make the trip for nothing. But I came here to meet with, um . . . Drake. At *his* suggestion. He wanted to clear up a personal matter between the two of us. So sending a substitute isn't going to cut it."

"Just give me ten minutes," said Hansen. "If at the end of ten minutes you still think meeting with me instead of Drake is a waste of your time, I'll leave. But I really can clear up everything." He sounded sincere and nonthreatening—although this could just be an act.

Erin took a deep breath and nodded. "Ten minutes," she said.

"I'm told there's a food court around here."

Erin gestured to the long building that paralleled the bookstore across a twenty-foot-wide concrete walkway. "Closer than you think," said Erin.

"Have you had lunch?"

She shook her head no.

"Then I'm buying," he said in a friendly tone.

"Look, I'm leaving after ten minutes, so you might want to get our food to go," she said pointedly.

He grinned, an easy, unself-conscious smile. "I'm willing to take that chance," he said, and there was undeniable charm in the way he said it. "Look . . . Erin . . . Drake filled me in, and I know you're confused. I also know he's given you plenty of reason not to be trusting. But if you just give me the chance, I'll explain everything to your satisfaction."

"I doubt that. This is about a sensitive matter."

Hansen pursed his lips and his face took on a more somber cast. "I know more than you think I do," he said. "And I'm a friend. More than a friend, as I think you'll soon discover. An ally. A comrade. I've been working with Drake even longer than you have."

"Drake told you we were working together?" she asked, squinting in confusion, as though unable to fathom why Drake would lie about something like this.

"That's right. And although I know you'll see this as another betrayal, I know the exact nature of your collaboration. And that you've just made a major breakthrough."

15

ERIN TOOK A long drink from a bottle of cold water and then bit into the turkey sandwich she had purchased, or Hansen had purchased for her, spending all of seven dollars. "Okay . . . Kyle," she said. "Now that we're settled in, I'm all ears."

They were sitting at a small rectangular table and there was a cacophony of conversation from hundreds of locations in the massive open food court. There were several groups of students within earshot, but they were self-absorbed—laughing, debating, flirting, working on their Facebook accounts, playing or talking on their phones, or watching one of the many television screens that descended from the ceiling in a seemingly haphazard fashion, and Erin wasn't worried in the slightest that anyone would listen in, or have any idea what they were hearing if they did.

So Drake had told this Kyle Hansen about work that could get her thrown in jail. After he had sworn he would never mention this to another soul. So what was another huge betrayal among friends? And this also begged the question, who else knew? Was there anyone who *didn't*?

Hansen seemed famished, and had finished a large bag of chips while they were waiting in line and had almost finished half of his chicken-salad sandwich in the brief time they had been sitting. "There's no easy way to start," he said. "Let me just say that you won't believe me at first. But I plan to prove everything I say. I'm not crazy. So if you could just pretend to believe me until the proof comes, that would be a big help."

"Go on," said Erin.

Hansen blew out a long breath. "Drake isn't human," he said simply, watching her face for a reaction as he did so.

Erin rolled her eyes. She must still be asleep in some kind of crazy, extended dream, she decided. Either she had entered the Twilight Zone, or she had used up her life's quota of bizarre, surreal surprises in the past four days, during which her life had been turned upside down and twisted into a pretzel. "Come on, Kyle. I'm not in the mood."

"Remember, I did tell you you wouldn't believe me. Anyway, that's why he didn't come himself. He can pass as human for a time, but it's a risk to do so for too long."

"So what is he?" said Erin, deciding to play along. "An elf?"

Hansen actually laughed. "No. He's from a planet about thirty-seven light years away from here he calls Suran."

"*Suran,*" she repeated, as if testing the word out on her tongue. "What, like the wrap?" she said, rolling her eyes once again.

Hansen's eyes widened. "*Very good.* Spelled with a *u* instead of an *a,* but it's funny you should say that, Erin. Because that's actually what I call Drake and his species. Wraps." He grinned. "Beats the hell out of Suranians."

Erin studied him for several long seconds, as if he were a science experiment, looking for some telltale sign that he had recently escaped from a mental institution. He returned her penetrating gaze with a relaxed patience, looking anything but crazy. Still, it was becoming obvious that he was, despite any appearances to the contrary. She looked at her wrist pointedly, even though she didn't have a watch. "You know your ten minutes are about up."

"I'm not wasting your time. And if you'd humor me as I asked, this would go a lot faster. I get it. This is crazy and you're waiting for the curtain to fall. It isn't, and it won't. Humor me," he repeated.

She tensed her muscles to rise from the chair and leave, but there was something about his eyes that stopped her. A confidence. An easy intelligence. A self-awareness of how insane he must sound to her, but also a deep courage of his convictions and a certainty that he would ultimately convince her. She blew out a long breath. "Okay, Kyle. It's hard for me to imagine I'll ever believe you, no matter what you tell me, but I'll humor you just a little longer."

"Thank you," he said.

"So if Drake's from this Suran, how can he pass for human for even a minute? All the aliens on *Star Trek* looked human, but that's just because they didn't have a big enough budget for more imaginative aliens."

"Not entirely true. There is such a thing as convergent evolution. The Wraps are fairly close to us in appearance, yes. Close enough that the extensive plastic surgery and genetic engineering he underwent before he came here allows him to pass as human for a short time. But there are other alien species whose appearance couldn't be any more, ah . . . alien . . . to us. Drake's problem passing for human isn't his appearance as much as his mannerisms. We've evolved to pick up on dozens of subtle cues regarding human expressions and appearance. That's why it was such a challenge for Pixar and others in the early days to animate humans. If an animated animal is slightly off, it isn't a problem. But make a human just a little bit wrong and we can sense this somehow, and it gets under our skin. Weirds us out. That's one of the reasons he took the appearance of Hugh Raborn when you Skyped. That and to buy credibility when you Googled him."

For the first time, Erin's expression wasn't one of complete skepticism, and Hansen seemed to pick up on this. "Drake told me when he explained how he had used software to transform his face into Raborn's, you said it couldn't be done. Not so convincingly, so seamlessly. Not in real time during a conversation. Well you're right. It can't be done. At least not with *human* technology."

This gave Erin pause. It had been one hell of a magic trick, however he had pulled it off.

"When I've finished explaining everything," continued Hansen, "I hope you'll trust me enough to let me take you to Yuma to meet Drake in person. It's the only way you'll be absolutely convinced I'm telling you the truth. You'll see for yourself he's not human. A short time with him and you'll have absolutely no doubt."

Erin studied him once again. She was far from convinced he was telling the truth, but if his purpose had been to get her to come to Yuma with him, there were far simpler lies that could have done the trick. In fact, he had to have known that the approach he was taking was certain to make her *more* suspicious of him rather than less.

Hansen seemed to read the indecision in her eyes. "The ten minutes you agreed to give me are up. If you'd like, I'll leave right now. Or *you* can. I won't stop you. But I can't believe that someone with your kind of curiosity, your passion for knowledge, would refuse to at least hear me out the rest of the way. Not unless you really think I'm certifiably insane. Which I don't think you do."

Erin sighed, realizing that he was right. "Go on," she said in surrender.

"To be honest, Drake is trying to limit the number of people who know of his origins. For obvious reasons. And you weren't supposed to be among them."

"So why are you telling me this now?"

"He had no other choice. You saw the real Hugh Raborn and then, being understandably suspicious and feeling betrayed, you weren't willing to give him the dosage combination for the cure. So he knew he had to come clean. He set up this meeting, knowing all along he was going to send me. Inviting you to Yuma to meet him and verify what I'm now telling you would have been the most direct route. But he knew you didn't trust him enough to do that. You needed to be eased into what is an entirely new and earth-shattering reality for you. A two-step process, begun on your home turf, where you would feel reasonably comfortable."

"Okay," said Erin. "In the interest of humoring you some more, you mentioned other alien species. Are representatives of *all of them* on Earth?" She leaned toward him and raised her eyebrows. "You're not a member of the Men in Black, are you?"

Hansen laughed. "No. Black isn't my color. And I'm afraid Drake is it. Period. I'll tell you why later on, but he's the only nonhuman on the planet."

"Uh-huh. Well somebody gave him bad directions to end up in Yuma. He does realize that Area 51 is to the west of him and Roswell is to the east, right?"

A warm, genuine smile flashed across Hansen's face

once again, revealing two rows of perfectly straight teeth, no doubt perfected after years of wearing metal in his mouth when he was young. "No aliens at either of those places, I'm afraid."

Hansen paused as if searching for the best way to bring Erin up to speed. "Now that you're willing to hear me out, let me start at the beginning. There are seventeen known intelligent species in our section of the galaxy. The level of their technology is all basically equivalent. The growth in our science and technology has been exponential, but you can't maintain that forever. And any significant differences in the technology of these seventeen civilizations has been smoothed away over thousands of years of trade, so now it's all perfectly homogeneous. Some arrived at this level thousands of years before others, but progress has slowed to a crawl now that they're pressing up against the maximum capacity the universe will allow in many fields."

Erin was fascinated despite herself. If it was a hoax, at least it was a well-thought-out hoax.

Hansen finished the last of his sandwich, washed it down with a long drink of Coke, and continued. "Recently—at least in the scheme of things—our closest intelligent neighbors caught our transmissions and began to relay them to the other sixteen known intelligences. Now they are all aware there is an *eighteenth* intelligence in the stellar neighborhood—which is a *very* big deal. A species which still has quite a ways to go before reaching the level of technology of galactic civilization. They'd like to welcome us into the galactic community. But they became alarmed upon viewing our transmissions."

"They didn't view any of our reality TV, did they?"

said Erin with mock seriousness. "That would alarm *any* intelligence."

Hansen laughed. "I sure hope not. The good news is that they do recognize fiction from nonfiction. Although I'm not sure how they would classify reality television. But anyway, even after factoring out the endless violence and destruction we tend to depict in fiction, we're the most violent, troubled species they have yet run across. Capable of atrocities the other species can barely comprehend. Mass genocides, tortures, and unspeakable cruelty. They find us gifted, but brutal."

"So they've matured beyond this stage?"

"I'm not an expert, but my understanding is that none of them were ever *at* this stage. Evolution can work through competition, but it can work through cooperation also. Take a beehive. Total cooperation, and they've done brilliantly in the scheme of evolution. Most species have a mix of brutal, survival-of-the-fittest competition, and good-for-the-long-term-survival-of-the-entire-species-and-its-genes cooperation. We're apparently much closer to the survival-of-the-fittest side of the ledger than the other seventeen intelligent species."

Erin digested this statement but didn't respond. She swallowed the last of her sandwich, not taking her eyes from the man across from her.

"But here's the thing," continued Hansen. "The Seventeen . . ." He paused. "That's what I call them: the Seventeen. I don't know why, but I feel a little ridiculous calling them Galactics or anything similar. The Seventeen have computers that are millions of times more powerful than ours. And their computers have predicted a ninety-two percent probability that we'll destroy ourselves."

Erin nodded. She could have told him that.

"Intelligence is rare in the galaxy. They would love for us to mature enough to join the galactic community. And they would hate for us to self-destruct."

Erin's eyes widened as her agile mind leaped ahead. She suddenly had a very good idea where this Kyle Hansen was headed. But she decided to let him get there in his own time.

"The problem is that they can't do much to stop us from committing suicide. Interstellar distances are interstellar distances, and the speed of light is even more of a bitch to get around than we all thought. The Seventeen can travel at a good fraction of the speed of light, but that's it. Even a ship from Suran would take several hundred years to arrive. This being said, their scientists have made a breakthrough allowing them to bypass the speed of light. But at a monumental cost in energy and resources. Their equivalent of the *Apollo* project just to send a single citizen here through a singularity. Requiring the equivalent of the entire energy output of their star for several years."

"So you're suggesting they mounted this *Apollo* project and sent Drake?"

"Right. They were convinced if they arrived by slowboat it would be too late."

"And this community of seventeen species, they only sent a single, um . . . Wrap?"

"Yes. Wraps are the unofficial leaders of the Seventeen. The species who has probably contributed the most to the group. And Suran is relatively close to Earth, at least compared to the home planets of most of the Seventeen. Most importantly, Wraps are one of the closest matches to us physically."

"Okay. So Drake was sent here, defying the laws of physics, sucking up a substantial amount of resources from an entire civilization, just to save us from ourselves. Is that what you're telling me?"

"That's right. The Seventeen weren't positive humanity's self-destructive tendencies could be reined in, but if there was an answer, Drake was sent here to find it."

A slight smile played over Erin's lips. The moment of truth had finally arrived. If it really was truth, that is. "Let me guess. Drake determined that the answer was finding a cure for psychopathy? Am I right?"

"Yes. With the help of a quantum computer he brought with him. That's what did the seamless conversion of Drake's face into Hugh Raborn's. Its capabilities are truly astonishing."

"Quantum computer. Sounds fancy, but I know nothing about computers."

"Then I won't waste my breath explaining it to you. It works on principles of quantum physics that are far from intuitive, and far different from the principles governing computing today. And orders of magnitude more powerful. We've been working on them for decades, but haven't gotten very far. And this computer has calculated that a cure for psychopathy would reduce our chances of self-destruction by a considerable amount, making it almost certain we could take our place in this galactic community in a few hundred years. When Wraps and others are finally able to reach us."

"If it takes hundreds of years for one ship to reach us, how does that constitute a community? Of Galactics, or Seventeens, or whatever you want to call them? Unless you like playing chess through the mail, making a single move every few centuries."

"First, while they can't routinely travel faster than light, they *have* cracked faster-than-light communication. Using the same type of technology that made the quantum computer possible. Although Drake hasn't spent the time or resources building such a transmitter, which is a daunting challenge using only current human technology, eventually he will, and can report back. If he is successful in saving us from ourselves, all seventeen known civilizations will send ships here to our solar system, the farthest away not reaching us for several thousand years. Each of the Seventeen now have sixteen of these ships in their systems. So each member of the Seventeen has a full intergalactic community orbiting its star. It really is the only way to make it happen."

Erin had a blank look on her face. "I must be missing something."

Hansen flashed a sheepish smile. "If you are, that just means I'm not explaining it well. I've already come to the conclusion that you don't miss anything."

Inexplicably, Erin found herself responding warmly to the compliment.

"The ships are interstellar arks," clarified Hansen. "We've imagined ships like these for many decades, but they've put them into practice. Basically you just hollow out an asteroid and turn it into a mini planet—but one you can drive through space like a ship. You can fit millions, or even hundreds of millions of people very comfortably inside a hollowed-out asteroid far, far smaller even than our moon. Imagine a sphere only twenty miles in diameter. If you layered the inside like an onion, or honeycombed it, the total surface area available inside would be staggering. And that's for a ship only twenty miles in diameter. Ships like these that transport huge

populations over hundreds of years are called generation ships, or interstellar arks. The aliens who sign on are
committing themselves and their offspring for all eternity
to live in a foreign solar system. But this is the only way
to achieve cross-cultural exchange, given the distances
involved."

Erin realized that her mind was now officially blown.
This Kyle Hansen was so convincing. His description of
this galactic society was so well-reasoned, and held together so well. It was mesmerizing to imagine, and she
found herself hoping it was true. But she had to remind
herself that just because she wished it were true didn't
necessarily make it so. Science fiction and fantasy writers
had fabricated societies that were every bit as complex and
well-reasoned as this, and which were incredibly rich in
detail.

Hansen's phone vibrated but he ignored it, his total focus on Erin not wavering for an instant. A fraction of her
mind noted this with approval. So many people these
days couldn't possibly resist glancing at their phones to
see what was coming in, no matter what the circumstances. There were a few people Erin knew who would
check a ringing phone even if they were on fire at the
time.

Erin stared into Hansen's expressive blue eyes, which
continued to be alive with an easy intelligence. "Let me
make sure I understand," she said. "So now you have
seventeen species living together, in each of seventeen
different solar systems. Basically each species flying
heavily populated mini planets to sixteen different neigh-
borhoods. And they all live in perfect harmony?" she said,
a note of skepticism in her voice.

"Great question. Again, I'm not the expert. But it's my

understanding that although these alien species are all much more peaceful and cooperative than humans, it isn't a perfect world. Or a perfect galaxy in this case. So the answer is no. Two of the seventeen keep almost entirely to themselves. They send out generation ships, but with only thousands, not millions of inhabitants. And they have almost no interaction with other species. Almost as if they're just making sure to have an observation post on the outskirts of civilization, keeping tabs. Some species hit it off with each other like humans and dogs, becoming fast friends, inseparable. Other pairings have an instinctive aversion to each other. Either due to their respective appearances, or to minds that are so incompatibly alien to each other there is instant hatred and combustion whenever they meet. There are a number of cases in which culture A is friends with B. And B is friends with C. But A and C haven't interacted at all in a hundred thousand years."

There was almost a minute of silence as Erin digested the enormity of seventeen civilizations living together in seventeen regions of the galaxy.

"All of this is fascinating," she said finally. "Incredible. Very thought-provoking for someone who has studied psychology and sociology. So even if it isn't true, hats off to you for a stunning vision of cross-culturalism in a galaxy with a prohibitive speed limit."

"Thanks, Erin. But it's all true. You already have all the evidence you need if you really think about it. I know nothing about genetic engineering or medicine, but didn't you ever question how Drake could have done what he did? Identify the precise genes that contribute to the condition and then find a way to reverse them—at the genetic level?"

Erin frowned. She had. She had guessed that it was pure luck, plus the novel approach of sequencing entire genomes, which would have been impossible only years earlier. A dovetailing of knowledge about the physical basis of psychopathy, advances in sequencing, an impressive algorithm, and lots of luck—which scientists liked to call "serendipity" for some reason.

But the odds of being able to do what he had done, when she really thought about it in a fully sober manner, were millions to one against. She had been so eager to believe. And his animal data was so compelling. But Kyle Hansen's story would explain a lot.

"Am I detecting some faint stirrings of belief on your face?" asked Hansen.

Erin raised her eyebrows. "Maybe," she replied. "But even if Drake *is* an alien, even if you prove this beyond a doubt, that still doesn't mean any of this is true," she pointed out. "He could have lied about all of it."

Hansen looked uncomfortable. "True. But I've worked with him closely for years and have come to trust him implicitly. He's aboveboard, unless he's forced to use deception out of necessity, like in your case." He leaned forward. "The important point here is that you have the key to saving the human race. I know that sounds preposterous and melodramatic, but it happens to be true. So let me take you to our headquarters, so you can meet this alien you've been collaborating with. Let me cement the truth of what I'm telling you even more firmly in your mind. So you can join our efforts without any reservations. And tell Drake about your breakthrough. So we can get on with saving ourselves."

Erin shook her head. "I'm not sure I'm all that impressed with that computer of his. The cure he's come up with is stunning. Nothing short of a miracle. This much is true. But it's still years away from approval."

Erin had discussed this at length with Raborn many times. First they needed to prove it worked. But even with a working cure in hand, it would take some doing to get the FDA to agree to clinical trials to demonstrate this, while at the same time keeping her out of jail.

They planned to introduce the cure into a population of psychopaths some *other* research group was studying, far away from Erin Palmer. When these other researchers realized what was going on and announced the impossible, that their subjects had somehow miraculously been cured, it would make worldwide news. It would be huge. Then Raborn would send vials with the cure and animal data to the head of the FDA, anonymously, explaining that this was responsible. The FDA would be forced to take it seriously. It might take a decade, but eventually the treatment would become available.

But even if they succeeded, Erin had come to believe this wouldn't matter much anyway. "Even if such a treatment were approved today," explained Erin, "psychopaths don't see anything wrong with the way they are. They think they're superior. And when it comes to looking out for number one, and being able to operate without remorse, without conscience, without soul, maybe they are. And the ones whose cure would have the biggest impact on society—the dictators of the world, leaders of drug cartels, and the like—would be the very last to agree to use it. Unless you think the FDA, or our government, or Drake for that matter, has jurisdiction over a Middle Eastern psychopathic dictator."

How many dictators and tyrants throughout history had been psychopathic? Erin suspected almost all of them. *Sociopath* was a word that was often used interchangeably with *psychopath,* but there was a difference, although it was subtle and not well-known, even among those in the profession. Sociopaths also suffered from antisocial disorder, but their upbringing and environment played a role in this. This wasn't true for psychopaths. They could have an idyllic upbringing and it wouldn't change a thing. Their mother could have been Mother Teresa and their father Gandhi. It wouldn't matter. Because for them it was all about wiring.

But their environments did dictate where they would ply their psychopathy in many cases. Those raised in educated, loving homes might turn to white-collar crime, cons, corporate backstabbing, insider trading, and corruption. They might go on to become doctors and lawyers and accountants, because this was a clear path to get ahead. If blending in and stabbing people in the back, metaphorically, was what was needed, this was what they would do.

But they especially thrived in environments for which butchery was in fashion. A psychopath raised in a gang environment, or a mob environment, or in a brutal society in Iran or Syria, would have no trouble becoming the most ruthless among the ruthless. Whatever it took to climb the ladder. If getting a law degree was what it took, fine. But if cutting off heads was required, this wouldn't trouble them a bit. If brutal rape and torture would cement fear in their subjects, no problem at all.

In brutal regimes, those capable of rising to the top were invariably psychopathic. And they preyed on the ignorance of the West. The quote that Apgar had given her during their first meeting from *The Bad Seed* was exactly right. These people appeared to be charming and reasonable men, not monsters. And normal people could never imagine a mind so alien to their own.

So when Saddam Hussein or Mahmoud Ahmadinejad had given interviews to eager Western journalists, the journalists were putty in their hands, along with a huge number of the viewers of these programs. The psychopaths were warm, articulate, and smooth. So reasonable and unthreatening, that what was said about them had to be a gross exaggeration, a lie. "Am I responsible for personally using an axe to behead dozens of dissidents, smiling as the blood spurted over my face? Impossible. Look how clean I look in my pressed uniform. Look how nonthreatening my posture and smile are. This is just Western propaganda, of course. Our society is quite progressive."

And the West ate it up.

Ironically, those whose genes made them the *most* compassionate, the *most* empathetic, who were the most removed from the psychopathic mentality, were the easiest to fool. These minds were unable to fathom a mind whose operation was so impossibly different than their own, whose motivations were so foreign. These empathetic elements could easily believe the lies—it was the *truth* their very genetic makeup wouldn't allow them to believe. And when public relations were required, the most dangerous psychopaths of all could play the good people of the world like a Stradivarius in the hands of a master.

"So a cure is an incredible accomplishment," continued Erin. "And the possibilities, although limited, are intriguing. But it won't accomplish what Drake and his computer think it will. Those capable of destroying mankind with less remorse than you or I would feel over swatting a fly will still remain."

Hansen sighed. "You make some valid points. But there's more to this than you've been told." A guilty look came over his face. "And I have a feeling that, necessary as it is, it's something that will take you some time to get comfortable with."

16

FOR JUST A moment, Erin wasn't sure if she even wanted Hansen to continue. The surprises, the tectonic shifts in her reality, were coming too rapidly. And this latest sounded worrisome. What had she missed this time? She wasn't sure she could handle any more psychological shocks to her system. But regardless, she knew there was no closing Pandora's box now.

"I have an idea," she said. "Let me regroup for a minute. Brace myself for whatever you're about to throw at me. You know what always helps with shocks to the system? With having everything you thought you knew about your life and the world turned upside down?"

Hansen's forehead wrinkled in thought. "No. What?" he said finally.

"Cheesecake," replied Erin, the corners of her mouth turning up into a smile. "You bought lunch, how about I buy dessert? Then you can throw the next grenade while I take comfort in my food. A bad habit to turn to sweets when you're stressed, but there you have it."

"You clearly haven't abused it," said Hansen appreciatively. "I'd have guessed you ate like a model." He paused. "Hell, I'd have guessed you *were* a model."

"Okay, flattery helps also," she admitted. "But not as much as cheesecake. Let's go."

They were standing in line to order when Hansen's phone issued two short vibrations and then stopped, alerting him to a new text message. "Sorry," he said, "but I'd better check this. Drake must have left a message. I think he was checking in on us and called earlier. It's not like we have a curfew or anything," he added with the hint of a smile. "But he believes you to be the most important person on the planet right now."

"Why? Even if I dropped dead this instant, he could still recreate my work, using another researcher for confirmation."

"Even forgetting about the risk involved in conducting the testing, which admittedly, you took the brunt of, it would take years. And we may not *have* years," he added pointedly as he began to read the message on his phone.

Kyle Hansen's eyes widened and his face became ashen.

"What is it?" she asked.

Hansen didn't reply. Instead he handed her the phone. It was open to a text message.

Yuma compound attacked. SF responsible. Rest
of team down. I'm on run, can't risk voice msg.
Abandoning phone. Don't try to contact me. Go to
MB in CO asap & get started. He'll expect you. I'll

contact u there in 48 hours. If I'm late, start w/out me. Keep Erin safe!! She's the key.

Erin handed the phone back to Hansen. She wasn't sure what to believe, but the timing was far too unlikely for her taste. "So I guess we can't go back to your head-quarters in Yuma now, after all. We suddenly can't prove what you've told me is true, can we?"

Hansen shook his head, but the stunned, horrified look still hadn't left his face. "Let's take a rain check on the dessert," he said leaving the line and motioning for Erin to follow. They found a nearby table that was free and sat down once again.

"This can't be," said Hansen the moment they were seated. "It's too much of a coincidence that this happened right when you found the cure and were about to tell Drake. I don't believe in coincidences," he said.

Erin gazed at Kyle Hansen with a new respect. Of all the responses he could have had to this situation, this was the one that restored her belief in his veracity the fastest. She couldn't have said it better herself. As she stared into Hansen's eyes, she realized that there was something about him that she trusted. He seemed to have a keen mind, good sense of humor, and an unpretentious, friendly personality. She found herself drawn to him. Drawn to him more than she was prepared to admit, even to herself.

"Yuma was totally off the grid," he continued. "Until now. So you have to be involved in what happened somehow."

"What *did* happen?" asked Erin. "And what's the connection between San Francisco and Yuma? Was Drake working with somebody there?"

"San Francisco?"

"Yes. Drake texted that San Francisco was responsible."

Hansen looked at her in confusion for several seconds before the light of comprehension finally gleamed in his eyes. "You're thinking about his use of the letters *SF*. Drake didn't mean San Francisco. In this case, *SF* stands for Steve Fuller."

Erin gasped.

"How do you know Steve Fuller?" demanded Hansen immediately.

"Wow," said Erin, annoyed with herself. "I think we've established that I wouldn't make a good poker player. I'll admit it. I have heard the name. But why don't you go first. What does he have to do with any of this?"

Hansen considered her for an extended period. "Okay," he said at last. "I guess I can go first. Fuller is an international arms dealer. And a psychopath." He hesitated again, as though uncertain what to say next. Erin hoped he was weighing the best way to tell her the truth, rather than taking time to concoct the best lie. "While Drake has been working on this project with you, he's been keeping track of those who pose the greatest threat to our survival. And Fuller is among a handful of the world's most dangerous players. I'm sure that's what he meant by *SF*."

"How does Drake know this guy's behind it?"

Hansen shrugged. "I don't know. Maybe he recognized him during the attack."

"But why? Why would Fuller attack Drake?"

"I have no idea how he would even know of Drake's existence. But maybe he got wind that Drake was trying to cure psychopathy."

Erin stared at him blankly.

"If psychopathy were cured," explained Hansen, "this would have a big negative impact on an arms dealer. If his best customers suddenly grew a conscience, stopped buying weapons, and started singing folk songs around the campfire, this would be very bad for business. And Fuller is a psychopath himself. Like you said, the last thing they want is to be cured. So what would a brutal, powerful, psychopathic arms dealer do if he found out Drake intended to rid the planet of this condition?"

Erin had to admit that if the attack was real, this reasoning did provide a logical underpinning for it. Perhaps even a compelling one.

"That's all I know about Steve Fuller," said Hansen. "So now it's your turn."

Erin stared deeply into his eyes. She had the feeling he knew more, but decided not to press. For now. Her gut told her that if he was withholding information, it was only because he didn't perceive it to be relevant. And the fact that he didn't seem to be a talented or practiced liar was a hugely positive personality trait in her book, and a great change of pace after working with the world's smoothest liars for so many years.

Erin launched into the story of how she happened to know of Steve Fuller, beginning with his call, when he posed as someone trying to recruit her to his company, Advanced Science Applications. When Erin described the events in the church parking lot, and how she had escaped and made it to Tucson, Hansen listened with an expression of awe, and was unabashedly complimentary of her courage and resourcefulness.

When she had finished she said, "The timing of Fuller's call is just as unlikely as everything else. I assumed the *Wall Street Journal* article had been the trigger, but the trigger for what? And why?"

"What *Wall Street Journal* article?"

She told Hansen how the paper had republished her thoughts on a device to remotely identify psychopaths, the interview that had originally drawn Drake to her.

"For some reason," continued Erin, "I had just assumed you—meaning you and Drake—had seen it. But, anyway, I guess this wasn't the reason for the call, after all. Fuller must have already known about the cure. Although I have no idea how."

Hansen rubbed his chin absently in thought. It was now almost three o'clock, but neither had any awareness of the passage of time, or of the many groups of students and faculty that had come and gone, scurrying around them unnoticed like a large and noisy group of ants. They had maintained their position at the table while hundreds of others zoomed in and out and around, as though they had been filmed using time-lapse photography.

"Not necessarily," said Hansen finally. "The *Wall Street Journal* article would have been enough."

"Enough for what?"

"Enough to get Fuller interested in recruiting you. Think if you really could perfect the psychopath detector you described in the article. That would be quite a valuable tool."

Erin shook her head. "I thought so too when I proposed it. But it turns out there are far too many ethical issues for it to ever be used."

"Maybe so," said Hansen, "but that wouldn't trouble a psychopathic arms dealer. And this device would be far more valuable to him, even, than to the normal person.

Many of the people he deals with on a daily basis—terrorists, dictators, and even their intermediaries—are psychopathic. But some are not. It would be useful for him and his people to be able to identify those who have a conscience from those who don't. In his dealings with potential customers and when recruiting subordinates."

"Okay, I can see that. He reads the article, decides this would be a useful tool, and tries to get me to perfect it away from a university. Having no idea that I abandoned this project before it began years ago."

"So you agree to meet with him. Then what?" Hansen threw out his hands, as if unable to find his way forward. "How do we go from that to where we are now?"

Erin's eyes widened. "They were monitoring me prior to my meeting with them," she said in alarm. "That's how they found me in the church lot. So it isn't a stretch to believe they were monitoring me the entire time I was in San Diego. Even before they contacted me. Why not? Gathering intel, getting a sense for my personality. Deciding the best levers to push to get me to come aboard their fictitious company, either by using a carrot or showing me the stick."

"So when you called Drake from San Diego, they were listening in?"

Erin nodded. "I can't be certain, but I'd sure bet on it."

"Do you remember what you said?"

"Not exactly. But I was furious about his Hugh Raborn deception." She frowned deeply. "And I'm *positive* I told him I had come to San Diego because we had succeeded. Because we had the cure."

Hansen blew out a breath. "That would do it," he said. "Fuller's people monitored you because he wanted you to build a remote diagnostic test. But when they learned that you and Drake had developed a cure instead, that must have thrown Fuller, proud psychopath that he is, into a panic. You went from a possible asset to a threat."

"And if they traced my call to Drake, this would explain how they found him. And why they attacked." It was all beginning to make a sort of twisted sense. "But why wait?" asked Erin. She knew this could still be an elaborate hoax concocted by Drake and Hansen. But she had no other choice for the moment but to assume it wasn't.

"They were able to schedule an innocent meeting with you. They probably decided to get as much information from you as they could before they attacked. They just didn't count on you being so suspicious. Or so elusive."

"That makes sense. But after they lost me, why didn't they hit Drake then?"

Hansen thought about this, but couldn't come up with a good answer.

Erin, on the other hand, arrived at an answer to her own question, and a chill went up her spine. She leaned closer to Hansen. "The reason they timed this the way they did just hit me, Kyle." An anxious look appeared in her eyes. "It's because they're *here,*" she said, making a small circle with her head, a gesture meant to encompass the entire food court. "Right now. Patiently waiting until we aren't in a crowd to take us out."

—~~~—

17

ERIN GLANCED AROUND furtively, focusing especially on fit men who were older than the typical student. Fuller would have someone surveilling them, keeping track of them in the sprawling food court, following them when they left and making sure to alert others outside to their position when they did.

"I'm not sure I understand," said Hansen. "Are you saying they waited to strike at Drake because they hoped you'd keep this meeting?"

"Exactly. So they could, um . . . reacquire me. They expected Drake to be meeting with me, so they could take us both out at the same time. Without any warnings being exchanged between us. When they discovered you had made the trip to Tucson instead of him, they must have decided to do this in stages."

Erin realized as she said this that they had probably recovered her phone from the pickup truck into which she had launched it. In this case, Fuller would have known that Kyle Hansen was coming to meet her rather than Drake. But this wouldn't have mattered. They just had to delay their strike on Drake until she and Hansen were in sight. If their attack was 100 percent effective, Drake wouldn't be able to alert Hansen that anything was amiss. The two of them would be blissfully ignorant and easy pickings. But even if Drake did inform Hansen of the attack in Yuma, which he *had,* they would either fail to ferret out that the danger extended to their own location, or be unable to extricate themselves, even if they realized they were surrounded.

Hansen didn't look entirely convinced. "Why would they ever believe you'd still keep this meeting after what happened? Or have the balls . . . courage," he amended, "to try to get past them to keep your appointment? Even if you wanted to? Wouldn't they think you were still hiding out in LA? Laying low?"

"From my conversation with Drake, they probably realized how important this meeting was to me. I might be wrong, but we have to assume I'm not. We have to assume they're here. Right now. I can't imagine they'll make a move as long as we're in this crowd. And they can afford to be patient."

Hansen gazed at her with open admiration. She sensed that he was attracted to her, but not in the usual way. She was used to men falling for her physically. But he had never once given her the sense this was about physical attraction, even when he had complimented her looks.

"Drake told me that you were very impressive," said Hansen. "For a human," he added wryly. "But I think he undersold you. What you did to get to LA and then Tucson was remarkable. And you think like a master detective, or a master spy. Like you've been engaged in cloak-and-dagger your entire life. I've seen your background. I know you have some pretty impressive fighting skills, but nothing suggests you've had any kind of actual experience with this sort of thing."

Erin frowned. "Yeah, well, don't congratulate me just yet. I've just identified the woods. I haven't come close to getting us out of them. My secret weapon is that I read a lot of thrillers. I know this sounds crazy, but I really think it's helped."

Erin knew her appearance was deceiving, so maybe his was as well. He was cute, but in a down-to-earth, friendly, not particularly hardened or athletic-looking sort of way, and she had the distinct impression he was *not* the hired muscle. He was too smart, and seemed too thoughtful—not that physical and intellectual skills were mutually incompatible.

"What about you?" she said. "Are you a bodyguard in Drake's organization?"

Hansen looked amused at the thought. "No. I'm afraid not."

"Any experience with these types of situations at all? Any fighting skills? I don't suppose you're ex–Special Forces?"

Hansen laughed. "No. But I'll take that as a huge compliment. I'm afraid I wasn't even a Boy Scout. Worse, I read nothing but science fiction, so you're ahead of me there too. I don't know how to operate a gun, don't know how to use a knife, and I'm pretty sure a ninety-year-old woman in a wheelchair could take me in hand-to-hand combat."

"Okay," said Erin with a twinkle in her eye. "I admire your . . . *pathetic* . . . honesty."

"So any ideas about what we do now?" asked Hansen.

Erin turned her head away from him, wanting to pause any conversation so she could have some quality time for thought. She reexamined her logic to this point, and still found it sound. Except for one point. Would they really go to all this trouble: attack Drake, send a team to surveil them here, and everything else, just because of a few words spoken over a phone? Maybe she *was* letting her imagination run away with her. Fuller wouldn't commit these kinds of resources, and take this kind of risk—openly attacking a compound in Yuma, committing a military assault on U.S. soil—unless he was certain she hadn't just hallucinated the cure.

If her assumptions and logic were correct, they drove straight to a prediction. One that would be simple enough to test. And if it panned out, she could be nearly certain the attack on Drake wasn't a hoax, there really were men watching them, and she wasn't getting herself and Hansen worked up over bogeymen that didn't actually exist.

Erin decided to continue to operate under the assumption that they did exist while she checked out her hypothesis.

She turned back to Kyle Hansen, who continued to gaze at her with a steady confidence, sure after her daring escape from San Diego she would find some way to pull a rabbit out of the hat. She found herself not wanting to disappoint him, and for reasons beyond just their personal safety.

"I need to make a phone call," she said. "While I do, I need you to walk back to the bookstore. But take a circuitous route. Like you're trying to decide if you should get something else to eat first. Try to spot whoever is watching us in here. My guess is he'll be fit, won't be a student, and will look totally occupied. As though he couldn't possibly be watching us. Act natural and don't be obvious."

Hansen nodded. "I'll try," he said.

"My guess is that the watcher in here will alert the team outside when you leave, and they'll be watching the entrance to the bookstore. So when you do cross between here and there, make sure you're with a crowd so they don't decide to try anything. When you're inside the store get a U of A duffel bag and fill it with two large Wildcat T-shirts and two hats."

The large shirts could be easily slipped over their current ones while adding bulk to both of them, enhancing the disguise.

"We want to be chameleons," continued Erin. "Blend in with the students. Try not to let anyone see what you're doing—especially not that you're acquiring clothing."

Hansen listened in rapt attention.

Erin paused to gather her thoughts. "The checkout is near the exit," she continued, "so don't check out. The watchers will see the items you're getting if you do. Just shoplift the whole duffel and get back here as fast as you can."

Hansen blew out a breath. "You know you're not cut out to be Jason Bourne when the thought of shoplifting fifty dollars' worth of clothing makes you want to vomit."

Erin couldn't help but smile, but she quickly became serious once again. "You know what?" she said. "Maybe don't do the duffel bag thing. It would be too obvious a shoplift. Get a standard backpack and remove all the tags. Put the shirts and hats in there. Half the bookstore's customers wear backpacks on a perpetual basis. And be sure to get the cheapest clothing you can find, so they don't bother imbedding any of those shoplifting deterrent devices. You know, the super-clearance stuff they half *hope* someone will shoplift just so they can be rid of it. Try to wrinkle it up a bit too."

"Are you sure you've never done this before?"

"Not even a candy bar. But don't worry, Kyle. If we get out of this we can reimburse the poor university."

Kyle Hansen pulled out his chair and rose. "If we get out of this," he said, "I'll throw the university a party." He took a deep breath. "I'll be back in five or ten minutes."

As he was walking away, under his breath, he couldn't help but add, "I hope."

18

THE MOMENT HANSEN left, Erin dialed Alejandro's personal cell phone number at the prison, using her pre-paid phone. She was more relieved than she had expected to be when he answered.

"Alejandro," she said excitedly. "It's Erin Palmer. I'm so glad I caught you. Do you have a minute?"

"Sure. Glad I answered. For some reason my phone didn't recognize you. How's the vacation going? Having fun?"

Erin almost laughed out loud. *Yeah, I'm having the time of my life,* she thought sarcastically.

"I'm having a great time," she said, trying to sound as sincere as possible. "I'm glad you convinced me to do this. Except I dropped my phone in a pool," she added. "Not too smart. Anyway, I'll tell you all about it later. I don't have a lot of time right now. So here's the reason for my call: were there any unusual visitors to the prison in the past few days?"

"If you mean the FBI, then I already know about it. You don't have to fish around."

The FBI? If her reasoning had been correct, she expected Fuller to have sent someone to visit the prison. But she wouldn't have guessed this person would be able to impersonate the FBI.

"Great," said Erin. "So, ah . . . what, exactly, do you know?" she said.

"The warden told me. The FBI is training someone to do what you do. So just to be sure he's ready, they wanted him to conduct MRIs on the last five prisoners you saw the day you left. I brought them to him myself. Just this morning. He left about four hours ago."

"Oh . . . good," stammered Erin. "And did he have any problem doing the MRIs?"

"Not that I know of. I guess he'll compare them with your results to make sure he's doing it right, huh?"

"Exactly," said Erin.

"You should feel proud, being the gold standard and all."

"I do, thanks. I just wasn't sure the FBI was going to tell you why they were there. I didn't want you to think they were checking up on me."

Alejandro laughed. "On you? I'd never think that."

His absolute confidence in her integrity made Erin feel even more guilty about what she had done.

"Did you get a look at this guy's credentials?" she asked. "I mean, was he really with the FBI? Or was he more of a consultant?"

"I don't know. He didn't show me any credentials. But he must have satisfied the warden. He was scheduled on very short notice."

"Okay then. Well, thanks a lot, Alejandro. You have a great week."

She returned the phone to her pocket and a sick feeling penetrated the deepest recesses of her gut. This call had really brought it home. Before, trying to elude shadowy, hypothesized surveillance seemed like nothing more than a challenging intellectual exercise. But it had suddenly become very real. Now the likelihood of the attack on Drake being a hoax was vanishingly small. Her logic had been correct. Fuller hadn't made his final move until he had confirmed that the cure was real, that she wasn't delusional. Whoever he had pressed into service as an FBI imposter knew his way around an MRI scanner enough to verify that the brains of the last few inmates she had seen suddenly read normal.

Kyle Hansen returned less than a minute later carrying a black canvas backpack, with a blue-and-red *A* stenciled on it proudly, his face flush from adrenaline. He took the chair he had occupied before and faced Erin. "Mission accomplished," he said happily.

She congratulated him and then quickly filled him in on her conversation with the prison guard.

"Brilliant deducing," he said. "This really cements it. You've connected the last dot from this Steve Fuller to us." He paused. "And I think I found the guy watching us on this level."

"How sure are you?"

"Not positive, but as confident as I can be. He's one of the few people here who aren't nineteen or fat old professors. Imagine a Navy SEAL trying hard not to look like a Navy SEAL."

Erin paused in thought. "Did you drive here from Yuma?" she asked.

"No. I took a puddle jumper and then cabbed it from Tucson International."

Erin thought about this. It didn't matter, she realized,

because even if he had driven, they would be watching his car.

"How much cash do you have?" she asked.

It took Hansen a second to adjust to this change of subject. "A few hundred, I think."

"Well, sure," she said playfully. "With all the shop-lifting you do it's no wonder you're loaded."

Hansen laughed.

"Two hundred is good," she continued. "That's plenty for cab fare. Or to bribe a student to become a cabbie for you."

She quickly told him her plan. He tried to hide his anxiety, but he couldn't quite do it.

"You sure you're okay with this?" she asked.

Hansen nodded. "Look, Erin, too much is at stake for me not to be. I won't let us down."

Erin waited ten minutes until the precise time the classes currently in session around campus had ended and the students were released back into the wild. The next round of classes would begin soon. For a square mile around them, undergraduates, graduates, and fac-ulty poured from buildings—as though these buildings were anthills kicked by a giant—and began swarming in every direction. Like a change of shift at a crowded factory, in just a few minutes throngs of young men and young women would be flooding in and out of the stu-dent union and the food court area.

Erin forced herself to wait three minutes and then said, "Let's go."

Without another word they rapidly approached the man Hansen had identified as the professional watching them. He had his nose in a textbook and barely gave them a glance as they approached, but Erin was confident Hansen had been right: this guy belonged in this particular food court about as much as a grade-schooler belonged rappelling down from a military helicopter. The man continued to ignore them until they both pulled up a chair on either side of him.

"We're willing to come with you," said Erin without preamble. "But I want your word that if we cooperate, we won't be hurt."

"I'm sorry, Miss, but I have no idea what you're talking about."

"You're really going to let this chance go by, just to avoid breaking cover?" said Erin disdainfully. "Really?"

The man stared intently at Erin for several seconds. "Okay," he said. "It's a deal. No one will touch you."

With the last word of this confirmation that he was, indeed, the man they were seeking, Hansen pressed the Taser he had concealed in his hand—the one Erin had slipped to him before they had crossed the food court— against the man's leg, and held it there until the man slid off the chair to the smooth floor, convulsing. Erin knew her martial arts reputation would have preceded her and that she'd be the focus of attention, so Hansen would have to wield the Taser.

She followed the man rapidly to the floor, hastily locating and removing his wallet and weapon, an H&K .45, and slipped them both into an open pocket in the black canvas backpack, just seconds after he completed his fall.

"Someone help!" shouted Erin, now playing the concerned citizen.

Dozens of pairs of eyes turned to witness her and Hansen kneeling by a muscular man lying on the floor.

Hansen hit him with another long dose of electricity, using the backpack to shield the activity from onlookers, and the man convulsed yet again.

Dozens of onlookers gravitated toward the scene in a rough circle, like fish swimming to spilled food. "He's having epileptic seizures!" shouted Erin. "Someone call nine-one-one."

As phones began dialing, Kyle Hansen hit the man on the floor with several more jolts, once again under cover of the canvas pack.

"I'm gonna find a doctor," announced Erin, lifting the backpack and quietly slipping away from the paralyzed man and into the crowd, with Hansen close behind. The second they were through the first wall of spectators, Erin handed Hansen a stolen shirt and hat from the backpack and they broke in opposite directions, slipping the shirts over their own clothing as they walked.

Erin slid her arms through the straps of the backpack, took a random exit far from where they had entered, and glommed onto a group of four girls who all sported backpacks of their own. She melted into the group as though she'd been part of it for years. "Do any of you know that guy in there?" she asked so they would continue walking and not question her presence in their midst.

"What guy?" said the girl closest to her.

"The guy having the seizures. Poor guy. None of you saw that?"

"No, we were just cutting through on the way to the dorm."

Erin heard a faint siren off in the distance. "That must be the ambulance now," she said for the benefit of her new walking companions.

Erin continued moving with the group and chatting

about anything she could come up with, not once glancing around to see if she was being followed.

Ten minutes later she arrived at Apache, one of several nearby dorms, with the group of four freshmen. And none too soon. She suspected they had been very close to ignoring their manners and asking her to leave them alone.

As soon as they were through the doors she approached a different group of students at the far end of the lobby, telling them that she was late for an important meeting, and that if any of them had ready access to a car, she'd be willing to pay fifty bucks to anyone willing to drive her six miles—so she wouldn't have to wait for a cab.

Within five minutes she was in the passenger seat of a car, on her way back to the Saguaro Inn. She checked the mirrors the entire drive but saw no sign of followers.

About halfway to the motel, she realized she was still carrying the dime-sized GPS tracking device she had planned to plant on Drake in her pocket. She shook her head, realizing that this plan had been made obsolete three realities ago, and tossed the tiny device out of the window.

As they pulled into the motel, Erin closed her eyes for just a few seconds, letting relief wash over her for the first time, and prayed that Kyle Hansen would have similar success and would be joining her shortly.

19

~~

ERIN PALMER SAT cross-legged on the bed, on top of a faded yellow-and-orange floral bedspread, while Kyle Hansen was parked on a small wooden chair that was in front of a cheap, laminated, particle-board desk.

"Well, no risk of anyone thinking of looking for us here," said Hansen, making a show of looking around the room in mock horror. A slow smile came over his face. "Big risk of the entire motel being condemned or falling down around us."

Erin couldn't help but return his warm smile. He seemed more genuine than most people she had met, and charming in an unpolished way. Which was a good thing. After years of working with psychopaths, too much polish hit her the wrong way.

As she gazed into his eyes, a momentary image came into her mind of a naked Kyle Hansen holding her equally naked body in his arms and kissing her passionately, and she could almost feel the smoothness of his body against hers.

Where did that come from? she thought.

Lisa Renner had been so right. Two years without sex—with little human contact of *any* kind—started to wear on the psyche. Which is why she had been intent on seducing her collaborator, Hugh Raborn, who turned out—maybe—to be an alien named Drake. It was a good thing she hadn't met with him in San Diego, she decided, because even though she didn't think of herself as overly choosy, she still insisted that the body parts of her sexual partners be 100 percent human. You just didn't compromise on certain things.

Was she really so desperate, though, that she could switch gears from Drake to Kyle Hansen so quickly? In her heart, she knew the answer to this wasn't desperation. In only a few hours she already found Kyle to be more appealing than any man she'd met in the past two or three years, including Drake. And working together to escape a dragnet and holing up together in a motel seemed to accelerate the bonding process, as did sharing any number of world-shattering, mind-blowing secrets.

Hansen had managed a clean escape from the student union in a similar fashion to her own, but his arrival at the motel had been thirty minutes behind hers. It was one of the longest thirty minutes of her life, and the suffocating, mind-numbing fear she had felt during this entire period was not due to what his capture or death would mean for her own prospects of survival, or any lofty cause, but was felt for him alone. This wait had exposed her emerging feelings more surely than a rational self-examination of her emotions ever would, as much as she refused to fully acknowledge it.

She wondered what he was thinking. Was he picturing *her* naked as well? She suspected that wasn't an uncommon occurrence, even among men who didn't know her. Only when she used makeup and disguise to purposely make herself look unappealing was she free from the male libido. Had she been more of a free spirit, had a psychopath never ripped her life away from the path it was on, she wondered what her life might be like. She wondered if she would enjoy the interest from men instead of wishing it would go away. She certainly wouldn't be in the field she was in, doing the work she was doing. A veterinarian perhaps, working with the animals she loved rather than with human monsters she loathed. And she certainly wouldn't be collaborating unlawfully with someone of uncertain . . . species.

"Any more messages from Drake?" she asked.

Hansen shook his head. "I ditched my phone. It was the one thing you forgot to tell me to do."

"Oh. Right. Good thinking." Erin raised her eyebrows. "Maybe you've read some thrillers, after all."

"I'm not *that* lame," protested Hansen. "Doesn't everyone know that cell phones can be used to track people nowadays?"

"I guess so."

"And Drake ditched his as well. And so did you. So it was an obvious thing to do."

"So how are we going to connect with Drake?"

"We go to the designated location and he'll contact *us*."

Erin reflected on Drake's text message. "So *SF* wasn't San Francisco. But *CO* did mean Colorado, right?"

"Right. We need to get there. But let me explain more about that part of the message later. Right now, I'd love to finish our conversation."

"Me too," said Erin.

Hansen left the chair and slid down onto the worn beige carpet, sitting cross-legged with his back against the wall, facing Erin on the bed five feet away.

Erin decided the chair he had abandoned did look uncomfortable, although she was still sure the ones in Dean Borland's office were more so, despite their far more welcoming appearance. The two of them both sitting cross-legged in a bedroom reminded her of slumber parties she had had as a little girl, only she doubted the air would soon be filled with delighted giggling, nor that the conversation would turn to who was the cutest boy in class.

"Where were we?" said Hansen, breaking Erin from her reverie.

"I believe we left off when I was saying that Drake had miscalculated. That his cure wasn't the panacea he thought it would be." Erin shook her head, almost imperceptibly. Had she really just used the word *panacea*? Maybe she had been in academia too long. "And you told me I didn't have the full picture," she continued. "*Yet again.*"

A thoughtful look came over Hansen's face as he considered the best way to move the conversation forward from this point. "Everything you said before we were interrupted is absolutely true," he began. "As far as it goes. Just having a cure isn't enough. And approval could take a decade, even if a corporate sponsor stepped up right away based on an anonymous tip, and the FDA allowed it to happen. This is time we, as a species, probably don't have. And you're also right that the very people we need to cure are the ones who would refuse to take it."

Hansen paused for several long seconds, as though not eager to continue.

"So tell me where I've gone wrong," prompted Erin. "Come on, Kyle, don't keep me in suspense."

Hansen sighed. "Drake wasn't planning to give them a choice."

Erin rolled her eyes. "Okay, shoving it down the throats of millions of psychopaths won't work either. Not that they'd identify themselves. And even if they did, and you could force them in some other way, it's ridiculous. Unless you really do believe that Santa can visit every kid on earth in a single night."

"There is a way," Hansen assured her. "One whose delivery doesn't involve chimneys. Drake has engineered a cold virus to carry the cure. A *hypercontagious* cold virus. Within a year, probably less, it will infect every man, woman, and child on earth. It's designed to be very mild, so ninety-nine percent of the population will get nothing more from it than a runny nose and maybe sneeze for a few days. One percent of the population, however, a few weeks after being infected, will no longer be psychopathic."

The enormity of this vision was mind-numbing. Erin's mouth fell open and stayed there for an extended period as she wrestled with the sheer audacity and scope of the concept. "You can't do that," she whispered.

"Maybe *we* can't," he acknowledged. "But Drake and his computer, after coming up to speed on our genetic code, can. The Wraps have developed genetic engineering to a level we can't yet begin to approach."

Erin shook her head. "I don't mean you can't do that because of the technology hurdle. I mean even if you *could* do that—you *can't* do that. My actions have breached ethics, I know that. But this would be a breach of ethics on one of the grandest scales in history."

Hansen nodded. "Which is why Drake didn't tell you about it. He knew you'd feel this way. Which is surprising given what you've been through at the hands of one of these monsters."

Erin's eyes widened and she visibly shrank back on the bed. The expression on Hansen's face made it clear he regretted saying these words the instant they had come out of his mouth.

"What do you know about that?" she demanded. "Those records are sealed."

Hansen lowered his eyes. "Nothing is sealed when it comes to Drake and his advanced computer," he said softly. "And I am truly sorry. I'm sorry that we abused your privacy in this way. And I'm sorry that this happened to you. I can't even imagine. But the way you picked yourself up and recovered from this is unbelievable. Inspiring. How you could trust anyone ever again, especially a man, I'll never know. I couldn't in your shoes."

Erin wasn't sure *she* could in her shoes either, which probably explained her lack of any kind of meaningful, long-term relationship. She blamed it on her dedication to her work, and that was part of it—but there was far more to it than that . . .

She looked away. She felt more violated than she had in years—possibly since the incident had occurred. But she needed to shake it off. It wasn't Kyle's fault for reading a profile that Drake had thrust in front of him.

Or was she already going out of her way to find reasons to forgive Kyle Hansen? To minimize his part in this? Was that why Drake had sent him? Did he and his computer predict she would be attracted to Kyle's warmth and obvious sincerity? Was Drake even more adept at manipulation than a human?

"Is that why Drake chose me to be his partner in crime?" said Erin. "Because he figured I'd have a grudge to bear? That I'd be easier to convince to ditch my principles for a cure?"

Hansen opened his mouth to answer and then closed it again. A few seconds later he said, "That's something you'll have to ask him. I wasn't involved in this decision. Drake likes to keep things compartmentalized, and until recently, I had no need to know just who it was that was testing psychopaths."

In a rush Erin realized that while it seemed in some ways that she had known Kyle Hansen forever—her libido certainly thought so—she had just met him. She had gained a strong sense of his personality, his sense of humor, and his intelligence, but she knew absolutely nothing more about him. There was so much going on she hadn't bothered to ask him a single question about himself.

"Time out," she said. "Before we go any further, let's do something I should have done a while ago. You know *everything* about me. But who are *you*? And how did you get involved in this?"

Hansen smiled. "You know, it never occurred to me I hadn't told you already. Sorry. Let me give you the short version. I'm a physicist. Thirty years old. Single. Currently unattached," he added, and as soon as he did a look of disbelief came over his face. "I'm not sure how my relationship status made it into a CliffsNotes summary of my entire life," he said in embarrassment. "Must just be a Facebook-generation thing."

Erin's heart had picked up speed at this indication of interest on his part, so unsubtle even he was surprised it had come out of his mouth. "Right," she said with an amused twinkle in her eye.

"I grew up in the Midwest. Indianapolis, Indiana, to be exact. My father was a mathematician and my mother a nurse, and I have two older brothers. Grew up loving science and science fiction. Completed my undergraduate at Purdue, and then went on to do graduate work in computer science and physics at Carnegie Mellon University in Pittsburgh. Working on making advances in quantum computing."

"That's an interesting coincidence given what you've told me about Drake's magic computer."

"Not a coincidence. That's how I found him. I had a theory about how to isolate quantum events. If I was right, my theory predicted a certain type of quantum pattern when I searched a particular . . ." He stopped himself in midsentence. "Unless you've spent years studying physics this isn't going to mean much to you. So let's just use the word *spectrum* for simplicity's sake, even though this isn't technically correct. I had a theory for how to identify certain quantum spectra and what this might mean. My thesis advisor, who was British, thought my ideas were *rubbish*."

"They have such a beautiful way with words over there, don't they?"

Hansen laughed. "He had some other choice words as well—this was just the nicest. Anyway, I went on to find what my theory predicted I would find—but more organized, and while still at vanishingly small levels, a far clearer signal than I had expected. When I plugged these results into my theory, it suggested a quantum computer was operating. Not the fledgling attempts we were currently making, but a far more sophisticated version."

"What did your advisor say to that?"

"That it was more rubbish. He said it was obviously an artifact. To him, this was even greater proof I was wrong. After all, for me to be right, a quantum computer had to be operating. And we were decades away from something on that level. In fact, the one we were working on at CMU was the most advanced in the world."

"He didn't immediately jump to the conclusion it was an alien design?" said Erin, rolling her eyes. "Talk about lack of imagination."

"Exactly," said Hansen with a smile. "Anyway, long story short, I was stubborn. I was able to localize the source to . . ."

He stopped as though considering what he should say next, and there was something about his expression that made Erin believe there was more to his story than he was telling. On the other hand, this was the abbreviated version, after all, so this was to be expected.

"To Yuma," he finished. "So I went there and began looking for a source. And I kept digging. Drake took notice. Finally he brought me into the fold. I left the graduate program and my old life behind, and removed myself from the grid. For the past four years I've been working with him, and learning quantum physics well beyond what human science has achieved."

Erin realized so much was going on that she hadn't really internalized just how monumental it was, how epoch-making, for humankind to finally have unambiguous proof, not just of alien life, but of intelligent alien life—although she still needed to verify for herself just how unambiguous this proof really was. But assuming it was true, it would change the course of human thought forever. She remembered reading a quote from a famous scientist, she couldn't remember who, speculating about intelligent life in the universe, that was particularly apt to this situation: *Sometimes I think we're alone. Sometimes I think we're not. In either case, the thought is staggering.*

"You mentioned you read a lot of science fiction," said Erin.

"That's right."

"I imagine it has to be a thrill to know what this part of the galaxy is really like. To know we aren't alone. To know that seventeen civilizations exist out there."

Hansen nodded, and a euphoric glow spread over his face. "I feel like the luckiest man in the world."

"So how many people work with him, besides you?"

"Indirectly, several dozen. Directly, just me, and only because I forced myself on him. He couldn't risk that I would keep pressing, trying to get others to take my theory seriously. He knew he might be discovered if I succeeded, so he decided he had to take me on. More as damage control than anything else."

"So what's your role?"

"Well, I learn quantum physics and help in any way I can. Which usually involves interacting with other humans, like his security detail, so he doesn't have to take this risk." Hansen grinned. "I have an easier time seeming like a normal human than he does. But not by much."

Erin laughed. For an expert on quantum physics—whatever that really was—she thought he impersonated a human quite well.

"But Drake does have his tentacles—and I do mean tentacles—into a lot of pies," continued Hansen. "He's working with a number of people he doesn't tell me about. As I said, he likes to keep things compartmentalized. Humans are less trustworthy than any species in the Seventeen, so he makes no exceptions in maintaining an ultra-paranoid level of secrecy and security. And that includes me. As integral as I am to his organization in many ways, information is still on a need-to-know basis."

"So you knew he had someone testing different dosage combinations, but you didn't know who?"

"Exactly. Drake is dedicated to seeing that we survive and mature and become part of the diversity of galactic civilization. But maintaining absolute anonymity is vital. So he takes the fewest possible chances."

There was silence in the room as Hansen allowed Erin to ponder all he had told her.

"So is our time out over?" he said finally. "Did I give you at least some sense of who I am?"

"You mean beyond your relationship status?" she said dryly.

Hansen winced. "Uh-huh."

"Yes, you did. That helped a lot."

"Good," said Hansen. "So let's get back to the main topic. Eradicating psychopathy forever. Drake predicted it would take some effort to persuade you. Despite . . ." He stopped, realizing he was about to make the same mistake he had made earlier, bringing up her tragic past.

He visibly switched gears. "Explain to me your ethical issues with this. Let's forget for a moment that taking this step is necessary to save the entire species from self-destruction. I do get how it's unethical to cure someone without their consent. But these are *psychopaths*. It seems like they and the world would be far better off—again, even if the stakes weren't what they are."

"I've done more thinking about this over the past few years than you can imagine," said Erin. "You do realize that as horrific as these people are, the ones who end up being serial killers are the tip of the tip of the iceberg. All psychopaths are monsters without souls, I'll give you that. And they typically do leave a trail of shattered lives behind them. But many haven't been *convicted* of any crimes."

"You emphasized the word *convicted*. So you're saying they've all committed them, it's just that most don't get caught?"

"Pretty much. There is plenty of corruption out there that people get away with. And if it's bad in this country, it's far worse in many others." She paused. "But you're changing the personalities and brain structure of people who, *technically,* haven't done anything wrong. They probably have or will, but they haven't been convicted. And with Drake's virus they aren't given a choice. My dean thought using a device to remotely identify psychopaths was like being the thought police, or the pre-crime unit. But this is the ultimate manifestation of that. The virus would be judge, jury, and—well, not executioner. But let's say—remodeler."

Kyle Hansen nodded, deep in thought, but remained silent.

"And this is where it gets really tricky," she continued. "Curing a Jeffrey Dahmer just might be a crueler punishment than imprisonment. Psychopaths in prison are relatively content. They love themselves and never doubt anything." She looked away. "But recently I witnessed a number of the prisoners I cured. And it's made me question all of my thinking. I work with the most violent offenders. I've come to see that being cured is the ultimate curse for them. They suddenly have a conscience—for the first time. Imagine if I slip you a pill that turns you into a berserker and you savagely kill your wife and kids. Then you wake up and return to normal. For the rest of your life you'd have to live with the memory of killing those who were the closest to you."

She waited for him to consider this and she could tell that imagining this scenario was making an impression on him.

"I've been seeing that lately. The inmates don't know they're cured, of course. All they know is that suddenly they're feeling true empathy and remorse. For the first time in their lives they reflect back on their actions and feel the same horror at what they've done as the rest of us would. The pain is *enormous*." She lowered her head. "I wouldn't be surprised if many of the inmates I cured commit suicide before too long. You should have seen them. We've had a lifetime with a conscience. We've become somewhat acclimated, built up a tolerance. Someone who drinks every day can withstand the effects of alcohol far better than a teetotaler. The systems of these psychopaths aren't prepared for a soul. Suddenly they know fear. They know uncertainty. They know what they've done to others, and why it's so terribly wrong. And they know remorse."

"Are you saying you actually feel *sorry* for them?" said Hansen in dismay. "After what they've *done*? Perhaps being made aware of their atrocities, and having to feel empathy for their victims is the best punishment of all."

Erin nodded. "I thought that for the first few weeks I wrestled with this. It does seem like what they deserve. It seems like poetic justice." She turned away for several seconds and her face turned into a mask of pure anguish. "Poetic justice for the lives and potential they so callously destroy," she finished, her voice breaking with emotion.

For the first time in years Erin's psychological defense system had broken down and images of her lost family, in different poses of death, had flashed into her mind. Her beautiful mother shot in the face at close range. Her sweet sister, Anna, with her head lolling lifelessly on her shoulder, her innocent face wet from tears. And her father literally stabbing out with his last ounce of strength.

The potency of her loss returned for just a moment, and if she had been standing she would have sunk to the ground. This was followed, inevitably, by a searing hatred that coursed through her veins like a drug. She had found a way to come to terms with her hatred on an intellectual level, but on a visceral level she knew she never would. Tears pooled in her eyes as she visibly fought to regain emotional control.

"Erin?" said Hansen softly. "Are you okay?"

Erin slammed her mental defenses into place, her right hand curling into a fist, and she shook her head in a short, violent motion for just a second, like a dog shaking off water. "I'm fine," she said weakly.

She took a few breaths and steadied herself. "As I was saying," she continued, her voice regaining its strength and composure, "I thought being forced to feel pain for what they had done was the ultimate poetic justice. But I'm not so sure anymore. Of anything. Part of me has begun to think of these people as a violent force of nature. I hated them for a long, long time. And the truth is, deep down, I still do. But what's the point? The ones who murder have less free will about it than you might imagine. That's what research like mine and others is showing.

Their brains are different. I'm not trying to absolve them, or make excuses for them, I'm just stating a fact.

"You don't hate a hurricane for destroying your town," she continued. "You may curse the fates and mourn your losses. But you can't hate a storm. If your friend falls into a river and is stripped clean by a school of piranha, you don't hate the piranha. You fear them, sure. You avoid them at all costs. You might even try to wipe them out if you can. But you don't *hate* them. They're just being piranha, after all."

She paused for several seconds to gather her thoughts. "So now you make these monsters human—for the first time. And yes, this is more than a fitting punishment for what they've done. But the cured ones weren't the ones who committed these savage acts now, were they? That was a different version of them. You're turning a monster into a human, and then punishing the human for the actions of the monster."

"Whoa," said Hansen. "Saying you've given this some thought is an understatement."

He rose from the carpet, stretched, and returned to the desk chair, his eyes never leaving Erin's. "It almost sounds as though you think killing them all might be more humane than curing them all."

"It just might be," she replied. "I don't know. Only God could know something like that. But I'm guessing you're able to see the moral issues involved with *killing* one percent of the population. Even without my help."

"Yeah, I think I'm on top of that one," he said. "But kidding aside, I have to believe they'd rather be cured than killed."

"Absolutely. But that's because, just like they can't fathom the suffering of others, they can't possibly fathom what it will be like to suddenly have a conscience. Maybe if they knew, they *would* prefer death. As I said, my prediction is that there will be a significant number of suicides."

"It's a horrible aberration, and situation, no matter how you slice it," said Hansen thoughtfully.

"I'm not sure if I believe in God," said Erin. "When you experience what I did before you're twelve, belief doesn't come easily. I find it hard to imagine any God taking the time to create a soul in ninety-nine percent of the population, but allowing a perfect storm of genetic errors to make monsters of the others."

"You're probably right. But I've heard it said that without evil, we wouldn't be able to recognize or appreciate good."

Erin twisted her head and stared at him in wonder. For all the thinking she had done recently, this was a thought she had not yet had.

"You make some compelling points," said Hansen. "About a cure bringing untold misery to the compassionate humans these people will now become. And about the risk of suicide. But isn't it true these effects will be the most severe in those who have committed the most severe, violent crimes? Didn't you say the majority of psychopaths are engaged in less-violent offenses?"

Erin nodded. "You're right. There is a certain symmetry there. Poetic justice again. The psychopaths who have done the least damage will feel the least pain when they gain a soul. Those who've *caused* the most pain, will *feel* the most pain."

"To be honest," said Hansen, "you've raised a number of points I wouldn't have considered. You've opened up more cans of worms than I expected. Until I've had time to really think this through, I can't argue with anything you've said. But I started this by asking you to forget about the fate of the world hanging in the balance. But now let's bring that back in. Are you saying you'd still have misgivings, even if it came down to this: either cure them, or lose the entire species *because* of them?"

"I'd have misgivings, but of course I'd cure them. Provided that I was absolutely certain that Drake and his computer were correct, and these really were the stakes, this is a simple trade-off to make. The world's easiest trolley problem."

"Trolley problem?"

"You've never done any readings on ethics?"

"What part about carefree geek physicist who loves science fiction and working with an alien visitor didn't you get?"

Erin laughed. "Jeremy Bentham? John Stuart Mill? Those names ring a bell?"

"I've definitely heard of Mill," he said. "But I couldn't tell you anything about him."

"These men came up with a theory of ethics called utilitarianism. The goal of which is basically the greatest good for the greatest number. In choosing between courses of action, this should be the guiding principle. A huge series of thought experiments have been constructed over the years to test this out. Many of these involve trolleys. These techniques are actually known as *trolleyology*."

"You've got to be kidding me."

"Yeah, you tell me about an alien visitor and seventeen alien species, in seventeen locations, hanging out together in hollowed-out asteroids, and *I'm* the one who's far-fetched. At least you can Google 'trolleyology' to confirm it."

Hansen laughed. "I can't say you don't have a point."

"Anyway," continued Erin, "these trolleyology problems reveal some interesting facets of human nature." She stared at him intently. "Let me give you a few examples. Suppose a runaway trolley is out of control and is coming to a fork in the tracks. You happen to be standing by a lever that can switch them. If the trolley stays on course it will kill five workmen standing on the tracks. If you cause it to *switch* tracks, it will kill a single workman. Do you switch the track?"

Hansen thought about this for a few seconds and finally nodded.

"Most people agree on this one. Even though you're taking an action that will kill a man, you're saving five lives at the same time." She paused. "What if the five were strangers to you, and the lone person on the other track was your mother?"

"Wow," said Hansen after a few seconds. "I'm not sure I can answer that."

Erin smiled. "Sure you can. The answer is that in that case, you'd let the five men die, rather than flip a switch that would kill your own mother. Admit it to yourself."

Hansen nodded, but looked troubled.

"This is what the majority of people say as well. Final one: Suppose you're now *above* the tracks standing beside a very heavy guy. The runaway trolley is heading toward five people. You realize two things: if *you* jump in front of it, you're too light to stop it. But if you push the heavy guy next to you down onto the tracks, his body will derail the trolley and the five will be saved. Do you push him?"

There was a long silence. Finally, Hansen shook his head. "No. I don't see myself doing that."

"Neither do ninety percent of people from around the world. It's one thing to throw a switch. It's another to throw someone under the bus—literally. But if you really think about it using pure reason, you *should* do it. In both cases one person dies so five can live. What's interesting is that psychopaths are born utilitarians. Emotions or conscience would never come between them and the math. Two researchers named Bartels and Pizarro studied the ten percent of people who said they *would* throw the heavy guy onto the tracks. They found them to score high on the scales of psychopathy and Machiavellianism."

"So what are you saying?"

"I'm saying that for these types of decisions, you'd actually *want* to have a psychopath in charge. Anyway, this was just an aside. The real point is that the problem you pose is an easy one. I, and anyone else for that matter, would be willing to do anything—*anything*—if I was convinced I was preventing species extinction. The math in this case easily outweighs my issues of conscience, any possible weighting of right and wrong." She paused. "But here's the thing. I have to be absolutely convinced."

"Makes sense."

"But as far as I'm concerned, this could still be just a very elaborate hoax. And even if I was convinced Drake is really an alien, we still can't be sure of anything else. His projections for our species. His motives. To a normal, the motives of a psychopath are impossible to comprehend. So if the minds of psychopaths are totally alien to us, what about the mind of an actual alien? How do we know anything? Maybe the virus is a cold virus to cure psychopathy." She paused. "Then again, maybe it's a virus that will wipe out the human species," she added, raising her eyebrows. "And you've been lied to."

20

HANSEN DIDN'T RESPOND right away.

Erin shifted on the bed, stretching her legs out while he considered what she had said. She continued to be impressed by him. She fully expected he would defend the alien he had worked with for years, but he didn't do so immediately. She could tell he was searching his mind, and his emotions, and taking her challenge to Drake's possible motives seriously.

Finally, he fixed a steady gaze on her and said, "All I can tell you is that I've come to trust Drake implicitly. And I have confidence that when you meet him, all of your remaining doubt will be wiped away as well."

"I hope you're right," she said. "I really do. And speaking of meeting him, are you ready to finish explaining the instructions in his text message?"

"Yes. I'd read the message back, but I don't have my phone anymore. Do you remember it?"

"Not the exact wording, maybe, but at least the gist."

Hansen nodded. "Okay. So Drake wrote something to the effect of *get to the MB*—molecular biologist—*in Colorado.* He added that he would contact us there, forty-eight hours from when he sent the text, and that the guy would be expecting us. So Drake must have managed to get a message to him also."

"We should contact this molecular biologist right now."

"Can't. Drake told me he was working with a genetic engineer in Colorado and had me memorize his address. But he wouldn't tell me his name or phone number."

"Compartmentalization?" said Erin.

"Compartmentalization," agreed Hansen.

Erin pursed her lips in thought. "Drake also said something about starting right away when we got there."

"Right. This is the guy he's been working with to have the viral construct ready. Everything is set to go."

"Does that mean if I were to tell him the proper doses required for each of the eight genes, he'll know how to engineer them all so they'll be expressed at precisely these levels?"

"If that's what *set to go* means, then yes. I'm not a molecular biologist."

"So Drake wants us to work with his genetic engineer to finish the virus immediately. Without necessarily waiting for him."

"Right."

"Which means he assumed that you could convince me to divulge the combination. He's confident you'll get me to overlook his unfortunate Hugh Raborn impersonation and join your efforts."

"I suppose so," said Hansen. He stared at Erin and spread his hands out in front of him. "About that," he continued. "About convincing you. How am I doing?"

"You're doing great. You're as persuasive as they come. At this point I think everything you've said and believe are probably correct. But the penalty for being wrong about this is too high not to be sure. So I'll give up the cure. But first I want to at least verify that the virus he's putting it into is actually a cold virus, and not something more . . . deadly."

"And how would you go about doing that?"

"Your molecular biologist in Colorado will have state-of-the-art genetic engineering equipment," she said. "Which has really come a long way. You can build long chains of DNA to your specifications very quickly, using a device built for just this purpose. It used to be a lot more complicated—you'd have to piece together snippets of sequence from various places, but now you can just synthesize it, base pair by base pair. And there are devices that can do the reverse, take a given stretch of DNA and tell you the composition—break it down to a long stream of A's, G's, C's, and T's."

Erin finally noticed Hansen's knowing nods and stopped. "I'm getting the sense you're already familiar with this," she said.

"Given my background, I shouldn't be. But Drake sent me to a company called Seq-Magic in Houston to check out their new model; the Seq-Magic Ultra. So I actually got to see one of these devices in action. Drake wanted the best equipment available. The Ultra does both synthesis and sequencing."

"In the same device?"

Hansen nodded.

"The equipment has come even further than I thought."

"It really is amazing what this thing can do," agreed Hansen. "It's fast and insanely accurate." He paused. "Drake did end up buying one. I only found out recently it had ended up in Colorado." He gestured toward Erin. "But you were saying . . ."

"To verify this is on the level, all I'll need to do is have your genetic engineer give me a sample of the viral construct he's using. I'll have your fancy device sequence it. Then I just have to have a computer compare the result to the known sequences of cold viruses, which are called *rhinoviruses*. There are differences between strains, but they're slight—just enough to get past your immune system each time so you get a new cold every year. This will verify the virus is what Drake says it is."

"Sounds easy enough," said Hansen.

"Well, I oversimplified a bit. The rhinovirus is an RNA virus, not DNA, so the sequence will be the inverse, so to speak, of the DNA sequence. And Drake's version will have been further engineered. Which means I'll have to use an algorithm that can compare sequences and allow for interruptions. But the core of the sequence should be identical to known rhinoviruses. And the stretches that aren't had better not match any known pathogens. If they do . . ." She paused. "Well, let's just say that this would be a problem."

Hansen spent several minutes trying to convince her that this would be an unnecessary waste of time, but he didn't get anywhere, and finally gave up. "If you insist on testing, we'll test. But I'm telling you, you have nothing to worry about."

"Well, I guess we've gotten ahead of ourselves anyway. Because verifying the virus will be straightforward. The hard part will be surviving long enough to get to your address in Colorado."

"I'm not worried about that either," said Hansen. "Not given *your* skills," he said appreciatively. He glanced at his watch. "But with respect to our next move, I think we should lie low for tonight."

"I agree."

There was a long silence.

Hansen looked uncertain. "So, um . . . I guess we'll be forced to spend the night together in this room, then," he said awkwardly.

"It's the only safe thing to do," agreed Erin.

Hansen blew out a breath. "I'll sleep on the floor, of course."

Erin smiled. "Of course," she repeated firmly.

Erin Palmer had never been the type to sleep with a guy on a first date. Or even a sixth. But there was a first time for everything. And in her heart, she knew that before the night was through, no power on earth would keep her from confirming that Kyle Hansen's physiology was 100 percent human.

PART TWO

We have here an unusual opportunity to appraise the human mind, or to examine, in Earth terms, the roles of good and evil in a man: his negative side, which you call hostility, lust, violence, and his positive side, which Earth people express as compassion, love, tenderness.

—*Star Trek*, "The Enemy Within" (Spock)

Suppose some mathematical creature from the moon were to reckon up the human body; he would at once see that the essential thing about it was that it was duplicate. A man is two men, he on the right exactly resembling him on the left. Having noted that there was an arm on the right and one on the left, a leg on the right and one on the left, he might go further and still find on each side the same number of fingers, the same number of toes, twin eyes, twin ears, twin nostrils, and even twin lobes of the brain. At last he would take it as a law; and then, where he found a heart on one side, would deduce that there was another heart on the other. And just then, where he most felt he was right, he would be wrong.

—Gilbert Keith Chesterton

21

~~~

ALL THINGS CONSIDERED, Captain Ryan Brock felt like shit as the helicopter he was in banked to the north to continue its trip back to Palm Springs. He was pretty sure he had taken more electricity in a sixty-second period than the entire power grid of the Eastern Seaboard. Four jolts in quick succession from a Taser set to maximum power wasn't something he was eager to try again.

And now Steve Fuller was in his vision, projected in front of the lower part of his eye as a tiny image in the specialized glasses he was wearing under his headphones. Like bifocals, when he looked straight ahead his view was unobstructed, but when he shifted his eyes downward the tiny imagine of Fuller, only centimeters away, looked like it was projected on an eighty-inch screen made of air.

Big Brother? *Very* Big Brother, with a face the size of a car tire.

But even if Fuller's face had been tiny, Brock would have no trouble telling that the man was not happy. Not happy at all. Probably worried about Brock's health after the unfortunate Taser incident, he thought wryly to himself.

Fuller was in the back of a stretch limo, using a section of the lacquered bar as a table for his laptop, which

showed Brock's image and transmitted his own. Not unexpectedly, Fuller wasted no time on pleasantries. "Please
tell me I've been misinformed," he said icily, barely above
a whisper. Brock had never known the man to explode or
even raise his voice. It was when the opposite happened
you knew you were in trouble. The quieter and colder his
voice got, the more infuriated he was. If you had to lean
forward to hear him, you weren't going to enjoy the out-
come. "Please tell me you didn't lose *everybody*? Tell me
that on the most critical mission you've ever led, with
unlimited resources at your disposal, you and your teams
didn't go oh-for-three. Or was it oh-for-four? I may have
lost count."

Brock knew it was a rhetorical question, but he also
knew it called for a response—and one that ignored the
sarcasm of the question. "We were unsuccessful in all of
our mission objectives," he said simply.

"Let's recap, shall we?" said Fuller, absently swirling
a glass of unknown liquid in his right hand. "You let this
girl, this Ph.D. student named Erin Palmer, escape from
your men in San Diego. No, *escape* isn't the right word.
I think the word I'm looking for is *overpower*. She *over-
powered* your men. And outmaneuvered them. She was
playing chess and they were playing checkers. It was
supposed to be the other way around."

Brock fought to keep his face impassive. Yes, they
had been outplayed at the heliport in San Diego, but
their mission briefing had been woefully inadequate.
Not just in describing the extent of Erin Palmer's fighting skills but in the very nature of the assignment. It
was presented to be as routine as a walk on the beach.
She had agreed to an interview and was willingly, and
happily, coming on board the helo.

But given the secrecy Fuller operated under, Brock rarely knew the reason for what he was asked to do. Which was just plain stupid. Why did Fuller have such a hard-on for this girl? Understanding what was going on, the bigger picture, helped a team understand the motivations of the people they were trailing or trying to capture, and enhanced their own motivations. It allowed them to anticipate the unexpected in many cases, or react better to it if they couldn't anticipate it. Turning Brock into a pair of remote hands, without a brain, was crippling.

He had been told nothing other than Erin Palmer's name, background as a scientist, and that she was not to be harmed. So when things changed, when the mission went to hell and the rug was pulled out from under, it would have been nice to know what the fuck was really going on. Otherwise, Fuller had to know the options open to Brock's team had been limited to the point of being nonexistent.

"Then your team let her disappear in LA," continued Fuller, still barely above a whisper. "Just disappear. You knew exactly where she landed—in real time. You had more people hunting for her than hunted for bin Laden. And she just slipped through like Houdini. This is a fucking grad student, not Carlos the fucking Jackal."

Brock didn't respond.

"So I make that oh-for-two. But that isn't the end of the world, is it? Because we know *exactly* where she's going to be. And we even learn that Drake is sending a surrogate to the meeting. We even get you deep background on the surrogate."

The helicopter Brock was in banked again and continued cutting through the cloudless blue sky.

"And both of them got through your trap? Both of them?"

"Yes, sir. I'm afraid so."

"You're *afraid* so. What we need to find out is if she's just that good, or if you're just that bad. Did I not make it clear just how fucking important this was?" he whispered, and if Brock hadn't turned the volume of his headphones to their maximum level, he couldn't have begun to make this out. "I know I didn't tell you *why* they were important. But am I given to fits of hyperbole? Do I seem the type to alarm easily? To cry wolf?"

Brock shook his head, but didn't reply.

"How many men did you have on site at the student union?" asked Fuller.

"We had ten," came the reply. Brock had almost said, "ten of my best," but had stopped himself from walking into *that* particular verbal trap.

"Ten," repeated Fuller. "And how many in direct visual contact with the targets?"

"One. Only me."

"Only you. So what genius decided that would be a good idea?"

The question this time didn't deserve a response. Fuller knew full well it was Brock's operation and he had made this decision.

"This girl was already paranoid after what happened in San Diego," said Brock. "And even having one person at the food court, big as it is, was a risk, as we found out. How conspicuous did we want to be? If there had been any way to blend in, we'd have had five men in direct visual contact."

Brock was still convinced he had made the right decision. All of his men had that mercenary, Special Forces, *stick-out-like-a-neon-sore-thumb* look to them. Not the old professor look, and not the look of an undergrad only a few years removed from the acne phase of life.

"As it was," continued Brock, "they had no trouble picking me out of the hundreds of people in the food court. They came to me straight as an arrow." He paused. "But even so, this should have worked. Even when they took me out. There are a number of exits from where they were, the literal heart of the student union, but I had men on all of them, so they couldn't slip through."

"Wow," said Fuller sarcastically, "you and I must not have the same definition of the word *couldn't*. Any guesses how they did, in fact, slip through?"

Brock and his team had easily been able to piece together their quarry's strategy after the fact, once every muscle in his body wasn't paralyzed from taking a million fucking volts. They had incapacitated him in a way they knew would draw gawkers, not to mention emergency personnel, to the food court area. They had timed their assault right after classes had let out all over the university, when there was a dramatic upsurge in movement in and out. And they must have changed clothing and disguised themselves, blending in with the crowd.

After Brock explained to Fuller how they had escaped, he added, "I know she's supposed to be an amateur, but she seems to be a natural. Or else she's had training of which we weren't aware."

"She hasn't," said Fuller simply.

"How can you be absolutely sure?"

"Haven't you been listening? This woman is now the most important woman in existence. I've pulled out all the stops in the past few days learning about her. I've climbed up her ass with a microscope. I know what fucking condiments she puts on her cheeseburger. Every movie she's seen in the past twenty years. And I am absolutely certain that, while she has some martial arts training, she has absolutely zero experience."

The conversation continued, with Brock outlining the steps he was taking to reacquire the targets. Just when it was nearing an end, the limo stopped and another man slid in beside Fuller. Brock recognized the newcomer as Robert Hernandez, an enigmatic member of Homeland Security, with a rank and responsibilities that were not entirely clear, at least not to Brock.

Hernandez acknowledged Brock, and Fuller asked the man from Homeland Security to hold tight until he and Brock had finished their discussion.

Five minutes later, when Brock had finished his briefing, Fuller put him on hold, and both video and audio went dark. It was infuriating. Whatever Fuller was discussing with Hernandez was apparently out of his pay grade. Which once again, only served to make his job harder. The less he knew about what was really going on, the more handicapped he became.

22

ONCE BROCK WAS on hold, Fuller filled his visitor in on recent events while Hernandez reached for several bottles on the bar and mixed himself a drink. The limo's ride was so smooth it was hard to tell it was even moving much of the time.

"So your people missed everywhere?" said Hernandez, shaking his head in disbelief. "They missed at the university *and* they missed getting Drake in Yuma?"

Fuller nodded.

"I thought you had him dead to rights. I assumed you'd make sure to use overwhelming force."

"He was very clever. He had booby traps we didn't see coming. And the men he had, while they couldn't stand up to our force for more than a token few minutes, bought him enough time to escape through a system of tunnels."

"You're positive it was him?"

"Yes. And we're all but certain we're not dealing with a squeamish, tree-hugging pacifist anymore who wouldn't know sound military strategy from his asshole. Assuming he has one, of course. I'm not an exobiologist. But we're now dealing with a different animal altogether. Plus he had access to a lot of money, and his preparations showed. And he only cared about his own escape. Didn't seem to give a shit about the rest of his people at all."

Fuller paused to sip from the glass he was holding. "Even with all of this, we still aren't absolutely sure how he did it. He might have used advanced technology, but we don't think so. We really only have a sketchy idea of what we're up against. Even after he escaped, four members of the team picked up his trail. Three of the four are still unconscious—have been for hours. We think we'll be able to revive them, but how long this will take is unclear. The thing is, they don't appear to have been touched. We have no idea what happened to them. The good news is that one of them did come to about ten minutes ago, and I'm expecting a preliminary report any second."

"Any guesses?"

"None. Maybe Drake used some kind of fucking Jedi mind trick. Anything is possible."

"So where do we go from here?" said Hernandez.

Fuller was about to reply when he was interrupted by a call. He stayed on the phone for several minutes and then hung up. "That was my preliminary report," he told Hernandez. "Right on schedule. The commando who regained consciousness said he was closing in on Drake when he was overcome by the most intense pain and fear he had ever felt; so intense that he passed out from it."

"Must have been what happened to all of them."

"Almost certainly," agreed Fuller. "And these men are hardened soldiers with a tolerance for pain that is off the charts, not weak-kneed schoolgirls fainting when they see a needle. *Intense* must be an understatement."

"Was any kind of device pointed at him?"

Fuller shook his head. "Not that he remembers. But he isn't positive. We'll learn more when the rest regain consciousness." He paused. "Anyway, before the interruption, I believe you were asking me where we go from here."

"That's right."

"The answer is that we pull out all the stops to reacquire Drake, Erin Palmer, and Kyle Hansen, that's where. All the stops. We found Hansen's phone. Drake had sent him a text message instructing him to bring Erin Palmer to a certain destination, and that Drake would contact them there." Fuller checked his watch. "In a little over thirty-two hours from now."

"Certain destination?"

"We think it might be Colorado, but we can't be sure. *CO* could well be a code for something else. The good news is that Drake told them not to attempt to contact him until then."

"Why is this good news? If they attempt to communicate, this gives us a better chance of finding them."

"Because only Erin Palmer knows which treatment works. So we have thirty-two hours to find either Drake or her. As long as they're isolated from each other, incommunicado, we have nothing to worry about. But if Drake gets the information he's after, he'll deploy the cure as soon as possible. We're not sure exactly how, but our best guess is a genetically engineered virus. Probably the common cold."

"So she and Drake are like binary liquid explosives," said Hernandez. "As long as they don't touch, they're safe. Mix them together and you've got a problem."

"Right. She knows which therapeutic mixture works, but has no means to spread it. We assume he has the virus ready to go—just needs to put on the finishing touches. So he has the means to spread it as soon as he learns the combination. Together—well, let's just say we're fucked."

"And you have no doubt that this treatment will perform as advertised? And that the effect will be permanent?"

"None," replied Fuller. "The inmates I had examined had normal brain physiology. And the repaired genome will maintain its integrity all the way into the germ line."

"Any leads on Drake?"

"None. But I have a feeling this girl will be the easier target of the two."

"Why?" asked the man from Homeland Security. "She's done a great job of playing hard to get so far."

"Just intuition. The other target has an alien mind—more alien than we can begin to imagine—and unclear capabilities. But we can make some educated guesses with respect to Erin Palmer's behavior. Put ourselves in her shoes and try to predict her moves. But trying to think like an alien, or outguess one, is a fool's errand." Fuller paused. "But she is key to his plans. So if we catch her, he'll have to come after her."

"Just for the sake of argument, wouldn't it be safer to kill her? *Before* she gives up what she knows? Then her knowledge dies with her."

Fuller shook his head. "And then Drake goes to ground and we don't know what he'll do next. But it's likely that he'll just find another way to identify the right therapy. Without using a patsy this time."

"No chance. Not when we're alerted to this possibility."

"He won't use inmates," said Fuller in a tone that suggested his patience was wearing thin. "He could just kidnap subjects off the street. From gangs, cartels, and other groups enriched for psychopaths. Separate out the true psychopaths from the pretenders, and test the shit out of them."

"So you think if we acquire her and keep her alive, she'll be bait he won't be able to resist?"

"Exactly. He's only days away from releasing this virus. *If* he has her information. Being this close, he'll decide it's worth the risk mounting a rescue attempt. And we'll make sure we have some obvious weaknesses in our security—to make it even more tempting."

Hernandez nodded. "You're the boss. If you think keeping her alive at this point makes sense, we'll keep her alive."

A thoughtful expression came over Fuller's face. "There's also the potential for a much deeper game.

Higher risk, but higher gain. Winning would be a good thing, don't get me wrong." He pursed his lips. "But we may be in a position to do more than just win."

Hernandez nodded thoughtfully. "I'm listening," he said.

23

~~~

THE HELICOPTER HAD landed, but Brock was still in his seat, feeling like an idiot. The pilot had already left the craft. Finally, five minutes after they were on the ground, the image in front of his eyes came to life. Fuller and Hernandez filled his world once again.

"Okay, Captain Brock," said Fuller, still inside the limo. "I've decided to let you redeem yourself. First, you're already in the inner circle, but you know how much I value secrecy. And I wanted the nature of the current situation to be on a need-to-know basis. Well, now that this simple operation has gone completely off the fucking tracks, I've decided you need to know."

Finally, thought Brock. It was about time Fuller came to his senses.

Fuller spent the next twenty minutes bringing Brock fully up to speed, while Hernandez sat beside him in silence, nursing his drink. "So here's the drill with Erin Palmer," Fuller told Brock when his briefing was completed. "We're going to make this girl radioactive. We'll have the cops and everyone else in the Southwest turning over every last cacti to find her. We'll put out a very public fifty-thousand-dollar reward for information as to her whereabouts. If this doesn't force her to panic and make mistakes, nothing will."

"Given her importance," said Brock, finally understanding exactly how Erin Palmer fit into the scheme of things, "why only fifty thousand?"

"Any more and it would raise eyebrows. Fifty is the right amount. But here is the key. I want her captured, not killed. This hasn't changed. So like before, make sure every man on your team has nonlethal weaponry. If one of your men shoots her by accident, I'll shoot the bastard myself—*on purpose*. Have I made myself clear?"

"Perfectly."

"Good. So we'll make sure the cops have very clear instructions that their job is to help locate her. If they do, they act as spotters. You're the hunter. Even if we told them not to kill her, if she starts resisting arrest, who knows what could happen. So they don't move in under *any circumstances*. Robert here will use Homeland Security to make sure this gets the attention—and care—it deserves. Everyone will be told that you're the point person from DHS, and not to take a piss without your say-so. Got it?"

"Got it."

"And there is something else. Something that will require some skill on your end, but could be extremely important. It'll make your job more challenging." He went on to describe what he wanted. "You know how much is riding on this," said Fuller. He leaned closer to the camera embedded in his laptop and spread his hands. "I'm a generous, forgiving man by nature," he added with a humorless smile. "But don't test me. This is your last chance. See that you don't let me down again."

24

KYLE HANSEN'S HEAD wouldn't stop spinning. Everything was happening so fast. He hadn't dated in years, ever since he had joined Drake's efforts, knowing that certain sacrifices came with the privilege of working with an alien emissary, and also of staying off the grid. The most important of these involved giving up entanglements with other human beings—particularly those of the opposite sex. Unless, of course, he was able to develop a romantic connection with one of the women who were also part of the team, even though they wouldn't be aware of Drake's identity as an alien.

But talk about your small dating population. Hansen now knew how Adam and Eve's kids must have felt. Lots of excitement to be a part of something new—in their case, the human race—but when the only people on the planet were in your immediate family, it couldn't have been easy to find a date for the prom. So far only three women had been part of the team since he had begun to work with Drake, and he had had zero interest in any of them.

Erin would be the fourth. The odds of finding your perfect match in a population of four women were too long to bother calculating. Yet here she was. And here he was, having made love to her repeatedly, first ravenously and then tenderly. Both of them insatiable.

Yet his interest in her went far beyond the physical—which given her looks, was saying quite a lot. She was bright and had a sense of humor he hadn't expected, given she spent most of her life inside a bleak prison, and given the trauma she had suffered at a young age. She truly was remarkable. But he still could be deluding himself. After all, they were in a tense situation, with adrenaline and emotions running high.

But if he *was* deluding himself, he decided, he never wanted the delusion to end.

They had slept soundly through the night, sometimes entwined in each other's arms and sometimes on separate sides of the bed, neither clingy nor making it a point to show a need for space. Usually this was the point in a budding relationship when a couple—who really sensed an emotional and not just physical connection—would stay up for hours trading intimate stories about their lives, hopes, and aspirations. Getting to know each other on a deeper level. But this hadn't happened. They had both been utterly spent after sex, physically and emotionally, and had quickly drifted into a deep sleep.

This was interrupted when Erin awoke at three thirty in the morning, shrieking as if someone were twisting a corkscrew into her eye. The screams had gone directly to the panic center of Hansen's brain and he had jumped out of bed like he was shot from a cannon.

He had held her and tried to comfort her, telling her it was only a nightmare. He knew their long philosophical discussion on the ethics of curing psychopathy must have brought painful memories to the surface. He wasn't surprised that the ultimate waking nightmare she had experienced as a child would escape from her subconscious once she was asleep, eager to haunt her yet again.

She had said he was right, and this had to be nothing more than a nightmare. But she also insisted that while she had had nightmares as a girl, she hadn't had one in her adult life. And if it had been a dream, she couldn't recall a single element of it.

"If I had any self-esteem issues," he had joked, "the fact that I had sex with you and then you had the only nightmare of your adult life might be seen as a bad sign."

She had laughed, kissed him gently on the lips, and told him the only nightmare she might have in connection with him was learning she had only imagined him, after which they slept through the night without any further incident.

They had awakened, made love yet again, this time more tenderly, and she was now getting ready for the day. He heard the shower running in the tiny bathroom next to the bed, and he had the small television turned on for background noise and to reestablish a connection to the real world. His shower would be next. He had thought to suggest they shower together, but he didn't want to act like a horny eighteen-year-old, and they *were* running for their lives, so he decided to keep this thought to himself.

He was feeling too many conflicting emotions to keep track of. The fate of humanity depended on launching this virus, which might never happen if he and Erin, and separately Drake, couldn't stay out of Fuller's way. He was on the run facing a deadly and powerful adversary. And at the same time he felt euphoric at having found Erin. Physically his entire body was practically singing it was so satisfied. Given they had both been suffering through a long drought, the sex had been epic. In fact, the word *epic* didn't even do justice to what it had been.

And interspersed with these other emotions was one of guilt. He hadn't really been thinking ahead when he had given Erin an abbreviated version of what had happened, and of his knowledge of Steve Fuller. He hadn't considered he might end up in an extended relationship with her—if they lived through the next twenty-four hours, that was. He could always go back and tell her the full story. She would understand that he had captured the essence of the situation even though he had skipped parts of the tale. Understand that they had not been long on time, and that he had doubted she trusted him completely—or at all, for that matter—so he had decided to cut corners; decided it was best to keep things simple and straightforward and not confuse the issue.

Still, he hated to think she might consider the abbreviated version of the story a deception, even if he had done it for the right reasons. How relevant were the parts he left out anyway? His mind drifted back to when it had all begun. He decided to replay what had actually happened in his mind and compare it to what he had told her.

Hansen's eyes were fixed on the motel television, on which a morning show was being broadcast. A plump, cheerful woman was teaching the audience how to whip up healthy desserts. But his mind's eye was seeing the inside of a small apartment, furnished with IKEA furniture—all the rage in the underfunded graduate school community—and a woman named Morgan Campbell, whom he had dated for many months, but with whom he had never reached the level of infatuation he already felt for a woman named Erin Palmer.

25

"So what do you have planned today while I'm killing myself changing bedpans and dealing with asshole doctors?" said Morgan Campbell, already knowing the answer. "Staying in?"

Kyle Hansen nodded. "Another brutal day of thinking."

Morgan shook her head as she adjusted her white nurse's uniform, which he had to admit she filled out quite nicely. "Well, don't hurt yourself," she said enviously.

Sitting around thinking about quantum physics and computer logic did seem like a cushy job, Hansen knew. But he really did find it brutal most of the time. Even so, it wasn't wise to complain to someone who had to deal with a cranky boss or physical labor. The truth was that when he was engaged in physical labor, he was in heaven compared to the torture of trying to attack a problem mentally for hours on end. It was agony. And only the occasional epiphany made it all worthwhile. Not only did these come far too infrequently, but even after he had hit on an astonishing insight to move things forward, the next unsolvable problem would immediately present itself.

He had read a description of the life of a novelist, and decided his life wasn't too far different. *Writing is easy,* Gene Fowler had famously observed. *All you do is stare at a blank sheet of paper until drops of blood form on your forehead.* Kyle knew this was true of theoretical physics as well. But there was no way Morgan would ever understand this, and he couldn't very well whine about staying home in his cushy apartment suffering all day.

"Dinner tonight?" asked Morgan.

He sighed. "Maybe. Let's play it by ear. I'll call you around three."

Hansen planted a perfunctory kiss on her lips and closed the door to his apartment gently behind him. They had been dating for nine months now, and he suspected they both knew it wasn't working all that well. He didn't believe in love at first sight, but after nine months of dense dating, and spending maybe half of their nights together, no spark had ignited. He couldn't imagine what might change. They knew each other very well, and either they were capable of falling madly in love with each other or not—in this case *not*.

Which actually was a good thing when he really thought about it. Morgan seemed pretty dead set against children. Not that they had had too many talks about their possible future—another telltale sign. Her not wanting to have children was a deal breaker as far as he was concerned.

When he had been fourteen, an aunt, much younger than his mother, had moved nearby with two toddlers in tow. Until that point he had had few experiences with kids, and those few had been negative, mostly involving sitting in airplanes while unruly toddlers kicked the back of his seat for an entire flight, or having them wail nearby and ruin his meal in a restaurant.

But these two kids, Michael and Jana, had visited often and spent the night frequently. He had forged an instant bond that only strengthened as they aged. They were adorable. Endlessly charming and amusing. He had always loved dogs, but he grew to love tiny ambulating humans even more, who were always saying adorable things and who saw the world in such fresh and interesting ways.

So it was good it wasn't working out with Morgan, because in their hearts they both knew it was time to move on. He needed to find someone with whom he could settle down, and Morgan was a trap. Comfortable but not exciting. The sex and companionship were nice, so instead of having to spend time and psychic energy on the dating scene, he could focus on his work. But if he wasn't careful, he could find himself waking up in three or four years without anything having changed in the relationship. He needed to grow some balls and end this. It was the humane thing to do for both of them, and he didn't think this was just a rationalization.

A loud rap on the door broke Hansen from his thoughts. He pulled it open, certain he would find Morgan standing there, having forgotten to tell him something. Instead a tall, distinguished-looking man of about forty appeared, his short hair prematurely peppered with white. "Mr. Hansen?" he said, his voice soothing and confident. Not waiting for a reply he added, "My name is Steve Fuller."

"What can I do for you?" said Hansen.

"I'm glad you asked that," said Fuller smoothly, with an insincere smile. And then, too fast for Hansen's eyes to follow, Fuller's right hand darted from his side, where he had concealed a tiny syringe, and jabbed a sharp needle through Hansen's slacks and into his upper thigh.

Hansen felt himself go wobbly and lowered himself to the carpet while he could still cushion his landing.

"As it turns out, you can do quite a lot for me," said Fuller, and these last words were as ephemeral to Hansen as writing on water as he slipped into a dreamless oblivion.

26

~~~

INSIDE A ROOM at the Saguaro Inn, Kyle Hansen's mind was wrenched back into the present and his heart leaped to his throat.

At first he couldn't grasp why this had happened, searching for a cause for this sudden arrhythmia and panic. But an instant later he realized what his subconscious, and his racing heart, had realized already: a picture of Erin Palmer was on the television he had been facing. He grabbed the remote beside him and cranked up the volume.

Erin's picture filled the entire screen, while the unseen female anchor of the local Tucson news station did a voiceover: ". . . and a reward of fifty thousand dollars has been offered for any valid information about the location of Miss Palmer, who is thought to be in Arizona or adjoining states. Authorities have also said that this is not a recent photo of Miss Palmer . . ."

Bull, thought Hansen. The photo looked as if it had been taken yesterday.

". . . so she could now have a different hair color, style, etc. If anyone thinks they have seen this woman, or has any information as to her whereabouts, please call nine-one-one, or the number on the screen."

The message ended and returned to the morning show where a short, balding man was now talking about his toy train collection—the largest in the country.

Kyle threw himself from the bed and began dressing. As he did he heard the shower stop. He rapped on the door and then opened it to find Erin toweling off. She looked self-conscious for just a moment, even though the towel was draped around parts he had seen very closely the night before, and in his opinion were far too flawless for any self-consciousness.

"Your picture was on TV," he blurted out. "They're offering a reward for any information that can help find you. Which means that every cop in the Southwest is looking for you as well."

Erin's jaw dropped. Kyle turned away to give her some privacy as she hurriedly finished toweling off and began to dress. "How is that possible?" she asked.

"Steve Fuller must be very well connected. And he's pulling out all the stops. You've done worse than threaten his life. You've threatened his very being. His personality. His mind. Apparently he's taking this personally."

"Did they say I committed a crime?"

"I came in late to the broadcast, but I doubt it. I think they want to keep you as mysterious as possible."

"Do you think we should lay low here even longer?"

"Not unless you were wearing a mask when you checked in. You're face is pretty unforgettable if you ask me."

"Shit!" said Erin as the full realization hit. She was in some kind of mad death spiral. Her life had become a runaway train.

How had it come to this? She had been a model citizen all of her life until she had let Drake, in the guise of Hugh Raborn, suck her in, convince her to rethink her ethics, and break the law. And now she was in the center of a nightmare with no end in sight. But that was the danger of electing to set foot on a slippery slope. And it wasn't as though she hadn't been able to see that the walls of this particular slope were made of pure ice— she had just chosen to ignore this.

So she had been drawn in. Inexorably. As though in her zeal to understand and attack the condition of mind that had destroyed her family, her reason had been impaired. When the first inmate died in his sleep, she had already taken that first step from the cliff, and gravity had taken hold. She couldn't find a way to reverse course. And even as her thinking evolved, she had gotten herself in so deep she felt she had no other option but to see it through to the end. And she had developed a relationship with a man she had thought to be Hugh Raborn, biotechnology executive.

Part of her didn't want to let him down. And the more she expressed her concerns to him, the more zealous and impatient he became. He applied subtle psychological pressures for her to continue, so much so that her subconscious wasn't eager to find out what he might do if she did pull the plug. Would he threaten her with blackmail?

And all the while she was continuing to immerse herself in philosophy and ethics; to evolve, grow, and see the world differently than she ever had before.

Now she was being hunted by an arms dealer intent on killing her, and by every citizen and police officer in the area.

She thought of her advisor, Jason Apgar. Of her ray of sunshine, Lisa Renner, whom she already loved, after knowing her only a short time. What would they be thinking when they saw her face on TV?

Would Erin ever be able to explain? *Could* she explain? After all, she had to face the truth: she was one of the villains in this tale.

And she had to admit the very real possibility that she wouldn't live out the week.

"Kyle, I can't do this anymore," she whispered, now fully dressed. "I want out." Was her life really to be cut short just when she had found someone like Kyle Hansen? She felt cheated.

Hansen sighed and gave her an empathetic nod that said, "I feel your pain," but not one that said, "I support this decision."

Erin stared into his eyes. "I know how much is riding on seeing this through," she said. "But I can just give the winning gene mixture to you. I know I can count on you to check things out before you give it to Drake. I can turn myself in. Take my chances with the police. Explain everything. Do whatever time I have coming—God knows I know my way around a prison. The more I struggle, the tighter this noose is becoming, and the more criminal acts I commit in the name of staying free. And I'm endangering you as well."

Hansen sighed deeply. "No one wishes more than I do that you weren't caught up in this," he said. "But if you turn yourself in, Fuller will get to you. Period. It doesn't matter how honest the cop, he'll have the correct paperwork to have you delivered into his hands. Look at how easily one of his men was able to impersonate an FBI agent to confirm that the treatment works. He'll torture you to find out what you know about me and Drake." He turned away. "And then he'll kill you," he finished, his eyes becoming moist as he said this, as though the thought of losing Erin was unbearable to him.

Without knowing exactly how it happened, they found themselves in each other's arms.

"You're right," she acknowledged unhappily. "I know you're right. But it's never going to end, is it? We'll be on the run our entire lives." She managed to force a wry smile. "Which at this point will be very short—so at least there's that."

Hansen shook his head. "No. We'll have to survive for a month or two—which won't be easy. But once the genie is out of the bottle, killing us won't change anything. Psychopathic Fuller would do it anyway, just out of hatred and spite. And for the pleasure it would give him. But once he's cured, he won't be the same man. He'll call off the dogs."

Erin nodded and her strength and resolve seemed to return. "Sorry," she said. "I don't know what got into me. I guess it's been a stressful few days."

Hansen took her face gently in both hands and tilted it up, kissing her lightly on the lips. "No one has ever handled this much stress any better."

They separated. "So now what?" she asked with a sigh. "This room could already be surrounded for all we know."

"If that's the case then we're well and truly screwed. So let's imagine we still have at least a little more time before they learn we're here." He paused. "Think. What do we do? You're the brains of this outfit." He looked her up and down. "And the beauty as well," he added appreciatively.

"What are you?"

"Hopefully, the one who inspires the brains of the outfit to come up with an idea."

Erin smiled. "Okay. Let's think out loud." She paused. "I guess the first thing is, we need transportation. We won't stand a chance on foot."

"We can't use a rental car. We'd have to show our driver's licenses, and we'd be traced right away. Any idea how to steal a car?"

Erin frowned and shook her head.

"Isn't this kind of thing done all the time in the thrillers you read?"

"Yeah. They pick locks too. I don't know how to do that either." Her eyes narrowed. "And now that I think about it, transportation isn't the first order of business, after all. We have no idea how long it might take us to figure this out. So we need to get out of here. We're sitting ducks."

Hansen didn't respond. He tilted his head to the ceiling. Without a car, where would they go? They were in a sparsely populated part of Tucson with only a sprinkling of buildings and roads, and with long stretches of flat desert terrain in between. The motel was the only decent hiding place for quite a long stretch if they were on foot.

His pulse quickened as he arrived at a solution. "They didn't show *my* picture on TV," he pointed out. "The motel clerk doesn't know me from Adam. And no one knows I visited your room last night."

Erin looked confused. For once, her agile mind hadn't raced ahead to the punch line.

"So let me get out of here and get a room of my own. At this motel. Then I can sneak *you* in. When the bad guys crash through the door to this room, they'll find it empty. They'll assume you ran off during the night and continue their search elsewhere, while we lay low here for another night."

"Brilliant," said Erin admiringly. She leaned forward and wasted an additional twenty seconds kissing him with enough passion to melt his socks.

"Go!" she said when their lips had parted.

"Perfect," said Hansen wryly as he took the short walk to the door. "You get my motor revved up and then kick me out."

He opened the door and surveyed the area as well as he could. He didn't see anything suspicious. He knew it was still possible the room was being watched, but he had no other choice but to assume otherwise. He made his way to the small lobby and paid for a room, wanting to glance around furtively the entire time he was checking in, but fighting off the impulse so he wouldn't look like the fugitive he was.

When he had been given his plastic room key, he retrieved Erin and escorted her to the new room, making sure to stay out of sight of the lobby and the petite woman in her midthirties manning the desk. Entering the new room was like a magic trick. It was identical in every way to their last one, down to the framed painting of a desert sunset hanging on the wall, except the bed was now perfectly made and the towels were fresh and folded.

"I did a lot of thinking while you were gone," said Erin the moment the door was closed. "And I think I've come up with a workable plan. How much money do you have left?"

"Seventy-three dollars," he announced after a quick count.

"That's all?"

"I just paid ninety in cash for the room."

She pulled a wad of bills from her pocket. "I have seven hundred and eighteen," she said. "Or at least the various men whose wallets I took had this much. So I guess we should add petty theft to the charges against me."

"So we have seven hundred and ninety-one dollars all together."

"Not bad. But here is the question: Is that enough to buy an old beater of a car?"

Hansen shrugged. "Hard to imagine you could get a car that actually still ran for such a low amount. But I really don't know."

"It only has to run for a day," she said. "And it can be rusted, dented, it doesn't matter."

"So how do we buy this hypothetical car?" said Hansen.

"We need the Internet, and we don't have it. So you need to get the motel clerk to let you use their computer for a few minutes. Whatever you have to do. Charm her. Lie to her. Be creative."

"And then Google 'cheap used cars in Tucson' and see what I get?"

"Exactly. 'For sale by owner.' Try to get it for five hundred or less, because we want to keep some money— just in case. Don't bother coming back to the room after your Internet search. Just find a cheap car, and tell the seller you'll take it if it can leave their premises under its own power. Then cab it over there." She paused. "But make sure to meet the cab somewhere out of sight of the lobby."

"Okay. Anything else?"

"Yes. Once you have the car, there's a Walmart a few miles from here. Buy some shears and a razor so we can cut our hair. And hair dye. And see if they have any temporary tattoos we can apply. Or get an ink paint set and we can free-form it. And clothing. And anything else you can think of that can help us disguise ourselves."

Hansen's eyes narrowed in thought. "Maybe you're beginning to rub off on me, but if they haven't raided your old room yet, we can plant some things to misdirect them."

"Like what?"

"I don't know. Maybe I get some black hair dye and some blond hair dye. You can cut your hair and dye it black here, while I leave an empty bottle of the blond hair dye in your old room to throw them off."

Erin's eyes brightened. "I like it," she said. "Maybe we're in the wrong line of work." Then, with a broad grin she added, "And I like that I'm rubbing off on you. I guess we'll just have to make sure we keep rubbing."

27

HANSEN WAS STUNNED by the number of cars one could purchase for under a thousand dollars. There were dozens of them on the market in this general location. Some as low as three hundred and fifty dollars, which he didn't get at all. It seemed to him they'd be worth more in scrap metal than that, but what did he know?

He found a twenty-year-old Chevy Malibu with over a hundred and seventy thousand miles on the odometer. It had faded and peeling electric-blue paint, stained, thread-bare cloth seats, bald tires, crank-handle windows—one of which no longer cranked—and a nonworking air conditioner. It was hideous. If it had been a mythological figure it would have been named the Blue Medusa, and this is what he decided to call it. But on the bright side, it *would* allow them to remain completely off the grid. And it was only five hundred dollars, on the nose. The question was, would it actually still drive?

Hansen was relieved when he pulled it off the small slab of desert that served as a front yard to the seller's run-down house. The car didn't exactly purr like a kitten, but he was able to get it to sixty without any pieces falling off, so he was satisfied. If it could only continue to work for six or seven hundred miles they were in good shape.

As Hansen made his way to Walmart, his mind returned to his first meeting with Steve Fuller. And with someone who had called himself simply, Fermi.

HANSEN'S SENSES SLOWLY returned. He had no idea how much time had passed since his visitor, Steve Fallon—no, that wasn't it—Steve Fuller, had jammed the business end of a needle into his leg. Just as he was about to open his eyes, Fuller waved smelling salts under his nose and he was jolted awake as though he had been hit with a cattle prod.

Hansen found himself in what looked like a glass

conference room with a large oak table in the center. The man who had visited him lowered the smelling salts he had been holding and took a seat across from him at the table.

"Sorry about the abduction," said Fuller. "But I think you'll appreciate the necessity soon."

"Where am I?"

"At a very secure, very secret facility. You haven't been out for long. We used a private aircraft to fly you here from Pittsburgh."

Hansen noted that his hands weren't tied, nor was he restrained in any way. *Was this really happening?*

"What is this all about?" he demanded.

"It's about your work, Mr. Hansen. You have some very unusual theories regarding quantum physics and quantum computing that are very much out of the mainstream."

"If you think my theories are ridiculous, just say so. You won't be the first. Or the hundredth. But you *are* the first to try kidnapping. You could have just sent a nasty e-mail and saved yourself some trouble."

Fuller smiled. "I see you're able to keep your sense of humor about this. Very admirable. But to continue, your unique outlook prompted you to search for a quantum signature in ways others would not have. And you found one. And you keep pressing about it. And pressing. And trying to convince other physicists around the world to take you seriously. You make a pit bull look like a toy poodle."

"Yes, I'm stubborn. So what? I'm convinced that I'm right."

Steve Fuller leaned forward and considered his guest for several seconds. "You *are* right, Mr. Hansen. There is no doubt about it. Or can I call you Kyle?"

Hansen stared at him. "You can call me anything you like if you can tell me why you're so convinced I'm right."

"Because you're picking up an actual, working quantum computer. One that works on principles based on your evolving theory. The only one on Earth. One brought here by four aliens from a planet thirty-seven light years away."

Hansen shook his head as if to clear it. He opened his mouth to speak.

Fuller held out a forestalling hand. "This is a bold statement. So I would expect a certain degree of skepticism." He nodded through the glass wall at a man who had been standing outside the room, still as a lizard. Hansen had been so off balance and so focused on what Fuller was saying he hadn't even noticed him.

The man walked into the room and took a seat beside Steve Fuller. He looked very average: average height, weight, and coloring. No remarkable features good or bad. Thinning hairline. About forty years old. But there was something off in the way he walked, the way he sat, the way he carried himself. Hansen couldn't put a finger on it, but it made him slightly uneasy.

When no one spoke, Hansen decided to break the silence. "Who are you?" he asked.

"My name is unpronounceable. On Earth, I go by the name Fermi."

Hansen's face crinkled up in confusion. *On Earth?* Part of him wanted to laugh out loud, but part of him knew on some primal level that this really was an alien.

"I thought it would speed things along for you and Fermi to meet," explained Fuller. "If a picture paints a thousand words, then a few minutes with Fermi cuts through the most stubborn skepticism."

"I had extensive plastic surgery on my home planet, combined with sophisticated genetic engineering, to pass as a human. And as you can see, or hear at any rate, I can speak your language fairly well, with limited accent."

As he said this Hansen realized he did have an accent, but it was subtle and impossible to place.

"But evolution has honed your mind to be a remarkable tool to understand posture, body language, and other subtle cues to your fellow human," continued Fermi. "So the longer one spends with me the more wrong I seem. This can't be helped. I can pass a cursory examination, and if I don't move much and keep silent, I can go out in public, be a passenger in a car, or even an airplane. But extensive interaction, other than over an audio-only phone, doesn't really work."

The man claiming to be an alien was wearing a light blue button-down shirt. He unbuttoned it to just above his chest, exposing a mass of flesh about the size of a flattened-out baseball. It was repulsive.

"My genetic material isn't exactly the same as yours, but its principles are analogous. My colleagues and I each were subjects of extensive reconstructive surgery and genetically engineered alterations during a period of over seven of your years. My species has had many thousands of years to perfect the engineering of our genetic material and can do tricks you have yet to even guess at. We were each genetically engineered to produce this growth that you see here."

"What is it?" said Hansen, his voice betraying just the slightest hint of disgust.

"Think of it as a gill. There are trace elements of your

atmosphere that are poisonous to us. And we like less nitrogen in our air. So the air we breathe is shunted through this bio-filter, ensuring we get the mixture we require."

Hansen raised his eyebrows but said nothing. Just because the man said it didn't necessarily make it true.

"We have vestigial appendages that are somewhat analogous to your hands," said Fermi. "Which we've engineered back to functionality and converted into replicas of your hands. Even so," he added, unbuttoning his shirt farther, "our own version of hands are indispensible to us, since they give us far better fine-motor control than the ones engineered to mimic yours."

As he undid the fourth button down, twelve thin tendrils crept out in perfect coordination from two slits near where a belly button should have been. Hansen's mouth fell open. While Fermi's human hands had seemed clumsy while unbuttoning his shirt, the movements of the tendrils were fluid and elegant. He picked a pen up off the table with the tendrils, each moving independently, and spun it effortlessly in an intricate pattern that was mesmerizing.

"For us, a precision task like threading a needle could not be simpler. Your hands have greater strength, because your distant ancestors needed to swing from trees." A small smile played over his face. "There are no trees on our planet."

Hansen's eyes narrowed as he considered the smile he had just seen. In addition, he remembered Fermi had nodded appropriately to something he had said. How could this be? While an alien could learn English, no alien could possibly learn involuntary facial expressions. If Hansen were impersonating an alien who laughed by emitting a high-pitched growl, he couldn't train himself to do this if he genuinely was caught unprepared by something truly funny—he would revert to human laughter instead.

So was this just an elaborate hoax?

Despite the impossibility of mimicking spontaneous human expressions, Hansen was largely convinced it was not. There was still something off about Fermi's mimicry he couldn't put his finger on. And no special effect or artifice could possibly have created the tendrils he was seeing.

"You smile and you frown and you nod," said Hansen. "If you really are an alien, how is that possible?"

"Great observation," said Fermi, with another nod and another smile. "And great question. Through genetic engineering, our normal body language pathways have been subverted. Before I was modified, when I was amused or happy, my second and seventh tendril would wave to the left. But now, the involuntary impulses in my brain, triggered by amusement, are directed down a different pathway, causing my face to form a human smile instead. It's all quite complicated, but it is a subroutine that is run automatically." He sighed. "But as impressive as our capabilities are in this regard, my body language is not perfect, as you can tell. Close, but still a hair off. You can mold the bodies and brains of my species only so far into a human. To go any further, you actually have to be one. A perfect forgery is impossible."

Hansen nodded thoughtfully and realized the very last of his skepticism had now vanished. "What do you call yourselves?" he asked.

"What we call ourselves is unpronounceable to you. We come from a planet, however, whose closest pronunciation in English would be *Suran*."

"We've taken to calling them *Wraps*," said Fuller. "And this is now what they call themselves as well. I'm not sure who first started this, but it kind of stuck. Or you might say, *clung*."

Hansen couldn't help but smile. He had had no idea what to expect after being abducted, but hearing a joke about Saran Wrap hadn't been one of his guesses. He turned back to Fermi. "And there are four of you here? Four . . . Wraps?"

"Right," replied Fermi.

The alien went on to explain how they had been transported here, basically instantaneously, and the civilization-wide effort this had taken.

"With respect to your theories, Mr. Hansen, your insight into the nature of quantum mechanics is raw and embryonic, but it's on the right track. Your people don't know enough about dark matter and dark energy to be able to see the proper solutions, but your theory is correct: you *can* get useful information from quantum entanglement, after all."

Despite the situation he was in, Hansen couldn't hide his elation upon hearing this from a scientifically advanced alien. He felt as though he were floating on a cloud. He had been maligned for his ideas for years. And here Fermi had matter-of-factly confirmed that the theory he so stubbornly defended against a never-ending onslaught of criticism was right—or at least on the right track. It was a vindication of his most deeply held beliefs.

Quantum physics held that particles could be in many places at the same time and could pop into and out of existence spontaneously. But one of the most counterintuitive aspects of the theory, now proven beyond a shadow of a doubt, was quantum entanglement. When a pair of particles were entangled, they would take on opposite aspects when the act of observation forced them into a determinative state.

As a gross oversimplification, all particles in the universe were like spinning coins, in an indeterminate state between heads and tails. But the moment one was *observed,* it would randomly collapse into either a head or a tail. Quantum entanglement said that these coins were emitted and spun in pairs. And if one ended up landing on heads, the other would always end up landing on tails. Always. And instantly. Even if the entangled coins were now on opposite sides of the universe, if one collapsed to a head, the other would instantaneously collapse to a tail, somehow communicating this instruction between them far faster than the speed of light.

This caused Einstein and others no end of headaches, and entire schools of brilliant physicists refused to accept that this was really what was happening. Einstein didn't believe this was real, calling it "spooky action at a distance."

Even so, even after quantum entanglement was conclusively demonstrated, the physics community insisted it still didn't violate the speed-of-light barrier. Nothing could travel faster than light: not particles, energy, or information. But since information wasn't being conveyed in this case, the speed-of-light barrier held. Yes, if a coin landed on heads at one end of the universe, its entangled partner would instantly land on tails at the other end. But since the heads or tails nature of the first coin was random, what good did this do anyone? No real information could be transmitted by this process.

And the possible implications of quantum entangle-

ment were even more profound than these bizarre results suggested. Since at the time of the Big Bang, all
the matter of the universe was concentrated in a single
point, it was conceivable that every last particle in the
universe was entangled with every other.

Fermi went on to explain how information *could be*
transmitted faster than light using quantum entanglement, but that it had to be done through knowledge of
dark matter and dark energy, which humanity didn't
possess, having only discovered these major constitu-
ents of the universe very recently. Although completely
invisible, the Milky Way was thought to contain so much
dark matter that this mysterious material outweighed all
the stars in the galaxy ten to one.

And 73 percent of the universe was now thought to be
made up of mysterious energy called *dark energy,* hidden in the vacuum of space. If human physics was ever
in any danger of being impressed with itself, the fact
that the science, until recently, had been totally oblivious to the vast majority of matter and energy in the universe, was a humbling reminder of its limitations.

Fermi explained again that he and his colleagues had
transported here from Suran using once-in-a-generation
resources, so that every atom of extra weight had been
inconceivably expensive. The trip had required energy
and computational ability beyond even Fermi's comprehension. While they would have loved to have brought
advanced technology with them, the only technology
their civilization could afford to send, literally, was a
small quantum computer.

"And this is what I've detected?" said Hansen.

"That's right," replied Fermi. "We have computers
many orders of magnitude more powerful, but we could

only bring along what you might think of as a laptop. Still, because it operates on quantum principles, it's thousands of times more powerful than the computers you have here."

Steve Fuller cleared his throat and faced Hansen. "But bringing this discussion out of the clouds and down to earth for a minute," he said. "This is one of the reasons I needed to, ah . . . force a meeting with you. Without putting too fine a point on it, we need you to shut the fuck up about the quantum signature you've discovered. Do you think you can do that?"

Hansen was taken aback by the way this had been said. He considered several choice responses before choosing the most benign. "No one takes me seriously anyway."

"I do," said Fuller meaningfully. "Consider yourself lucky that no one else has to this point."

"What is *that* supposed to mean?"

"It means that in your zeal to localize this signal of yours, you've been trying to get permits and funds to dig underground just outside of Washington, D.C., for months. Where you think this mysterious signal is emanating from. And no matter how many times you're denied a permit you won't stop pressing. And you won't shut up about your theory either. Do you know how fucking annoying that is? Well, congratulations. You finally made it. Right now we're sitting in a facility three hundred feet underground, at the precise spot you wanted to dig. Dead center. And I can't tell you how much we don't want to be discovered down here."

Hansen swallowed hard. He was proud his theory had so accurately pinpointed the location of the signature, but he was beginning to get nervous.

"So we need you to tell your advisor and everyone else you've been pestering that you've made an error. And that you've now come to your senses. It's a good thing we're moving our headquarters out West in a few weeks," added Fuller. "Or we might have been forced to kill you."

He said it with a friendly smile, as though he was joking, so Hansen chose to believe him.

28

~~~

FULLER OPENED HIS mouth to continue when he was interrupted by a knock at the door. A woman stuck her head into the conference room and asked when she should serve lunch. Fuller glanced at this watch and asked her to return in thirty minutes.

The moment the door closed, Fuller took up where he had left off. "But I don't want you to decide if you'll do what I'm asking just yet," he said to Kyle Hansen. "Because you still don't know the big picture. After you do, I'm sure you'll *want* to cooperate."

Both Fuller and Fermi described the seventeen known civilizations in this arm of the galaxy and how interstellar comingling of the seventeen species was handled. And why the Seventeen believed it was vital that one of them send a contingent to Earth in order to save a savage but talented new species from self-destruction. The Wraps had been an obvious choice for this duty for a number of reasons.

Hansen had no sense of how much time was passing,

and was astonished when there was another knock on the door. Could thirty minutes have passed already?

Sure enough, the same woman who had visited before wheeled in a serving cart loaded with five metal plates, all of them covered by metal domes, and an assortment of drinks, along with plates, napkins, and silverware. The conversation ceased until she had left the room once again.

Fuller lifted the domes from two of the plates to reveal heaping mounds of two Chinese dishes, beef broccoli and cashew chicken, which had surprised Hansen since the only utensils that had accompanied the meal were Western.

Fuller turned to Hansen. "Hungry?" he asked. "Or would you rather wait for a better stopping place?"

"I'll wait," said Hansen immediately. He could always eat. But he couldn't always learn about the history of galactic civilization.

Fuller nodded approvingly. He covered the steaming dishes once again and continued where he had left off. "The Wraps came to our government and quickly demonstrated their bona fides," he explained. "Regardless of what you may have heard, this is the only visitation Earth has ever had. And as you've learned already, it wasn't by spaceship. The Wraps offered to use their skill and their quantum computer to help us protect us from ourselves."

"How?"

"They were short on explanations. Fortunately, they were long on results. First, their computer is somehow able to scan for nuclear and bioweapon signatures at incredible sensitivity. You identified their quantum computer based on its spectra. Their computer can identify

WMD basically the same way, although we have no idea how. And we provide all the inputs we have. Our entire huge database. All the information we have on known terrorists, along with every other piece of electronic data we can collect. And they have access to trillions of pages more on the Internet. Their computer can take these inputs and do magic with it. See patterns we can't. Make predictions with uncanny accuracy." He raised his eyebrows. "I've been begging them to pick a few stocks for me," he added with a smirk.

"I'm surprised you trusted them enough to give them total access to your data."

"They earned our trust. It didn't happen right away. As a show of good faith in the early days, Fermi and his friends alerted us to several terrorist actions that would have leveled one of our cities if not for them. As distrusting as we were inclined to be, it only took saving our bacon a few times before we became willing to be more open minded. Eventually we decided they were exactly what they presented themselves to be. Namely, friendly aliens trying to help."

"When did they arrive?"

"The exact date is classified, but it was after nine eleven, unfortunately. Not that we didn't have all the information we needed to stop that one ourselves. What I will tell you is that we are now the most classified department in the world, under the auspices of DHS; the Department of Homeland Security. We wait a few years after inauguration to even tell new *presidents* of our existence, and the rest of the agencies we serve will never know of us. And I should add that this is a global effort. The Wraps decide on the priorities and where we put resources. If, in their judgment, stopping a plot against

Israel or England or somewhere else is more important than stopping a plot against America, we do that. Not that we don't try to stop them all. We find a way to feed the intel to various protective agencies, our own and in other countries, in such a way that it looks homegrown. We've rooted out dozens and dozens of plots that could have spiraled out of control. Plots that through a domino effect could have led to a retardation of worldwide civilization and even the end of humanity. But no one knows we exist, or are providing intel behind the scenes."

Hansen wasn't sure he was totally buying it. He felt he was missing something. He loved science fiction and wanted with all his heart for this to be true—an advanced and benevolent species watching over us. It was the ultimate science fiction dream. But it was human nature to question things that seemed too good to be true. And Hansen didn't quite trust a species devoting huge amounts of energy and resources, on a scale at which the energy output of human civilization for all of history was just rounding error, without wanting anything in return.

"The Wraps are totally pacifistic," continued Fuller, unable to hide his disapproval. "So we don't tell them operational details. They like to think of this as an intellectual exercise. If they think people will get hurt, even those who have made themselves the enemy of civilization, they get squeamish. Like a vegan in a steak house. You and I are ordering the porterhouses and trying not to drool. *They're* trying not to vomit."

Fermi nodded. "It is true," he said. He went on to describe the toll just being on Earth was taking on them. They liked and even admired individual humans, who often had a great sense of humor and of duty. Impressive curiosity and drive. But in comparison to any member of the Seventeen, humanity as a whole was the most raw. The most passionate. The most ruthless, selfish, and malevolent.

But at the same time, there was a flip side to this passion. Individual humans were capable of astoundingly powerful displays of love, loyalty, self-sacrifice, and heroism. Still, being exposed to the single-minded brutality of the species, just watching the news for a single day, was extremely taxing to their psyche. Like having an exposed nerve being hit repeatedly with a needle.

The conversation dwindled and Hansen and Fuller decided to eat their fill of Chinese food before it got too cold. Fermi pulled a nondescript bar of food from his pocket, which looked to have the consistency of tar, explaining that Wraps had different dietary requirements than humans.

After Hansen finished the last of his beef broccoli, he turned to the alien and raised his eyebrows. "You chose the name *Fermi* as a wry statement, didn't you? As an ironic response to the Fermi paradox."

"Outstanding," said the alien approvingly. "A sense of humor is a trait shared by eleven of the seventeen known species. We Wraps have a very dry sense of humor. Something true of many humans, as well."

"Oh yeah," said Fuller. "Wraps are a real laugh riot. *An alien named Fermi.* Who *wouldn't* get a comedy gem like that?" he added, his voice dripping with sarcasm.

Enrico Fermi had been a brilliant, Nobel Prize–winning physicist who had worked on the Manhattan Project. One day, in 1951, he and some colleagues were discussing reports of UFOs, and whether or not they were real. His response was simple. If aliens existed, where were they? "Where *is* everybody?" he was reported to have said.

From anyone not as brilliant as Enrico Fermi, this might have just been a comment made in jest with no deeper meaning. From Fermi it was profound. The logic behind it very difficult to refute. This was ultimately called the *Fermi Paradox* and entire books were written speculating as to the answer to this simple question.

The universe had been around for fourteen billion years, and in the scheme of things, humanity for the blink of an eye. If intelligent life was common, it should have arisen all throughout the history of the universe. Eight billion years ago. Five billion. A hundred million. It didn't matter. Once intelligence arose, technology would arise an instant later, on cosmological time scales. Even assuming a species could only spread outward from their home planet at a tiny fraction of the speed of light, after several million years the universe, and the Milky Way galaxy, should still be *teeming* with intelligent life. So if intelligence was common, the local neighborhood should have been extensively colonized by at least one intelligent species, occupying every square millimeter of available real estate and advertising its presence. The fact that this wasn't the case spoke volumes.

But it occurred to Hansen that just because he was staring at an alien who embodied the answer to "Where is everybody?" and had chosen the name Fermi to be ironic, the Fermi Paradox was no less insightful, and no less demanding of an answer, than it ever was.

"So what *is* the solution?" said Hansen. "If Wraps have been around for millions of years, why didn't you, or one or more of the Seventeen, colonize this entire galaxy while we were still swinging through trees? Or were all eighteen of us born at basically the same minute of cosmic time?"

"The variation in birthdays among the seventeen— now eighteen—is very slight. Some of the seventeen civilizations were space-faring hundreds of thousands of years ago. Wraps have only been a part of the galactic community for about forty thousand years."

"Can I assume you're all at different levels of technology?"

Fermi shook his head. "Virtually the same. Part of this is because intermingling brings homogenization. But mostly it's because the universe allows rapid technological advance—to a point. Once you hit barriers built into the fabric of reality—like the speed of light or absolute zero, progress bunches up. Our species arrived at these barriers relatively quickly. Others very slowly. But it doesn't matter. Imagine running a marathon, at the end of which is an impenetrable barrier. The fast runners reach it very quickly, while the tortoise might take a thousand times as long. But either way, they all end up at the same place."

Hansen considered. He had never thought about it in this way, but Fermi made a lot of sense.

"But back to your original question about the paradox described by my namesake," continued the alien. "Given the ubiquity of intelligence, we are certain it has arisen multiple times in multiple places. So why *hasn't* the presence of those who were born billions of years before us been felt? We think for a number of reasons. We believe there are three categories of civilizations. The vast majority we believe are stillborn, self-destructing before they leave their planets, either through overpopulation, war, pollution, or other means of suicide. The same path your civilization is traveling now. Only when such a species happens to be discovered by more mature civilizations in time for them to intervene, before the point of no return, will this type of species survive. We hope this will be the case with you."

"So you're saying it's just a great piece of cosmic dumb luck that you found us when you did?"

Fermi nodded.

"And the other categories?"

"In the second category are those few species who managed not to self-destruct and became space-faring many millions or billions of years ago. These have most likely advanced to such a transcendent level that they can easily hide from us, or create entirely new universes to inhabit. Leaving this one as an incubator for future intelligent life."

"So the Seventeen must be in the third category."

"Correct. The third category consists of civilizations that are mature. Not self-destructive. But stagnant. Not driven enough to reach the next level, as the super-species may have done. And not expansionary. Fermi assumed that there would be exponential population growth and an unquenchable desire to explore and expand the frontier. This drive isn't present in any of the Seventeen. None are growing in population. And most are shrinking. All are extremely comfortable as technology and access to nearly unlimited energy creates almost unlimited options for personal growth."

Hansen considered. On Earth, the populations of many third-world countries were skyrocketing, but in many of the more comfortable and established countries population wasn't growing at all, or was even declining. This had never been the case in Fermi's time, but intelligent species with declining populations and no interest in colonization would answer his question quite nicely.

"Our cultures are unambitious," continued Fermi. "Largely content with the status quo. After many thousands of years of stagnation, our greatest source of entertainment and stimulation is intermingling with each other. But the Seventeen haven't welcomed a new member in twenty-five thousand years, and the current interactions are growing more and more routine, which is one reason *you're* so important. A new species added to the mix adds diversity, a new way of thought, and creates endless permutations and combinations between and among all the others that reinvigorates them all. Even if you and another culture mix worse than oil and water, this still shakes things up. Makes things interesting. And with respect to advances in technology, new cultures, even those whose technology is relatively unsophisticated, bring fresh blood, and new ways of thinking about things. Which inevitably leads to some additional progress being made."

"Fascinating," said Hansen. "I only wish the real Enrico Fermi could be here to discuss this with you."

"He was one of your most brilliant scientists, without a doubt. The other three travelers from Suran also adopted names of famous humans who have speculated about the existence of aliens."

"I can't wait to hear what they are."

"They took the names Drake, Sagan, and Roddenberry. To honor these visionaries of your species."

Hansen nodded. It was perhaps a measure of his level

of geekiness that he was familiar with all three, as he had been with Fermi. Frank Drake had founded the Search for Extraterrestrial Intelligence, SETI, and had come up with what was known as the Drake equation, used to attempt to estimate the number of intelligent species in the universe. Carl Sagan had been one of the founders of the Planetary Society, which was partly dedicated to the search for extraterrestrial life. A pretty heady bunch to use as namesakes. But Roddenberry? *Star Trek* had been groundbreaking, but the creator of a piece of entertainment seemed out of place with the other three.

"Roddenberry?" said Hansen aloud. "Why? For his depiction of aliens?"

Unexpectedly, Fuller jumped in to answer this question before Fermi did. "No, for his *prime directive* concept." Fuller said it with a measure of contempt, making no attempt to hide his disapproval. "The Seventeen apparently have a similar concept. You know, an edict about not mucking too much in our scientific development, since we're so primitive."

"Not primitive," corrected Fermi. "Just unpolished and not quite . . . ready. There are certain basic tenets of science a species has to learn the hard way to be able to build from there."

"Which is why they haven't shared their computer or methods with you, correct?" guessed Hansen.

Fuller didn't answer, but his face darkened.

"We could jump humanity ahead," explained Fermi. "But this would be like cheating in school. Things learned the hard way tend to be learned more thoroughly."

"You can get an A in algebra by cheating," clarified Fuller. "But then you're screwed in Algebra II."

"Interesting," said Hansen.

"Yeah?" said Fuller. "Well, what's even more interesting is they seem to want to make a minor exception for *you*. When we were trying to decide what to do about you, they suggested that you were important. That your theories were correct and might get wiped out by the establishment if not given encouragement. That regardless of your stubbornness, you would eventually get drummed out of the mainstream and shunted to the scrap heap of history."

Hansen shook his head as if he hadn't heard right. "So one of the few times they've chosen to intervene—other than to watch for WMD—was on *my* account?"

It was all too much to digest, and Hansen's emotions were spinning like a kaleidoscope: pride, vindication, shock, disbelief, and several others.

"You came up with your theories without their help," said Fuller. "And you basically discovered us without their help as well. So by seeing that you're nurtured rather than snuffed out—snuffed out *scientifically*," he quickly clarified, "they aren't breaching their ethics. It goes without saying we'd love to know how to build a quantum computer. And it looks like the only way we'll be able to do that is through you. So we're making an effort to turn the biggest thorn in our side—you—into an asset."

Hansen studied Fuller's face. "So what are you proposing?"

"You tell your advisor and others you've pestered that you were wrong about this quantum signature thing. Fermi and his associates are now constructing a device to block this signature, by the way, but it will take a year or two to complete. So you agree not to do experiments that will allow you to locate our new headquarters in the interim." He paused to let this percolate. "In exchange, we'll pull strings to get you funded for your research needs when it comes to quantum computing. Even though everyone will still think you're a crackpot, you'll miraculously get funding. Over the objections of the entire establishment."

"So I go back to my life, forget this ever happened, and have a fairy godmother looking out for me?"

"Exactly. Finish your Ph.D. According to the Wraps, you'll need all of what you'll be learning in your graduate courses at CMU. In subjects the Wraps have no interest, or willingness, to teach you. Once you've graduated, we'll sign you up under a joint project through DHS and DARPA to design a quantum computer. Which you'll do at our headquarters, so you can consult with the Wraps. As ridiculous as it sounds, it will be like twenty questions. They won't tell you the answer. But if you guess the right answer, they'll wink at you."

Fuller paused. "But from here on out, if you ever breathe a word about any of this, we'll know. And we'll make sure you're put in a mental institution where God himself won't be able to spring you—or even find you."

Hansen offered a weak smile. "That doesn't sound too constitutional," he said.

"According to the Wraps' computer—the granddaddy one back at their home planet, not the laptop version they have here—there is a much better than even chance we won't survive as a species another ten years. These Wraps are our benefactors. The U.S. Constitution is an impressive document, but when survival of the nation is at stake, people like me have a little extra leeway. The Constitution isn't a suicide pact."

Hansen pursed his lips in thought, making sure he wasn't missing anything. "Okay. I accept. You make a compelling proposal. And I *will* keep your secret. You can count on it." He raised his eyebrows. "But just out of curiosity, what would have happened if I had rejected your offer?"

Fuller didn't respond for several seconds. Finally, just the hint of a smile flickered over his face and he said, "Let's just say it's a good thing that none of us ever have to find out."

29

HANSEN PARKED THE Blue Medusa in the expansive Walmart lot and his mind returned to the present. He bought a prepaid disposable cell phone, not identical to Erin's but with the same limited functionality, and called her while pacing through the store's endless aisles.

"Has anyone kicked down the door of your old room yet?" he asked.

"I don't know. I haven't opened the curtain as much as an inch to peer out and see what might be happening. This motel could be blanketed with twenty commandoes, and I wouldn't know it."

Just hearing her melodious voice was causing stirrings of arousal within him. It was a wonder mankind had to wait for Pavlov to understand the whole stimulus-response thing.

Hansen told her he had had second thoughts about

attempting misdirection by planting false leads in her old room. Returning to this room was too risky.

"I agree," she said. "I came to the same conclusion after you left."

"I'll drive by the motel a few times and do some reconnaissance. If there are hostiles in the parking lot, I'll wait until they leave. If not, we can change our appearances and get the hell out of there."

"Did you just use the words *reconnaissance* and *hostiles*?" said Erin in amusement.

Hansen laughed. "I thought you'd like that. I may not read your genre, but I don't live in a cave. I have seen movies with military themes."

"Those wouldn't be the ones where Hasbro toys come to life, would they?"

"Nah. I'd never watch mindless stuff like that. If it doesn't have subtitles and isn't showing at an art house theater, I won't go. It's as simple as that. My favorites are arty French films with German subtitles."

"Let me guess. You don't speak a word of either language?"

"Good guess," he replied with a chuckle.

Hansen knew they were wasting precious time on banter, but they were both under tremendous stress, and this was a way to defuse the tension a bit and continue to solidify the deep connection that was rapidly developing between them.

"Stay on the phone while you shop, so I can know exactly what you're getting and make sure you get the right sizes. Knowing what you've bought will help me plot out the most efficient way for us to transform ourselves."

"Sounds good."

"I figure once you're back, we should be able to get shorn, colored, tattooed, and clothed in less than ten minutes."

"Roger that," said Hansen with a heavy sigh.

30

RYAN BROCK WATCHED as his team left the vicinity of the Saguaro Inn to pursue other leads. He and the man he had chosen to partner with on this mission, Lieutenant Jim Blessinger, would be doing the same soon. But before doing so, he wanted to be absolutely certain he had left no stone unturned. The petite woman at the front desk, who had recognized Erin Palmer's photo on TV, had told them that Erin had checked in, using an alias, paid in cash, and was now gone, not bothering to stop by the front desk when checkout time had rolled around just minutes earlier. A maid had been about to begin cleaning Erin's room, but they had arrived in time to stop her, so nothing inside had been disturbed.

Erin Palmer could have left half an hour before they arrived or ten hours before. There was no way to tell.

According to the desk clerk, Erin had checked in alone. The clerk had also happened to see her return to the motel by cab, within an hour or so of when she had disappeared from their sight at the union. She had been alone this time as well.

This matched their expectations. She and Kyle Hansen

would have almost had to have gone their separate ways to have any chance of slipping by them. And splitting up made by far the most sense strategically. Given her almost preternatural strategic abilities in this area, Brock was convinced they would split up and make things more difficult for them.

Brock had gained considerable respect for this girl, who continued to make seasoned veterans look like rookie assholes. He suspected she was long gone. There was always the chance the clerk had misidentified her, but given this guest's arrival by cab, without bags, and payments in cash, he was convinced it really had been Erin Palmer.

So now he and Blessinger were in the room she had checked into, trying to find tea leaves to read: tiny balled-up pieces of paper with writing on them, a book of matches; anything.

The TV station that Erin had last watched was a local one. Brock wondered if she had seen herself on the screen. If so, she would be even harder to catch, since she would be more careful than ever. But it didn't matter. The dragnet for her was so extensive she didn't stand a chance. This wasn't football, where a great defense could win the day. This was a game of cat and mouse. With five thousands cats. And a single mouse. Didn't matter how clever a mouse, it was only a matter of time—and not much time at that.

Brock inspected the room with a fine-tooth comb but found nothing useful. It was time to go. Somehow they would catch her trail again. He took one last look around. Everything was neat and tidy, for the most part. A few towels had been used. And the sheets looked as though a war had been fought on them. But Brock didn't doubt Erin Palmer had done a lot of tossing and turning before she had managed to fall asleep.

The outline of a small stain caught his eye on the cotton sheet, like a small bit of soda had been spilled and had left a faint, amorphous outline when it had dried. He tilted his head. It could have been a permanent feature of the sheet, but he doubted it.

Would water have left this kind of outline? Maybe. He hadn't seen any spent soda bottles or other drinks. Had she tried to disguise herself? He knew nothing about dying hair, but perhaps she had spilled a clear ingredient in this process—maybe a base before the new color was applied. He had already turned over the sheets and the yellow-and-orange floral bedspread once to be sure nothing had been left in their folds, but he did so again, even more carefully this time. He found no other evidence that would suggest hair dye had been applied here.

He leaned over the bed and put his nose close to the faint outline on the bed. His eyes widened. What an idiot he had been. How could he be so fucking stupid?

"Jim, smell this and tell me what you think it is."

Blessinger repeated Brock's maneuver and wrinkled his nose in disgust. "Jesus, Ryan. Really?"

"I'll take that as a confirmation. It seems our little grad student got laid last night."

"Yeah. No shit. But I would have taken your fucking word for it," said Blessinger, looking toward the sink as though he wanted to scrub his nose with soap.

Brock ignored him. They had been careless. Just because the desk clerk had said Erin had checked in alone, didn't mean she couldn't have met up with Hansen later. Brock should have checked, just to be sure. Erin Palmer and Kyle Hansen had obviously joined up again here—in more ways than one. Very interesting.

"I'll let the team know we think they're traveling together," said Blessinger. "And have become . . . good friends."

"Do that," said Brock. No matter what, they had uncovered useful information, but maybe he could get lucky. "While you're calling the team, I'm going to talk to the desk clerk one more time. What was her name?"

"Whitney. You know, like the inventor of the cotton gin."

"Really? That's how you remember it?"

"It worked, didn't it?"

Brock rolled his eyes. Minutes later he was sliding a tablet computer into the hands of the woman named Whitney at the front desk. "Have you ever seen this man?"

She studied the photo with a funny look on her face. "Yeah. He just checked in a little while ago."

Brock thought he would jump out of his skin. "He checked in? Here? Are you sure?"

"Positive."

"No kidding," he said, forcing himself to sound relaxed and barely interested. "What room did you put him in?"

She checked a computer. "Room one forty-eight."

"Was he alone?"

"Yes. I think he might have walked here—I don't know from where. Then, after he checked in, he came back and gave me a whole routine about losing his phone, and needing to check a few urgent e-mails. He practically begged me to let him use a computer for five minutes."

"Interesting," said Brock, trying to hide his eagerness. "I assume you let him."

"Yes."

"The computer he used," said Brock. "Has anyone used it since he did?"

Whitney shook her head.

"Can I see it?" asked Brock.

Whitney led him through the desk area into a small office. Brock worked the mouse and within seconds had the recent browsing history for the computer up on the screen. He smiled as he clicked on the last page Hansen had viewed. It showed a used car for sale, a blue Chevy Malibu long past its prime. It was quite an eyesore. But to Brock it was the most beautiful sight he had seen in quite some time.

He left the small office. "Thanks, Whitney, you've been very helpful," he said as he passed the front desk. He paused at the glass double doors serving the motel lobby. "And I'll make sure you get the fifty-thousand-dollar reward. For now, though, do me a favor. Don't leave this office until I give you the green light. Hopefully, it won't be too long. And light up the No Vacancy sign."

Whitney swallowed hard. "Will I be in any danger?" she asked.

"Stay put and you'll be just fine," he said reassuringly. "I promise."

And with that he pushed through the lobby doors and began dialing his cell phone.

—◆—

31

HANSEN PURCHASED THE items in his cart and returned to the Blue Medusa in the Walmart parking lot. As he entered the car, he wondered what Drake was doing right now. A being he had worked with far more closely than any human.

While Drake had helped him achieve unbelievable things, Hansen had also often been relegated to the position of a lowly hired hand. But this couldn't be helped. Someone needed to take care of mundane interactions with humans, since it was always best to keep Drake's interactions with members of the host planet to a minimum.

Besides, if it weren't for him being Drake's errand boy, he never would have had the chance to meet Erin Palmer.

But Hansen had been worried about his alien associate for some time now, even prior to this attack, which elevated his anxiety to the stratosphere. Drake had seemed to be getting more and more unstable as the psychological burden of living among the constant savagery of humanity took its toll. And now this. Not only having to witness, and escape, a brutal attack, but being forced to go on the run. Being hunted like an animal.

And the attack in Yuma wasn't the first time Drake had experienced such savagery up close and personal. As Hansen pulled out of the parking lot, vivid memories of Drake's first exposure to human ruthlessness came to the forefront of his consciousness.

* * *

TWO YEARS HAD gone by since Hansen had met with Fuller and Fermi. Two years in which he had worked harder than ever before, and during which progress was slower, and more painful, than ever before.

The Wraps had been right to intervene when they had. If he didn't know for sure that he was on the right track, he would have given up months earlier, as stubborn as he was. This was sheer torture, made even worse by knowing that beings existed somewhere close by who could give him the answers he needed instantly.

Generous funding had magically appeared, as promised, to support Hansen and to purchase expensive equipment for his advisor's lab. Even so, his advisor was embarrassed by Hansen. He appreciated the funding, although he was convinced a crackpot who knew nothing about physics was responsible, but insisted that Hansen would never earn his Ph.D. unless he switched gears immediately. Unless he got with the program and worked on something that wasn't unanimously thought to be preposterous.

Hansen had finally broken up with Morgan, and while he did date on occasion, he hadn't found anyone special. He still lived in an apartment, and he was soaking up as much knowledge as he could from some truly brilliant professors, skeptical of his own work though they might be.

Steve Fuller hadn't attempted to communicate with him even once since that first meeting, but Hansen felt certain he was being observed, at least periodically. But he couldn't bring himself to feel outraged. They'd be fools to trust him entirely.

Not that he wasn't trustworthy, but too much was riding on him keeping quiet. He could only imagine how often the Wraps and their computer were helping to break up terrorist plots around the world, carefully tracking WMD in the hands of crazed regimes, and using inconceivable computing power to predict pockets of global tension and suggest ways to defuse them before they spiraled out of control.

The Wraps were like benevolent fairy godmothers watching over humanity, guiding them away from the self-destruction an even greater computer on Suran had predicted with such certainty. Given the importance of Fuller's operation, and the lives it was saving in both the short and the long run, Hansen would have kept tabs on someone like himself if he were in their shoes, making sure he didn't betray them.

When he had started to pry, Fuller could have just put a bullet in his head. So the fact that his head still only had the usual five openings, and not a bullet-shaped sixth between his eyes, made the prospect of being under surveillance a lot easier to bear.

And instead of eliminating him as a risk, Fuller and Fermi had vindicated his beliefs and given him a purpose. He would be instrumental in making epic breakthroughs in quantum physics for mankind. Yes, he was just repeating what members of the Seventeen had discovered hundreds of thousands of years earlier, and other races, perhaps, millions or billions of years before that. But it was like watching a stunning magic trick performed by a master illusionist and being the first to figure out how it was done. There was still some satisfaction to be had from this endeavor.

And by pushing the boundaries of current knowledge, he was hastening the day when humanity would reach a stage of maturity and scientific development that would allow them to be welcomed as the eighteenth member of galactic society.

Hansen was in his apartment one morning, staring off into space and hoping that some divine intervention would give him insight into a problem that had stumped him for weeks, when there was a single light rap on his door.

He threw it open, expecting to see a solicitor. Instead, the first thing he saw was a yellow spiral notebook, being held open and thrust toward his face. DON'T SAY A WORD was written in big capital letters on the page facing him.

Hansen's breath was knocked out of him just as surely as if he had been hit in the stomach. The notebook was being held up by twelve thin, supple tentacles, protruding from the midsection of the man standing there.

At first he thought it was Fermi, whose visage was seared into his memory, but it was not. It must have been one of the other three Wraps on Earth. They were artificially constructed to look like humans, and the surgeons and genetic engineers responsible back on Suran had obviously not seen any reason to deviate much from a single template.

The Wrap turned to a blank page and scribbled more words hastily, his tendrils balletic in their movements. He held the page out to Hansen.

DRIVE ME SOMEWHERE WE CAN TALK. BUT STAY SILENT IN YOUR CAR.

Hansen nodded, and without saying a word, grabbed his keys and wallet from a table near the door and closed it softly behind him.

The Wrap transferred the notebook to a ham-fisted human hand and his tendrils retreated under his shirt.

His face was bruised, his clothing was filthy, and he smelled of petroleum. He looked as though he was burned in several places.

Hansen could only imagine what had happened, but whatever it was, it was very bad. The Wrap got into the passenger seat of his car, and Hansen turned on the radio, pretending he was alone and out for a drive.

He chose a destination almost immediately, and fifteen minutes later he and his guest were sitting on a bench in Schenley Park, a four-hundred-and-fifty-acre municipal park that bordered the campuses of Carnegie Mellon and Pittsburgh Universities. The bench had a view of a tranquil man-made lake surrounded by lush trees, dense with dark-green leaves.

"My name is Drake," said the Wrap a moment after they had lowered themselves to the bench, apparently satisfied that it was finally safe to speak. "I need your help."

Just as with Fermi, he had a slight accent, impossible to place, and a way about him that Hansen's subconscious suggested was wrong. Something he wouldn't have picked up on nearly this quickly had he not been exposed to it before.

"What *happened*?" asked Hansen.

"It was barbaric," replied his guest, a faraway, haunted look in his eyes. "A carnage. An atrocity. Humanity is . . . brutal. Barbaric. I'm not even sure your species *should* be saved from itself anymore. I can't even imagine loosing you on the galaxy. You're like a plague."

"Slow down," said Hansen, his heart and mind racing. "First of all, are you okay? Physically?" he added, since it was clear that the alien was an emotional wreck.

"I'm battered but I'll live."

"Okay, what happened to you? Why are you here?"

The alien named Drake looked away for several seconds, the haunted look returning. "The others . . ." He halted as though he couldn't go on. He turned away. "The others are all dead."

"What others?" said Hansen. "The other Wraps?"

"Yes. And scores of humans as well. Humans who were working with us."

Hansen felt like he had been hit with a baseball bat. Fermi dead? The emissaries who had been sent here at enormous cost to an entire civilization dead? How? Hansen didn't have a clue about the details of their security, but it had to be unprecedented. These had been the most important four beings on the planet—apparently now down to one.

"How?" asked Hansen.

"We were betrayed," said Drake in horror. "Utterly betrayed. By Steve Fuller."

"What?" said Hansen, his eyebrows coming together in confusion. "Fuller is the head of the entire operation."

But even as he said it he realized for this to have happened it almost had to have been Steve Fuller. The only person who could beat impenetrable security was the head of that security. Which explained the how. But not the why.

"Yes," agreed Drake. "Fuller *was* in charge. But I've learned he was doing more than just working with us. For years, he was also using his extensive military connections to trade arms. He and his shadow organization have their hands in every pie across the globe."

"That's insane. You're here to keep track of WMD,

dictators, and disruptive elements. And you're saying the man you were working with, the man in charge of the whole program, *was the man who was supplying these same elements*?"

"Yes. But not with WMD. That's why our computer never made the connection. But when we were giving Fuller extensive lists of dangerous players around the world, we were basically putting together a customer list for him."

"How do you know all this?" said Hansen.

"He told us. His men wiped out our bodyguards and anyone else not in his organization. They captured us. He was after our quantum computer. With it in his hands, he would have unlimited power."

"Did he get it?"

"Physically, yes. He had been insisting that we let him use it since we arrived. Insisting that we break our own version of your prime directive. But we never gave in."

"So he decided to take it from you?"

"Yes. But once he pulled his coup, really on himself since he was in charge, he discovered it was worthless to him. It's programmed to only respond to Wraps. To him, it might as well be a paperweight."

Drake looked away again. "He was furious," continued the alien. "And when we wouldn't tell him how to access the computer, he tortured Fermi. In front of us."

His eyes glazed over as though this was a trauma from which he would never recover. The fact that it hadn't driven him mad already was a miracle, given his more delicate constitution and sensibilities, and after having experienced something that would be traumatic to the most jaded human.

"Did Fermi give him what he wanted?"

"No. We were all programmed, at the genetic level, to be incapable of giving in to coercion of this type. In the end Fuller killed him. But he told us all about his arms operation while he was at it."

The alien shook his head in horror. "I don't understand," he said. "Steve Fuller was our *partner*. How could he do this? It was like he was two people. He was so friendly and fair-minded. We all thought he was among the best of your people. How could we have been fooled so totally?"

Hansen thought of Jeffrey Dahmer and others like him. So smooth. So well liked. And yet monsters beyond compare on the inside. "I don't know," said Hansen. "Some people can look and act normal, even come across as compassionate, when inside they're pure evil. I don't understand it either."

Drake stared at him incomprehensibly, unable to believe such evil could reside in any living thing, let along in someone able to wear the facade of good so convincingly.

"So how did you escape?" asked Hansen. "And what happened to the others?"

"The military was aware security was breached. Those independent of Fuller. They mounted a rescue attempt. During the attempt, the other two members of my species were killed, as were all of the rescuers. One man, severely injured, was able to get me out."

The alien looked as though he was crying but no tears came out. Apparently, the Wraps had engineered this emotional cue but had forgotten to install human tear ducts, which made this act look totally surreal. "I tried to save his life," continued Drake. "But I couldn't. After he had saved *my* life."

Hansen nodded woodenly. "And Fuller?" he asked.

Drake shook his head. "I don't know. There was gunfire and explosions. I had my eyes closed most of the time—most on both sides were killed. Entire sections of buildings were burned to the ground or exploded into fragments. Fuller may have escaped, or he may have been killed. But without me to tell them, I'm not sure if anyone will ever know he was responsible."

"Even if he escaped," said Hansen with a frown, "if he decided not to resurface, the government might assume he had died trying to fight off the attack. Died a hero. One of the many who died but were unidentifiable. You have to tell them about him."

"No," said Drake simply. "I've learned from this experience. From now on I plan to limit the number of humans I trust to the absolute minimum. Especially those in a position of power. The good news is that when they don't hear from me, they will assume I was killed and mixed in with the rubble as well."

Hansen wondered what it would be like, not only for this to happen, but to be the last of your kind on a strange planet, without any way home.

"Okay," said Hansen, "so you take yourself off the grid. But then what?"

"I came here sworn to a mission," said Drake. "To save your species from itself. To be honest, I need to re-evaluate if this is as laudable a goal as I had thought. I may ultimately determine the universe would be better off without you. But after giving it considerable thought I've decided that, for now, I will honor my commitment." He paused. "Which is why I came to see you."

"I don't understand."

"First, I had to trust someone, some human. And we've been watching you. You may be fooling us as much as Fuller did, but we are very impressed with your aura. In short, you're someone I think I can trust. And you also happen to be vital to my mission. I need your expertise."

"*My* expertise? You have to be kidding."

"I need you to build a quantum computer for me. Our only one was destroyed in the battle. At least Fuller didn't get it," he muttered to himself.

"I'm the primitive, remember? If anyone can construct one, it's you—not me."

Drake shook his head. "Not true. It's us together." He paused as if considering how to explain. "I'm not a physicist or computer scientist on my world. And we brought a computer with us. Suppose you crash-landed on a primitive island. Just because you've used a cell phone your entire life, could you build one from scratch? Or a microwave oven? Or a television?"

"I get your point. But if you don't have the skills, I certainly don't."

"That's why I said *together*. I'm not a physicist, but I was taught big-picture things in school that can direct you. Newton was maybe the most capable and brilliant of your scientists. He invented calculus. Something you now learn in high school. But the average high school student isn't even close to the genius he was, and couldn't possibly understand calculus, and build upon it, the way Newton could. But if the student went back in time to when Newton was just developing his ideas, he would still know enough big-picture concepts to guide the true genius."

"So you know enough quantum physics to guide me, from your equivalent of high school?"

"Right. But I need you to put it all together and truly understand it. I have the big-picture knowledge. You have the working knowledge. And you've now spent years headed in the right direction. But even if I had an exact blueprint, I would still need you. Materials and components readily available on Suran are not available here. You know what Earth materials might serve the same purposes, and how to get them. And we'll need to work extensively with other humans; contractors, suppliers, collaborators. I can't do that. You can."

Hansen shook his head. "I appreciate what you're saying. But recreating your computer can't be done."

"You are right. You and me working for a thousand years couldn't do it. But that computer was overkill. Even a fraction of its capabilities will still exceed Earth's computers. Without such a computer, I won't be able to do my job. But with my guidance and your genius, I'm confident we can build a makeshift version powerful enough to do what needs to be done."

Hansen considered. He could spend the next fifty years stumbling blindly through the dark, but Drake could accelerate this dramatically. Yes, it would mean working off the grid. Falling out of existence. Changing the course of his life forever. Still, it was a no-brainer. How could he say no?

They would need money and eventually a headquarters. But as they discussed this, the plan became clear. A quantum computer, once perfected, would allow them access to unlimited funds. They could build a fortress after that. It would take years and enormous effort, but they could do it.

So Hansen agreed.

Drake vanished into the woodwork and Hansen went back to his life at CMU. If he had fallen off the grid immediately it would look too suspicious. And this gave him a chance to stockpile supplies he would need in a secret warehouse. Six months later, with Drake's help, he faked his own death.

Now there was no turning back.

He and Drake worked around the clock. Within a year they had developed a crude quantum computer that, primitive though it was, could easily break through the security encryption of any native computer, allowing them to siphon off all the money they needed from huge government slush funds that might not be fully deployed for a decade. From there they added contractors and collaborators on different pieces of the puzzle, and built a fortress in Yuma, Arizona.

Four months after that, while they continued to work toward a more refined, second-level computer, Drake reached a decision.

His experiences with Steve Fuller had caused him to study everything he could on the human condition, focusing solely on humanity's seedy underbelly. He was horrified. He did a lot of the Suran equivalent of vomiting along the way, but he kept at it. And it took an obvious toll. He began to harden. To become less squeamish. And his resolve grew.

"We need to accelerate our work on the next-generation computer," he announced one evening. "It's more urgent than ever."

"What's changed?" said Hansen.

"I've become convinced that humanity will fall no matter what I do. Our computer can't look everywhere at all times. And even the one we brought with us missed Fuller completely. Playing defense is doomed to failure. So it's time to play offense."

"Offense?" said Hansen.

"Yes. In the end, we're battling human violence, human aggression, human brutality. But the worst of this, the most dangerous, has a name." Drake paused. "It's called psychopathy. And it's impossible to defend against." He stared at Hansen with a fierce resolve burning in his eyes. "That's why I intend to cure it," he said.

32

HANSEN DROVE BY the Saguaro Inn a few times from a distance, trying not to draw attention to himself while he scanned the parking lot and area leading up to the entrance to room one forty-eight. While there were other cars on the roads in the vicinity of the motel, the Blue Medusa was so memorable Hansen thought it would be foolish to risk driving around another time. Besides, he hadn't seen any evidence of anyone waiting there.

But even so, he knew that watchers could be slumped down in one of the many cars parked in the lot. The coast was probably clear, but there was no way to be sure. The good news was that even if someone was there, they'd be watching the room Erin had checked into and not the one they were in now. On the other hand, there were a number of cars that could probably see both rooms from the same vantage point.

Hansen decided there had to be some brilliant strategy he could use to find out for sure. He may have been a boring physicist and not Jason Bourne, but he was nothing if not creative. Binoculars would have been a good idea, he realized. If only he had thought of this while he was at Walmart.

An idea began to coalesce in his head. He thought it through from several angles and decided it was worth a shot. If this worked he was prepared to be very impressed with himself. He parked out of sight of the motel and dialed information. A few seconds later he had the number he needed.

"Saguaro Inn, Whitney speaking," said the woman who had checked him in.

Hansen deepened his voice. "Whitney, hi. This is Detective Ericson of the Tucson Police Department. I think you may have called our hotline, but I'm not sure. The return number was smudged and I had to guess at some of the digits. We get a lot of false reports and I'm afraid the switchboard is getting sloppy."

"No, you got it right. I did call."

Hansen frowned. He had hoped to learn she hadn't seen the bulletin on Erin, or hadn't made the connection if she had. But Erin's face was memorable, and he wasn't surprised. "Okay. Good. What can I do for you?" he said.

"Some guy called me back already. I told him I had checked the girl everyone was looking for into the motel. He asked me some questions, and then ten minutes later two guys showed up."

Hansen took a deep breath and tried to remain calm. After all, this wasn't a surprise either. The whole point was for the people after them to come to the motel, find nothing, and then leave. And this was his chance to learn more about what they were up against. "Uniformed officers?"

"No. Looked like Secret Service agents if you ask me."

"Did they show you ID? I only ask because there are a number of agencies on this, and I can't be sure who was sent."

"They didn't show me ID and I never thought to ask. I called and they came. That was good enough for me." She paused. "But I'm pretty sure they're still here. You can ask them yourself."

Hansen fought off panic. He reminded himself this was still a good thing. When he saw them leave, the coast would be clear. "No need to bother them," said Hansen. "Did they find the girl they were looking for?"

"No. She left without checking out. But one of them showed me the picture of another guy. When I told him this guy had checked in a little while ago, he was pretty excited."

A chill went up Hansen's spine. "Okay, thanks," he croaked, suddenly having trouble taking in air. "Sounds like they have everything under control. Sorry to trouble you," he added, ending the connection.

Hansen felt dizzy. The people who were after them were there. *Now.*

And they knew Erin was in room one forty-eight.

Hansen called her immediately. "Bad news," he said when she answered. "Two men are on the premises and they know what room you're in." He quickly explained how he had found out. "Any ideas?"

She paused for a long moment. "No. I'm betting they're sitting in a car, watching the room right now. Unless you can whip up an invisibility cloak, there's no way out."

"So why are they waiting? Why not charge the room?"

"I can think of two reasons. One, they know you're gone and they're waiting for you to return before springing a trap. Or two, they're waiting for reinforcements. Either way, it's bad for us."

"I think we need to force their hand," said Hansen, finding it hard to believe he had spoken these words.

"Interesting thought," murmured Erin. A few seconds later her voice picked up enthusiasm. "I know. What if you called the cops on them?"

"They may *be* cops. Plainclothes. Remember, Fuller has everyone involved."

"Maybe. But I doubt it. I think we should do it."

"Okay," said Hansen. "It's definitely worth a try. If we're lucky the cops will respond quickly. When they get here, I'll call you. While these guys are distracted by the cops, you can sneak around the building and I'll pick you up."

Erin sighed deeply, and he knew she didn't like it.

No kidding. He didn't like it either. It was a crappy plan. But since it was currently their *only* plan, it would have to do. Hansen should have known that just because his face wasn't on TV, this didn't mean those after Erin had forgotten about him. He had been stupid not to think of this. And here he was, patting himself on the back. He was too far out of his league to even know how far out of his league he was.

Hansen hung up and called 911. He was a guest in the Saguaro Inn, he explained, and overheard two men talking about jumping some pretty girl in room one forty-eight. They sounded deadly serious. They were in the parking lot, in a car, stalking her now. Could the police send over a car to check it out? He said he wanted to stay anonymous and hung up before anyone could ask questions.

He pulled up to a curb and became one of six or seven parked cars spaced along its edge. A sidewalk a few feet in from the curb paralleled it and ran in a ruler-straight line for a significant distance in both directions.

Hansen turned off the car, leaving the keys in the ignition, slumped down low in the seat so he would be as inconspicuous as possible, and surveyed the Saguaro Inn parking lot off in the distance. He was far enough away where he was confident he wouldn't be spotted, but close enough that he could see a single person, even though only as a tiny, nondescript object. He wondered if the cops would really come, and if so, how long it would take them. Hopefully no more than five or ten minutes.

Hansen kept his eyes on the entire lot, which he could easily view panoramically from this distance, and played out what would happen in his head. At least what he *hoped* would happen. The cops would come, carefully surveying each car in the parking lot. The two men who had been so chatty with the front desk clerk would likely be in one of them. The cops would approach cautiously, ask them to step out of the car, and then ask for ID. Would the cops frisk them? Was that legal? After all, the cops wouldn't have a warrant, and only an anonymous 911 call would have implicated the suspects in any wrongdoing.

Anyway, it didn't matter. The moment Hansen saw cops approaching any car with a purpose, he would alert Erin to break for the backside of the motel.

He had only been parked for a minute or two, but he

was becoming more and more uneasy by the second. He felt so helpless. What would he do if the two men did break for the door to room one forty-eight? He had better have a plan.

These men were very professional, so they must have a reason for their delay. Erin had suggested they might somehow know he was out and were waiting for him to return. There was no question the front desk clerk, Whitney, would be as helpful as possible to the man who had questioned her. But when Hansen had left the premises to buy a car, he had purposely boarded the cab well out of her sight.

A horrible thought hit him with the force of a high-caliber bullet to the gut. *Shit!* he thought, as his stomach began churning. Just how helpful had Whitney been? Had she told them that he had returned to the lobby after checking in to use her computer?

Of course she had. And this information would be like waving raw steak in front of a tiger. The professionals after them would take the obvious next steps immediately.

Hansen's heart thundered in his chest, and for a moment the entire world seemed to spin around him.

He had failed to erase his browsing history.

He'd bet his life these men now knew exactly what car he had bought. What an idiot he had been!

Hansen had fancied himself stealthy, off the radar, but now he imagined dozens of eyes on him, laughing at his false sense of security. He rapidly scanned the area and then carefully examined his mirrors.

Two men, in their late twenties and very fit, were fifty feet behind him, walking along the sidewalk, seemingly engaged in quiet conversation and not paying the slight-est attention to any of the cars parked on the street.

Hansen had absolutely no doubt they were coming for *him*. And if he hadn't just now realized the people after them knew what car he had bought, he would have been oblivious.

Hansen turned the key in the ignition with more ur-gency than he had ever felt before and glanced toward the motel, where two men had just exited a car and were stretching and milling about.

Their strategy was so clear to him now. The men ap-proaching him would take him out—eliminating Erin's early warning system—and then the men in the parking lot would take *her* out seconds later, relying on preci-sion timing.

Hansen peeled away from the curb like a Formula One race car reacting to the starting gun. The men be-hind him immediately broke into a sprint and began shooting, hitting his back windshield but missing with further shots as the car raced away down the street. The two men tore after him with remarkable speed, but they had started well behind, and even with the poor acceleration of the Malibu they quickly receded behind him.

Hansen called Erin, who answered on the first ring. "Two men are on their way to your room," he said breath-lessly. "Do whatever you have to do to slow them down. I'm on my way in the car."

He accelerated around the corner to the parking lot. Should he meet her around back, as planned?

The instant he thought this he rejected it. Penned in the way she was, the odds of her ever making it out of the room were not good, despite the fact that they had to come to her and her file had said she was a skilled marksman.

Hansen gunned the engine, knowing in his heart that only a bold frontal assault would win the day. They had expected to take him out of the equation before they went for her. Now he would use the only weapon available to him: the Blue Medusa. He and Erin were all out of other options.

As he approached the parking lot several earsplitting gunshots rang out, accompanied by an explosion of shattering glass. Erin had opened the drapes just enough to see out of and was firing the weapon she had taken from the downed man in the student union.

One of her assailants went down, shot in the forearm. Erin had shot him so that his gun went flying and he would now have to use his left hand to fire any further, but had not done any permanent damage to him. From such close range, Hansen was fairly certain she could have put a hole through his forehead. But she apparently couldn't bring herself to do this, regardless of the stakes, since these could well have been good men who had been misled by Fuller.

As soon as the wounded attacker fell to the pavement, his partner dived to the side, just as another round exploded from room one forty-eight and came within a millimeter of his thigh.

He continued to roll across the unforgiving concrete for fifteen or twenty feet before stopping. Just as he rose to make a move, Hansen was on him, driving the car into and through his body.

The man was an incredible athlete. He had just avoided a gunshot and had virtually no warning but managed to dive onto the hood of the Malibu and roll up on the curved front windshield, deflecting the force of the strike. He rolled off the side of the car and crashed hard onto the cement.

Hansen was maneuvering for another try, squealing the tires as he did so, when the two men who had been racing after him arrived on the scene, now in front of him.

Two quick gunshots rang out and drove through the front windshield, both missing Hansen as he ducked down. Unable to see where he was going, he instinctively slammed on the brakes. As the car screeched to a halt, he knew that both he and Erin Palmer were dead, and with them the chance for humanity to be diverted from its own deadly path.

But as terrified as Hansen was, as much out of his element as he was, adrenaline was flooding into his bloodstream. If he was going to die, he was going to go out fighting, not only for his own life and that of a woman he had come to care for in a short period of time, but for a cause he believed in.

He threw open the door and dived from the Malibu before it had stopped completely. He was vaguely aware of additional gunshots coming from room one forty-eight. Erin wasn't going down easily either.

Hansen came out of the roll on his back. When he stopped, one of the men who had chased his car was standing three feet away, crouched behind the Blue Medusa to avoid any flying bullets. He calmly raised his gun and pointed it dead center at Hansen.

"Please," croaked Hansen. "Don't shoot. I surrender."

"Good to know," said the man. And with that he calmly squeezed the trigger.

33

HANSEN OPENED HIS eyes with a start and was totally disoriented. It was night. Where was he?

Who was he?

His mind groped around in horror trying to get his bearings and remember what had preceded his awakening.

It all came rushing back to him. The motel. The Blue Medusa. The gun pointed at him at point-blank range.

How was he still alive?

He felt around his body for bullet holes or blood but found none.

He realized he was lying across the backseat of a car, which was outside and not moving. The windows were open and cool night air surrounded him, although he was unable to see the moon from his vantage point.

The air felt strangely cool against his head. It was the oddest thing. Still in a daze, he brought his right hand to his head and touched it.

He gasped, thrown fully awake instantly. *He was bald*. He moved his hand around the unfamiliar contours of his skull, covering all real estate above his ears. No hair anywhere.

Erin Palmer had been resting her eyes in the front seat, which was fully reclined. When she heard him in the backseat her eyes shot open. "Kyle, *thank God*," she said. "You've been out for over ten hours. I was beginning to think you'd never wake up."

Hansen pushed himself up to a seated position in the

back of the car. Since his eyes had been closed they were adjusted for night vision—at least to the limits that human anatomy would allow—and he stared out of the window, straining to get his bearings. There were no lights of civilization. In the dim illumination provided by moonlight and starlight alone, he saw the outline of a massive concrete pillar with mighty steel struts extending upward into the blackness, just a foot from the car.

"You're probably wondering where we are and how we got here," said Erin.

Hansen turned to her and noticed that her hair was cut to just below the ears.

"I thought I was dead," he said simply. And then, shaking his head as though he didn't believe it still, he said, "How is it that I'm not dead?"

Erin spread her hands. "I don't know. I was surprised too. *Pleasantly* surprised," she hastened to add, and then, deciding this wasn't nearly a strong enough sentiment, added, "Ecstatic. Relieved out of my mind." She paused. "Anyway, our attackers—the *hostiles* as you put it—were armed to the teeth and shot up this car pretty good. Took me a long time to clean up the glass once we arrived. But they only used a tranquilizer gun on you."

Hansen blew out a long breath. "Boy, it sure looked like a regular gun to me."

"I don't doubt it," she replied. "But for some reason they wanted to take us alive."

"For some very *unpleasant* reason I'm sure. Aren't there a small portion of psychopaths who are not only indifferent to suffering, but actually get off on it?"

She nodded. "Yeah."

"So go on. How did you possibly get us out of that?"

"You helped a lot. You took one of them out with the car. And I had already injured one. While you were getting shot I was able to hit another of them in the thigh. Turns out I was in a far better tactical position than I realized. They couldn't see where I was in the room. To root me out, they had to cover territory without adequate cover. I might have been able to get them all before they got me, but I was out of ammo. Their man at the student union probably had some extra clips somewhere. In hindsight, I should have looked for them."

"What, in the two seconds you had before a hundred pairs of eyes turned to you and the twitching bad guy on the ground?"

She smiled. "I guess I can't beat myself up too much for that. So far, things have worked out. I realized I was out of ammo, but your stunt with the car had them second-guessing themselves, and they pulled back to regroup. This gave me the chance to leave the room and retrieve a gun from the guy you had hit. Turns out it was a tranquilizer gun. Didn't know it, but those things are *great*. Much better than a real gun."

Hansen raised his eyebrows. "How so?"

"If you hit someone, anywhere, they're out of the picture. With a real gun, that isn't necessarily the case. You might hit them, but if the shot is off even a little they remain a threat. With a tranquilizer gun it's one and done. Within seconds."

Hansen nodded. "So you were able to hit them all?"

"Well, you get credit for one. And without you, I wouldn't have had a chance. Thanks," she said warmly. "That was incredibly brave of you."

"I was absolutely terrified. But there were no other options."

She turned away, and Hansen imagined he saw a tear in her eye, but in the poor light, even this close, he could well have been wrong.

"There *were* other options," she said softly, her voice now distant. "You could have frozen. Until you're faced with a situation like that, you never know how you'll react." There was a long silence. "I froze up once." She paused once more and then shook her head. "*Never again.*"

The car was as silent as a tomb for several long seconds. Finally, Hansen decided to change the subject. "Did the cops ever show up?"

"No. You need to work on your nine-one-one calls," she chided him. "They may have arrived after the fact. Who knows? Time seemed to work in slow motion. I think the entire attack, from start to finish, only took a minute or two. When they were all down I pulled you back into your car and drove off. You know what they say about adrenaline making you many times stronger than normal?"

Hansen nodded.

"They're *lying.* I can't *believe* how hard it was to move you. And you don't have a pound of excess weight on you. Unconscious bodies need to come with a handle. Or a dolly would have been nice."

"Sorry about that. Good thing we never got that cheesecake at the union."

Erin smiled. "So then I drove for a few miles, parked in an alley behind a Dumpster so I could think for a bit, and decided to come here."

"And where is here?"

"We're in the center of the Santa Cruz River. Directly under a bridge that doesn't see much use anymore.

Pretty good, huh?" she said happily. "Even the few drivers crossing the bridge have no way of seeing us under here."

"Two things. One, Tucson has a river? Really? And two, if we're in a river, why aren't we floating? Or sinking to our deaths more like it?"

"It's a dry riverbed for most of the year. Some good rain in the Tucson mountains above us and it floods. That would be very bad for us, but I didn't think it was very likely. The river is over two hundred miles long, in a U shape, and some is underground, but Tucson was originally settled along its banks."

"Why did it dry up?"

"When more settlers came, they needed more water. They pumped it, they diverted it, they forced it into unnatural channels. And it wasn't exactly the mighty Mississippi to begin with."

A sad look came over her face, barely detectable in the dull light.

"What's wrong?" said Hansen.

"I only know any of this because of my new roommate. A history grad student named Lisa."

"So naturally she'd be interested in the history of the city she's living in?"

"Right. The kindest, warmest person you'd ever want to meet." Erin paused. "Are you familiar with the story of Sodom and Gomorrah?"

"Sure. I think. They were totally corrupt cities, and God destroyed them. I think the word *sodomy* comes from this story. What does that have to do with anything?"

"My mother was Jewish and my father Catholic. My mother used to joke about certain hallmarks of being

Jewish. One is that if you have two Jews in a room, you have three opinions."

Hansen chuckled.

"And the second involved this story," said Erin.

"Sodom and Gomorrah? In what way?"

"Well, the thing about this story is, God tells Abraham he's going to nuke the cities. Because the citizens are so wicked. Abraham says, 'Yeah, that's true and all, but what if there are fifty righteous men there? How can you destroy *them* along with the evil ones?' And God agrees. If God can find fifty righteous men, he'll spare the cities. So then Abraham says, 'Well, what if you can only find forty-five?' And God agrees again. Over a series of steps, they get down to ten righteous men. Of course, God isn't able to find even ten in these cities, so he wipes them out. But the point is, Abraham is basically arguing—with *God*." She paused. "My mom would laugh and say that only a Jew would have the chutzpah—the balls—to argue with God. And not only argue, but win some points."

Hansen smiled. "I see why she liked this story so much. I've never heard that part of it."

"So back to my roommate, Lisa. I study the evil that humans do. I work with murderers and rapists. My family was wiped out by pure evil. You know all that. But even those who aren't psychopathic can be pretty violent and selfish and cruel. Sometimes it gets so depressing, I think to myself, to hell with the species. Sometimes I just want to curl up into a shell and give up on life. After all I've been through, given the current situation, it's tempting to say, 'Drake thinks we're self-destructing? So what? Good riddance.'"

There was more silence, and once again Hansen suspected tears had come to Erin's eyes. "But then I meet people like Lisa. Wonderful people. People who are kind, and gentle, and caring. Who would do anything for others." She paused. "And I remember my family. My parents were the warmest, most generous people I've ever known. My father, so filled with love, that in the end . . ."

She faltered, and after a lengthy period of silence it became clear she would not continue.

Hansen now understood why Erin had shared this particular biblical story with him. "So you're saying the world is Sodom and Gomorrah," he whispered finally. "And people like Lisa and your family are the ten righteous men."

"Exactly," said Erin, her voice still thick with emotion. "So maybe we are worth saving. Because of them. And people like them."

Erin took some additional time to gather herself. "Anyway," she said, "I should probably continue filling you in. As I was saying, I knew about this river because of Lisa." She paused. "So I came here to wait for you to regain consciousness. I had no idea it would take so long. That was one hell of a potent dose. I was getting worried."

"Glad to be conscious again," he said. Then, grinning, he gestured to the concrete pillar beside them and added, "But why do I feel like a troll?"

Erin laughed. "What? You've never hung out under a bridge before?"

Hansen rubbed his bald head. "No. And I usually go to better barbers too. I see you kept busy while I was out."

"I had your goodie bags from Walmart. I was seriously thinking of disguising you as a woman, but I didn't have a dress."

"So you went with the bald look?"

"Yeah, bald with black tattoos. I used the rearview mirror to give myself some as well. I'm not a great artist, so I used the ink pens you got and stuck with simple designs."

She had inked a giant cross on both sides of his neck and printed a stylized *Carpe* on one of her forearms and *Diem* on the other, large enough to be unmistakable. She had cut her hair short but hadn't dyed it.

"Now that you're finally up, we can move," she said. "While you were out I came up with a plan. But the plan works a lot better if I don't have to move you around in a wheelbarrow."

"I'm sure it does," said Hansen. "I'm dying to hear it."

Erin winced. "From now on, let's try hard not to use that particular phrase."

34

"PULL IN HERE," Erin Palmer instructed the driver of the cab they had called, a tall, unshaven man with a Russian accent. Erin had provided the address of their destination over the phone, and she and Kyle Hansen had remained silent in the backseat after the cab had picked them up on the little used bridge over the now-dry Santa Cruz River. Since Erin's face, disguised though it was, had appeared on every television station in the Southwest, Hansen had screened her from view when they had entered the cab and she had immediately shut her eyes and dropped her head to her chin, pretending to be taking a nap.

Twenty minutes later they arrived at their destination; the back end of the University of Arizona's psychology building, near the loading dock.

"She just needs to grab something from her office," explained Hansen as Erin exited the cab, turned away from the driver, and strode behind a corner and out of sight. "Shouldn't be more than five or ten minutes."

"I'll wait as long as you want," said the driver in a thick accent. "The meter's running."

Hansen nodded. They had checked their cash reserves, and guessed they'd be down to their last fifty bucks after paying the cabbie.

Hansen tried to act bored, but couldn't help glancing around nervously. It was hard to imagine Fuller would expect Erin to return to her office. Fuller had probably had her apartment under surveillance in the beginning, but Hansen wondered if he was continuing to waste manpower on such an effort. Erin had shown herself as far too capable to be foolish enough to return there. If she were in a horror film, Hansen knew, she wouldn't be the dumb hot chick who went into the dark basement alone after hearing all the screaming.

Given the considerable territory Fuller's people now had to cover, it was unlikely they were still watching the psychology building, if they ever had been, but just to be on the safe side they had decided to use the back entrance. All the door locks around the entire building were the same, and Erin's pass code would gain her access to any entrance.

Even though Hansen believed this analysis intellectually, it was still hard not to be on the jumpy side, and he didn't want to give the cabbie any reason to suspect he wasn't completely relaxed. You'd think the man would wonder how they had come to need a cab where he had picked them up, but the cabbie had probably seen just about *everything* before, so had stopped wondering how people ended up in the unlikely circumstances they did long ago.

Seven minutes later, Erin rounded the corner of the building. When she approached the cab, Hansen said, "I'm sorry, but do you take credit cards?" knowing that this would distract the cabbie from studying her face as she returned.

It worked. The cabbie's eyes left Erin and glanced at Hansen in his rearview mirror with a distasteful expression that said, *what kind of shit are you trying to pull here—you'll pay your fare if I have to beat it out of you.* But aloud he simply shook his head and grunted, "Cash only."

"Oh, okay," said Hansen as Erin slid in beside him. "No problem."

"Downtown Hilton please," said Erin, throwing Hansen a nod that indicated she had been successful.

Erin had told him that during the long period she had waited for him to regain consciousness, she had reflected on a number of subjects: her life, her research, how she had ended up where she was, and her advisor, Jason Apgar. And then it had hit her.

Apgar was at a scientific conference the entire week. In Boston. Erin had told Hansen it was all she could do not to scream for joy at the top of her lungs, which would have risked giving away their position, even though she suspected she could have screamed for hours and never been heard.

This was incredibly lucky, she had explained, because she knew where Apgar kept a spare set of car keys in the office. And the exact lot at which he parked whenever he flew out of Tucson International Airport. He was a creature of habit, and they had attended conferences together on several occasions, during which he had taken her to the airport. And parked in the same lot each time.

It was too good to be true. If she had remembered this from the very beginning, they'd be well on their way to Colorado already.

But they couldn't go directly to the airport. If the abandoned Malibu was found, Fuller's people would quickly find the cabbie who had picked them up, and he would tell them of their trip to Erin's lab and then to the airport. Better to pretend to be going to a large hotel first, to kill any possible trail.

They arrived at the Hilton, a beautiful stone structure honeycombed with rooms and surrounded by stately palm trees, and Hansen paid the cabbie while shielding Erin once again from his view. They waited until the cab was out of sight, made sure no one was watching, and slid into another cab, directing it to the airport.

Only twenty minutes later they had paid the second cabbie, and Hansen was pulling out of the airport lot in a gunmetal-gray Lexus with leather seats and all the electronic gadgets and extras anyone could ever want. A smooth-driving, sleek luxury car, the exact opposite of the Blue Medusa, although he had to admit that that car had done its job well.

"I'm pretty beat," said Erin, as Hansen accelerated onto the onramp to I-10 East, a highway they would take for the next two hundred miles on the long journey to Boulder. "How would you feel about turning into a chauffeur in about thirty minutes?"

"Well, let's see. You saved my life back at the Saguaro

Inn. And you watched over me while I was unconscious for most of the past twelve hours. So . . . even though it will be an incredible sacrifice . . . I'll do it." He raised his eyebrows. "But just this one time."

Erin smiled. "Just let me sleep for four or five hours and then I'll drive and let you get some rest. In the meanwhile, how are you doing? Any aftereffects from whatever was in that dart? Which apparently had enough juice to put out an elephant."

"I feel fine. A little sore here and there from throwing myself out of a car onto pavement. But, really, I'm just happy to be alive."

It was also true that his entire psyche was still humming blissfully, despite their recent close calls and current desperate situation. He had met a phenomenal woman and had spent a night with her—after a considerable stretch in the sexual desert—that he would never forget. She had done wonders for him: physically, emotionally, psychologically . . . and every other way he could name, and he was well on his way to infatuation. He thought about voicing this sentiment but decided against it. He didn't want to come across as giddy, and while he knew she wasn't the type to jump into bed on a whim, and that she had definite feelings for him, he didn't know just how deep these feelings went. They had just met, after all.

"Other than being tired, how are *you* holding up?" he asked instead.

"Surprisingly well," she replied. "It's funny, but this life-and-death stuff really does focus the mind. There is a certain appeal to it. A certain simplicity. Life is so complicated. So many decisions. But when you're fighting for your life things become very straightforward. Priorities become very clear. And the excitement and adrenaline are there too."

Hansen nodded. "I've heard that soldiers can get addicted to it."

"There is still a large part of us that is animal. A will to live in the moment. And that's what the survival instinct does for you. It frees you from petty daily worries and having to struggle with thorny ethical issues."

"It didn't free you from ethical issues at the motel," Hansen pointed out. "You could have taken those guys out and you didn't."

"I have too much blood on my hands already," said Erin. "Even if it is the blood of monsters."

They drove in silence for a time, the highway nearly deserted at this late hour, and the all-enveloping night, broken only by their headlights lancing through the darkness, was hypnotic.

"So before I fall asleep on you," said Erin as they passed an eighteen-wheeler, "tell me more about yourself. You haven't really told me much." Breaking into a smile, she added, "You know, other than your relationship status."

Hansen groaned. "I'm never gonna live that one down, am I?"

She shook her head no.

"Well, I'm the youngest of three brothers. Grew up in Indy as I've said. I was a good long-distance runner on the track team in high school. Not because of my great athleticism, but because I was persistent enough to put in the hours needed."

"And I'm guessing you were a chick magnet."

Hansen laughed. "Well, yeah," he said in amusement. "That goes without saying. I mean look at me," he added, waving his hand past his bald head and down to the crosses inked on his neck. "What girl could possibly resist?"

"That's why I shaved you," said Erin. "So you'd be less appealing to the competition."

Hansen smiled. With her in the game, there *was no* competition, he thought. Aloud he said, "Anyway, to continue, my father died in a car accident when I was seventeen."

"I'm so sorry," said Erin.

"Me too. I just wish I had fonder memories of him. He treated the family pretty badly. He wasn't physically abusive, he could just be bitter and nasty a lot of the time. A brilliant guy, but he was the oldest boy of a family of eight when *his* father passed away. He had earned an academic scholarship to Indiana University, but he had to come home and take over the family furniture business, to support his mother and siblings."

"That's rough."

"He didn't take it well. He felt he never had the chance to live up to his potential, and resented the world for it." He paused. "I was determined not to be like him in that way. That even if my dreams were crushed, I wouldn't take it out on others."

Erin opened her mouth to ask another question when Hansen said, "What about you? Yes, I started out knowing more about you than you did about me. But only on paper. What was it like growing up with your aunt and uncle?"

Erin sighed. "Complicated," she said. "I was a real

mess for quite a while. And while I had lost my immediate family in the most horrible way possible, my aunt had suffered the loss of a sister, brother-in-law, and niece. And they had three kids of their own, so integrating into the family was . . . complicated."

"I can't even begin to imagine."

"I was also just about to enter puberty. A time when most kids are struggling to fit in and figure things out. My aunt and uncle were, and are, good people. But in the early days I found myself resenting them for not being my parents. And I hated myself for not doing more to save my sister, Anna. So I lashed out. I got into trouble in school. I got into drugs. I got into . . . well, let's just say it's a wonder I lived to see fourteen."

"So how did you turn yourself into the well-adjusted, remarkable woman you've become?"

Erin laughed. "Well-adjusted is debatable. Remarkable is, too, but I'll take it. But the answer is, I found a way to come to terms with the trauma I'd experienced. Which was obviously responsible for my increasingly reckless behavior. I decided to deal with these memories, with this trauma, head-on. To dedicate my life to studying the force that had destroyed the people I loved. To help society root out these monsters, identify them for what they were, before they could destroy other lives. To make myself strong, mentally and physically, so I would never feel helpless again."

She stopped, and Hansen waited patiently for her to continue at her own pace.

"And now I find myself living the definition of the word *irony*. I would never have dreamed that I'd actually be in a position, not just to root out these monsters, but to eradicate their condition from the face of the earth. And if you would have told the sixteen-year-old me that I would grow to actually resist the idea, I'd have said you were crazy." She sighed. "I guess the future is more unpredictable than any of us can imagine."

"As someone who's been working with an alien for many years now," said Hansen, "you won't get an argument from me."

"It isn't just that you never know what the future will hold," said Erin. "It's that people can be so dogmatic in their beliefs. So certain of their views they can't imagine these could ever change, no matter what the circumstances. And convinced anyone who believes otherwise is either stupid or misinformed. But I've talked to any number of people whose most deeply held beliefs of early adulthood have changed over the years, through repeated exposure to new and different experiences, and to new ways of thought. I'm just struck by how absolutely certain we can be about things for which there is no objective certainty. How stubborn. And how often we can fool ourselves."

Hansen nodded. "I think it's even worse than that," he said. "We're all guilty of being absolutely sure of things we have no business being sure of. But I think most of us also cling to these cherished beliefs with superhuman tenacity. Even in the face of overwhelming evidence that we're wrong."

Erin eyed him appreciatively. "Superhuman tenacity. I like that. Very eloquent for a physicist," she said. "I find you to be a wise, fun, brave, and slightly geeky man, Kyle Hansen. Exactly the type of man I've been looking for." She paused. "Only I didn't know it until we met."

She turned away and sighed as the Lexus continued to

slice smoothly through the star-filled night. "You'd just better be the man I think you are," she added under her breath.

35

HANSEN CHECKED THE address again and nodded. "This is the place," he said.

Erin squinted through the tall wrought-iron gate, but the pavement twisted just beyond it, and a thick barrier of various pine trees and other foliage surrounded and completely obscured the residence within, which was clearly the intent.

A keypad and monitor stood as a sentry before the gate and Hansen pulled up alongside it, lowered the window of Apgar's Lexus, and pushed a button on the keypad. They had been driving for twelve hours without incident and had seen no sign of pursuit.

After almost a minute's wait, a male voice came through the monitor, but the video remained off. "What can I do for you?" said the voice suspiciously.

Hansen cleared his throat. "My name is Kyle Hansen. An associate of mine named Drake said you'd be expecting me."

There was a long pause. "I'm afraid I have no idea what you're talking about. You must have the wrong place."

Hansen eyed Erin in confusion. He was sure he had the right address.

Erin determined the source of the problem before he did, pointing to her head and then to his.

Hansen rolled his eyes and turned back to the electronic sentry. "I'm guessing I'm on camera right now," he said. "And you were probably sent my picture. Do me a favor and mentally subtract all hair from the picture, and add some large neck tattoos. And then look at me again. I had some close calls getting here and I changed my appearance, ah . . . slightly."

"Slightly?" said the voice after another few seconds. "I don't think your own mother would recognized you—or claim you," he added. "You should have a passenger with you. I need to see her and have her introduce herself."

Erin leaned across Hansen so her face would register on the camera. "Hi," she said. "Erin Palmer here."

There was a loud click and the gate began to swing inward. "Welcome," said the voice as Hansen drove through. "Can't say I love either of your new hairstyles," he added.

Yeah, tell me about it, thought Hansen.

After winding along the private driveway for only thirty yards the residence came into full view. "Wow," said Hansen appreciatively.

The mansion was the height of opulence. It appeared to Hansen as if three ordinary luxury homes had been linked together into one, although in a jagged pattern rather than a perfectly straight line. Stone, brick, and wood combined to form pillars, turrets, and balconies.

"This is where Drake keeps his genetic engineer?" said Erin in disbelief.

"Apparently so," said Hansen as he inched toward the circular drive that abutted the front rotunda entrance. "But trust me, he keeps his quantum physicist in a twelve-by-twelve room in a small underground facility in Yuma. I should have studied genetic engineering," he added with a smile.

"Well, at least he put the money you guys stole to good use," she said with a playful twinkle in her eye. Erin had teased him the night before about feeling more guilty about stealing fifty bucks' worth of T-shirts from the U of A bookstore than about skimming millions of dollars from government slush funds. He had explained that he'd been able to make peace with that theft, even though he knew it was a rationalization. He figured, if the government were to know about Drake and his mission, they would have funded him to at least this high of a level.

As they pulled up in front of two stately cherry-wood doors, a good ten or twelve feet tall, two men emerged from the house, weapons drawn. They were dressed casually, but had a hard edge to their features and demeanor. One was thin and wiry while the other, taller man, looked to be a bodybuilder, with his musculature showing even through clothes not designed to put this on display.

"Out," ordered the bodybuilder, and both Hansen and Erin exited the car, their hands in front of them.

The thinner man looked inside the car, while his partner said, "Open the trunk."

Hansen studied Apgar's car remote and pushed a button with a picture of a trunk on it. Both men inspected the trunk, but it was totally empty.

The thinner man now had a phone in his palm. "Any sign they were followed?" he said into it without bringing it any closer to his mouth, indicating it was on speaker.

"No," said a distant voice. "They look to be clean."

Both men holstered their weapons. "Sorry about that," said the thinner man, holding out his hand. "Greg Gibb. I head the security detail."

After Hansen and Erin had shaken his hand, he gestured to his partner. "And this is Slade Zalinsky," he added, after which the handshaking ceremony was repeated.

Hansen wasn't at all surprised that Drake had hired these men to protect this property. He certainly hadn't skimped on security in Yuma, for all the good it had ended up doing him.

Gibb led them through the towering doors into the house, which was just as spectacular inside as out. "Tough duty," said Gibb, noticing his guests gawking. "But somebody has to do it."

As they walked through the residence, Hansen couldn't help but notice that the spectacular bookshelves they passed were largely empty. No paintings hung on the walls and no knickknacks adorned shelves. Most of the rooms didn't contain a single piece of furniture. The size and opulence of the mansion was just a cover, ensuring the outer gate and presence of a security detail wouldn't be out of place. But when Drake had purchased it and the previous owners had moved their belongings out, no one had taken the time to personalize the place in any way.

A short, heavyset man with glasses rushed down a magnificent spiral staircase and greeted them, introducing himself as Max Burghardt. Minutes later Gibb and Zalinsky had gone back to their duties while Burghardt and the two newcomers gathered around a marble-and-glass table in a kitchen the size of two large living rooms. The short molecular biologist procured three sixteen-ounce bottles of Coke from a stainless-steel refrigerator and handed them out.

"I take it Drake hasn't made it here yet," said Hansen as he unscrewed the lid.

"No," said Burghardt. "But he's acquired a smart-phone and has been calling in."

"And you know how to reach him?" said Hansen.

"Yes. You can call and say hello soon." He checked his watch. "I'm scheduled to call him in forty minutes. First things first, though. We're on the verge of an epic transformation of the human race. With respect to speed and impact, unquestionably the most profound change in the history of the species. Revolutionary. *Evolutionary*."

It was surreal to hear this, but Hansen knew that as over the top as he sounded, Burghardt was absolutely accurate.

"But Drake has filled me in on current events. He tells me there's someone who is ruthless and controls vast re-sources trying to prevent us from succeeding. So our window of opportunity may not be very wide. So as much as I'd like to spend time getting to know you both, we really don't have that luxury. I have everything ready to go. With the help of Drake's computer again, I've just finished engineering the most infectious agent the world has ever seen."

Burghardt turned to Erin. "So if you tell me the pre-cise relative concentrations needed of the eight genes, I can see that they are modulated in exactly this way after being released from my viral construct."

"How is that done?" asked Erin.

"Are you a molecular biologist?" he asked.

"No, but I have some background."

"As you know," explained Burghardt, "the levels of gene expression are controlled by promoter sequences in the DNA upstream of the open reading frames of interest. Another factor is how many introns are in the sequence, and how efficiently they are removed. With the help of Drake's advanced computer, I've come up with an algorithm that tells me the exact sequence and placement of promoters to use to dial in any required expression level. With breathtaking accuracy. I've perfected it through tests on hundreds of insertions so that it's now absolutely foolproof."

"Once I give you the required levels for all eight," said Erin, "how long for the algorithm to spit out the answer?"

"Fifteen or twenty minutes. The algorithm is very complex, and the number of calculations required is mind-boggling. Even so, fifteen minutes is an eternity for a modern computer."

"Then how long to finish your construct?"

"Say . . . twenty-four hours. Working around the clock."

"Somehow I imagined it being faster than that. Isn't the synthesis all automated?"

"Yes, but I have to cut open the DNA for each gene where the program instructs me to, insert the proper sequences, and close them up again. Then I have to insert all of this into the virus. Then I have to ramp up production so huge numbers of infectious constructs are synthesized. And finally, I have to put the finished product in aerosol form to enhance the spread of infection." He paused. "So no time like the present. If you tell me the combination now, I can enter it into my program and have my algorithm solve it by the time we contact Drake."

Erin took a deep breath. "Look, Max," she began. "I understand the importance of this. I understand the monumental impact this will have. But because of that, I'm going to need to slow the express train for just a few hours."

Burghardt looked at her in horror, as if she had just informed him he was dying of an incurable cancer. "Why?" he said in absolute dismay.

"Because before I tell anyone anything, I need to talk to Drake. I'm the only one of us who's never done so. I've spoken with a human projection of him, but never to him in his alien form. I also need to confirm that the viral construct you're using is actually the common cold, and not something more deadly."

"It's absolutely the common cold," said Burghardt, as though offended. "I can vouch for that. And you do understand that Drake is trying to save the human race, right?" He turned to Hansen for help, but Hansen returned a helpless look that said, *I've already tried to convince her—you're on your own here.*

"That's almost certainly true," said Erin. "But if I'm going to be part of releasing a hyperinfectious agent, I need to be absolutely certain it's on the benign side."

"If Drake wanted to spread something deadly," said Burghardt in exasperation, "he would just spread something deadly. Why would he even need the information you have?"

"I don't know. I admit I'm being paranoid. But I won't risk the world's population if there's even a one in a million chance we're being deceived. Drake's powerful computer has obviously been a huge benefit to you. But without *your* help, he couldn't have gotten this far, correct? You wouldn't have been able to design the most infectious agent in history. Or control gene expression with such precision."

Burghardt nodded.

"So maybe he needed the fiction of curing psychopathy to get you to help. To get you to perfect these things. And then slipped in something else. Who knows?"

"So what do you propose exactly?"

"First, I need to speak with Drake. Then, I want you to run your construct through your sequencer. I'll take the sequence it generates and check it online against the known sequences of rhinoviruses. Any extended bit of sequence that isn't a match, I'll check against all known pathogens. Just to be sure."

Burghardt digested this for some time. Finally, he glared at Erin and said, "Is there any possible argument I can make that will persuade you to change your mind?"

Erin sighed. "I'm afraid not. I guess I can be pretty stubborn," she said.

Burghardt turned to Hansen. "And you don't have *any* pull with her?"

"I'm on your side on this," replied Hansen. "But without her skills, she and I would be long dead. And it's probably only a two- or three-hour delay. So I'm going to have to support her on this." He smiled. "Besides, I think I *will* sleep just the tiniest bit easier knowing your construct is what you think it is."

~~~~~

36

WHILE THEY WAITED to call Drake, the three scientists took the time to exchange backgrounds. Burghardt had earned his Ph.D. in molecular biology from UCLA, specializing in the study of rhinoviruses. Much of his work involved understanding differences in infectivity levels between the numerous minor variations of the common cold. Why were some strains so much more infectious than others?

It was obvious why Drake would want to recruit someone with his expertise. Drake had approached him, Burghardt explained, revealed himself as an alien, and described his goals. Burghardt would be one of only a handful of people to have knowledge of an alien on Earth. He would be saving the species. And he would have access, at least remotely through Drake, to the world's most powerful computer, propelling his work to levels impossible otherwise.

It hadn't been a hard choice for Burghardt to stop applying for postdoc positions and come live in a mansion a movie star would envy.

Besides, he had always been a vocal fan of science fiction, even to the extent of posting reviews on his own blog, so working with Drake was as cool as it got. At that point Erin had interrupted. "Drake seems to like recruiting science fiction fans, doesn't he?"

Hansen shrugged. "Not necessarily. Max has some unique skills."

She turned to the short molecular biologist. "Are

there any other genetic engineers in the U.S. who are as expert with rhinoviruses as you are?"

"Four or five."

"I'll bet he chose you to approach because he knew you liked science fiction," said Erin.

"Most scientists like science fiction," said Hansen.

"Yes. But not all. I wonder if he thinks science fiction fans will be more receptive to the alien angle?"

Both men agreed that this was possible, although they seemed to think it unlikely, and the discussion moved on to other subjects, as the three of them continued to try to get to know one another prior to their scheduled call with Drake. Before they knew it, it was time, and Burghardt led them to his home office.

The room had built-in desks, cabinetry, and bookshelves throughout, although once again the cabinets and bookshelves were mostly empty. An expensive computer and several large monitors looked lonely on the desk.

Burghardt manipulated the computer and soon had its audio and video output thrown up on a forty-inch monitor, the room's largest. Hansen approved. When Skyping with an alien, Erin might as well get the full effect.

Burghardt positioned himself in front of the camera first and warned Drake that he wouldn't immediately recognize his colleagues. When they did appear, Drake looked them up and down but didn't comment on their new looks. "Congratulations on making it to Colorado. Are you both okay?"

Erin caught Hansen's eye and gave him a quick nod. She had recognized the voice and odd accent of the man she had known as Hugh Raborn immediately.

"We're fine," said Hansen. "Although I was hoping you would make it here before we did."

"Far less urgency for *me* to get there," said Drake, who appeared the way Hansen had described: just about average in every way. "You two are the rate-limiting step. With any luck I'll be able to make it there before too long. But Steve Fuller is expending considerable resources to find me. And you two have an advantage over me while on the run. You don't make other humans uncomfortable. So you can interact with them for extended periods if you have to, and maybe even enlist their help. I can't."

"Kyle told me the sight of you might give me the willies," said Erin by way of greeting. "And he was right. Even on the video."

"I know," replied Drake. He unbuttoned his shirt to reveal the alien nature of his physique, as he had done with Hansen and Burghardt. As usual, his tendrils whipped through the air with a grace that couldn't be faked. Hansen glanced over at Erin. She was hypnotized, and wore a crooked smile on her face.

"I'm sorry I had to resort to the Hugh Raborn deception with you, Erin," said the alien. "But now you see the necessity."

"Why didn't you give me this demonstration from the beginning?" asked Erin. "Like you did with these two?"

"I had to interact with them far more extensively on this project than with you. Your activities were largely autonomous." He paused. "So Max, can I assume the Seq-Magic Ultra is already in high gear, synthesizing our construct?"

"No," said Erin, sparing the short molecular biologist from having to be the bearer of bad news. "I haven't given him the combination yet."

"*Why not?*" demanded Drake. "Surely by this point

Kyle has explained the importance of this project? The overarching goals?"

Erin nodded. "He has. But I wanted to talk to you first. Hear your voice. See your, ah . . . tendrils."

"Okay. You've done that. Now let's end this call so you can tell Max what he needs to know without further delay."

"I need him to sequence the construct with me looking over his shoulder first."

"What?" thundered Drake. Hansen had never seen him react this way to anything before. The stress of the last few days must be driving him near the edge.

"It's only a few hours' further delay, if that. And I'll be honest, I now have zero doubt you're an alien. And your motives are probably pure. But then again, you *are* an alien. And the Hugh Raborn in you knows that even human motives can sometimes be impossible for other humans to fathom. So just because your expressed motives walk like a duck, and quack like a duck . . ."

"And if Fuller catches up to you because of your few hours' delay?" said Drake.

"I have to take that chance. The longer we argue about it, the longer the delay," she pointed out.

Drake glared at Erin Palmer for a few additional seconds, but she retained a look of resolve, and he reached a decision quickly. "Max," he said. "Sequence the construct in front of her. Make it quick. Get us all back on the line the moment she's satisfied."

"Will do," said Burghardt, ending the connection.

—◦—

37

ONE OF TWO palatial master bedrooms in the mansion had been converted into a biotech lab, which Erin noted was as fully equipped as any she had ever seen. A fume hood sat over a table at one end of the room. Lined up against the wall at the other end were several stainless-steel refrigerators and freezers, each set to a different degree of coldness, all the way down to negative seventy-six degrees Fahrenheit. Glass cabinets above a long lab bench were stuffed with chemicals, flasks, beakers, and petri dishes, and a large glass incubator sat catty-corner to the refrigeration units. Inside the incubator, liquid-filled two-liter flasks were growing huge numbers of *E. coli* bacteria, the workhorse of biotech, at their preferred growth temperature of ninety-five degrees Fahrenheit.

In the center of the room stood a stainless-steel device about the size of a large refrigerator, with a touch-screen monitor attached. Seq-Magic Ultra was emblazoned in blue, stylized letters across its front. The device contained a variety of cabinets that slid open at the touch of an icon to reveal slots for key reagents, which its internal robotics would use to build long stretches of DNA, one nucleotide letter at a time. The series of chemical reactions inside the state-of-the-art device occurred at breathtaking speeds, but couldn't come close to matching the speed of the simple *E. coli* bacterium, which could replicate an entire genome of over four million bases in less than thirty minutes.

Burghardt slid a pair of disposable latex gloves onto his hands, and removed a box of inch-long, sealed plastic tubes from a freezer rack. He selected a vial and showed Erin the tiny, carefully written label on the side, which read Cure Construct—Final, along with a date. Hansen read the label as well, although he was determined to be a silent observer during this process.

Burghardt dialed a micropipetter to draw up a single microliter from the vial, popped on a sterile plastic tip, and removed an almost imaginary amount of fluid. Ten minutes and several ministrations later, the Seq-Magic Ultra was digesting the sequence of the construct with superhuman speed, and strings of A's, G's, C's, and T's were streaming across the monitor faster than human eyes could follow, each letter appearing in a different color.

Within thirty minutes the sequence had been completed, over six thousand base pairs long, and checked for accuracy twice.

"Can I assume the sequence can be directly uploaded to an online site?" said Erin.

"Of course," replied Burghardt. "This device is wirelessly connected to the Internet," he added, a statement Hansen thought was unnecessary. What device *wasn't* connected wirelessly to the Internet these days?

"Good," said Erin. "Go to GeneRepository-dot-com," she instructed.

"Never heard of it," said Burghardt.

Erin shrugged. "So what?"

"So, while there isn't a single database that contains all known gene sequences, CodeMaestro comes the closest."

"GeneRepository has the complete sequences of more pathogens," said Erin. "And better software."

Burghardt stared at Erin in contempt. "How do you know anything about any of these databases?" he said. "When do *you* do molecular biology?"

"Not as often as you," replied Erin with a scowl, clearly annoyed at the short genetic engineer. "But my field uses these tools also. It seems I know more about what you do than the other way around."

Hansen finally decided it was time to step in. "This is ridiculous," he said. "Who cares? Both sites will have rhinovirus sequences, correct? So let Erin use the one she likes. This is for her benefit anyway."

Burghardt nodded. "You're right," he said, but couldn't help turning to Erin and adding, "but you're still wrong about this. If I haven't heard about a sequence database, it can't be very good."

Within two minutes they were on the site Erin had wanted. It was a bare-bones, no-frills site that was very simple to use—which had been Google's claim to fame. *Maybe this was why she liked it so much*, thought Hansen.

The Seq-Magic Ultra uploaded the sequence to the Web site. Given that the long stretch of DNA had to be checked at different starting and stopping points, and thus different permutations, even checking against the rhinovirus database took several minutes. But in the end the site confirmed that the sequence was 84 percent homologous to conserved rhinovirus regions.

Burghardt beamed. "Satisfied?"

Erin nodded. "Almost," she said, instructing the software to check the sequence against all known pathogens, looking for 50 percent or greater homology. This was a far bigger and more complex job and took almost an hour before the site reported back that there were no matches.

The construct was based on the common cold, just as advertised. With no known deadly sequences inserted.

They had Drake back on Skype within minutes.

"Congratulations," said Erin cheerfully to the alien when he appeared on the monitor. "Your construct checks out. So grab a pen and paper. Because we're about to change the course of human history."

38

~~~

ERIN HAD MEMORIZED the precise dosages necessary for each of the eight genes, and carefully provided this information, making sure it was read back to her twice. When she was through, Drake asked to confer with Burghardt in private, probably about his plan for disbursing the virus, which he refused to disclose to either Hansen or Erin.

Compartmentalization.

While Burghardt would now be working furiously for twenty to thirty hours, Erin and Hansen no longer had any responsibilities. Since it was unwise for them to risk leaving the premises, they sent Zalinsky on a shopping errand to pick up clothing they had chosen online at a local Target store, including underwear, so they could change out of garments that had been worn hard for several days and were about as fresh as month-old cheese.

They both took naps, cooked up omelets using the ample ingredients found in Burghardt's well-stocked kitchen, and after their change of clothing arrived, took long, hot showers.

Hansen felt fantastic. Against all odds, they had prevailed. In less than a day they would achieve their goal. And if it took a while for them to create a new base of operations completely off the grid, he was prepared to live with that. The residence they were in could house dozens of people in comfort, so if Hansen had to choose a place to hole up in, and a female companion to hole up *with,* he could do a lot worse than this spectacular mansion and a remarkable woman named Erin Palmer.

Burghardt came downstairs as night was falling to tell them Drake had requested another call with them. The short molecular biologist set up the call and then left, disappearing once again into his lab.

When Drake's face appeared on the monitor, Hansen said, "How's it coming?"

"You're in the same house as Max. Why are you asking me?"

Hansen glanced at Erin. "Well," he replied, looking a little embarrassed. "He's holed himself up in the lab, and he's working so hard we didn't want to bother him. Even to ask how it's going."

"I approve," said Drake. "I'm told it's going great. Max is ahead of schedule." He sighed. "But let me tell you why I called. I've decided on a change of plans. Instead of meeting you out there, I'm going to need you both to bring the finished virus to me. The three of us can implement the release plan together."

"What *is* the release plan?" said Erin.

Drake smiled. "I'll tell you when we're about to release it," he replied. "The point is, you two are the only ones I trust to do this. Other than Max, of course. But he's been working around the clock. You two are fresher."

"Where are you?" asked Hansen

"Near San Francisco."

Erin and Hansen traded glances. They had barely survived traveling from Arizona to Colorado. They were still the subject of a massive manhunt.

As if reading their minds, Drake said, "This should be very simple. I'm at a safe house I set up a while back for emergencies. This will probably ultimately become the new Yuma. So I have access to my resources again, including our quantum computer. Which I managed to save, by the way."

Hansen's eyes widened. How had he forgotten to even ask about this?

"This includes financial resources," continued the alien. "So I'll have one of the men in my employ deliver a van to your location. All you have to do is get in the back and let him drive you here. No one will stop him. And no man, woman, highway camera, or satellite will be able to see you while you're hidden in the back."

"Sounds like a stress-free trip," said Hansen. "We could use one of those."

"Great," said Drake. "Max thinks everything will be ready by noon tomorrow. Be in his garage at one, and my man will meet you there."

They agreed and ended the connection.

As soon as Drake's face disappeared from the monitor, Hansen took Erin in his arms and kissed her gently, savoring the feel of her soft lips and tongue and the clean scent of her hair. "I guess it's going to be a long, boring night," he said playfully. "I just wish I could think of something fun to do that would help us get through it."

He raised his eyebrows. "Something that would provide healthy exercise and burn calories."

"Normally, I'd think this was a great idea," said Erin. She paused for a few seconds, blew out a long breath, and added, "But this is an important night. We're on the eve of a momentous change. So what I'd really like is if you would just hold me tonight. We can lie together and watch a movie. Get to know each other better."

Hansen was all for them getting to know each other, and this plan sounded great. But it would sound even greater if it was implemented *after* they had made love. "We can do that," said Hansen, trying unsuccessfully to hide his disappointment.

What did this mean? Did she regret their night together? Was she trying to pull back? Given the warmth he had felt from her, and the sentiment toward him she had openly expressed, this was the last thing he had expected.

As if reading his mind she leaned in and kissed him, only separating several minutes later.

"Don't get me wrong," she said. "The other night was great. And I hope to have many more nights just like it. Besides, I've never been with a bald guy before. But let's wait until tomorrow night. After we've successfully changed the world. We'll be even happier, and more eager."

The corners of Hansen's mouth turned up into the hint of a smile. "I don't know, Erin. I'm pretty sure it isn't possible for me to get any *more* eager. Especially after that last kiss. But I understand what you're saying."

"I promise you. When we have something to celebrate tomorrow, we'll celebrate in a way that you'll remember for the rest of your life."

Hansen drew her to his chest and wrapped his arms around her. "I'm going to hold you to that. But for the time being, we'll just, ah . . . cuddle," he said.

"Thanks, Kyle," she replied.

Hansen sighed. All of her reassurances aside, there was still something about this that didn't make sense to him. Oh well, he thought. This wasn't the first time he had failed to understand where a woman was coming from. And he guessed it wouldn't be the last.

39

MAX BURGHARDT WAS bleary-eyed and disheveled, not looking much better than Hansen and Erin had after they had battled thugs at the Saguaro Inn and spent more than ten hours under a bridge. He carried a four-foot-long steel canister under one arm, packed with uncountable infectious agents, which could serve as the epicenter of a worldwide infection millions of times over.

Having been notified that the van was only a few minutes out, the three scientists stepped through a door at the far end of the mansion that opened to a ten-car garage, which Hansen guessed was as spacious as his entire apartment had been.

The garage was spectacular. The floor was not lowly concrete, but rather a honey-colored, smooth, glossy surface that Hansen thought just might be marble. Oak cabinets lined one wall and were so stylish they would have felt at home in the nicest living room. A short, glass display case sat against the wall near the door to the main house, and Hansen could only guess the use the previous owner had made of it, since it was totally empty now.

The only way one could tell this was a garage and not a small house, other than the presence of two cars at the far end of the structure—the latest Mercedes convertible and a four-door Jaguar—was the presence of a home gym in one corner, although it, too, was top of the line. Eight-foot-high stacks of black, rectangular weights were enclosed within a central steel structure, and four or five black chairs and benches extended from the center all around. Various white steel bars and levers attached to pulleys protruded from steel beams in a seemingly haphazard fashion.

Burghardt had been holding a closed duffel along with the virus canister, but Hansen had no idea what was inside. The mystery was cleared up, however, when the short molecular biologist extended it toward Erin. "I fixed up a goodie bag for your trip," he said. "Mostly junk food. But it's a long way to San Francisco."

"Very thoughtful," said Erin.

They were waiting in silence for the van to arrive a minute later when the door to the main house flew open and Gibb and Zalinsky entered, commando style, automatic weapons extended.

It took a second for Hansen to assimilate what was happening.

The weapons were pointed at him. And at Erin.

Hansen was more confused and angry than he was alarmed. *"What's going on here?"* he demanded. *"Have you lost your minds?"*

"Hands where I can see them," said Gibb calmly in response.

Hansen made sure he kept his hands away from his pockets, and Erin did the same, first lowering Burghardt's goodie bag to the glossy floor. The short molecular biologist backed a few steps away, but didn't look surprised or troubled.

While Gibb continued to hold a gun on them, Zalinsky quickly and expertly frisked them both, leaving no intimate body part unchecked. He pulled a .45 from Erin's belt and a small stainless-steel tube from her pocket, about the size of a bloated pencil.

Hansen was taken aback, having no idea Erin had been carrying a gun. She must have taken it from one of the men she had incapacitated at the Saguaro Inn.

Zalinsky placed the .45 and the silver tube on top of the short display case behind him. He nodded toward the gun. "I guess what I was told is true," he said to Erin. "You *are* more dangerous than you look."

A chill went up Hansen's spine as he realized what was going on. Somehow, these men were working for Fuller. There was no other explanation for their actions.

But as he considered this further, he realized that Burghardt would now be in their gun sights as well if this were the case. And the molecular biologist would not be reacting with such equanimity.

As Hansen's mind flailed, trying to make sense of things, the expected van arrived and pulled into the garage. The side door of the van slid open and an average-looking man emerged onto the polished floor, facing Kyle Hansen and Erin Palmer.

It was Drake.

Just when Hansen thought things couldn't get any stranger. "What is this all about?" he demanded once again, turning to the newcomer. "Drake? What's going on?"

The alien stared deeply into Hansen's eyes. "I'm not sure I believe that you don't know, Kyle. But if you truly don't, you should ask your traveling companion."

All eyes turned to Erin.

"Me?" she said with an incredulous note in her voice. "I have absolutely no idea. Other than to say that it looks like aliens can go just as crazy as humans."

Drake ignored this comment. "So how long have you been working for Steve Fuller?" he asked her.

The color drained from Hansen's face. Had he entered a surreal, parallel universe where black was white?

"Can you hear how ridiculous you sound?" protested Erin. "I had no idea Steve Fuller even existed until a few days ago when he called me in San Diego. I don't know what this is about. But either you've been misled, or you're very, very confused."

"Drake," said Hansen. "She's right. I've come to trust Erin with my life. And if she were working for Fuller, nothing that has happened since she called you from San Diego makes any sense. It's out-and-out impossible."

"I don't know, Kyle," replied Drake. "Maybe *you* were working with Fuller. Maybe you recruited Erin during your journey together. All I know for sure is that she's working with him now. I'm still not sure about you."

Hansen's mind was spinning in circles, and he couldn't even begin to understand where Drake was coming from. "You're sure she's working with Fuller based on *what*?"

The alien was about to answer when Erin interrupted. "Look, Drake, Kyle told me how difficult it's been for you living among humans. Being exposed to our violent natures. He told me it's having a negative effect on you. But you have to fight it," she insisted. "Are you familiar with the story of Sodom and Gomorrah?"

Drake laughed. "If I understand the word correctly, I think what you're trying to do is called a *filibuster*. Nice try, Erin. I see you glancing outside. Waiting. Hoping you can stall me long enough for help to arrive. But that's not going to happen." He paused. "Show her, Gibb," he said.

Hansen suddenly realized from the nonreaction of Gibb, Zalinsky, and the driver of the van to the word *alien* being thrown around that Drake must have let them in on his little secret. This was astonishing in and of itself.

Gibb pulled a sophisticated electronic device from his pocket, the size of a cell phone. A red light glowed on its surface.

"That device is blocking the bug you have on you, Erin," said Drake. "So your transmission is no longer getting through to Fuller. No rescue squad is coming. They'll just think the bug malfunctioned. Happens all the time. So no need to stall with boring stories or armchair psychobabble."

Erin didn't respond, but Hansen had never seen her look as worried as she did now, and they had been through some desperate situations together.

"But we didn't want Fuller to worry about you," continued Drake. "Or suspect you might have had a change in plans. So we timed it so the last thing he'd hear before the bug's unfortunate malfunction is your colleague giving you a goodie bag filled with food. For your imminent trip to San Francisco. This should be very reassuring to him."

"You're out of your little alien mind," said Erin.

Drake simply smiled but said nothing.

"Drake, Erin may be right," said Hansen. "You know you aren't well-suited, psychologically, for living on this planet. And you've had stretches, ever since I've known you, where you don't quite seem to be yourself." He gestured to Gibb, Zalinsky, and the driver of the van. "The Drake I know would never risk telling these men who you really are."

"I appreciate the concern, Kyle. But these men are mercenaries. Ex-military. Their loyalty is absolute. They don't care about lofty ideals. They just know I've paid them very well. And that if they do everything I ask of them for the next six months, they'll get a bonus that will enable them to retire three times over."

Drake turned to Gibb and Zalinsky. "And speaking of doing everything I ask of you," he said. "It's time to strip Erin Palmer of her electronics," he said.

Gibb nodded and faced Erin. "Okay," he said. "My partner is going to remove a bug and two homing devices from you. He's wearing body armor, so if you try something cute, I'll just shoot you. If you're able to block the shot with his body, he'll be just fine, and I'll shoot again."

The muscular mercenary approached her and shoved her head down roughly. He picked through her hair to her scalp, like a gibbon grooming a mate. Finally he stopped. Keeping a finger pressed down on an exact spot on her skull, he removed a pair of tweezers from his pocket, obviously having been forewarned as to what the removal would require. He brought the tips of the tweezers to Erin's head, gripped a small growth like one might grip a greedy tick, and pulled.

Erin cursed as a tiny piece of her head was ripped out

along with Zalinsky's target, and a fissure of blood appeared. Less than a minute later, Zalinsky had removed two additional small devices he found pinned to the inside of her clothing.

Zalinsky placed all three in his hand and held it open for all to see. The electronic devices were so small they were dwarfed by his palm.

"You know what these are, Kyle?" said Drake.

Hansen frowned deeply. "Gibb said he was removing a bug and two homing devices. So I assume that's what they are."

"Glad to see you were paying attention," said Drake dryly.

"I've never seen any of these in my life," said Erin. "Somebody must have planted them. Maybe while I was sleeping."

"Why don't I believe you, Erin?" said Drake, shaking his head sadly. "Imbedding the legs of an electronic bug like this in someone's skull, deep under the hairline, is Steve Fuller's signature move. I worked with him for years. Believe me, I know."

Erin turned to Hansen in surprise. "He worked with Steve Fuller?"

"I'm afraid so," replied Hansen, looking guilty.

"I thought you said he only knew Fuller because he'd put him on some kind of list?"

Hansen winced. He had planned to tell her the parts of the story he had omitted. He had no idea it would come out like this.

But more importantly, how could they have found these devices on Erin Palmer? Had she been playing him for a fool the entire time? He refused to believe it. It just wasn't possible.

"We discovered these electronics yesterday during a routine scan," explained Drake. "Imagine my surprise." His voice darkened. "And my disappointment."

"I'm being framed," said Erin softly.

"Save your breath," said Drake. "I'm not buying it. You were wearing a bug that I'm sure was broadcasting straight to Fuller. And a homing beacon as well. And as soon as you met me in person, I have no doubt you were planning to plant the second beacon on me."

Erin just shook her head helplessly, her eyes filled with horror.

"But now your plan has completely backfired. Because the bug has transmitted the false information I gave you. The bit about coming to San Francisco to meet me. Fuller is nearby, I'm sure, but he won't move in. He has no idea I'm here. He thinks I'm in California right now."

He walked over to Zalinsky and several tendrils snaked out from under his shirt and swept up the two homing beacons in the mercenary's hand. He quickly transferred them to his human hand and the tendrils disappeared under his shirt once again. He carried the homing beacons over to the driver of the van, who had remained still and silent since he had arrived, as had Burghardt. The driver lowered the window even farther and Drake handed him the small electronic devices, which the man put in his shirt pocket.

"Watch this," said Drake. He nodded to the driver, and the van exited the garage and was soon out of sight.

"You get what's happening here?" the alien said to his two prisoners. "He's going to San Francisco. With Erin's homing devices. Her bug is no longer working, but fortunately, both of her homing devices are working fine. So given that Fuller overheard you were going on a long journey, when the homing devices start moving in the direction of San Francisco, he'll be following that van every single mile of the way. I could *walk* from here to the border of Colorado right now with a giant neon sign that said, 'Attention Steve Fuller, Drake Here,' and I wouldn't be touched. Nice plan, huh?"

Hansen couldn't help but admit that if what he said was true about Erin, it *was* a nice plan. Using her electronics against her to lead whoever she might be working with on a wild-goose chase was inspired.

Drake turned to Burghardt for the first time, and gestured toward the metal canister under his arm. "The aerosolized virus, I presume?"

Burghardt smiled. "That it is."

"Great." Drake walked over to Burghardt and held out a human hand, and the molecular biologist passed him the canister.

"Let's get out of here, Max," said Drake.

They both walked to the door to the main residence. Drake gripped the handle on the door and then turned back to his two prisoners, still being held at gunpoint. "As much as I'd like to get to the bottom of this immediately, I have things to do. Conditions to cure. So I have to go now." He glared at Erin. "But I'll be back in about two hours. To interrogate the two of you properly."

"Drake, you have to believe me," said Hansen. "I had no idea about any of this. And I'm *positive* Erin has been framed somehow. She wouldn't do this."

"That's very sweet," said Drake. "And maybe you're telling the truth about your own involvement, as deluded as you are about hers. But maybe not." He shrugged. "I guess we'll all find out in about two hours."

40

~~~

ONCE THE ALIEN and the short genetic engineer left the garage, Gibb had the two prisoners move a good ten feet apart, after which Zalinsky approached Erin cautiously, giving her the respect she deserved. He ratcheted a single plastic bracelet around one of her wrists and then used a longer strip to connect this bracelet to a steel strut on the home gym, on the side facing the entrance to the main residence. This gave her a fair amount of freedom of motion, but ensured she wasn't going anywhere.

This completed, Zalinsky repeated this process with Hansen, strapping him on the same side of the home gym as Erin, but about six feet apart from each other.

Hansen considered pleading his case with these men, but decided it wouldn't get him anywhere.

When they were both chained by plastic to the immovable gym, Zalinsky returned to his partner's side. "Feel free to get in a good workout if you'd like," said the muscular mercenary with a sneer. "I recommend the leg press."

Hansen considered a caustic reply but decided against it. "You do realize that this is a big mistake," he said instead. "And it will get cleared up. And when it does, we'll all be on the same side again. So please keep that in mind."

"Could be," said Gibb. "But for right now, our orders are very clear. In any case, we'll be leaving you alone until Drake returns. But rest assured, we'll be very close by."

The two mercenaries walked to the door back into the mansion. Gibb paused to pocket the .45 Zalinsky had placed on top of the trophy case, and then they both exited, leaving Hansen alone in the room with Erin Palmer.

Hansen lowered his head, signaling to Erin he didn't want to engage in conversation for the time being. He needed to organize his thoughts. To analyze all that was going on in an attempt to understand how any of it could possibly make sense.

But no matter what angle he tried, he came up completely empty. Not only did none of it make sense, he couldn't imagine how it ever *could*.

Hansen finally lifted his head and locked his eyes on the woman who had come to mean so much to him in such a short time. "Erin," he began. "I can't tell you how sorry I am about this. Drake has clearly had a nervous breakdown. Or the alien equivalent. I wish I knew how those electronics came to be . . . attached . . . to you. But you were obviously framed. And we need to figure out how and why."

Erin let out a heavy sigh and shook her head. "I'm afraid I wasn't framed, Kyle," she said softly. "It turns out I *am* working with Steve Fuller."

41

HANSEN'S STOMACH LURCHED and he thought he might vomit. He stared at Erin Palmer in horror. He had been so sure about her. But how could this even be? She must have been working with Fuller before she had even met him. But then what was the point of the last few days?

"Everything Drake said is accurate," continued Erin. "I knew about the bug. Fuller did plant it. And I *was* trying to stall, hoping he would storm the place when he heard Drake was here. I had no idea Drake had blocked the bug's transmission. And I *was* planning to plant a homing device on him. I was just feigning innocence in the hope of throwing him off and buying some time."

"But why?" pleaded Hansen. "How?" He shook his head miserably. "I was actually thinking you were someone I could fall in love with someday," he whispered, almost inaudibly.

His eyes showed a hurt beyond hurt, a betrayal beyond betrayal. How could he have been fooled so completely?

"I had no other choice," said Erin. "It was necessary. And you have to admit, you withheld information from me as well."

"Is that what this is about? You thought I betrayed you? That wasn't it at all, I just—"

"Don't misunderstand," she interrupted. "I know why you did it. The details you left out weren't absolutely necessary to give me the gist of what you *thought* was going on. That had nothing to do with my decision to join Fuller." She paused. "I understand why you're so hurt," she said. "And I don't blame you."

She gazed into his eyes with a warmth and affection that sickened him. Was she still playing a game? Trying to draw him in, using his obvious attraction to her?

"You're the last person I'd ever want to hurt," said Erin, and she could not have looked more sincere. She paused, and then after a heavy sigh, added softly, "Because I can see myself falling in love with you someday as well."

Hansen wasn't sure how to react to this. Thirty minutes earlier he would have been on cloud nine. But now?

"Then why are you doing this?" he said.

"Because there's a lot you don't know."

"Okay. Like what?"

"Remember when you were shot with a dart at the Saguaro Inn?"

Hansen nodded. It wasn't something he was likely to ever forget.

"Well, the dose of tranquilizer in those darts only lasts for about an hour. Not ten or twelve."

Hansen struggled to comprehend. "What's that supposed to mean?"

"It means that a lot happened after you lost consciousness. A lot more than I told you."

"Was *anything* you told me after I woke up true?"

Erin winced. "Ah . . . not so much," she admitted. "I did try to escape from the motel. But while I think I'm pretty good, no one is *that* good."

Hansen stared at her with wide eyes, speechless.

"The good news," she continued, "is that it looks like we have some time." She gestured toward her cuffed hand. "And neither of us is going anywhere. So are you ready to learn what *really* happened between the time you were shot, and the time you woke up in a dry riverbed?"

Hansen was still reeling, but he managed to nod.

"Great," she said. "I think you'll find this extremely interesting." She raised her eyebrows. "And then some."

42

ERIN COULDN'T BELIEVE Kyle Hansen had just driven his newly acquired car into the middle of the fray outside of her motel room and was trying to use it as a weapon. The meek physicist who claimed he'd lose in hand-to-hand to a ninety-year-old woman in a wheelchair?

What courage. And what insanity, both.

Everything seemed to happen in slow motion. Hansen taking out one of their attackers with the car, and then screeching to a halt and rolling from the car before it stopped. The car blocking her view of where Hansen had landed, but being able to make out a man on the other side of the car, crouching down and pointing a gun toward the ground.

He must be aiming at Kyle!

Erin shot frantically at the crouching man behind the car, but had little chance of hitting him. Her angle was bad, the car was blocking her out, and she had to make sure she aimed high or risk hitting Hansen herself. It was hopeless.

The man standing over Hansen pulled the trigger.

"Noooo!"

The long, hysterical scream filled the air, and Erin realized only after the fact that the scream had come from her own mouth.

She kept squeezing the trigger long after the magazine was empty. A part of her realized she was now out of ammunition, but she didn't care. What did it matter?

She hadn't let herself truly care about anyone since she was eleven. But lately she had relented. She had begun to let people in. Lisa Renner. And now Kyle Hansen.

And now he was gone.

She was a *curse*. Whoever she cared for was taken away.

Reinforcements were suddenly coming from out of thin air and all of them were converging on her motel room. In seconds they realized she was out of ammo and broke down the door.

She decided not to even attempt to fight. What was the point?

Finally, one man, the man she had shot, entered the room, blood streaming from his arm, and Erin absently realized he was the same man they had Tasered at the student union. He looked relieved when she just stood there, showing no intent to demonstrate her impressive martial-arts skills.

"Hello again, Erin," he said. "My name is Ryan. Ryan Brock." He pointed a gun at her awkwardly with his left arm. "I need you to sit on the bed."

Of all the things she imagined he might have said, this was not among them.

"Why?" she said simply, moving to the bed and sitting on its edge.

"I don't want to take the chance that a fall might injure you," he said. And, inexplicably, he sounded almost . . . friendly.

This was the last thought she had when, almost apologetically, Ryan Brock pulled the trigger and everything went black.

* * *

Erin opened her eyes with a start. How was she still alive?

Two men sat across from her at a magnificent mahogany conference table. Two men she had never seen before. Her hands were loosely cuffed together by long strips of plastic, giving her considerable freedom of movement.

"Sorry about the restraints, Miss Palmer," said the taller of the two men. "But from what I understand, you could kick both of our asses without working up a sweat. And this is something we'd rather avoid."

"Who are you?" she demanded.

"My name is Steve Fuller. I'm the man who called you on the phone and invited you to meet with me in Palm Springs."

"I know who you are!" she hissed. Her eyes blazed with a fury, with a visceral hatred, that was stunning in its power. "I know all about you."

Fuller leaned back in his chair, as if desperate to put additional distance between himself and her withering glare. He looked truly taken aback. "What could you know about me that would bring out this kind of hatred?"

"I know you're an international arms dealer. I know you attacked Drake's compound in Yuma, killing everyone there." She lowered her eyes, which had suddenly become moist. "And I know you killed Kyle Hansen," she whispered.

Fuller studied her for several seconds and threw a worried glance at his colleague. There was something about this other man that made Erin think he was more dangerous even than Steve Fuller, although she couldn't put her finger on what that was. Another gut instinct.

"First of all," said Fuller with a sigh. "We didn't kill anyone in Yuma. We used nonlethal gas. And second of all, Kyle Hansen is alive and well. Just like you. He's sleeping peacefully in the next room."

"Bullshit. You know I've studied psychopaths like you for years. You know I've spent every day in the company of the world's smoothest liars. I'm not impressed with your apparent sincerity. You'll have to do better than that."

Fuller sighed and rose from the chair. "Follow me and I'll show you."

Fuller led her from the room and down a hallway. Guards were stationed outside the door, but he gave them a stand-down signal with his eyes. He opened the door to another room, also with two guards outside.

Erin entered and then gasped. Sure enough, Kyle Hansen was sprawled out on a portable cot, his chest rising and falling steadily.

She rushed forward and examined him, bringing her cuffed hands to his face and stroking his cheek. He felt warm and looked to be uninjured.

"Believe me when I tell you," came Fuller's voice from behind her, "that you and Kyle are the last two people I would want harmed."

Erin turned to face him. "Where are we?" she said.

"We're in Palm Springs. At a very secure facility under the desert. The one I had hoped to meet you in when I called you." He shook his head. "If only I hadn't so grossly underestimated you, we could have all spared ourselves a lot of trouble. But I still say it was impossible to predict you'd be this gutsy and elusive."

He stared at her grimly. "But much, or maybe even all, of what you think you know is wrong. And it's more critical than you know that you learn the truth." He motioned toward the door. "So if we could return to where we were, we have a lot of ground to cover. And the faster we can finish, the faster we can return Kyle Hansen to consciousness."

43

THEY HAD RETURNED to the room Erin had been in when she had first come to, across from Steve Fuller and the strange man who had yet to be introduced. Fuller had freed her of her restraints, making sure she understood they were being watched through video monitors and she had no chance of escaping.

Erin's head was spinning. Was there really even more to this story than she knew? Somehow, she felt there must be, or she and Hansen wouldn't be alive. But what could it possibly be?

"So can I assume it was Kyle who told you I was an arms dealer?" said Fuller.

Erin nodded. She had considered remaining silent, not answering his questions, but decided to cooperate—to a point. As long as she was only telling him things that were fairly obvious.

Fuller leaned in and stared at her intently. "Did Kyle happen to mention anything wild? You know, maybe something having to do visitors from another planet?"

"Funny you should mention that. In fact, he did. Pretty crazy, huh?"

The man beside Fuller began to unbutton his shirt,

although his fingers seemed clumsy. "Not as crazy as you might think," said the man, as twelve whiplike tentacles shot out from his stomach area and undid the last few buttons on the shirt with inhuman speed and elegance.

Erin's mouth dropped open and she didn't speak for several seconds. No wonder she had felt so uneasy around this man. Hansen had warned her this would be the case. Finally, with her eyes wider than she guessed they could open, she croaked, "Drake?"

The man—or clearly, the alien—shook his head. "No. My name is Fermi."

"I don't understand. I thought there was only one of you. Did the Wraps mount another Mount Everest expedition to send you after Drake?"

Steve Fuller turned to Fermi and raised his eyebrows. "She knows to call you a Wrap," he said. "And that it took a heroic effort by your people to get you here. Kyle seems to have told her quite a lot."

The alien frowned. "Erin, did Kyle just fail to mention any Wraps other than Drake, and you just assumed there was only one here? Or did he explicitly say that Drake was the only one?"

"Explicitly," said Erin, and even this word was hard to spit out. Why hadn't Kyle Hansen told her there were other aliens? Was there *no one* she could trust?

But suddenly she realized she was jumping to conclusions. "Drake must not have told Kyle about these others," she said. "That would explain it."

Fermi shook his head. "Erin, Steve and I met Kyle in a room very much like this one years ago. There are four Wraps on your planet. And Kyle knew that for certain."

Erin shrank back as though she had been slapped, the color draining from her face.

"Look, Miss Palmer," said Fuller. "Erin. I know you've been through a lot and don't know who to trust. But I think you would agree, clinging to a blind trust of events as told by Kyle Hansen would be a mistake. He told you only one Wrap was here. And clearly this isn't true. So if you could tell us what he told you, exactly, this would help us set the record straight."

Erin nodded, like a zombie. Why not? What harm could it do at this point?

She launched into everything Hansen had told her. A galactic community he called the Seventeen. Sixteen interstellar arks parked in each of seventeen different solar systems. Hansen's work with Drake, and the alien's insistence that ridding the species of psychopathy was the only way to prevent humanity's self-destruction. And Hansen's claim that Steve Fuller was an arms dealer, and his rationale for why such a man would want to eliminate Drake.

Fuller and his alien associate listened intently, raising eyebrows, shaking their heads, and glancing at each other knowingly on occasion, but saying very little.

When she had finished they informed her that everything Hansen had told her about the Wraps, the Seventeen, and how transit to Earth had been accomplished was accurate, as far as Hansen knew it, but his narrative veered off course when it came to the Wraps' expedition to Earth. There had been four Wraps, not one. And they had not gone it largely alone after arrival, as Hansen had described, but had immediately made contact with the government of the United States, since it was the strongest nation militarily.

Fuller and Fermi repeated almost all of what they had told Kyle Hansen those many years earlier about how the organization was set up, with Steve Fuller in charge, and the purpose and extent of their activities. They explained how and why they had abducted Hansen from his apartment near Carnegie Mellon, and the promise the Wraps had seen in him with respect to extending the frontiers of quantum mechanics and computing on Earth.

When they were finished, they waited silently while Erin pondered all that they had said. So many conflicting thoughts and emotions were wrestling for prominence she thought her head might explode.

"So why would Kyle mislead me?" she asked Fuller. "And why would he say you were an arms dealer? And Drake *is* real. Unless you're telling me he really wasn't the man—the being—I was working with to cure psychopathy. Which I'm not sure I'm willing to believe at this point. Kyle has said that only a Wrap—with a quantum computer—could have found the cure, and I believe it. So were you part of this also? Of curing psychopathy?"

Fuller took a deep breath. "I'll answer all of these questions, and more. But let me come about it in a more roundabout way. Let us first tell you some things we never shared with Kyle. This will put all of the rest into context. It's the only way you'll understand."

Erin waved her right hand toward the two men across from her in a classic, *you've-got-the-stage* gesture.

"The Seventeen, as you call them," began Fermi, "have been stagnant, ossified, for tens of thousands of years. Our societies, our science, is little different than it was thirty thousand years ago, when you and the Neanderthals were vying for supremacy on Earth. The early members of the Seventeen recognized an essential paradox hundreds of thousands of years ago. Imagine a species with the required drive, passion, and indomitable will to take the next step toward transcendence. A species refusing to take *no* from the laws of physics. A species who *demand*s that the galaxy and the universe yield before them. Any such a species would be ultracompetitive and aggressive. Insatiably driven. Reckless. And would self-destruct. With absolute inevitability. The computer simulations show this in every case. Such a species would develop weapons of mass destruction, experience dramatic overpopulation, and its immaturity, aggression, and recklessness would lead to Armageddon. Every time.

"The Seventeen survived self-destruction because they are timid, slow-thinking sheep in the scheme of things, compared to the wolves that are required to tame the galaxy. But we realized long ago that it was only a matter of time before we became extinct as well. Our populations are shrinking every year. We're old, in decline, tired. It may not happen for millions, or tens of millions of years. But our extinction is equally inevitable."

The alien paused and raised his eyebrows. "Thus the paradox. Timid species like the Seventeen who can survive their adolescences don't have the drive to colonize, the drive to blast through seemingly impenetrable scientific barriers through tenacity and force of will alone. Those that have the proper drive, like you, can't survive their adolescences."

Erin nodded, transfixed by the strange alien.

"We reasoned that the only chance for life in the long

term was if we could find a ruthlessly competitive species and intervene in its natural development. Help it survive its adolescence. Nurture it."

Erin nodded. "So this species can lead you to the next level," she whispered. "So it can make advances and provide a shot of vitality into the Seventeen. And however many more intelligences you may encounter over millions of years of scientific growth and colonization."

"Exactly," said Fermi. "Being too satisfied, too comfortable, and not ambitious enough was the disease. And such a species would be the cure. This hypothetical species of wolves, if you will, would be like a hydrogen bomb on the cusp of detonation. If the Seventeen could defuse it in time, and then channel its explosive power into constructive pursuits, this enormous power could be harnessed to drive all of us forward."

The alien held Erin's gaze. "That's not to say there was unanimity in this regard. A significant percentage worried that such a species unleashed upon the galaxy would accelerate our demise. That the cure would be worse than the disease. But they were voted down in favor of employing this strategy—if we were ever in a position to do so. But we weren't sure we would ever be able to find such a species. And even if one did arise, and we were lucky enough to find it, we would have little chance of reaching them in time to intervene.

"So with the last bit of our collective drive, we endeavored to be prepared if the chance ever did arise. To find a way to at least send a few emissaries faster than light to protect such a species. No matter what it took. Our top scientists, from a galactic population of almost a hundred billion, worked on the problem for tens of thousands of years. Finally, a method was found to transport a small number of beings, along with a modest quantum computer, faster than light. The resources required were tremendous. Unthinkable. But if we ever found a species capable of driving the galaxy to a new level, with all the adolescent baggage that inevitably came with this drive, they would be our only chance."

Incredible, thought Erin. It made a kind of bizarre sense. The yin and yang of human nature. The self-destructive qualities of humanity were the very qualities needed to grab the unconquerable laws of physics, the unconquerable galaxy, by the horns. A soft, unambitious species, kind and caring and gentle—everything humanity strived to be—could not. Only a species who was domineering, and arrogant, and competitive, and relentless, could hope to challenge the galaxy on its own terms.

"So I take it that we're the species you were looking for," said Erin.

Fermi sighed. "Yes. You are, indeed," he said. "But, unfortunately, we found something else first. Something that made things even more complicated. A form of life we hadn't predicted. One that would shorten the time we had to avoid extinction from millions of years to thousands." He leaned forward. "A form of life that would make the most malevolent members of your species seem like harmless saints by comparison."

44

ERIN'S EYEBROWS CAME together in confusion. "Intelligent?"

"Very much so," replied Fermi. "I won't explain the physics of it, but we detected strange quantum patterns coming from a region of space fifty-eight thousand light years away. Similar to the quantum pattern we expected to generate on the day we sent our emissaries out to a gifted but destructive civilization, if this day were ever to come. But far stronger. We soon realized what it was we were witnessing. A species was creating wormholes and holding them open as gates; gates allowing instantaneous travel between them. Using technology that we can't begin to match."

Fermi paused. "And now that we knew where to look," he continued, "we discovered this species occupied much of the galaxy behind them and were working their way toward our neck of the galactic woods. And they were annihilating intelligent species along the way. *Ruthless* wasn't even the right word. The species had as little regard for other intelligences as a raging wildfire would have for dry twigs in its path."

"How fast are they coming?" asked Erin.

"Fast," said Fermi. "They'll be here in thirty-two thousand years."

These Wraps were apparently more used to thinking in cosmological time scales than she was, thought Erin.

"And we knew we would have no chance when they arrived. They don't want to dominate other species, they simply want to annihilate them. Destroy them utterly."

"You said it was a form of life you hadn't predicted," said Erin. "What does that mean?"

"Are you familiar with insects on Earth you call army ants?" asked Fermi.

"Uh-oh," said Erin worriedly. "That can't be good."

"It isn't," said Fermi. "Army ants have a genetic need to march. To constantly move and seek out new territory, obliterating everything in their path. Locusts are the only other life form on Earth to come close. Or maybe viruses, which use cells to create more copies of themselves and then destroy the cells and move on. But army ants kill everything they encounter. *Everything*. To not kill would be an impossible concept to them."

"I've seen documentaries," said Erin grimly.

"Imagine a planet in which army ants developed a collective intelligence," said Fuller. "Maybe this conferred a selective advantage against other tribes of army ants."

"That is not to say that they resemble ants physically," added Fermi. "We have no idea as to their appearance. Just their behavior." He paused. "We call this species the Hive. For obvious reasons."

Erin nodded thoughtfully. "Okay," she said. "So you've got intelligent army ants—who may not look anything like ants, but are just as destructive—who find a way off planet. Pretty horrible to contemplate."

"Don't worry," said Steve Fuller. "It gets much worse."

"Hard to imagine that."

"I know," said Fermi. "That's why we never did. Imagine ants again for a moment. Each individual ant has some brain capacity, but not enough for sentience.

But the *colony* could gain sentience, if each ant member were able to combine its brain capacity collectively into some sort of neural network. Call it a hive-mind. On a planet rife with individual ant colonies, vying for supremacy, if evolution conferred this adaptation on one of these millions of colonies, it would soon dominate all others. Not just other ant colonies but all other forms of life on the planet. Eventually this winner of the evolutionary lottery would range over its entire globe. Just like humans range over Earth and Wraps over Suran. And now, as I mentioned, this single colony is ranging over thousands of light years." The alien leaned closer to Erin, his eyes locked on hers. "You've studied the human brain. Do you see any problem with that?"

"I'm not sure I understand the question."

"Remember, the colony has become a superorganism. Again, every last individual member, although physically separate, is somehow connected to form a single mind. A hive-mind. Do you see why the Seventeen never imagined this as a real possibility for a space-faring race?"

Erin's eyes widened. "Of course," she said. "Because it's impossible. Even over a single planet. If all the neurons in a human brain were spread out over the entire earth, you couldn't get the brain to work. Even at the speed of light, the communication between neurons wouldn't be fast enough. One of the reasons the brain is so compact is so signals can reach every last neuron as quickly as needed."

"That's right," said Fermi. "That's what I was getting at. The only way an abomination like this could exist is if the life form evolved the ability to send their equivalent of a neuronal firing faster than light. Instantaneously.

*If evolution provided the species with a way to take ad-
vantage of quantum entanglement."*

Erin blinked rapidly. "I'm sorry, but I don't know what
that is," she said.

Fermi described how every particle in the universe
was in some way connected with every other, and how
the Seventeen had eventually learned how to make use
of this entanglement to communicate instantaneously,
whether the communication was next door or at the edge
of the universe.

"So this is a species with an army ant nature and an
intuitive sense of quantum mechanics," said the alien.
"Which explains the superiority of its technology based
on this science."

"You said *its* technology," said Erin. "Not *their* technology."

"The members of the hive make up a single individual,"
said Fermi. "A single superorganism. You're made up of
trillions of individual cells, but when I speak of these tril-
lion cells in the collective sense, I'm speaking about you
in the singular."

"But then how can it be a species?"

Fermi smiled. "Excellent question. The semantics
are a little tricky. A species is defined as a group of or-
ganisms, so you are technically correct. The Hive began
as separate individuals, with separate minds, limited
though they must have been, but have become something else. But since this one superorganism has con-
quered thousands of light years of space, we consider it
both an individual and an entire species."

Erin decided to move on. She would have to ponder
semantics at another time. "But since it's intelligent,"
she said, deciding to use the singular, "won't it modify

its behavior? I understand its possible unwillingness to stop killing nonintelligent life. Even very compassionate humans still eat meat, or chicken, or fish. And plant life is life as well. So for a human to give up taking any life would be suicide. But an intelligent colony of army ants could at least bring itself to draw the line at fellow intelligences."

"One would think," said Fermi. "But that's not how it goes. Intelligent, nonintelligent, it's all the same to the Hive."

"How do you know that?"

"Because it's been able to infiltrate some of our societies," said Fermi simply.

45

THERE WAS A knock at the conference room door and a man brought in a tray of bottled water and cold soft drinks. There was a coffeemaker in the room, and Steve Fuller took the interruption as an excuse to pour himself a cup. Coffee was a drink for which Erin Palmer had never developed a taste, so she opened a bottle of the chilled water instead and poured it into a glass.

Fermi took a bottle of water as well, and Erin wondered if all members of the Seventeen had arisen from this liquid. She didn't know much about this subject, but for some reason she had a feeling that they would all enjoy a cold glass of water.

When everyone had settled in once again, Erin turned her eyes back to Fermi and said, "What do you mean, infiltrate? I thought they wouldn't get here for thirty-two thousand years. I mean *it* wouldn't get here."

"The infiltration wasn't physical," explained Fermi. "The physical members of the Hive can do short hops across space-time. But for longer ones the Hive needs to establish gates, which its physical members are building at an incredible pace. But fourteen hundred years ago, we discovered the Hive had another ability: it can enter a sentient mind from any distance, and suppress the mind of its host. Not easily. And, thankfully, not often.

"We soon discovered that twelve of the seventeen species had been infiltrated. The other five, for reasons which were not entirely clear, were resistant. When the few individuals who were being used as hosts were discovered, they were almost always killed by the portion of the hive mind that had controlled them. But a handful did survive. And this handful gained insight into the thought processes of the hive-mind."

Erin looked on expectantly.

"So fourteen hundred years ago," continued Fermi, "we discovered that the Hive was utterly selfish, utterly ruthless, and utterly without mercy, remorse, or compassion. It was a mentality that could not be understood. And although the hive-mind is one entity, it's a highly splintered one. It has its mental tendrils in thousands or millions of places, so only a fraction of its attention is devoted in our direction. But it was sending out feelers. Scouting parties. It was using the principles of quantum entanglement, through a method we still don't understand, to seize the minds of sentients to help prepare the way for its conquests, tens of thousands of years in the future."

Erin thought of the scouts in an ant colony, the advance

team, branching off from the main body. The army ant analogy was proving quite useful.

"Ultimately, we found foolproof means of identifying those few individuals controlled by the hive-mind in this way. And the twelve susceptible species found genetic countermeasures that they embedded in the DNA of their entire populations, making them resistant to this form of infiltration. When these genetic modifications had been completed, the Hive scouts were pushed out, never to return."

"Okay," said Erin. "So their last infiltration happened more than thirteen hundred years ago."

"Actually," said Fermi. "It took several hundred years to perfect and implement the countermeasures. So the Hive was fully blocked from entering any of the Seventeen's minds only about eleven hundred years ago." The alien frowned. "Not that it really mattered. We obviously couldn't let it control individuals and gather intelligence. But even without the use of its scouts we knew we were ripe for the taking. Maybe ants would need good intel going against something that could mount a challenge to them. But we were like a few soft grub worms in the path of an entire colony of seething army ants, millions strong. No intel needed in our case."

Fuller stared at Erin and raised his eyebrows. "I'm sure it didn't fail to register with you," he said, "that the description of the Hive's behavior sounds extremely . . . psychopathic."

"No. I got that," she replied.

It all made a horrible sense to her. This superorganism would *inevitably* be without mercy or remorse. When the *self*, the seat of intellect, was so massive—spread out over trillions of individuals and thousands of light years—its *selfishness* would be equally immense.

Erin knew many scientists believed insect colonies on Earth were the ultimate embodiment of cooperation. But she realized now it was just the opposite. Sure, if you looked at army ants as individuals, they were cooperative— with each other. They made bridges with their bodies so their brethren could cross. They were willing to readily die for the cause. But if you looked at them as a superorganism, as cells of a single being that just happened to be able to move independently, the actions of individuals weren't cooperative anymore. They were selfish. The cells in her own body displayed perfect cooperation, but they had a single purpose: preserving her as an individual.

The Hive would have the same relentless need to march as the army ant. And it would only care about its own needs, its own gratification. Anything outside of itself was for it to do with as it pleased. The hallmark of psychopathy.

In normals the words *chair* and *torture* would light up different areas of the brain; they were seen as being qualitatively distinct. But not to psychopaths. Similarly, to normal sentient species, sentient life and nonsentient life would be seen as being distinct. But not to a hive-mind.

"It seems to me that the Hive isn't *just* psychopathic," said Erin. "It's the *ultimate* psychopath. The ultimate, violent, rampaging psychopath."

"Right," said Fermi. "Although none of the Seventeen had any concept of this condition, being the sheep that we are."

"It doesn't bother you to call yourself sheep?" said Erin.

"No. Maybe that's what makes us sheep. We know that many humans would be irate if they were called this. But we know who we are. In the spectrum of societies, this is a fair analogy. And as I've said, wolves tear themselves to pieces before they become space-faring. Sheep don't."

Erin nodded. "Go on," she said.

"Given all that we knew," continued Fermi, "we resigned ourselves to our fate when the Hive arrived. We would be quickly exterminated." His demeanor brightened. "But then we discovered you. It was a miracle. You fit the exact scenario we were long hoping for. We wanted to save a species like you from itself, and groom you to lead us. So we wouldn't go extinct after millions of years of stagnation. But now this imperative had become far more urgent. So the four of us were chosen for the most important mission undertaken in the history of the Seventeen. To protect you so you could lead us against the Hive when they arrived. So we might have a chance of survival."

Erin shook her head. "But our science and technology are thousands of years behind yours. And it sounds as though you're thousands of years behind the Hive. I'm afraid we'll be just as helpless as you are. We might be wolves, but wolves going up against tanks become just as dead as sheep."

"No," said the alien firmly. "The progress you've made just since your first signals reached us is *ridiculous*. Breathtaking. Your first radio broadcasts took place only about a hundred years ago, using vacuum tubes, and in a cosmological blink you've managed relativity, quantum mechanics, genetic engineering, cell phones, supersonic jets, and baby steps toward quantum computers.

We were the fastest of the Seventeen to climb the technology ladder, and it took us four thousand years to make the progress you've made in a hundred. And your progress is accelerating. You have an insatiable curiosity. An endless drive. An itch you can never scratch. If you have a billion dollars you want a billion more. You're never satisfied. If we can help you through this critical period, you may well be a threat even to the Hive. Even if you only had a thousand years to prepare instead of thirty-two thousand."

There was silence in the room while Erin considered this. So the mission these four Wraps had been sent on had profound implications, not only for the future of their individual race, but for the future of the entire galaxy.

"So how were the four of you chosen to come here?" she asked Fermi. "You must have been pretty special."

Fermi smiled. "Yes, but ironically, in a way that made us stand out in a negative way on Suran. After extensive testing, we four were found to be the most aggressive, competitive, and driven members of our species. The least sheep-like among the sheep. We're still far to the left of the most pacifistic vegan on Earth, but we were rare individuals who might be able to handle the kind of onslaught of brutality we were sure to find here."

Erin couldn't help but smile. "No kidding?"

"No kidding," repeated Fermi.

"Getting back on topic," said Steve Fuller, "the Wraps only shared this information about the Hive with us recently. They didn't want to spring such a wild story until they had earned our trust. And they have. The world will never know just how critical their contributions have been. But once they did disclose this situation, we began putting our minds to the best strategic steps to take going forward. A sheep, and even a sheep's computer, can't possibly strategize like a wolf." Fuller raised his eyebrows. "This is where you enter the picture."

"I have to say that I haven't connected the dots to me yet at all."

"We decided we had to accelerate the process," said Fuller. "Add more humans to the team. Brainstorm. Analyze the enemy, starting now. The Wraps are nervous about giving us technology, so we don't play with fire and burn ourselves."

"We probably would, you know," said Erin. "Not wise to give a loaded gun to the crazed teenage version of your future savior."

"Regardless of whether it's wise or not," replied Fuller, "even without their technology, we can find better ways to accelerate our own development. My view is that if everyone knew the history of the galaxy and the Seventeen, and the leadership role we will be expected to play in this galactic community, along with the threat from the Hive in thirty-two thousand years, humanity would pull together. At least better than we are now." He sighed. "But that's a debate for another time. For now, we're in a position to help the Seventeen understand the coming enemy. Their computer contains all the intel ever gathered on the Hive. When we realized that it behaved in many ways like the rare, Hannibal Lecter–type psychopathic killer, it occurred to us that an expert on psychopathy might come in handy."

Of course, thought Erin. How could she have missed it?

"I saw the *Wall Street Journal* piece and did some

background checks," continued Fuller. "You were just what we were looking for. Brilliant. Single-minded in your goal of understanding psychopathy. Young. And your idea of finding remote ways to detect psychopathy could be helpful in what we're trying to do to stop the most dangerous people here on Earth."

"At last, your recruiting call begins to make sense," noted Erin.

"The more I learned about you, the more perfect I thought you were for this job. I saw you as forming the nucleus of a team that would try to get inside the heads of our enemy. At least better than the Seventeen possibly could. Analyze everything known about Hive behavior." He paused. "The larger team we plan to build will have exobiologists, of course. But we hoped you would be willing to lead a team of what we expect to call *exopsychologists.*"

Erin had to admit such a role sounded amazing. Challenging and important. Not as much fun as going into a prison every day . . .

"And as I mentioned," continued Fuller. "I'm arguing that we should consider the possible effects of full disclosure to the world. Study if this is something we should do in five or ten years. So we would want top psychologists and psychiatrists to predict how people would handle learning of this. Would it bring our species closer together? Create widespread panic? Would this knowledge increase our resolve? Even though the enemy won't be on the playing field for thirty thousand years?" He stared at Erin. "And I wanted you to be a part of this as well."

Erin nodded. "It all suddenly makes sense. But to even begin to recruit me for this effort, you knew I needed to meet a Wrap. So I would believe what you told me. So you decided to fly me to your headquarters to initiate me."

"Exactly. And we continued to vet you. Gather intel on you. We monitored your phone." Fuller shook his head. "Unfortunately, I didn't get the chance to listen to the recordings of your conversations until the day after I had set up the meeting with you. But you can't even begin to imagine how startled I was when I did play the recordings and I heard *Drake's* voice on the line."

"I assume Drake wasn't working with you anymore," said Erin, "or you wouldn't have been surprised. So what happened? Did he have a disagreement with the rest of the group?"

"No," said Fuller, shaking his head. "He was incinerated in an explosion."

46

KYLE HANSEN HAD been listening attentively to Erin's tale of her meeting in Palm Springs with Steve Fuller and a very much alive alien named Fermi. She had been standing when she had begun, but five minutes earlier she had slid her hand down the steel strut to which it was attached to sit cross-legged on the cool garage floor. Soon after this she had begun to slump even farther and her voice had noticeably weakened.

Finally, she stopped altogether, and Hansen could tell she was struggling to keep her eyes open.

"Erin?" he said anxiously. "Erin, are you okay?"

"No," she whispered, her voice barely audible. "I'm feeling . . . dizzy. Insulin shock," she mumbled.

"You're *diabetic*?" said Hansen in disbelief. How had Drake missed this? Even if it was adult-onset diabetes, this was something that should have been in her file.

"I keep it . . . secret. Don't like . . . showing . . . weakness."

Hansen couldn't believe it. He knew she didn't like to show weakness, but she hadn't seemed the type to hide something like *this*.

Could this really be happening? On top of everything else? Just when Erin was revealing to him the rationale for her seemingly inexplicable behavior. And given what she had said already, the rest of her story was critically important. If there was a God, he didn't appear to be a big fan of Kyle Hansen and Erin Palmer. What next, an earthquake?

But worse than her not finishing her story, her very life could be in danger. Hansen seemed to recall that insulin shock in diabetics could be fatal if not treated.

Erin pointed at the display case on which Zalinsky had set the items he had taken from her. A silver cylinder still rested there. "Glucagon injection," she whispered faintly. "For emergencies. In the . . . thigh." With that, her eyes slid shut again and she looked to be unconscious.

Hansen shouted at the top of his lungs and continued to do so until both Gibb and Zalinsky raced into the garage, guns drawn.

As soon as the door opened, Hansen stopped shouting. The two mercenaries surveyed the room for hidden danger and to make sure their prisoners were still restrained. Seeing no reason for alarm, they lowered their weapons.

Hansen gestured toward Erin with his free hand. "She's in insulin shock," he said rapidly. "That cylinder you took from her is an emergency dose of . . . I think she said glucagon. But whatever it is, you have to inject her. Now!"

The two men glanced at each other as if uncertain what to do.

"You know Drake wants to interrogate her," barked Hansen. "You think he'll be patting you on the back and giving you a bonus when he gets back here and she's *dead*? *Come on! Every second counts.*"

Gibb walked over to the steel cylinder and carried it gingerly to Hansen, as though it were booby-trapped and might explode at any second. "Open it," he said.

Hansen gestured for Gibb to put it in his right hand, which was cuffed to the home gym. When Gibb did so, Hansen held the metal tube between his thumb and index finger and used his free hand to press a small metal dot extending out from one end, hoping this would open it. Sure enough, one half of the silver tube rolled back inside the other half, lengthwise, to reveal a glass syringe, filled with a colorless liquid.

"Take it," said Hansen. "Carefully."

Seeing that the cylinder contained exactly what Hansen had said it would seemed to galvanize Gibb, and he took it as instructed.

"Now jam it into her thigh," ordered Hansen. "*Quickly! And make sure she gets it all. Go!*" he screamed.

Gibb pulled a combat knife from a sheath at his ankle and cut a seam in Erin's pants at the thigh so he wouldn't have to risk damage to the needle by stabbing through her clothing. He plunged the needle into her leg and emptied the entire contents of the syringe.

Hansen exhaled loudly. "Thank you," he whispered.

Both Gibb and Zalinsky remained in the garage to see what would happen. Within minutes Erin's eyes fluttered open.

She caught Hansen's eye and smiled weakly. "Thanks," she whispered. She noticed that Gibb still had an empty syringe in his hand. "And you too," she said to him.

"Will you be okay?" asked Hansen.

Erin nodded. "Feeling much better already."

After another few minutes of recovery, Erin rose from the floor and looked over at Gibb. "Thanks," she said again. "But I'm okay now. No need to babysit any further."

Gibb thought about this for a few seconds. Finally, reaching a decision, he turned to Zalinsky. "Let's go," he said. Seconds later they had exited back through the door into the mansion and were out of sight.

After they left, Hansen stared at Erin reproachfully. "I know you don't want to show weakness, Erin. But keeping something like that a secret is dangerous." He turned away. "Jesus, we could have lost you."

"It was stupid of me," admitted Erin. "And very bad timing. But let's talk about the wisdom of this another time," she continued, her voice regaining strength by the second. "Right now, I need to finish telling you what's really going on here."

Hansen nodded. "Go ahead," he said, eager to hear the rest. But also wondering what other obstacles the fates might choose to throw at them next.

47

"DRAKE WAS INCINERATED in an explosion?" repeated Erin. What did that mean?

"Obviously," continued Steve Fuller, "reports of his death were greatly exaggerated." He raised his eyebrows. "But we didn't know that at the time. We only learned this recently. When we were gathering further intel on you. Imagine our surprise when we heard his unmistakable voice over your phone."

"Did he stage his death so he could go AWOL?" asked Erin. "So he could take more dramatic steps than the rest of the Wraps were willing to take to save us?"

Fuller shook his head. "This was the most important assignment ever given to a Wrap in their history. There is zero chance this was his motive. And no one believed in what we're doing more than Drake."

"So what's your explanation?"

"The Hive," said Fermi grimly. "It must have found a way to penetrate his defenses and control him. Which is alarming on many, many levels."

Erin's eyes narrowed. "You actually think part of this hive-mind is present here on Earth?" she said.

"That *has* to be it," said Fermi. "How the Hive managed to learn about this mission we may never know. But the truth is, this is a pivotal point in a war that won't take place for thirty-two thousand years. So it wouldn't surprise me if the Hive attempted to infiltrate Drake's mind with more than the usual tiny fraction of its full capabilities. To gain a foothold. Given his genetically engineered defenses to this, the Hive must have had to work carefully over many years to breach. We didn't think this was possible no matter how long it tried, but we must have been wrong."

"But how can you be so sure this is true? You say yourself you thought a breach was impossible. So even an improbable solution makes more sense. Maybe Drake finally went crazy from being around us for so long."

"I wish that were the case," said Fermi. "But not only did we hear his voice, we heard what he's been up to. With you. Curing psychopathy. Which we quickly recognized as a stunningly brilliant plan by the Hive to win the war before it begins."

"I don't understand. Curing psychopathy sounds more like a plan from an *actual* Wrap. One pushed over the edge and wanting to go on offense rather than defense to protect humanity. If Drake were controlled by the Hive, why wouldn't he just nuke us into oblivion?"

"Too risky," said Fermi. "Let's walk through the scenario. The Hive finally succeeds in taking over Drake. All the Wraps on this planet are exceedingly well protected, and we're never allowed to all be together at the same physical location. Similar to your president and vice president never flying on the same plane. There is far more security around us right now than is evident, believe me. So Drake—let's now call him Hive Drake or H-Drake, since he's no longer in control of himself—can't be sure an attack on us will succeed. And if he fails, we'll be alerted that the hive-mind has circumvented our safeguards. And the Hive may never get another chance."

Erin pursed her lips. "That explains why he wouldn't try to attack the other Wraps on Earth. Not why he wouldn't try to wipe out the human race."

"Because he knows we're still out there, monitoring," said Fermi. "Even if he did manage to produce a lethal, infectious bioagent and slip it under our radar, when it started killing people we'd be on top of it. We could use our skills and computer to counteract it. Even if this wiped out half of humanity, which might be devastating to your civilization for hundreds of years, the Hive won't arrive for thirty-two *thousand* years, and our analysis suggests this setback would only make you stronger in the long run. Like a broken bone is stronger after healing, or a controlled burn can lead to a healthier forest." He paused. "But we don't need to speculate. Because we know what H-Drake has been up to. First, he faked Drake's death. Any ideas what he did next?"

Erin shrugged. "None."

"We're almost certain the first thing he did was recruit Kyle Hansen," said Fermi. "Kyle could help him build a primitive quantum computer, within the limitations of primitive Earth components, and work with the required human consultants and collaborators."

"Based on what you've told us," added Steve Fuller, "H-Drake must have convinced Kyle that along with running this show, I moonlighted as a dangerous arms dealer and killed off the other three Wraps. That's probably why Kyle didn't mention them to you. Not important at that point—at least given what he believed the truth to be." Fuller shook his head. "Kyle also faked his death about six months later, probably so he could join H-Drake full time."

Erin nodded, but remained silent.

"We had big plans for Kyle once he graduated from CMU," continued Fuller. "And his supposed death hit us all hard. And not just because we thought we lost his brilliance, which is considerable, although he's so modest you'd never guess it. But because we monitored and vetted the shit out of him, and had developed an affection for him. He's a good man."

Erin had quickly reached this same conclusion herself.

"Kyle spoke many times about Drake using a quantum computer," noted Erin. "So they must have succeeded." She furrowed her brow in confusion. "But I still don't get it. The Hive's grand plan after all of this is to cure psychopathy? How does this help them? Help *it*?" she corrected.

"Like I said, H-Drake knew we were still out there," replied Fermi. "Along with our quantum computer and all of its capabilities. We screen for everything that could cause widespread destruction; nuclear, biologic, chemical, anything. And we correlate purchases and other information. If he tried to unleash any kind of WMD attack, we'd probably stop it, along with the Hive's chances here. And as I said, even if not, if he didn't wipe out the entire population, you'd only grow back stronger over many thousands of years."

The alien shook his head. "But we weren't looking for someone constructing a crude quantum computer," he explained. "Or someone trying to come up with a *cure* rather than a biologic agent that kills. Basically, he knew a cure would sail right under our radar screen. We wouldn't be the slightest bit suspicious until it had infected everyone on Earth."

"Yes, *but so what*?" said Erin, still confused. "A cure for psychopathy just helps you in your goal of protecting us. *Decreases* the chances we'll commit suicide."

"*No,*" said Fermi adamantly. "A cure *defangs* you. A

cure takes away some of the elements that make you what you are. The positive of what you are."

"*No!*" barked Erin passionately. "I refuse to believe that! Yes, psychopaths are fearless. And boldness and fearlessness in business and other settings can be a positive. And they can be very articulate and persuasive, and can sometimes think outside the box. But they are so destructive that anything positive about their behavior is more than nullified."

Erin remembered telling Hansen that some trolleyology research had suggested psychopaths might be better utilitarians than normals. On the other hand, a nuclear bomb might make a better paperweight than a normal bomb. But so what? This was minor consolation to those it destroyed when it went off.

"We agree," said Fermi. "In those that are psychopathic, the negative brought on by their genes *far* outweighs any positive. But the way the Hive is curing this will remove all of these genes from the human gene pool forever. Not just for psychopaths. How many psychopathic genes did he discover?"

"Eight."

"Okay, imagine that if you're unfortunate enough to have all eight, you're a psychopath. Which is a huge negative to society. But what if you had four of the eight? Where would that put you? Maybe more selfish than average. More aggressive. More prone to take risks. Less compassionate. But in this case, the good these traits can do in moving society forward might outweigh the bad. We had our computer do an analysis, and if you wipe out all the genes from the human gene pool that in the right, unfortunate combination cause psychopathy, humans lose their edge. They never become as sheep-like as the members of the Seventeen. But they lose enough of their insatiable drive, their ultracompetitiveness, to no longer be a threat to the Hive."

Could this be true? Could psychopathy just be the unhappy extreme of traits that helped mankind dominate a hostile planet? It was something Erin had never considered.

"We put everything we know into our computer," said the alien. "And its analysis showed that in the Hive's shoes, the strategy H-Drake is attempting to deploy is the optimal one. The strategy with the maximum probability of achieving long-term success. Namely, neutralizing humanity as a threat when the physical components of the Hive arrive."

"Are you sure you and the Hive haven't overestimated the importance of some of these genes to our drive and ambition?" asked Erin.

"Positive," said Fermi. He paused in thought. "Did you ever see reruns of the original *Star Trek* television series?"

Erin shook her head no, wondering where this was going.

"I'm a huge fan," said Fermi. "Which is ironic, because one of my two Wrap colleagues took the name Roddenberry. And he *isn't* a fan."

"What?"

"Never mind," said Fermi. "Anyway, I've read all the scripts for this series. I don't watch the actual shows, because I can't handle the violence, but I can skip over the violent parts of the scripts rather easily."

"Okay, so what about it?"

"There was an episode called 'The Enemy Within,' which I believe provides a perfect sense of why negative traits, in proper moderation, need to be preserved in your species. In the episode, a transporter malfunction splits Kirk into two identical versions. At least identical physically. But one version is basically a psychopath. And the other is basically a sheep—with a constitution similar to members of the Seventeen. What's fascinating about the episode is that the empathetic Kirk can't make hard decisions. They paralyze him. He can barely make *any* decisions. He's impotent. On the other hand, the psychopathic Kirk is all rage and no reason."

"I have to admit," said Fuller, "Fermi had me watch this after we discovered what H-Drake was up to and it's a fascinating episode."

"If I ever get my life back," said Erin dryly. "I'll be sure to buy it."

"So to continue," said Fermi, "McCoy and Spock dissect the situation. McCoy tells the compassionate Kirk the following, and I quote: 'The intelligence, the logic. It appears your half has most of that. And perhaps that's where man's essential courage comes from.' But later, Spock, a student of humanity, tells McCoy the following, which is the most relevant for our discussion: 'And what is it that makes one man an exceptional leader? We see here indications that it's his negative side which makes him strong. That his evil side, if you will, properly controlled and disciplined, is vital to his strength.'"

Erin almost whistled. It was uncanny how this line exactly mirrored current events, and surreal to have an actual alien quoting lines from *Star Trek* like a fanboy. "Very interesting," she admitted.

And it *was*. Fermi's computer had confirmed her own certainty that any positives that might come from the perfect storm of genes that resulted in full-on psychopathy paled when compared to the negatives. But she could see the truth of his argument as well. A smattering of these same genes in the population was critical for human leadership, human vitality.

There was a long silence in the room. Finally, Fuller nodded at Erin and said, "So that's basically it. We've laid out the entire situation as well as we possibly can. I know we've given you a lot to think about. Do you believe us?"

Erin realized she did, and told him so.

"We need your help," said Fuller.

"Don't worry. I won't be giving Drake the dose information he needs. He won't be able to carry out his plan."

"For now," said Fuller. "But this won't stop him from blending back into the woodwork and trying it later. Or something else. We have no idea of the Hive's full capabilities, strategic or otherwise. We need to end this now."

Erin considered. "What do you want me to do?" she asked. "And why hasn't Kyle been part of this conversation? Why are you keeping him unconscious?"

"We're all but certain humans are one of the species not susceptible to infiltration by the hive-mind," said Fermi. "But until a few days ago, we didn't think Drake was susceptible either. So it is possible that a concerted effort by a greater than normal fraction of the hive-mind for a period of years might succeed. And Kyle has now been working with H-Drake for many years."

"You can't possibly think that *Kyle* is being controlled."

"No," said Fuller. "We think this is still very unlikely. But, unfortunately, the stakes are too high to assume anything else."

"It's impossible," insisted Erin. "Believe me. The two of us have . . ." She stopped in midsentence. "Well, let's just say that I've been, ah . . . involved with him. *Intimately,*" she added, and something about their expressions made her think this wasn't a surprise to them, although she had no idea how this could be. "There are certain reactions that can't be faked," she continued. "He's as human as they come."

"Wrap families had no idea fourteen hundred years ago when one of their members was infiltrated by the Hive," explained Fermi. "Even though it's in control, it can default to the being it's controlling for physical and social reactions. It's an emulator function. While in control the Hive can run a stimulus response routine that the being it's controlling can't stop. Whatever the real Kyle Hansen would have said, however he would have responded, the Hive can fire up these pathways and read the result. And choose to respond in exactly the same way. So in effect, it can *be* Kyle Hansen, down to his last personality quirk or physical reaction. Until it chooses to be otherwise. If any being the hive-mind infiltrated acted like the Hive for even a few minutes, the infiltration would be exposed."

This was troubling, but Erin was still all but certain Kyle was still Kyle, on the basis of logic alone. But she did understand why this group wanted to err on the side of caution. "Are you sure none of the other Wraps have been infiltrated?" she asked.

"Positive," said Fuller. "The Wraps know the telltale signs. They're as subtle as a quantum signature, but their computer knows how to find them. The Wraps are clean, unless all three are being controlled. And since they alerted us to the Hive and the current situation in the first place, we know that's not the case."

"If you know the telltale signature," said Erin, "why can't you clear Kyle?"

"We haven't yet zeroed in on the precise telltales for humans," replied Fermi. "Again, we're not even sure if infiltration is possible in your species."

"Okay," said Erin. "But I've been working with Drake for years also. How do you know I haven't been infiltrated?"

"We heard your conversation with Drake," replied Fuller. "He desperately wanted the cure and you didn't give it to him."

Erin nodded. "So what do you propose?"

"While we've been talking," said Fuller, "with the assumption that we'd be able to convince you to help us, we've had a team brainstorm a credible cover story to enable us to put you and Kyle back on the field of play."

"To do what?"

"We'll give you a thorough briefing on that in a few minutes," said Fuller. "But for now, I'd like to run a cover-story scenario by you and see if you think it will work."

Erin nodded.

Steve Fuller pulled a cell phone from his pocket and less than three minutes later a man joined them, his right arm in a sling. The same man who had entered her motel room.

"I gave Captain Brock here and his men a difficult challenge," said Fuller. "They needed to capture you both without harming either of you, but with a catch. They had to put Kyle to sleep before you, so that we could later convince him that you had prevailed and saved his bacon. So we couldn't use overwhelming force or he wouldn't buy it. The captain performed brilliantly, at great risk to himself, since the strategy severely tied his hands."

Brock nodded at Fuller, acknowledging the praise. He then turned to Erin. "I really want to thank you for not killing me when you could have," he said gratefully. He gestured toward his injured arm. "It was a brilliant shot. Taking me out of play without doing any permanent damage. I'm in your debt."

"Yeah, well . . . you're welcome," said Erin. A broad grin spread slowly across her face. "I have to admit, I'm not used to being thanked by someone after shooting them."

"Do you shoot a lot of people, ma'am?" said Brock.

Erin laughed. "No. You're the first."

"Good to know," said Brock with just the hint of a smile. "In any event, my team has come up with a cover story we think is workable." He went on to describe the fictional tale of Erin's heroic rescue of Kyle Hansen from the Saguaro Inn. "And we found a great location you can credibly say you were hiding at while waiting for Kyle to recover. We were really proud of this one. Did you know there's a dried-out river in Tucson?"

"Yes," said Erin. "My roommate told me all about its history. The Santa Cruz."

"Very good. Anyway, once we fly you back and set the stage, we were thinking of placing you there. Under a bridge. And leaving a Lexus for you at the airport."

"A Lexus? How will I explain *that*?"

"You ever fly to any conferences with your advisor?"

Erin shook her head no.

Brock smiled. "Well, Kyle Hansen won't know that, will he?" Then, with a shrug, he added, "And I've decided your advisor is the kind of man who would own a Lexus."

48

WHEN ERIN PALMER finally finished her account of what had transpired after Hansen had lost consciousness, he was speechless. For years he had believed Steve Fuller had turned on the Wraps, killing them all. All but Drake. And he had believed that Drake was dedicated to helping mankind.

And now this. Incredible. A ruthless species fifty-eight thousand light years distant. A species capable of seizing control of a Wrap emissary sent to Earth. As if the existence of Wraps on Earth, and the description of the Seventeen, weren't mind-blowing enough.

And Hansen believed every word. There was no other way Erin could know about Fermi, or that one of the other Wraps was named Roddenberry. This was the only way to explain her shifting of allegiances, and the electronic devices Drake had found on her.

And it all made perfect sense. Drake's actions in the garage were the most telling sign of all. Not only did he not behave as an avowed pacifist, but he seemed to take relish in their discomfort. Over the years, Hansen had caught Drake behaving in ways that clearly conflicted with what Hansen had originally been told about Wraps. But he had made excuses for Drake every time.

Hansen stared at Erin in wonder. "So they sent you back in as a mole," he said. "So you could locate this, ah . . . H-Drake, and help Fuller stop him."

Erin nodded.

"Is that why you wouldn't sleep with me last night?"

he asked suddenly. "Because you thought I might be, you know, H-Kyle?"

Erin laughed. "No. I'm convinced you're human and they were being too paranoid. But I had a bug partially implanted in my skull. I knew Fuller and his people were listening in. I found the thought of a group of men around a speaker listening to our . . . noises . . . while we were having sex a little . . . inhibiting."

Hansen made a face. "No kidding," he agreed. "That could make anyone self-conscious. But what made you so convinced I wasn't being controlled?"

"It has to be difficult to control a mind from fifty thousand light years away—even if you can send your thoughts out instantaneously. And, apparently, controlling a human is no easy task. The Hive would have had to start years ago. And what would be the point? It was already controlling Drake. Why expend the resources to control two people working side by side?"

"Well, let me reassure you. No one is controlling me."

"Which is exactly what you would say if the Hive *were* controlling you."

Hansen frowned. "Good point."

"Don't worry, Kyle," said Erin with a smile. "As I've said, I have zero doubt. But I promised Fuller I wouldn't risk telling you until after Drake was killed and your actions made it absolutely clear you hadn't been infiltrated."

"So the plan was to *kill* Drake?" said Hansen. "Killing him wouldn't hurt the Hive. It would just abandon his mind at the time of death. Is there any way to just push out the hive-mind and save him?"

"I'm afraid not. Not according to Fermi. At this point, the Hive's control is too strong. And if the Hive did leave Drake, it would be sure to kill him itself no matter what. Killing him is our only choice."

Hansen pondered this. "Any chance Fuller didn't buy Drake's head fake with the homing devices?"

"I don't think so," replied Erin with a frown. "I think we're totally on our own. Which Fuller promised me he wouldn't let happen. In his defense, he had no idea Drake would discover his electronics and come up with such a brilliant misdirection strategy."

"The Hive shows an impressive knack for deception."

"True. But I'll bet we're still the champions in that category. I think the Hive is just a talented amateur. Our species are the true professionals."

"Could be," said Hansen. "But maybe not for too much longer. We've lost. You know why Drake left. To release the virus. And with Fuller tracking a decoy van, there's nothing to stop him. The funny thing is that this cure will be a blessing to mankind in the short run. Even if it ultimately saps our drive and retards our scientific advancement. Even if it eventually causes us to lose a war we'll never live to see."

"Don't be so sure we've lost," said Erin. "Drake won the last round, true. And taking Fuller out of the picture hurts. But things may not be entirely what they seem."

"What do you mean?"

"I can't tell you," she said. "Because Drake almost certainly has this garage bugged."

Hansen's eyes widened. This had never occurred to him. But she was right. It was obvious. Why else would they be left alone together, without any guards posted within earshot?

Drake had wanted them to chat freely. He hoped they

would provide critical information before he even began an interrogation.

"Anyway," continued Erin. "That's the story. I may have left a few things out," she added, nodding slowly and giving Hansen a wink at the same time. "But I think I covered most of it."

Hansen stared at her intensely as though trying to read her mind. She had already disclosed there was a deeper picture, which she probably shouldn't have. But for the life of him, he couldn't figure out what it might be. They were restrained, weaponless, with no hope of backup. And Drake had doubtlessly finished releasing the virus.

Erin put a finger to her lips. Then she rolled her hand tight, the one that was lashed to the home gym. It was remarkable how small she could make it, and she had tilted her wrist slightly when the cuff was placed around it to gain extra room. Even so, even using her free hand to help pull her bound hand through the plastic bracelet, she could not remove it from her wrist.

Undeterred, her face a mask of pure concentration, she began to saw the skin of her wrist into the plastic. Blood began to seep out where she had cut herself, and she twisted her wrist in such a way as to coat all of it with a fine layer, using it as a lubricant. Hansen was amazed at her stoicism. She didn't cry out in pain and her face continued to show nothing but determination.

Erin was about to try to slide her wrist free once again when the door from the house opened, and Drake, Burghardt, Gibb, and Zalinsky entered the garage.

Zalinsky took one look at Erin and raised his gun. "Having trouble with your cuff?"

Erin shook her head. "No trouble. Why do you ask?"

Drake glared at the muscular mercenary. "Just keep the gun on her and assume she can slip her cuff whenever she wants," he said.

"Roger that," said Zalinsky.

"So," said Drake, facing the two prisoners. "Have you been having fun?"

"Don't pretend you weren't listening in," said Erin.

"I was. But I didn't catch all of it. I was busy releasing the virus, I'm afraid. And now it can't be stopped."

"How was it released?" asked Hansen with genuine curiosity.

Drake gestured to the short genetic engineer. "I had Max here separate it into thirty half-full perfume bottles," he replied. "We wanted to make sure that it was properly scented, for good measure. I had previously hired thirty women to go to all the terminals at Denver International Airport and spray the perfume around. Pretending to apply it to themselves. I explained I was doing market research for a perfume company, and would later ask questions of passengers to determine if they had smelled anything pleasant at the airport or not."

"Impressive," conceded Erin. "What better place to begin a global infection than at an international airport?"

"Exactly," said Drake. "Denver International is one of the top fifteen busiest airports on your planet. Even as we speak, infected passengers are jetting to every city in America, and most countries of the world. Within a few days, there will be infectious centers in thousands and thousands of locations worldwide. A virus this infectious doesn't really need such a big head start, but why not?"

Hansen turned his head toward the genetic engineer

and two mercenaries. "Did any of you hear our conversation in here?"

The three men all indicated they had not.

Figures, thought Hansen. Drake would be sure that the bug in the garage transmitted only to him. But the human members of Drake's team were here now. So maybe he could plant a seed of doubt. It would take considerable doing, but it might be possible. A malevolent hive-mind fifty-eight thousand light years away controlling Drake? The cure for psychopathy part of a grand plan to defang the human race? To get these men to believe this would be exceedingly challenging. But Hansen was determined to give it everything he had.

"You know I was Drake's biggest supporter," he said to the humans in the garage, speaking as quickly as he could since he didn't know long he would have before Drake found a way to stop him. "But Erin convinced me Drake has played me for a fool. And he's doing the same to you. So hear me out. Don't let Drake muzzle me. The stakes couldn't be higher. If you hear me out and I can't convince you, *shoot* me."

Gibb considered. "Okay," he said. "We'll hear you out. Why not? Tell us how we're being played."

"No." said Drake. "Shoot them immediately!"

"If Drake has nothing to hide," said Erin, "why is he suddenly so eager to kill us?"

Hansen caught the eye of the genetic engineer. "Drake told you he was the ultimate pacifist, didn't he, Max? Does *'shoot them immediately'* sound like the words of a pacifist?"

"I said to shoot them!" barked Drake.

Gibb hesitated.

Drake shook his head in disgust. "No matter," he said. "None of you would have been useful for much longer, anyway."

Suddenly, Burghardt and the two mercenaries sank to their knees, screaming in agony, the weapons held by the two mercenaries falling to the ground beside them. They continued screaming and writhing, as if their entire bodies were being sprayed with acid.

Hansen glanced at Drake, but he wasn't moving and looked bored.

The screaming continued for several seconds and then all three men passed out, all at about the same time. An eerie silence filled the enormous garage.

Drake walked over to the three unconscious men, lifted one of their guns from the floor, and put a single bullet into each of their skulls, his expression never changing.

While Drake was going about this with cold-blooded efficiency, Erin redoubled her previous efforts to slide her wrist through the cuff, tearing more skin as she did so, but making sure this occurred on the top of her wrist so she didn't cut through her radial artery. With one last heroic effort, shredding the skin on top of her wrist to the bone, she finally pulled it through.

As Drake shot the last of his three former associates, he dropped the gun and turned to face Erin, now free. A stream of bright red blood was running along her wrist and splattering on the glossy floor.

The Hive-controlled alien shook his head, as if disgusted by Erin's pathetic attempt at resistance. "Take one step toward me and I'll do the same thing to you as I did to them," he warned.

Erin didn't respond, but she remained where she was.

"So let me clear some things up for you, Kyle" said Drake, never taking his eyes from Erin Palmer. "What Erin meant when she alluded to having some tricks up her sleeve is that she gave me the wrong combination for the cure."

Hansen glanced over at Erin, whose eyes widened in shock.

"That's right, Erin. I know all about that. Why do you think I suspected you in the first place? When you gave me the wrong combination, I knew something was wrong. So I had Gibb scan you for bugs while you were napping."

"How could you know I gave you the wrong information?" mumbled Erin in dismay.

"There was no guarantee you would survive and make it here. So I decided I needed a backup, in case you didn't. I waited until Fuller pulled surveillance from your apartment and broke in, being careful not to disturb anything so no one would know I had been there. But I did pay a visit to your desktop computer. And I got the correct combination from your files. I had what I needed five hours before I spoke to you."

"So why didn't you put Max to work on this immediately?" asked Erin.

"I decided to wait for you to give me the information, since I had already told Kyle you were the key, and I didn't want to have to explain to him further. I have to say, I was very surprised when you fed me misinformation." He shook his head. "But make no mistake. Your pathetic attempt at deception gained you nothing. I gave Burghardt the correct information immediately after you left the call. So the virus I released will do *exactly* what it's supposed to do."

Hansen found himself unable to speak. Erin's ace in the hole had been countered effortlessly.

Erin's expression changed from nauseated to calm indifference, as if not wanting to give the Hive the satisfaction of seeing her beaten. She shrugged. "So what? I won't be around in thirty thousand years when you sweep through here anyway. In the meanwhile, by curing psychopathy, you'll have saved us a lot of trouble. So you outsmarted me. I couldn't care any less."

"Oh, I'm not done yet," said Drake. "Now that I've successfully completed my primary mission and I've been discovered, I have nothing to lose by using this host to wipe out as many of you as I can. This is my chance to see how good Fuller and the Wraps here really are. And I have to say, given this operation, I'm not impressed. They planted you as a mole and now they're blindly following an empty van. Perhaps I overestimated the potential of your species. Not that it matters now, since you've been neutered. But I'm willing to bet I can kill at least half of you in the next few years before my host is killed." He glared at Erin. "So do you care *now*? Is this imminent enough for you? Personal enough?"

"But why?" asked Erin. It was a question she had asked of the counselor who had carried her out of her father's veterinary clinic many years before. "Why must you obliterate all other intelligent life?"

"Because only *I* matter. Everything that isn't me or doesn't directly serve as fuel is an *abomination*. A pale imitation of true life. Of true intelligence. I will ultimately fill the entire galaxy. And in billions or trillions of years, the entire universe."

As Drake had been speaking, Erin had gradually inched her way toward the nearest fallen mercenary.

"I need to be going now," the alien said to Erin. "But I wanted you to know before you died just how profoundly you had been beaten. And that your failure will result in the deaths of billions of your fellow humans in the near term, and extinction when I come through to finish the job." He shook his head in disappointment. "I only regret having to kill Kyle Hansen so soon," he added. "He could have continued to be a useful pawn." Drake shrugged. "Oh well."

Once again Drake's expression didn't change, but Hansen's brain was flooded with pain signals that threatened to melt his body. It was as if a flamethrower were being used on the inside of his skull. As if millions of fire ants were tearing every cell of his body to pieces.

He screamed and fell to the floor like those before him, in more agony than he had imagined it was possible to feel. And fear. A deep, seeping, paralyzing fear to go along with the pain. He found himself praying for death. For anything that would end the overwhelming agony. Finally, his mind cooperated and he blacked out, falling the rest of the way to the smooth floor.

At the same time, Erin fell to her knees as well. Her eyes filled with tears from the excruciating pain. It was greater than any she had ever experienced. But not the fear. The fear she felt was immense, but she had been initiated into the realm of absolute fear before she had reached puberty.

She fought to retain consciousness. And although she succeeded, the Hive continued to exert pressure on the fear center of her brain, paralyzing her. When the Hive realized she was not yet unconscious she felt another burst of pain, even greater than the first. She saw Drake through nearly closed eyes walk over to the now-unconscious Kyle

Hansen and pick up the gun he had used to finish the other three men.

Erin willed herself to move, but could not. The fear and the pain were too great.

Memories of her parents and her beautiful little sister, Anna, rushed to the surface, and Erin knew from experience that no pain, no fear, could possibly be as debilitating as those losses had been. Or as debilitating as losing Kyle Hansen would be now. She could not allow history to repeat itself. *Not this time.*

Drake raised the gun and rested it against Hansen's forehead.

With a final burst of will, Erin broke through the fear-induced paralysis and dived on the ground, coming out of a roll with Gibb's gun in her hand and the trigger fully depressed. She emptied the entire magazine into the alien until he was hamburger, blown from his spot over Hansen, the gun that he had been holding falling harmlessly to the floor.

"*Never again,*" she whispered with her last reserve of strength.

And with that, Erin Palmer collapsed onto the cold garage floor, unconscious.

49

KYLE HANSEN'S EYES fluttered open and the world gradually came into focus. He realized he was lying on a bed—he had no idea where. Erin Palmer was sitting in a chair above him, reading a book on a small electronic tablet. He turned his head slightly and she caught the motion, launching herself at him and hugging him for all she was worth, albeit gently.

She separated and kissed him warmly on the lips. "Welcome back," she said happily. "How do you feel?"

"How long have I been out?"

She checked her watch. She had bandages around her wrist, but she looked great otherwise. Freshly scrubbed and alert. "Twenty hours," she replied.

Hansen glanced around. "Are we safe?"

"Couldn't be any safer."

He swung his legs over the side of the bed and pushed himself into a seated position facing Erin. "I feel like I'm having déjà vu," he said. "How many times will I pass out, sure I'm dead, only to wake up to you?"

"Well," she replied, a wide grin spreading over her face, "I've gotta believe that twice in a lifetime is already pushing it. Don't you think?"

Hansen laughed. "Okay, tell me how you got us out of that one," he said. "And just for a change of pace, tell me the truth this time. I don't want you to think that whenever I'm unconscious for an extended period, that means you can lie to me."

Erin nodded. "I'll keep that in mind. What happened is that I picked up Gibb's gun from the floor and I shot the alien bastard. Not Drake, but the Hive. You know."

"But how? Gibb and Zalinsky, two hardened mercenaries, couldn't fight through that level of fear and pain. And Burghardt and I collapsed like a house of cards. How could one woman be so extraordinary in so many ways?"

"Well," said Erin with a sly smile. "As much as I'd

like you to think I'm superwoman, I do have a more pedestrian explanation."

He stared at her in anticipation.

"I cheated."

"Come again?"

"I cheated. I told you that I had to edit out parts of my meeting with Fuller. So Drake wouldn't hear. Let me fill you in. Fuller had expressed surprise that the Hive hadn't tried to pry the combination from my mind. The Hive knew it couldn't control humans, but Fuller was surprised that it hadn't taken a shot at slipping in just to get that little snippet of information. A far simpler task than trying to take control." Erin paused. "That's when it hit me."

Hansen just blinked and waited for her to continue.

"It *had* tried. The night in the motel I woke up screaming. The pain was enormous. That must have been the Hive. Trying and failing."

Hansen nodded slowly. "It makes a horrible kind of sense," he said. "That was the most intense scream of pain I've ever heard. And you did say you didn't remember having any kind of a nightmare."

"Exactly. Fuller told me they suspected that when the Hive tries to enter a human mind, our minds automatically block it, but the attempt hits the fear and pain centers of our brains pretty hard. That's how Drake escaped in Yuma. Four of Fuller's best men experienced such a high level of pain they all passed out."

Hansen sighed. "Funny," he said. "I suddenly have no trouble imagining what that might be like." He paused. "Okay, so you were forewarned. I still don't see how that helped you."

"Forewarned is forearmed," said Erin. "You didn't think that injection was really glucagon, did you? Do you really think if I was diabetic I'd keep that such a big secret?"

"Come to think of it," said Hansen. "I did find that strange. So you faked the diabetic thing?"

"Right. We were screwed. Big-time. When Drake realized I'd given him the wrong recipe, and then discovered the bug and homing devices, the situation turned pretty ugly. I was really counting on Fuller and his team to come to the rescue if I needed them. And then Gibb frisked me and removed the syringe Fuller had given me in case of an emergency."

"What was in it?" asked Hansen.

Erin grinned. "A potent dose of morphine. *Very* potent," she added. "I *told you* I cheated. And even with enough morphine on board to choke a herd of buffalo, the pain was still more intense than any I'd ever experienced. I can't even imagine what it was like for you. Even with morphine on board, I still barely managed to fight through the pain and fear to shoot Drake."

Hansen nodded appreciatively. He had wondered how she could have been so stoic when she was purposely cutting into her wrist and tearing skin to free herself. And now he knew. Morphine.

"Amazing," he said. "But that doesn't make you any less extraordinary, Erin. When the morphine was taken from you, and knowing Drake was listening in, you had to come up with the idea of faking diabetes to get me to ensure you received the injection. In fact, using your wits to survive is more remarkable than just happening to have a high pain threshold."

"Thanks. I knew there was a reason I liked you so much," she said, and then leaned forward and kissed him again.

"Don't get me wrong," said Hansen. "I'm thrilled to be alive. And I plan to take you up on your promise to rock my world later on. But we *lost*. Humanity has been defanged. I know it won't affect us or our children or our grandchildren. But the Hive will end up the big winner in the galaxy without our more mature, but still relentless descendents around to lead the Seventeen against them."

Erin smiled broadly, and she looked so happy Hansen thought she might float off the ground. "No. I'm afraid *we* won," she said. "We won *huge*."

Hansen stared at her. "Okay. What did I miss this time?"

"Fuller knew no plan survived engagement with the enemy. And the stakes were too high not to cover every base twice. So he made sure there was redundancy. If Drake somehow did what he ended up doing, learning I had given him the wrong instructions for the cure, there was a backup plan. Any guesses?"

Hansen pursed his lips in thought for an extended period, but came up empty. He shook his head.

"I sabotaged his DNA synthesizer," said Erin happily. "After a few hours of brainstorming with Fuller and his team, we came up with the idea. I'd always planned to check the virus before Drake released it. You and I discussed it. And you explained how you had personally inspected the device they would use for this job, the Seq-Magic Ultra. And obviously, to give the virus a clean bill of health, I'd have to go online."

Hansen's eyes widened in wonder. "Brilliant," he said. "So while you were checking out Drake's *biological* virus online, you were exposing his DNA synthesizer to a *computer* virus."

"Pretty cool, huh? While you and I were being flown back to Tucson so we could end up under a bridge, and while we were driving through the night to Colorado, Fuller's people were busy. They awoke the engineer who wrote the software for the Seq-Magic Ultra from a sound sleep. National security and all that. He helped them navigate around his own safeguards and modify his software. They designed a bogus site for me to visit to— presumably—vet the virus. But while the site was pretending to check for pathogenic matches to a biological virus, it was sabotaging the synthesizer. So that it would put in wrong bases as it built DNA strands, but indicate the correct ones had been inserted when the sequences were double-checked."

"Incredible," said Hansen. "But if you were going to sabotage the synthesizer anyway, why give Drake false information?"

"Redundancy. What if the computer virus failed to work for some reason? Or if Max insisted we download the sequence to another computer and go online from there, rather from the Seq-Magic Ultra itself? Fuller called it a 'belt and suspenders' strategy."

Hansen laughed. "I believe you were saying that no species holds a candle to ours when it comes to deception. Or am I misremembering?"

"That's what I said, all right. And you haven't even heard the last of it. Because Fuller decided to attempt a very deep game. It wasn't enough for us to win. Not enough for us to stop the Hive from defanging us and drive it from its Wrap host. He wanted the Hive to think *it* had won."

Another look of wonder came over Hansen's face. "And that's what happened, isn't it? Fifty-eight thousand light years from here, the Hive is now removing us from the list of credible future threats."

"Exactly. Although things didn't exactly go the way Fuller had envisioned. We expected Drake to trust the information I gave him, and not suspect me. I would plant a homing device on him. Fuller would let Drake release the sabotaged virus, which now wouldn't even be able to cause a cold. The Hive would think it had won, and then a few days later, Fuller would move in and take Drake out. It didn't work out as planned, but we still got there."

"So now we're off the Hive radar?"

"Yes. The Wraps believe the effort involved in these scouting expeditions, in controlling another mind from this kind of distance, is immense. They don't think the Hive will waste the effort checking up on us for a long, long time—if ever. And once the Wraps build a faster-than-light transmission facility, they'll report back to the Seventeen, making sure they're on the lookout for possible infiltration. Their science isn't as advanced as the Hive's, but it's plenty advanced. They'll find ways to do a better job of blocking the hive-mind from infiltrating their citizenry, and they'll raise their guard. And after this they'll never lower it again."

Hansen nodded. "Brilliantly done, Erin."

"It was all Fuller," said Erin modestly.

"Really?" said Hansen. "Because it seems to me that Fuller was chasing a van to San Francisco while you were saving the day. And my life. Again."

"Well, technically, the first time I saved you was a fake, so we really can't count that."

Hansen laughed. "You're right. I guess you only saved my life once." He paused. "Good thing. Because I'll never be able to thank you enough as it is." His voice was soft and heartfelt, and his body language conveyed not only immense gratitude, but admiration as well.

"You're very welcome," whispered Erin, almost shyly.

Hansen took a deep breath. "So where exactly *are we* right now? For some reason, I'm thinking Palm Springs."

"Good guess. That's where we are. And we've both been invited to join Fuller's team. Interested?"

Hansen raised his eyebrows. "Maybe," he said, a playful smile coming over his face. "The work won't be boring, will it?"

"I'm gonna say . . . no. I think it might be *interesting* even. And I can promise you affectionate coworkers. Who won't mind if it takes you a few months to grow back your hair."

"Good to know."

"And our starting pay would be three hundred thousand a year. And because they aren't allowed to hire felons, I'm told we'll both be receiving presidential pardons for any and all crimes we've committed to this date."

Fuller had told her about the pardon the night before, and she had spent considerable time while waiting for Kyle to recover pondering recent events in her life. She still felt guilty about performing illegal experiments and causing the deaths of three inmates. And no pardon would make this guilt go away.

But if she dedicated herself to helping the Wraps bring humanity safely through its adolescence, and helping the

Seventeen better understand the psychopathic entity known as the Hive, this would go a long way toward assuaging that guilt.

In addition to the pardon, Fuller had promised to return her to good standing with the University of Arizona and the entire Southwest. They would post her picture once again and explain a terrible mistake had been made. And she would be allowed to complete her Ph.D. if the president of the United States himself had to intervene with Dean Borland.

She couldn't wait to see Lisa Renner again. And she already planned to speak with Steve Fuller about adding a Ph.D. historian to the team, at about the exact time Lisa would be earning her degree. Fuller was pushing to disclose publically the existence of the Seventeen. If this were ever to happen, it would be great if someone went through the hundreds of thousands of years of the history of galactic civilization available on the Wraps' computer and put the highlights in book form. Perhaps penning a gripping, informative, thousand-pager. Erin had no idea if she could convince Fuller that this would be a good idea, or if Lisa would ever be interested. But she was nothing if not stubborn, and she was determined to give it her best.

Her thinking on the subject of human psychopathy remained . . . complex. She would now be trying to perfect a device that could identify psychopaths, for the groups' use only. But she had been in a position to see this condition cured forever and she had stopped this from happening. Yes, she could now see that this condition was a necessary evil—in the truest sense of the word—so that a watered-down version of these genes could help spur mankind to greatness. But the cost in human misery would be enormous.

She had thought of her parents and little Anna. Would they applaud her actions, or be appalled? It was impossible to know.

But what if their suffering and premature deaths were not for nothing? She would trade the world to have them back for even a day, to erase what had happened. But if not for this tragedy, she wouldn't have chosen the field she had, and thus wouldn't have been in a position to help stop the Hive. Drake would have used another researcher, and maybe he would have succeeded.

If her family had to die in this horrible fashion, maybe she could at least take some solace in knowing that their deaths might have played a role in altering the future history of the entire galaxy in a decisive way. She didn't believe in the adage that things happened for a reason, that a certain event might serve a higher purpose, especially not an event as senseless and heinous as this had been. But could she absolutely rule it out? Maybe not.

Or maybe opening even a sliver of her mind to this idea was just another way of trying to make herself feel better for turning her back on the cure. For betraying the memory of her family.

As with all things having to do with psychopathy and the death of her family, she knew that there were no easy answers. These were issues that would always haunt her, and that would always remain . . . complicated.

But there was one more possibility that had occurred to her. She now understood why the set of genes that led to distilled evil when they were concentrated in a single individual needed to remain a part of the human genome. But was there a way to keep these genes in the germ lines of psychopaths—ensure they remained in circulation to give humanity its edge—but counteract their effect? Not on those who received them in moderation, but only on those who received them *all*. It was a task that was absolutely impossible for current human science and medicine. But the Seventeen were thousands of years more advanced in the art of genetic engineering than humankind. Yes, it was an exceedingly complex task that might forever be beyond even *their* capabilities. But maybe not. And Erin was determined not to rest until she found a way to make this a top priority, first for the Wraps on Earth, and then for the Seventeen. Even if such a miracle couldn't be accomplished for generations, no effort could ever be more worthwhile.

But she would have plenty of time to ponder all of this later. For now, she needed to bask in what she had accomplished, and the new purpose her life would soon take on. And finally let romance into her life.

"Three hundred thousand dollars and a presidential pardon," repeated Kyle Hansen as he sat facing her on the bed. "Sounds tempting. Will the pardon include the theft of a book bag, two T-shirts, and two hats from the University of Arizona bookstore?"

"Of course," replied Erin. "I insisted. It also covers buying a car that's a crime against eyesight."

Hansen laughed. "In that case, I'll take the job," he said happily. "But I did have one more question. When we were alone in the garage, I thought I heard you say you could see yourself falling in love with me someday. Did I hear that right?"

"What?" said Erin, feigning confusion. "Must be your imagination. I mean, that's *crazy*. I've only known you like, what, twenty seconds? I guess anything is possible in five or ten years. But *me*, thinking I might be capable of falling in love with a geeky computer physicist who couldn't best a wheelchair-bound ninety-year-old woman in hand-to-hand combat? Doesn't seem likely." Erin grinned. "But since you brought it up," she added, "I thought I heard you say something similar."

Hansen rose from the bed and faced her with a dazzling smile. "I guess we were both under a lot of pressure," he said in amusement. "Imagine that, both of us letting our imaginations run away with us." He paused and raised his eyebrows. "But I have an idea. Just to see if our relationship can lead to a . . . higher level. How about if I agree to change my relationship status to *committed*?"

"Wow. You make an interesting offer. And I know how important your relationship status is to you." Erin made a show of rubbing her chin as if this were a tough decision she was mulling over carefully, fighting to stop herself from breaking into laughter.

At that moment she realized she felt more exhilarated than she ever had in her adult life. And it occurred to her that as formidable as the Hive was, the one thing it could never experience was the joy of caring for someone outside of itself. Of being cared for in return. Of sacrificing for others. Of becoming infatuated. Of falling in love.

And while these things could be a source of weakness in humankind, they could be an even greater source of inspiration and strength.

"You've got yourself a deal, Kyle Hansen," she said finally, melting into his arms and kissing him warmly.

And the last thought she had, before she was swept up in the passion of the moment and the rational centers of her mind gave way entirely to the sensory experience of the kiss, was that she felt very sorry for the Hive.

TOR

Award-winning authors
Compelling stories

Please join us at the website
below for more information
about this author and other great
Tor selections, and to sign up for
our monthly newsletter!